I0630077

THE RANCHER

ALSO BY PETER BRANDVOLD

The Peter Brandvold Introductory Library

The Bells of El Diablo

Blood Mountin

Shotgun Rider

Spurr Morgan

The Weird West Double

.45 Caliber Series

Bloody Joe Mannion Series

The Saga of Colter Farrow

Lonnie Gentry Series

Lou Prophet Series

The Revenger Series

Rogue Lawman Series

Sheriff Ben Stillman Series

Yakima Henry Series

And many more...

THE RANCHER

NORDIC & FINN
BOOK THREE

PETER BRANDVOLD

WOLFPACK
PUBLISHING
— EST 2013 —

The Rancher
Paperback Edition
Copyright © 2025 by Peter Brandvold

Wolfpack Publishing
1707 E. Diana Street
Tampa, FL 33609

www.wolfpackpublishing.com

All rights reserved. No part of this book may be reproduced in any form
or by any electronic or mechanical means, including information
storage and retrieval systems, without express written permission from
the publisher, except for the use of brief quotations in reviews. Any use
of this publication to train generative artificial intelligence (AI)
technologies is expressly prohibited.

This book is a work of fiction. References to historical events, real
people, or real places are used fictitiously. Any similarity to real
persons, living or dead, is purely coincidental and not intended by the
author.

All brand names and product names used in this book are trademarks,
registered trademarks, or trade names of their respective holders.
Wolfpack Publishing is not associated with any product or vendor in
this book.

Paperback ISBN 979-8-89567-255-6
Ebook ISBN 979-8-89567-254-9
LCCN 2025948064

THE RANCHER

CHAPTER ONE

Finn ripped a haunch off the big jack lying limp beneath his paws and started to skin it, growling and snarling, the hunter proud of his prey.

Anders Nordic smiled inside his thick, shaggy, red-blond beard. He rode his prized Appaloosa, Apache, along the trail that skirted the Avalanche River on his left.

"Braggart," he teased the dog, a stray he'd saved from the horrors of masochistic little boys and had named Finn after a friend he'd liked.

One of the few people in this world he'd liked.

He and the dog, on their way back from checking the Comanche Ranch north range for rustlers, were only three miles from the big Dakotan's new home. Still hard to call such a grand place home. It was hard for a reclusive wanderer like Nordic to call any place home since he'd left Dakota. But that new "home" of his and Finn's was the headquarters of the sprawling Comanche Ranch here in the Never Summer Mountains of northern Colorado.

Finn ceased his bloody work to regard his trail partner dubiously.

Though they'd been together for a couple of years now, Finn often didn't know what to make of Nordic. Just as Nordic often didn't know what to make of Finn. He didn't know the dog's history. That was all right. Finn didn't know his. They both knew, however, that they were cut from the same coarse cloth. They'd found a good, quiet life together these past two years—when they hadn't been dodging rustlers' bullets or a crooked banker's posse.

A big, surly, trouble-attracting drifter defined quite differently than most.

Now the shaggy collie, mewling softly, returned to his work tearing hide and chewing flesh still steaming in the cool, high-country air.

Nordic chuckled.

He had just ridden past the dog where he lay on a slight rise above the trail, when the dog yelped suddenly, jerking his head up, ears pricked as far as he could raise them. A bullet had hammered the ledge of rock rising three feet above him—a tooth-gnashing *spang!* as the bullet ricochetted off stone.

Finn leaped to his feet, hackles raised, ready to go at it. He peered indignantly down the slope and across the trail toward the broad, fast-moving river thundering over boulders beyond a stand of spruce, fir, ponderosas, and aspens.

Nordic checked down the Appaloosa and looked down the bank toward the river.

Instantly, his Winchester Yellowboy .44 repeater was in his gloved right hand. He cocked it and aimed the rifle toward the river one-handed. All he could see down there was a puff of pale powder smoke rising from the far side of a mottled-gray boulder, dispersing into the pine boughs angled over the top of the rock.

Anders saw the smoke but not the shooter.

He turned to Finn and, covering the dog with his Yellowboy, slapped the slicker-wrapped bedroll strapped behind his saddle.

"Come on, boy!"

The dog didn't have to be called twice. Finn bounded off his rear feet, shot across the rocks and sage lining the trail, and leaped up onto Apache's back, plopping down behind Nordic and looking around warily, skittishly shifting his weight from one front paw to the other.

"Sit tight, boy!"

Anders rammed his heels against the Appaloosa's flanks and crouched low, trying to make himself as small a target as possible. Apache leaped off his rear hooves with a shrill whinny, turned his head slightly left, taking a quick look behind him, and shot like a cannonball up the trail through low buttes and towering pines. Nordic swung his gaze from left to right, looking for a good patch of high ground from which he could get the lay of the land...and whoever wanted him dead.

Could be rustlers or nesters. Possibly claim jumpers.

You never knew up here in these high, rugged reaches.

He and Finn were on Deveraux graze—Garth Deveraux's Comanche Ranch graze. It was Nordic's graze now, too, as improbable as that seemed. Roughly seven months ago he'd married Garth Deveraux's daughter, Alexandra. That had made Anders Nordic a landowner for the first time in his life. He'd married into it. He was still trying to get his mind around that nettling fact.

Married into it.

Truth be told, he hadn't considered how it would feel, marrying a rich woman with a rich father and his suddenly becoming a rich landowner himself.

Sure enough, a passel of suited attorneys had added his name to the deeds. And there was a passel of deeds, too—make no mistake. And not one word on any did Nordic understand!

He'd been so poor his entire thirty-five previous years that he'd bought new boots only when both sides had been slapping up against the toes like dogs licking their chops.

But this was no time to count his bonds, mineral rights, land parcels, and stock shares. He'd ridden no more than fifty yards from where Finn's meal had been so rudely interrupted, when two riders casually swung out of the forest on the trail's left side, fifty yards ahead. Holding rifles straight up from their right thighs, they spread out across the trail and turned their horses to face the hard-running Appaloosa.

"Whoa, 'Pache!" Nordic intoned, hauling back on the reins and curveting the mount.

Behind him, Finn gave three sharp, warning barks.

Anders glanced over his shoulder.

Finn was staring down the trail behind them over which Apache's dust was sifting. Two more riders were galloping toward Nordic and into Apache's dust, slowing now as they approached from fifty yards away. One was burly, thick-set. The other, rail thin with long, dark-brown hair.

Rage burned in Nordic. It was not an anger he was foreign to. He was a moody, quick-to-anger cuss, a man who'd lived in remote line shacks most of his adult life until he'd met his lovely bride, Alexandra Deveraux. He'd spent almost as much time in small-town jail cells than he'd spent in his tucked-away line cabins, nestled far and away from others—aside from rustlers, would-be land-grabbers, nesters, and every other form of nefarious owlhoot that populated the remotest regions of the Western frontier.

Nordic's wrath was an even hotter than usual one, however.

These men were trespassing on Deveraux range. On Anders's wife's and her father's range. On *his* range, if you wanted to get legal about it...and more than just a little embarrassing. Nordic hadn't paid a dime for the land nor done anything to manage it before he and Alexandra were married aside from hazing away nesters, prospectors, half-wild Indians who'd quit their reservation, and the always savage, degenerate frontier rustler.

Or "long looper," in the Western parlance. The kind who'd drop a hammer on a man as easily as swatting a fly.

Which group did these belong to? All Anders knew was they weren't Indians, which were getting fewer and farther between out here these days, which was both a good and a sad thing, to his own outsider way of thinking.

Finn was barking furiously, standing atop Nordic's bedroll, tail raised. After he'd had his meal so violently interrupted, Anders couldn't blame him. Nordic was mad in his own right.

"Easy, boy," Nordic said, caressing his Yellowboy's trigger with his gloved, right index finger. "Let's hear what these ringtails have to say for themselves."

"Hold it right there, fella," warned the thick-set man

riding up behind him. He drew back on his reins and stopped his paint gelding ten feet away from Anders. "Slide that long gun back down in its scabbard. Looked right at home there."

"Did I ask you?"

The big man flushed behind a thick tangle of cinnamon beard stubble. "No, but…" He frowned and hardened his voice, desperate to get the upper hand back. He aimed his Spencer repeater at Nordic's broad chest and clicked the heavy hammer back with his thumb. "But you'd best do it!"

"Why?"

"'Cause I'm tellin' you to!"

The man who'd just spoke was ahead of Nordic on the trail—a big man with a puffy, red face glowering at Nordic from beneath the thin brim of his bowler hat.

"I don't take orders from men I don't know. Especially them who shoot at me, shoot at my dog, an' box me in." Anders narrowed a frosty blue eye at the man. The direct retort of a man with four guns aimed at him, made the man flush a little.

The man opened and closed his hands around his Winchester carbine, which he kept aimed at Nordic. "Settle down, now," the man said slowly, apprehensively.

The long-haired man sitting behind Nordic said, "Easy! We was told he was quick to rile."

Nordic smiled at the bowler-hatted man. "That's true." His smile broadened. "You wanna see?"

The bowler-hatted man shouted, "Kill hi—"

Nordic had the next and last word on the matter—in the form of his thundering Yellowboy.

The bowler-hatted man jerked back in his saddle as a

puckered blue hole appeared in his left cheek, just below his eye.

Three more shots blasted, one after another, from the maw of the Dakotan's Yellowboy. As the smoke cleared and the echoes of the thunder died, three of the four men were down, two groaning and writhing before two more blasts roared off the surrounding ridges, quickly swallowed by the river's constant rush. The fourth man, on the back trail side and to Nordic's left, screamed and trained his Winchester on Nordic one-handed while blood oozed from his chest.

Anders whipped around, nudging Apache across the trail to the other side. That sudden, quick movement caused the fourth man to fire wide, the bullet whistling ominously as it caromed inches off Nordic's right ear to spang off a rock behind him.

The fourth man stayed mounted, sagging in his saddle from a belly wound, while the three other horses ran away, their reins bouncing along the ground behind them.

Apache whinnied and sidestepped, nervous.

Pale gun smoke wafted.

Wailing, the fourth man slammed the butt of his carbine against his shoulder and aimed at Anders, catching him with a fresh shell only halfway into his Winchester's action. Knowing another bullet would be on its way in a single flick of the devil's tail, Nordic shouted, "*Down, Finn!*" and threw himself from his saddle.

The fourth man's rifle roared, orange flames and pale smoke lapping from its barrel. The bullet wheezed through the air where Nordic's head had been a quarter second before.

Anders grunted and cursed as his right shoulder

slammed against the hard-packed, two-track trail. Finn landed beside Nordic with a thump, a grunt, and the crackle of coarse grass.

The dog turned and barked furiously at the fourth attacker.

Instantly upon striking the ground, Anders felt as though he'd been pile-driven by the giant fist of a large, angry god. Hearing his sole-surviving opponent curse shrilly as he cocked his own rifle again, Anders racked another round into the Yellowboy's action and rolled onto his back.

He rolled again and came up on his left side, pressing his cheek up hard against the Yellowboy's rear stock, and aimed down the barrel, pulling his right index finger back taut against the trigger.

He frowned.

All he saw was the bowler-hatted rider's horse, a blue roan, its saddle now empty, whip around as it whinnied shrilly and galloped back down the trail from which it had come. Its coal-black mane flashed gold in the early afternoon sun angling down through the pines, reins trailing, the rataplan of its galloping hooves gradually fading as the horse grew smaller and smaller with distance.

"What the hell...?" Nordic slid the Winchester right and left and back again, looking for his fourth assailant.

The man had disappeared as though he'd been snatched away by some invisible forest sprite.

Nordic froze and lowered his smoking Winchester slightly.

He turned his head to one side, frowning, pricking his ears. From up the ridge on his right, a rifle's thundering crash echoed as, like the thuds of his fleeing horse, the rifle's report died quickly on the still mountain air.

Ahead and to his left, a man grunted.

Nordic whipped his head in that direction.

The fourth man lay on the ground, in a deep patch of grass and sage, on the other side of the trail. He lay with his legs spread before him. His rifle lay beside him, his crushed hat beyond him.

He turned his head toward Anders, grimaced, cursed, arched his back, and ground his spurs into the high grass and aromatic pine duff.

Blood shone brightly on the chest of his brown wool shirt, between the flaps of his brown vest and his cream duster.

The man grunted again, sharply. He turned his head toward Nordic, and his half-open eyes became glassy in death.

Mewling his worry, Finn trotted up and sniffed Anders's face and ears.

"I'm all right." Anders patted the thick fur along the dog's neck then ran his reassuring hand down his back to his shaggy tail. "No worse fer the wear, I reckon…"

He winced at the ache in his shoulder and hip.

Nordic stared at the fourth man, befuddled.

He hadn't shot him.

At least, he didn't *think* he had.

Had he just not *realized* it?

He raked a gloved thumb along his jawline, pensive.

He hadn't had a drink since breakfast, the obligatory one with his old bull buffalo father-in-law, Garth Deveraux. The obligatory *two*, rather—one *before* breakfast and one *following* breakfast—while they sat out on the veranda of the sprawling log lodge that was the centerpiece of Deveraux's vast ranch holdings and that sat atop the pristine, sun-washed, forested Comanche Ranch.

That was where Nordic's beloved wife—he still had to chuckle at the improbable sound of that, this aging loner's *beloved wife*—had grown up before she'd gone east to a finishing school and an art college. A year ago, she'd returned to the Comanche Ranch on which Anders had been manning a remote line shack, culling the herd of rustlers that forever plagued the ranges of these vast reaches so far from civilization.

He and the rancher's daughter had met, fallen in love, and...

The thud of galloping hooves plucked Nordic out of the reverie likely caused by the sudden violence of his head smacking the ground.

Dazed. Maybe a concussion. There was a shrill ringing in his ears...

Finn was growling.

He'd already detected the horse and rider moving down the near slope toward him, horse and rider silhouetted against the afternoon's thickening shadows as they wended their way through the forest.

"Hold on, boy, hold on," Nordic urged, laying a placating hand on the collie's back peppered with pine needles and flecks of crushed pinecones. Finn was a dog of the outdoors.

Anders picked up his Yellowboy from where he'd stretched it across his thighs and finished racking the round into the breech. He left the hammer at full cock.

"Let's hear what he has to say fer himself!"

A sudden, bright smile blossomed on the man from Dakota's red-blond-bearded face weathered by years under the open skies on the northern plains and then in the western mountains.

"Or"—his smile grew brighter and his blue eyes glinted—"what she has to say fer *herself*."

He depressed the Winchester's hammer. Creakily, he rose.

Finn howled and wagged his tail.

Apache turned to the slope and whinnied, giving his own tail an excited switch.

Gone for that rich man's daughter, they were.

Purely gone for her.

But then, Anders was, too…

CHAPTER TWO

Alexandra Deveraux Nordic—she'd even taken a step down namewise when she'd married this Norski from Dakota—stopped her leggy sorrel mare about twenty feet up the slope from where Anders stood, Yellowboy resting on his shoulder. Finn sat beside him, thumping his tail.

The dog was mewling his delight at seeing his favorite lady. Apache lifted his fine snout, whinnied gleefully, and stomped a rear hoof.

"Ah, don't make fools of yourselves!" Nordic scolded the dog and the horse, both of whom ignored him. The rancher placed a fist on his hip, turned to his wife, and said, "Now, don't go thinkin' we needed help. That fella there"—he indicated the man lying in the sage on the other side of the trail—"the next shell in my breech had his name on it!"

The former Alexandra Deveraux scrutinized the four dead men and pulled down the corners of her mouth. Her chestnut hair was pulled back behind her head in a loosely tied chignon just below her gray Stetson adorned with rawhide stitching along the brim. She wore a white blouse with lace running down the front and on the cuffs. She always wore her blouses loose, but they did little to hide the contours of her beguiling figure.

Her smile may have been sarcastic, but it was still pretty. "Out making friends again, boys?"

Nordic wasn't surprised to find her out here. She usually took one of her horses, most of them blooded, for a long, hard ride in the mountains to stave off the stable green. And just for fun.

He didn't worry about her. She was always on a fast horse born and bred in these mountains, and she kept a Winchester carbine in a saddle holster. When a long time ago it had become clear she wasn't going to confine herself to the drawing room with her books, sketch journals, and piano, her father had taught her how to shoot— a necessity when riding anywhere in the mountains rife with outlaws, mountain lions, and grizzly bears.

That's what she'd been doing today. Just riding. Getting away from the lodge and her father.

Nordic glanced at the dead men then shuttled his puzzled gaze back to his wife. "If they wanted to make friends, they had an odd way of showin' it."

"Rustlers, nesters, claim jumpers…?"

Nordic shrugged. "Who knows?"

It was Alex's turn to shrug.

Anders looked around at the would-be killers. "I don't think they're rustlers. None of 'em look like rustlers."

"How do rustlers look, Nordic? And how do these men *not* look like them?"

Glancing at the dead men again, Anders said, "They, uh…well, they don't have the desperate *look* of rustlers.

Rustlers are usually cow-stupid, but they have enough *imagination* to realize the consequences of their actions. You want to pick a rustler out of a busy saloon? Just look for the men—the really *bad sunburned* men!!—sittin' in shadowy corners using cheap tonsil varnish to ease their nervous twitches. Those fellas ride all day expectin' to be *hung*!"

Alex gave a throaty chuckle, her eyes riveted on this big handsome man she'd so improbably fallen in love with. Whom she'd so desperately fallen for. "I've lived out here all my life, and I've never heard them described that way. But...to use a phrase of my father's...I'll be hanged if you're not right."

Nordic scowled and ran a gloved, frustrated hand through his beard. "There's somethin' else about these fellas."

"You've piqued my curiosity." Alex tipped her head to one side and smiled with bemused but genuine curiosity. "What is it about these fellas, Nordic?"

He seemed a font of endless speculation and curiosity to her, and she to him.

His billowy red neckerchief fluttered in the breeze which nudged the ends of his thick, blond mustache. He wore a light-blue tunic with green piping above each breast and brown leather suspenders. The cuffs of his worn, loose-fitting, deerskin pants were tucked down into the high tops of his worn brown boots.

He looked at the first man he'd killed. "That there was the leader. He's a killer, or I've missed my guess. These others...yeah, killers. Your average killer. Nothin' to get all worked up about."

"They ambushed you!"

Her husband smiled. "Yeah, but they missed."

Finn turned to him, indignant.

"All right, all right. They came *close* to you, but they weren't aimin' for *me*!"

"*Why?*" Alex asked.

Nordic shrugged. "'Cause I am who I am."

Something…or some*one* stirred on the trail behind Nordic.

He swung around to see one of the fallen men move his head from side to side, grunting and grinding his spurs into the trail beneath him. It was one of the two who'd ridden up behind him. He'd ridden to the left of the round-faced man with the Spencer repeater.

The man grunted, groaned, and cursed softly under his breath.

Nordic glanced at his wife, who shuttled her own puzzled gaze to the surviving outlaw and arched a curious brow at her husband. She was wondering how he was going to handle this one. But though they hadn't been married long, she knew. Oh, she knew.

Alex pursed her lips and nodded.

Finn turned to the moving man, yipped, raised his hackles, and growled, showing his snow-white canines.

Anders hauled his Winchester down off his shoulder. He cocked it and, holding it straight out from his right hip, walked over to where the big, burly man lay on the two-track trail, near a small cedar curling up out of the trail's shaggy center. Hatless, he had long, tangled, cinnamon hair and a bulging forehead mantling his round, beard-carpeted face. Two streams of blood ran down from the wound in his right temple, over his eye, and down his cheek.

The wounded man looked at the big man whose long shadow angled over him. Lines of exasperation cut deeply across his forehead, nut brown below where his hat usually sat, powder white above.

"What's your name?" Anders asked.

He gritted his teeth. "Go to hell!"

"Who sent you?"

The man lifted his head and coughed. Wincing, stretching chapped lips back from coffee- and tobacco-stained teeth, he said, "Gotta...gotta shot o'...whiskey, partner?"

Anders sighed and finished him. He wasn't going to get anything out of him.

Finn walked up to the dead man and made water on his leg. The dog turned to Anders, sat down, and gave a puzzled yip.

Alexandra looked around. "I don't like this."

Anders sighed. "That's the way of it. I have enemies. Your father has enemies. Coulda been after us both."

"Don't be so cool about it! Someone's after you. These men were hired. They were cannon fodder for some man with a bone to chew. If he sent four, he'll send more."

Nordic shook his head. "Could just be rustlers who wanted to get me out of their way."

"I admit you have a reputation, Anders. But they want you out of the way so they could get to father. I have a sense about these things!"

"Nothin' here tells you that!"

"My intuition does!"

Nordic snorted. "Ah, Jesus."

Alex hardened her jaws at him. "It's a real thing, you mastodon."

"Well, now that we got that question answered,"

Anders said, "why are...er, *were*...they after him?" He studied the dead men again and glowered his chagrin. "I acted like a tinhorn. I shoulda found out what they were up to. They graveled me. I lost my head. Usually, it's men like *them* that shoots first an' asks questions *later*. Not me!"

Alex gave him a skeptical look, narrowing one knowing eye.

Nordic kicked a rock and said, "Purely piss burns me!"

Cheeks warming, he muttered a reprimand to himself. He was trying not to curse so much in front of Alex. He, however unlikely, had married a cultivated girl. Eastern education. But then, she'd grown up out here, heard her father's men cursing around the bunkhouse even late at night when the feathers flew over a disagreement over a girl in town or poker.

Anders knew from having heard them himself through his and Alexandra's open bedroom window.

Her old man never bothered to hold his tongue, either...

Garth Deveraux, an Englishman with roots in Scottish aristocracy, got downright artistic with his black tongue enhanced with his spattering of his mother's Germanic Gaelic. Not that Nordic could understand those tongues, but he knew an obscenity when he heard one. The Irish and Scottish languages seemed to have been born around them.

He wasn't about to admonish the men for their "farm talk," however. The men worked hard at the Comanche Ranch—all under Anders Nordic's charge now. He was their boss, all right, another little fact difficult for him to reconcile with himself, a man who'd always worked for just enough money to get himself, his dog, and his horse fed from month to month.

Now he was in charge—in partnership with his wife and father-in-law, of course—of the largest spread in the Never Summer Mountains.

Alex turned her head to look up the trail and down. She turned to her husband, who was a full head taller than she even in her undershot, high-heeled stockman's boots, and said, "There are more where these men came from."

"Intuition again."

She nodded. "The best kind."

She turned to him, her fine cheeks red with frustration. "Purely *piss burns* me not to know!"

Anders chuckled.

Alex smiled. "Such talk ain't fit fer a lady?"

He chuckled and caressed her smooth cheeks with his thumbs.

"By now, mister"—she rose onto her toes, flicked the brim of his cream *sombrero* with her thumb and index finger, and added in a low, sultry tone—"you should know I'm no lady!"

She gave him a peck on the mouth.

Nordic's ears warmed. Imagine that. This hardened Westerner by way of Dakota with familial roots amid the northern fjords—his wife making his ears warm. When he and she were alone, his ears could get a lot warmer than this...

Alex read his amorous thoughts. "This is neither the time nor the place, you cad."

That only made him more uncomfortable.

He busied himself with going through the men's pockets, finding nothing that identified them. No bill of sale, nothing. Only a few playing cards, a broken comb, a single bullet, some coins, some greenbacks, a leather wallet that contained a girl's name scribbled on a scrap of notepaper—*Nadeene from Glendive*—and that was it.

"Whoever sent 'em didn't pay 'em. Leastways not yet." He toed the pile of coins and wrinkled, wadded up greenbacks. "Men like this—dull-eyed, *stupid* killers—can make this much in a month punchin' cows."

Alex regarded her husband with apprehension.

He wished she hadn't been here to see this nor to *take part* in it. He didn't want her to worry about him. That was another change marriage made, one hard to get accustomed to—being with someone who loved you and worried about you.

Being with someone you loved and worried about.

That hadn't been in the papers written up as part of their marriage license.

Finn stared up at Anders. The dog turned his head to one side, gave him a crosswise study through those intelligent, chocolate eyes cast with understanding and no little remonstration.

Too late, those eyes seemed to say. *You married her. You got yourself into this. No turning back now. Not for anyone but a coward.*

If a dog could smile, Finn smiled.

The dog leaped up and very gently placed one understanding paw on Nordic's right thigh. The other front leg dangled groundward as Finn balanced himself on his hind legs. The dog gave his trail pard a single bark, drilling his dark-brown, admonishing gaze into the wintry, Northlander blues of his master.

Anders returned the dog's smile with a reassuring one of his own. He patted Finn's head.

The dog lifted his snout and gave a soft mewling from deep in his throat.

Alex turned to Anders, frowning. "What's he telling you?"

"Not to be a fool," Anders said, obliquely. "And that it's time for a drink!"

CHAPTER THREE

Nordic and Alex mounted their horses and gathered the four dead men's mounts grazing quietly in the forest off both sides of the trail. The only one that gave them any trouble had belonged to the man who'd just expired. The zebra dun was skittish.

Nordic grabbed his riata off his saddle horn, paid out a loop, and gave Apache his head, galloping after the fleeing, snorting, buck-kicking mount.

His first loop dropped down over the dun's head. A half hour later, Anders and his wife, with Finn running along beside them, started back up the trail, following the course of the broad, blue, white-frothed Avalanche River in the direction of the Comanche Ranch. They led the four horses by their bridle reins. The dead men, wrapped in their own bedrolls, lay slumped belly down across their saddles. They were tied ankle to wrist beneath their mounts' bellies.

The Avalanche rumbled near the trail on Anders's and Alex's left. The river had long ago cut the idyllic and

legendary Kawuneeche Valley in the heart of the Never
Summers.

Nordic and Alexandra were horse people. This was
likely foreign territory to the mounts. Nordic would take
them to town in the morning and see if he could learn
anything about the identities of the men they belonged to,
and find homes, if only a livery barn, for the horses themselves. Three of the four were branded but neither Anders
nor Alex recognized the brands, which meant the mounts
were probably not from around here, just as their riders
probably weren't either.

Nordic hadn't recognized any of them. He doubted
they were from here. He'd like to go through the wanted
dodgers in Marshal Glen Conagher's office in Camp
Collins. Anders and the marshal had a rocky history, for
Anders had trouble keeping his wolf loose in town—*any*
town with their loud, annoying masses—but since
becoming part owner of the Comanche Ranch, he'd been
doing his best to keep his wolf on its leash.

Finn helped, knowing instinctively when his big
partner from Dakota was wading into shallow water, that
Anders's frustration was building...

It was in this valley that Alex and her two brothers,
Billy and Brian, had been sent by their mother to pick the
succulent wild berries—chokecherries, thimbleberries,
saskatoons, and wild raspberries and strawberries—that
grew thick among the willow shrubs lining the river,
feeding off the verdant, high-country grass.

There was much history in this vast, beautiful country
for Nordic's young wife. He had to admit feeling jealous
of the idyllic life she'd lived here. His life in Dakota had
been a harsh one, but the way he saw it, it had toughened
him and had made him capable of making sure Alex's

good life here at the Comanche would go on and on...
with "a passel of ranch urchins," as Nordic's seemingly
gruff but bighearted father-in-law would add.

Part of Garth Deveraux's deal to let Anders marry his
daughter was that he, Deveraux, would have plenty of
offspring for carrying on the Comanche Ranch's tradi-
tions as well as to keep the ranch alive and healthy.

The ranch was already one of the most successful
ranches in northern Colorado. Garth Deveraux wouldn't
be satisfied until it was the most prosperous spread in the
West, with a big, boisterous family to keep it going
through the ages.

He may live only to see the beginnings of that, but
he'd know it, by God. Even from six feet under, he'd
know it. He'd punctuated that promise with a self-assured
wink, a raise of his brandy glass, and a deep swallow and
sigh, his broad mouth corners quirking a forthright smile.

An old bull buffalo was Garth Deveraux, a man to
ride the river with, even now in his later years and failing
health.

Anders hoped those four dead men weren't a sign of
trouble ahead for the old rancher.

"What are you thinking about?" Alex asked her
husband as they turned their horses off the main trail that
followed the Avalanche. They were riding south,
upstream. If they were riding north, downstream, they'd
meet up with the Cache la Poudre River and the trail
down the mountains to Camp Collins, the only settlement
of any size in these parts.

Anders gave Alex a skeptical look. "What do you
think?"

She pursed her lips, nodded, and turned her head
forward as they followed the trail up Comanche Ranch

toward the ranch headquarters spread out on top of it. In the last afternoon, the trail was shaded by tall evergreens. The firs, pines, aspens, and spruces were a furry, dark green now as the sun dropped behind the bald, stony crags jutting in the west.

They rode under the crossbar arching over the trail at the edge of the yard, and into the headquarters. The bunkhouse windows on their right were shimmering behind flour sack curtains with guttering lantern light. It got dark early beneath those high, western peaks. Nordic could hear from within the hum of conversation, an occasional voice raised in jest or jeering and ribald laughter.

A birdlike whistle sounded from the heavy, dusky shadows ahead.

A picket's signal that someone had entered the yard.

Responding to the well-concealed picket's signal, boots thudded inside the bunkhouse. The door opened, casting more light into the near-dark yard. Two men stepped out onto the boardwalk fronting the long, L-shaped, mud-brick building, wearing hats and holding rifles across their chests.

"That you, boss?" one of the men from the bunkhouse said. They were silhouetted against the wavering lantern light behind them, but Nordic recognized the deep, burly voice of the Comanche Ranch foreman, Zeb McGreevey.

"It's us," Nordic said.

"Hi, Zeb," Alex said.

"Ma'am." The burly man with long, shaggy gray hair dropping down from a battered green Stetson pinched his hat brim to her. He wore a wool-lined mountain lion vest against the high-country chill. He still wore cracked leather chaps, which meant he hadn't been in from the range long. Ranching was all too often nearly a full-day's job. "You're out late."

The foreman's gaze had drifted to the four horses flanking Nordic and Alex carrying dead men.

McGreevey looked again at the two Comanche ranchers and said, "Ran into trouble, I see."

Nordic sighed.

"Who are they?"

Anders shook his head. "Don't know. I thought maybe you'd recognize 'em, Zeb." McGreevey had spent most of his life in these mountains working for one outfit or another. He pretty much knew everyone.

The aging foreman said, "Hmm," which came out as a deep, rumbling grunt.

McGreevey handed his rifle to Ryan LaPlante, the youngest man on the Comanche roll. The foreman walked out and, opening folds in their bedrolls and pulling their heads up by handfuls of hair, inspected each dead man's face.

When he'd scrutinized the last face, he rose with a grunt from a crouch, turned to Nordic and Alex, and shook his head.

Nordic sighed and shared a frustrated look with his wife.

To the foreman, Anders said, "Have your men lay 'em out in the barn. Put up their horses. Ours, as well. Have 'em ready to ride in the mornin'. I'm gonna take 'em to town, talk to the liverymen and Conagher."

The old foreman raised a skeptical brow.

Nordic grimaced and shrugged a shoulder. "Yeah, well…"

McGreevey turned to the younger man and gave his head a toss. Ryan LaPlante leaned his rifle against the bunkhouse wall then ran out to take the reins of the dead men's horses.

"I'll come back for yours, boss," the young man told Nordic, then began leading the dead men's horses off to the barn.

Nordic stepped down from his saddle, extended his hand to Alex, and helped her down as well, liking the feel of her slender waist as well as her body's supple warmth, clamped between his hands.

"Come on up," called a burly, raspy, English-accented male voice from the direction of the lodge.

Anders turned to see his tall, broad-chested father-in-law standing at the top of the lodge's veranda steps. He was silhouetted against the thumbnail moon rising over his left shoulder. An orange glow shone up near his head. Smoke from the cigar he was smoking wreathed his face. He bent forward a little, coughing, lightly pounding his chest with the end of his fist.

Again, in his burly voice, raspier than before, "Let's palaver. If we got trouble, I wanna know about it."

Again, he coughed. More loudly. As though he'd taken a puff of especially acrid tobacco smoke.

Nordic and his wife batted their hats against their denim trousers and leather chaps as they started up the sloping rise toward the lodge, beyond a fringe of spruces and pines silhouetted against the shimmering starlight. There was a rustling in the trees. Finn gave a bark and dashed off to chase a rabbit.

Ahead of Nordic and his lady, most of the lodge's windows were lit against the now-dark night—though as far as Nordic knew, only Deveraux and the big Black man who served as his butler as well as coach driver were here. For several months, a young pioneer mother and her infant son, Robert, who'd come from Nordic's home territory of Dakota, had stayed here with them at the ranch. Nordic, holed up in a line shack, east of the headquarters, had saved them from Deveraux himself, who had hard and firm rules when it came to nesters.

He'd come around, however, when Sarah Nordstrom's entire family was killed by Deveraux's own outlaw foreman and the gang of rustlers he'd led. The big, gray, leonine-headed Deveraux stood atop the porch steps in a ratty robe over wash-worn longhandles. Elkhide slippers stretched across his swollen feet. He'd had a heart stroke a few months ago, and had slowly, excruciatingly been wasting away ever since.

Riley Otis, the Black man who tended old Deveraux as well as the lodge, stood in the shadows back by the doors. A big man, Riley was old—Alex had never known how old—but tough as a Brahman bull. Gray-headed, gray-mustached, and with gray cataracts in his eyes, he had helped raise Alexandra when her mother had been suffering from the infirmities that had plagued her in her later years.

Riley was still that tough, capable, protective man—just older. The glow from his pipe bowl touched his face and the warm, black, old eyes regarding Alex affectionately. Gray smoke jetted from one corner of his mouth.

Deveraux held his proscribed cigar in his right hand, a stout green goblet in the other. There was only an inch or so of French brandy—the once formidable rancher's favorite nightly drink—left in it. Anders could sense the worry in the young woman standing beside him.

"Father, have you eaten?"

"No, he ain't," answered Riley Otis behind him, puffing his pipe.

Deveraux glanced down at his goblet, shook his big head, his thick, gray muttonchops standing out in contrast to the sun-seasoned darkness of his fleshy face. His face used to be even darker, before his post-heart stroke vituperation had settled in. "I preferred a liquid supper this evening." He looked at the glass again. "Speaking of which…come in, come in. I'll buy!"

He gave a ragged chuckle then turned and strode a little uncertainly toward one of the lodge's thick, oak doors adorned with carved oak handles in the shape of a lion's head. The door was propped open with a stone. A small table and two wicker chairs sat to the right of the open door.

A chess game was laid out on it. That's what Deveraux and Riley Otis did at night. They played chess and drank French brandy till Riley practically had to carry the rancher to bed.

Alex looked up at her husband, hardened her jaws, and gave a deep, raking growl of frustration. "That man…" she said.

She walked up the porch steps. Nordic followed her across the porch and into the lodge, turning to see Finn standing on the porch behind him, an expectant look in the dog's eyes, tongue drooping over his bottom jaw as he panted in the wake of his rabbit hunt. His quarry had apparently eluded its hunter.

"You're gettin' soft with all this pamperin'," Anders told him. He jerked his chin. "Come on."

Finn ran through the open door, which Anders promptly closed behind them. The dog paused in the foyer to lap water from the steel bowl Riley always kept filled for him. When the dog had had his fill, he followed his trail pard, who was now apparently his tony *lodge* pard, into the sprawling, well-appointed house's deep shadows relieved by guttering light from the gas lamps.

He turned through the open door of his father-in-law's office, Finn on his heels, just as Alex was filling three goblets on the large liquor cabinet abutting the wall ahead and on Nordic's left. An oil painting of a coal-black, fierce-eyed, bucking stallion, hung on the wall above the cabinet. Other such paintings adorned the masculinely appointed office's walls. Ancient British pistols, muskets, a fancy red British military tunic with gilt trim, and a plumed helmet sat on shelves and stone pedestals.

Manuscript pages from Ben Franklin's autobiography were housed behind glass atop one of the bookshelves.

Leather-covered books choked shelves and were piled atop the rancher's desk, which, as large as a lumber dray, fronted the stone fireplace in the wall to Anders's right. The dancing flames filled the room with penetrating heat and the delicious aroma of piñon pine and oak. As soon as Nordic stepped into the room, he felt sweat beads pop out on his forehead. The old rancher's poor circulation kept him from ever getting warm enough.

Alex turned away from the cabinet, holding two stout, half-filled goblets. She set one on the cherry table in front of Nordic, the other beside the leather chair with carved horse-head arms her father occupied, holding the robe close around him, legs crossed, one slipper nearly falling off one wool-socked foot. In fact, upon closer inspection as he accepted a drink from his wife, Nordic thought the grand old Englishman of the Colorado manor was wearing *two* socks!

The big Dakotan's own feet sweated in sympathy for the rancher's own...

Alex read her husband's mind. She widened her eyes, waved a hand to fan her face, then fetched her own drink from the liquor cabinet.

She sat down in a brocade-upholstered chair to the right of her father, whose own chair backed up against the log wall from which several copper spikes protruded, six feet up from the floor. His big, cream Stetson hung from one. His brown leather holster and cartridge belt, every loop filled with brass, hung from another. The holster was filled with his old, walnut-butted, cap-and-ball conversion .36. Deveraux could have afforded the latest Colt, but it was sometimes hard for the old fellas to change with the times.

The old man, having seen his daughter's reaction to the over-stoked hearth, gave her an angry scowl. "You can turn the place into an icebox when I'm gone," he growled. Raising his glass to his lips, he added as though offhandedly, "Prob'ly be sooner rather than later, you'll be happy to know."

"Oh, Father!"

Alex turned to her husband who stood behind the chair opposite her own, which matched the masculinity of the old man's, that awaited him.

Saucily, she regarded him from beneath her brows and said, "You can sit anywhere you please, my darling. After all, the house, the ranch, is yours." She canted her head at her father and in a good-natured jeering tone, added, "You even landed the old bastard's daughter." She raised her goblet and winked at Anders. "Cheers!"

"If you two are gonna make bedroom eyes at each other," old Deveraux growled, "go to bed! And while you're there, make me a grandchild. I'd like to know I have at least one in the oven before they turn me under!"

"Turn you under?" Alex said. "Oh, no, we're gonna have Zeb drag you out to a pasture and lay you on a manure pile!"

She winked at Nordic.

One of Alex's favorite hobbies was getting the old man's goat.

"Bullshit," Deveraux said, narrowing a warning eye at his daughter. "My attorneys will be here to make sure my wishes are fulfilled...and my debts placed in your name!"

He had a good, hacking laugh over that.

Nordic's cheeks warmed with embarrassment. Being of the more moderate Scandinavian temperament, he wasn't accustomed to such immoderate talk outside of a saloon or a brothel. He didn't think the old man was naturally foul-mouthed, either, being a Brit from such lofty roots and all. But Deveraux's age and the always present specter of his annihilation caused him to revel in speaking his mind, no matter how salty.

"Father, you out devil me every time," Alex said.

He stared at her hard and for a long time. "I'm going to miss you."

Alex looked away quickly. "Shut up with that."

Anders sank down in his chair. Finn turned in three full circles, head to tail, then lay down with a grunt at Anders's feet, planting his chin on the Dakota man's boot.

Alex smiled at the dog, who was snoring instantly.

"Wish I could sleep like that," Deveraux said, and took another sip of his brandy. "Just once more before I'm—"

"Oh, I know, Father," Alex said. "Before you're six feet under!"

"You're going to miss my counsel when it's no longer here, young lady."

She leaned forward, elbows on her knees, her eyes and hair glinting in the firelight. "I already do, you old Satan!"

Deveraux turned to his son-in-law. "Good luck with this one."

Anders sipped his brandy and turned to the old man, who had the traces of a self-satisfied smile lingering on his mouth. He was still thinking about that bun in the oven, Nordic knew. He hoped though he doubted he'd live to see the first one.

"We'll get down to it, sir," Anders said, cutting his own devious glance at Alex. Then he shuttled his direct gaze to his father-in-law. "Make any fresh enemies recently?"

"Every time I turn around. You don't recognize 'em?"

Nordic shook his head. "McGreevey doesn't, either."

"Hmm." The old man stared straight out before him, nodding slowly. He turned his gaze to his big, blond son-in-law. "You're ramrod of the Comanch' Ranch." He gave a dry chuckle and shook his head. "That means with all my land and stock…this whole big house an' the corrals an' outbuildings…the men…you've taken on my enemies, too."

The older rancher smiled without mirth. "An' there's a goodly lot of them." His smile faded as he stared down at the glass in his hand. "A good lot of them."

He smiled again. This time with mirth.

Why, the old bastard, Nordic thought, took some sort of sick pride in his uncompromising reputation. Alex must have had a similar thought. She stared at her father, thin brows beetled, then turned to Anders and shook her head in stunned exasperation. "I believe he's enjoying this."

Deveraux grinned dreamily. "Soon, we'll know who sent them. One last challenge." He looked at Nordic. "Unless they were just after you. God knows you've made as many enemies as I have in your relatively short time. Your reputation precedes you, young man." The rancher shaped another devious smile. "That's partly why I hired you." He slid the smile to Alex. "That's why I let you marry my daughter."

Alex grimaced.

Deveraux barked out another raking laugh.

"Maybe," Nordic said, and threw back the rest of his brandy.

The old man might be a genuine pain in the ass, but he knew his liquor.

Deveraux finished his drink and leaned forward, reaching for the bottle.

"No," Alex said.

The old man scowled at her. "Huh?"

"No!"

"Pshaw!" Deveraux sank back in his chair, parched. He cut an indignant glance at Nordic. "Get the upper hand now, while you still can, son. If you don't, this is what you have to look forward to in your old age!"

Finn looked at the old man, whom he loved for some reason, and thumped his tail on the floor.

Nordic glanced at his wife.

She regarded him with one brow raised.

The Dakotan thought this was a good time to take his leave.

"I believe I'll head to the bunkhouse, warn the men to

keep an eye on their back trail and a finger on their triggers…just in case."

He turned to Alex. "You keep a careful eye out, too. Don't ride out alone till this has played itself out."

Alex drew her mouth corners down. She did not like being confined. But she nodded. She didn't want to worry him. That didn't mean, however, she'd obey him…

"I won't be late." Nordic strode out of the study. "Come on, Finn."

The dog barked and followed him out.

CHAPTER FOUR

When Alex and her father had heard the heavy front door close, Deveraux hooked an arm behind his head.

He turned to his daughter. He studied her for a time. She looked away, feeling his penetrating gaze. She knew what was on his mind. It was on hers, too.

It weighed heavily on her from time to time.

"How's he doing?" the old man wanted to know.

Alexandra looked at him quickly, as though she hadn't been expecting the question. "All right," she said with a casual shrug. "Everything's fine."

Garth Deveraux curled one side of his upper lip in a lopsided smile. "Do you ever feel you've taken a wild animal out of the forest with the intention of giving it a better home only to realize it was most at home where it was?"

"Oh, please!" Alex bounded to her feet, glass in hand.

She filled the goblet half full, set the decanter back on the table, and stopped. She felt the old man's eyes on her.

"What the hell!"

She'd been raised around rough men. Her mother and younger brother had been the only two grace notes in her life—outside of her animals, that was.

Why should she not talk like those ruffians she'd been raised around?

Who had, in fact, had a large hand in raising her, for she'd never felt at home anywhere than in the barn with her "babies," as she'd called her horses, dogs, cats, geese, pigs, chickens, and everything else she'd mothered and raised, including orphaned wolves, coyotes, badgers, and, at one time, a beautiful bald eagle who, with a mate, had built a nest high up in a spruce tree not far from her bedroom window.

"You're going to kill yourself. You've been killing yourself for years. Now…with Mother gone, I know you're ready for the manure pile!"

"After one last challenge," he said, his devious grin in place.

Alex filled his glass and thrust it at him. "Never mind you might get Nordic killed, too."

"He knew what he was getting into. Besides"—Deveraux chuckled—"he's had a few blue whistlers sent his way in the past." He grasped his glass in both hands, looked down at it, and smiled. "Ahhh…"

"And, to answer your question, I'm just not sure."

The rancher arched a brow at her.

"About how he's doing," she said. "I think he's fine."

"He loves you. By God, if he doesn't!" That devious smile again. "Though only the good Lord knows why…"

She sank slowly back down in her chair. She drew a deep breath, took a big drink from her glass. Suddenly, emotion nearly overwhelmed her. She drew another, deeper, sharper breath. The gaze she turned to her father glistened with tears shimmering in the reflected light of a near oil lamp.

"All I know is I love him," she said in a thin voice in which she tried to put some of her usual steel, so she didn't start babbling like an idiot. "And I know, by God, he loves me!"

"He does."

"Imagine, after all these years of not finding a man I even half liked, only a few, much older men I admired but could never find myself sharing a bed with, I found him out in your squalid line shack infiltrated by mice and surrounded by long-looping killers!"

Deveraux gave a wry snort as he ran the tip of his thick index finger around on the rim of his glass. That cockeyed smile again. "Go ahead and say it the way it comes to you, Alex." He chuckled again. "Couldn't get any honesty out of the boys. You're a font of it."

He laughed, coughed, and held his glass out to one side so it wouldn't spill. He pounded his chest then sat back in his chair again with a phlegmy sigh.

Alex brushed tears from her cheeks with the backs of her hands and sniffed.

"If he wasn't who he is, you wouldn't love him."

"I don't want to change him. A man like that you can't change. You can't change him because changing him would be breaking him." She shook her head slowly. "And there's no breaking Anders Nordic."

"So don't change him. Give him his head." Deveraux looked around. "Maybe it's this place that needs changing."

Pensively, Alex looked around as well.

She turned to her father, smiling. "Urchins in every

room, screaming, yelling, playing with barking dogs, screeching cats…"

That smile again, a heavy-lidded blink. "Badgers?"

She laughed and sipped from her glass.

"You two are cut from the same cloth," Deveraux said. "I just didn't realize it till I saw the looks on both your faces, that first day you met at the line shack. That's why, try as I might, I could never find you a suitable suiter. You didn't care about wealth, power, money…or to help your old man stay connected to the world beyond the Comanche Ranch—"

"Sorry, Father," she said with a sympathetic scowl. "I owed you more."

"Bullshit. You wanted a good life for yourself…with a man you could…hell…*love*!" He looked at her. "You've grown up and become the woman you were meant to become *despite* me."

"This current situation," Alex said, her eyes grave. "It's bad, isn't it? It feels…bad. Four men…probably sent by someone else."

Deveraux shrugged. "It might be bad." He took two deep sips from his glass. "There are men in powerful places who don't care for me. I've made enemies same as anyone else who rises to my level of success. Yes, it could be bad. No use mincing words."

He ran his index finger around the brim of his glass again. "Maybe it's just what I needed to keep me alive."

"One last do-si-do?" It troubled her, but she was enough like her father that she understood him.

But, yes, it troubled her.

Deveraux nodded. "For forty years your mother sustained me. Now that she's gone, I still have my enemies."

Alex looked off and nodded.

"Go to bed," he told her. "He'll be along soon." Deveraux chuckled. "Him an' that dog of his."

———

A lex had performed her nightly ablutions and was in bed, almost ready to nod off, when she heard the front door open and close. Footsteps sounded from downstairs. He went into the kitchen and had a glass of water.

Then his boots were on the stairs, thumping as he climbed. The thumps were accompanied by the padding of four paws, the ticking of claws on wood.

Nordic's footsteps grew louder in the hall, stopped outside her…no, *their*…door.

The latch clicked, the door squawked open a foot. He shoved his head in. Finn peered into the room from between his legs. Nordic held his hat in his hand. The light from the lantern on the dresser near the door shone in his eyes the blue of lakes high up in the mountains over which jutted stony ridges still touched with the ermine of the previous winter's snows.

"Still awake?"

She smiled, nodded, and slapped the bed beside her.

He moved into the room. Finn followed, panting quietly. Anders latched the door, and hooked his hat on a wall peg. "We had us a palaver, me an' the boys. They know what to do. They'll be ready."

"I'm ready, too," she said. "I'm ready for you to be my husband."

"I've had a few drinks," he warned. "A quirley or two."

"So've I." Alex often had a cigarette of peppery Mexican tobacco rolled in brown wheat paper before bed, with a whiskey.

She owned a highborn beauty and the rustic direct-ness of a girl who'd been raised in the mountains among men like the hands Nordic had just visited in the bunkhouse, several pairs of whom were arm wrestling...and her father. If it hadn't been for her beloved mother, she likely would have been as wild as that badger or those orphan coyotes and wolf cubs she'd raised and turned back into the wild to prove themselves or die.

Which was the way of the world, Anders Nordic had learned long ago.

He'd never enjoyed anything as much as being a husband to Alexandra Deveraux.

An hour afterward, Alex rolled dreamily toward him and tried to wrap her arms around his neck, to rest her head on his chest. The room was dark, and her arms found only air.

She sat up and looked around.

There he was on the floor before the fire, head propped back against his saddlebags, his shell belt wrapped around his two Smith & Wesson Russian .44s laid out to his right. Finn lay curled up to his left. The dog, too, snored softly. Nordic's weathered soogan was pulled up taut against his chin. He snored softly, his snores and the dog's snores competed with the crackling of the flames in the hearth.

Content.

Alexandra rested back against her pillow. She smiled and drifted back to sleep.

Content.

Nordic opened his eyes.

He lay with his ears pricked, listening. All he could hear was the soft crackling of the burned down fire.

That was the problem. That was all he could hear.

Alexandra whispered from the bed. "Hear that?"

"Yeah."

"Nothing."

He turned his head slightly to glance out the curtained window behind him. The very light, soft blue of the false dawn shone through the sheer, lacy fabric. Birds should be singing. Almost annoyingly loudly. It was probably near five. The forests around the lodge should be alive with their voices.

But they were not. Something...or someone...had hushed them.

Finn growled softly as he stood and gazed at the window.

"Easy, boy. Stay here."

The dog mewled and continued showing his teeth at the window.

Quietly, slowly, Anders slid his soogan off and gained his feet.

"Stay here," he told Alex, reaching for his trousers.

"All right."

He thought he could trust her. They'd sort of come to a nonverbal agreement that in times of trouble, he called the shots. What he said, goes. He'd been in many more dire predicaments, deadly situations than she had. At such times, he could not fracture his mind with worry about her.

He strapped his cartridge belt bristling with both

Russians around his lean waist, grabbed his Winchester and donned his hat. He picked up his boots, held them in his left hand, and went out, leaving the door unlatched behind him. He turned to head for the stairs but stopped when the big silhouette of Garth Deveraux, who'd been standing at the top of the stairs and peering down the dark well, turned to him sharply.

He wore a long-tailed, cream night sock that was too small for his big head. Comically small.

The cold steel of the revolver he held glinted in the ambient light from the window at the hall's far end, behind Anders.

Recognizing his son-in-law, the rancher, clad in the same longhandles and slippers he'd been wearing earlier, turned back to peer down the stairs. Nordic walked up to him.

"You heard?" Deveraux asked.

"Yeah, nothin'."

"Two of our men on the porch. I heard 'em whispering from here, with these old ears. Tell them to shut the hell up an'…" He let his voice trail off as he turned his head to peer at his son-in-law, taller than the older man by a good four inches. "Well, you know what to do."

Anders nodded. Clutching the Yellowboy in one hand, his boots in the other hand, he moved slowly down the stairs, wincing at every wooden chirp, groan, and creak. He paused in the foyer to step into his boots. He pulled each on tightly before continuing his trek to the front door, which he unlocked and opened slowly.

The two men standing on the porch before the door swung their heads toward him quickly, eyes widening beneath their hat brims, gloved hands tightening around the necks of their rifles.

Nordic stepped outside and drew the big door quietly closed behind him.

He heard Deveraux ease the locking bar into place.

"Keep it down out here," Anders said, annoyed by their lack of caution. Deveraux hired only seasoned men. These two were not acting seasoned. They sensed their boss's annoyance, both flushing in the dim but strengthening light.

Nordic turned to the man who'd been stationed here. "You man your post." To the other man, he said, "Move around slowly. Tell the other two pickets to hold their ground. I'm going to scout around the yard. Tell those men not to shoot unless they have a clear target." He gave a steely smile. "And know it's not me!"

Both men nodded.

Nordic moved on down the porch steps. He stuck to the shadows. Crouching and holding a gloved hand over the Winchester's breech to keep the gradually intensifying blue light from reflecting off the brass, he moved down the grade toward the bunkhouse.

He didn't like the silence he heard in the night around him.

Not even a coyote or a hunting owl.

No.

He didn't like it a bit.

CHAPTER FIVE

The steadfast, always-alert Zeb McGreevey stood just outside the closed bunkhouse door.

The sashed windows were dark but Nordic saw a couple of shadows, including that of the young string bean, Ryan LaPlante, the foreman's young sidekick, moving around inside. Anders walked up to his foreman who looked every bit his fifty-something age out here in the faint dawn light, but, despite the bulge of his hard belly, was still fit and strong and could work from sunup to sundown and require only a few hours' sleep if needed.

Nordic had hunted with him, and he could climb some of the steepest grades in the Never Summers after elk and bighorn sheep and haul their carcasses down on his back. The man humbled Anders.

He also had the respect of the Comanche Ranch men and that was often all that stood between a foreman and the long trail to the next possible job.

"Keep the men inside—will ya, Zeb? I'm gonna look around...real quietlike."

The taciturn foreman nodded. He knew how it went. This wasn't his first rodeo.

McGreevey had been a foreman here at the Comanche Ranch when the ranch was first established but had moved on when he'd been offered better pay elsewhere. He'd returned another time over the years and returned again last year when it had turned out Deveraux's foreman at the time was trying to rustle him beefless. The old man wouldn't have respected any man who didn't follow the money.

Men like Zeb McGreevey didn't have a lot of years in them. The job wrung them out, left them cripples before their time.

Such men were the least qualified to live out their last years in boardinghouses and charity wards. They had to lay in nest eggs before their working years were up and all they had was a meager savings to live on—most of which, of course, would be spent on cigarettes, whiskey, and giggling young women.

"Don't get excited, Zeb. I know how you miss those Injun-fightin' years." Nordic shook his head, his own wry smile quirking his mouth corners. "Had a few of those in Dakota. Let's hope that's not what silenced the birds here."

"I don't know, boss…"

Anders placed a hand on the man's stout shoulder. He could feel the strength in the man. McGreevey could take down the best young bull in the stable, hogtie him, and leave him howling for mama.

"When it's just us, it's Anders. All right, Zeb?"

"You got it."

"You know more about this job than I do."

"That's not what I've heard."

"I know how to man a line shack up in the higher reaches, an' I can feed a hungry dog a fine elk bone." Anders shook his head. "But I know my limitations with men."

"I heard you liked it alone." McGreevey was a quiet, straight-shooting man, but not a man without humor. He frowned with fake curiosity. "Whatever made you decide to leave the line shack, Anders?"

Anders just snorted and moved off, keeping his hand wrapped around the Winchester's magazine.

He slowly circled the ranch headquarters, staying hidden in the shadows of tree and brush clumps, and in the shadows of outbuildings like the blacksmith shop and harness shop, as well. The old, original bunkhouse hunched remotely in a stand of ponderosas and spruce.

The ancient hovel with its sagging shake roof and small, dilapidated porch was overgrown with brush and cedars. It was only a little larger than the line shack Nordic and Finn had lived in their first few months on the Comanche Ranch, scouting for nesters and rustlers…until a chestnut-haired mountain sprite had ridden up to the cabin one early mountain morning with her father…and into the solitary life of the big, standoffish Norski from Dakota.

Neither he nor she had ever loved before. They'd taught each other how to do it.

The lessons stuck.

He was maybe a hundred yards from the current bunkhouse when a horse whickered behind him.

He swung around suddenly, dropped to a knee, raising the Yellowboy to his shoulder, and peeled the hammer back to full cock.

He peered over the stirrup-high grass, weeds, and the

dense, green chokecherry and gooseberry shrubs before him. He frowned, seeing nothing but the gradually thinning shadows retreating toward the objects that cast them —trees, rocks, abandoned pens and corrals...a moldering chicken coop in which Alexandra's mother had raised chickens back when the ranch and she were still young.

Oh, but the stories first told here. Now, they were legend as was the old rancher who had lived them. His daughter, lovely in a heartrendingly ethereal way and as much a part of these mountains as its long, forested slopes, lakes, and streams, would become as much of the legend as her old man was.

Maybe her own sons and daughters, as well...

If Nordic could remain alive long enough to father them, that was.

Hooves pounded behind Anders.

He swung back around to face east, the direction he'd been heading when he'd heard the horse whicker. A hard-pounding rider galloped toward him. He was a small man crouched low in the saddle, with long, black hair blowing crazily out behind him in the wind of his own passing.

Was that a beaded headband he wore?

Aiming down his Yellowboy's barrel, Anders blinked, incredulous.

An *Indian*?

He suddenly felt as though he'd unwittingly stepped through some unseen portal and was now on the Comanche Ranch back when Deveraux and his father had first established the place and the pounding of hammers tacking the timbers of the main lodge together echoed between the ridges.

The Indian galloping toward Anders raised a rifle to his shoulder. Smoke and flames lapped from the barrel.

Anders had ducked and rolled just in time.

Another bullet tore into the turf from the opposite direction as the first.

Both bullets cut into the weeds he'd just been kneeling in. More bullets tore into the brush behind him now as he faced the first rider who'd fired. There was a second one, barreling toward him from behind.

Anders rose to a knee, snapped the Yellowboy up and hammered off three quick rounds before throwing himself to his left. He struck the brush-covered ground on his left shoulder and hip. He sat up and, levering and firing, levering and firing, sent two rounds toward the second rider who was roughly twenty yards away from him and, reins in his teeth, was levering another round into his Spencer repeater's chamber.

Like Nordic's first attacker, he was dark-skinned. Not even ever-so-vaguely Indian. He was pure if he had an *ounce*!

He wore a bowler hat and broadcloth coat over a cream, tanned leather tunic adorned with died porcupine quills. He yelped as Anders's bullets tore into him and threw his rifle into the air above his head and flew backward over his horse's arched tail, his long, coal-black hair winging out madly around him.

He hit the ground and rolled then lay on his back with an arm folded beneath him. Both bullets had taken him through his chest, shredding his heart.

Running footsteps sounded beyond the dead brave.

Punching fresh .44 rounds through his Yellowboy's loading gate, Anders looked up to see the squarely built, broad-shouldered McGreevey running toward him, pumping his left arm, holding his Henry repeater down low by his right side. Occasionally, he reached up to snug his weathered hat down lower on his head.

He stopped and stared down at the dead, dusky-featured Indian whom Anders had guessed was somewhere in his early to late twenties.

McGreevey lifted his head to stare disbelievingly at Nordic. "An Injun, sure a-damn-nuff! Felt it in my *bones*!"

Anders didn't doubt it a bit.

"Those horses are ours," Nordic said, jerking his chin toward where both mounts, wearing only blankets and rope halters, had fled, buck kicking indignantly.

He rose and tramped off through the brush, looking around cautiously and taking long, fluid, purposeful strides. He and McGreevey stopped to stare down at the first man Nordic had shot. He was dressed like a white cowboy—blue shirt, denims, a red, neck-knotted bandanna. A broad-brimmed, low-crowned, black Stetson lay crushed beneath his right shoulder. He was dressed like a white man, but his skin was as dark as the other Indian's.

A rawhide medicine pouch, so old its seams were unraveling, hung down against his chest from a braided leather thong around his neck. Twin braids curled beneath the brave's head. His half-open, deep-brown eyes gazed at the anthill aswarm with ants beneath his chin.

Ranch hands appeared in the brush between the bunkhouse and Nordic and his foreman. All looked tentatively around, Winchesters in their hands. Anders could see only four or five.

McGreevey turned to them. He had that old, Indian fighting look in his eyes. Nordic knew that look. He knew many white men who'd acquired that look in the bloody, uncertain years when Indians were battling with everything they had, every ounce of fury, revenge, and the driving desire to hold on to their ancestral homes.

Anders had never begrudged them that. He'd have done the same thing.

"Injuns," McGreevey called to his men. "Two of 'em. They was stealin' horses out of the rough string remuda. Circle the headquarters nice and slow. Could be more!"

As the men separated, each heading in their own direction, an old man's voice barked hoarsely, "What in tarnation. Who is it?"

There was movement in the brush between Nordic and the house.

Finn barked.

Anders could see him leaping along behind the old man who was stomping toward his foreman and son-in-law, trying to see above the tall grass. Deveraux came within thirty yards and kept walking, stiffly, on sore feet. He was dressed in his baggy denims and black shirt pulled down over his building paunch and tucked into his pants, which were held up by a wide, brown leather belt with a brass buckle trimmed with the Comanche Ranch brand, a bucking stallion with the letters C and R to each side of the horse.

His high-crowned cream Stetson sat on his gray head.

"Who is it?" the rancher demanded as he approached Nordic and McGreevey, Finn still leaping and barking excitedly.

Nordic spied more movement in the brush behind the old man and Finn. Alexandra was striding toward them, her hair pulled back. She wore a red-and-white checked shirt, suspenders, and, like father like daughter, a crisp pair of blue denims that looked a helluva lot better on her than on her father.

Deveraux gave a loud, breathless, exhalation and leaned forward, hands on his knees. He had his old .36 Colt tucked behind his brown leather belt, to the left of the buckle.

"Pa!" Alex called, running toward him, holding her carbine up high in her right hand, above the weed tips that bent now in a building breeze as the weeds themselves gained more definition as the sun continued its climb. "Pa!" Alex called again, stopping beside her father, crouching and placing her left hand on the ailing man's back. "You have men for this!"

"Two young Indian males, Mr. Deveraux," McGreevey informed the rancher. "Judgin' by their facial features and the tattoos on their hands and necks—Utes that just come to fightin' age. Looks like they was tryin' to steal a coupla horses."

Still bent forward, Deveraux spat into the brush ahead of him and nodded. "They'll do that." He paused, breathing. "Young Utes. Out to prove themselves. Countin' coup!" He shook his head. "Damn."

McGreevey said, "I haven't seen Injuns out in three, four years. They used to jump the reservation now an' then, come up here huntin' for the winter. If they left our cattle alone, we didn't begrudge them. But these two were after horses and instead of just runnin' with 'em, they came after Anders." He stopped abruptly, embarrassed. "Nordic."

Deveraux glanced at Alex and smiled. Alex didn't react to the foreman using his husband's first name. Men could turn on each other like two male grizzlies fishing the same stream.

McGreevey gave his head a single, dark shake and glanced at Nordic, who walked over to where his wife stood with her father. Deveraux's breathing was starting to slow.

Anders said, "Well, you know what they say…or used to say…where there's two Injuns…"

"There's more." Deveraux straightened, wincing at the hitch in his lower spine that Nordic could hear making small creaking sounds. The old man shook his head. "Wherever these two braves are from, an' I ain't sure I even wanna know—hell, I've outlived Injun fightin' *ain't I?*—there's more of 'em. Yep."

Nordic looked at McGreevey. "Keep a few men at home today." He doubted there was a war party around. He hadn't heard war drums. But, hell, with Indians, you never knew.

"Right."

"Oh, boy…" Deveraux winced sharply as pain bit him. He coughed and shook his head. Nordic didn't think there was any joint in the oldster untouched by arthritis. It reminded him of his old saw and admonishment to never grow old. From what he'd seen on the frontier, where men abused themselves horribly for years on end, it wasn't worth it.

The screams at the end weren't worth it.

When the pain got too great, he'd take a bottle and a bag of jerky, ride into some deep canyon, unsaddle his horse and send it home with a slap to its rear. Finn would be long gone by then. Such was the curse of our dogs passing before us.

Anders would hunker down at the edge of a notch cave and, alone, spend his last hours sipping whiskey and staring out at nature, watching the light change, the shadows slide. He'd listen to the breeze in the mesquites and cottonwoods, and when it was good dark, when he was good and drunk, and when the wolves and mountain lions came, he'd call it a life.

Nordic looked at McGreevey. "Trouble on two fronts, maybe. I'm gonna see to the first front in town. Shouldn't be late. Keep the men on their toes."

"Got it."

Deveraux bent over and coughed again.

McGreevey glanced at Nordic, gave his head a single wag, and strode back in the direction of the bunkhouse.

Alex steadied her father with one arm around his waist.

She looked at her tall, blond husband, whose blue eyes were pensive, troubled. "You're gonna ride to town alone? First those four who attacked you yesterday and now...and I can't believe I'm going to say this... *Indians?*"

"Gonna see if Conagher or any of the liverymen in town recognize the four. I'd like to know where they came from. Might give me an' idea if more are comin' an' who sent 'em."

Nordic kissed his wife.

"Don't ignore my question," she admonished.

Nordic smiled, kissed her again, set his rifle on his shoulder, and strode off through the brush, heading for one of the headquarters' two stables. "Come on, Finn! Let's rustle up 'Pache!"

The dog, who'd been sniffing and marking his territory around the two dead Utes, barked and went running after his partner.

CHAPTER SIX

"Here ya go, Mr. Nordic," said Ike Galvin, the Comanche Ranch head stableman and hostler.

The tall, gaunt, leathery man in a blue overalls led two of the dead men's horses out of the stable. His sidekick and nephew, sixteen-year-old Charlie Bates, followed him trailing the two other dead men's horses, an understandably grim expression on his pale, drawn face.

Finn sat several feet off, regarding the horses and the dead men wrapped in their own soogans and tied belly down across their saddles. The dog mewled anxiously. He wasn't fond of seeing dead men, either. Neither was Apache, who drew his sleek head up, sniffed, and whickered.

Nordic leaned out from Apache's back to accept the reins from the stableman and glanced at young Bates leading two more horses out of the stable. He was dressed like his uncle in overalls over a work shirt, a badly weathered, funnel-brimmed Stetson on his head. A cinnamon stick drooped from one corner of his mouth. He worked in the sun all day with the horses and with a pair of bulls he and his uncle were doctoring, but he never seemed to tan. His nose just burned. Red pimples spread out from around his mouth and across his soft pale cheeks—the bane of every boy's teenage years.

"You sure you should have had your nephew assist in such a task?" Anders asked the older hostler before the boy was in earshot. Galvin had a lump of chaw bulging out from behind his right cheek. "Might give him nightmares."

"Mr. Nordic," Galvin said, "I watched my pap get impaled by the painted spear of a Ute warrior when I was only seven years old. Our cabin was burnin' behind me. I had to listen to my ma's screams until the flames silenced her. I buried 'em both. That's just how life is out here."

The older man, somewhere in his early fifties though, like so many on the frontier, looked a good fifteen years older. He glanced at his nephew, who appeared a little green around the gills. To Anders, the hostler said, "I give him that cinnamon stick to suck. Dulls the dead-man stench. I don't need one anymore. Can't even smell 'em."

The boy walked up and, unable to meet his boss's gaze directly, handed Nordic the reins of the other two horses.

"Thanks, boy," Anders said.

The boy just stepped back and turned to Finn, who'd run up on him, rose onto his back legs, and pressed his front paws into the boy's chest. The dog yipped and panted, tail wagging. That broke the ice in the boy. He turned to Nordic, looked at him directly for the first time the man from Dakota could remember, and smiled brightly, with unabashed delight.

"He likes me," the boy said in his crackling teenager's voice.

"He's a good judge of character, Finn is," Nordic said.

He pinched his hat brim to Galvin then swung Apache around. "Come on, Finn!"

As Finn kicked off the still-laughing youngster's chest, Nordic booted the Appaloosa in the direction of the gateway arch over the trail leading out of the yard and down the mountain toward the Avalanche River and the town of Camp Collins beyond. He slowed the mount from a trot to a fast walk when he saw Zeb McGreevey and his tall sidekick, Ryan LaPlante, in his early twenties, sitting their horses to the right of the gateway arch. Into the arching crossbar over the trail, the Comanche Ranch brand—the bucking stallion sidled up on both sides by the letters *C* and *R*—had been burned.

"Boss, I think we should ride with you," the foreman said in his deep, gravelly voice bespeaking much late-night whiskey and cigarettes rolled with dark, peppery Mexican tobacco. He'd once ranched down along the Rio Grande and had bought and sold cattle and horses on both sides of the border.

He'd once described it to Nordic as a more or less legitimate business. He'd given an oblique smile inside his thick, untrimmed, salt-and-pepper beard.

"Sure Shot'll tag along. You know as well as I do, he's the best shot on the roll."

The tall, fair-skinned kid shifted uncomfortably in his saddle and flushed.

"I have the men all set," McGreevey continued. Fancy Dan's in charge. He's up just now havin' coffee with your wife an' father-in-law. If anyone can protect that house"—McGreevey arched his brows and canted his head toward the big, log lodge showing through the

pines and spruces jutting along the side of the rise—
"Fancy Dan can."

"Yeah, but can he leave my wife alone?" Nordic
smiled.

"That there's another problem. On the other hand, he
helped teach her to shoot and knows she can knock a
bean tin off a corral post with a Bisley Flattop .44 from
fifty yards." The foreman's eyes glittered ironically as he
shook his head. "Hell, I can't even do that." He chuckled.
"Fancy Dan'll be on his best behavior. Prob'ly even help
her with laundry."

Fancy Dan often came up from the yard around the
bunkhouse to help Alex hang her freshly washed sheets
and everything else in her laundry basket from the
clothesline running across the lodge's backyard. Fancy
Dan's name was ironic. Daniel Simon Girty, born and
half-raised in Germany, had acquired the deprecatory
handle in the army when he'd been docked pay and
even demoted a rank for wearing his uniform
improperly.

He was maybe six feet and stout, with a big, hard,
rounded gut, an infamous love of blood sausage, and a
thick, red beard. He wore a high-crowned Confederate
kepi—he'd fought for the north, but a hat was a hat—
with three bullet holes in the crown.

He'd led Crow scouts in Montana against the Lakota
and Cheyenne and had adopted not only the Crow tongue
but their war methods, which were, to put it politely,
uncompromising.

"All right," Nordic said. "Since Fancy Dan's up
there..." He lifted his chin to indicate the lodge then
tossed the older man the reins of two of the dead men's
horses. He glanced at young LaPlante. "Sure Shot, you

stay an' keep an eye on the headquarters with Fancy Dan. Don't let him get too close to my wife."

He smiled to soften the blow for the boy. Every young rider wanted to be close to his bosses, whom they naturally hero-worshipped, sometimes, as Nordic was afraid in Sure Shot's case, to his own detriment.

Sure Shot grimaced, deeply disappointed. He said, "Oh, but, boss, I…you fellas might need me. You know —for long-range work."

"There won't be any long-range work today," Nordic said. "And I don't want too many men in town."

That often drew the ire of Marshal Conagher, who'd never liked either the Deverauxs or Nordic. He thought the Deverauxs were too big for their britches, since they owned, or had a good interest in, a good third of the businesses in town and he'd always felt the need to kiss their asses. He didn't like Nordic for more personal reasons. Nordic had broken the nose of one of the man's deputies and humiliated Conagher himself in front of the other deputy when he'd taken the marshal's own gun and had "convinced" him to let him out of jail.

"Good idea," McGreevey said now, understanding how his boss looked at things. He didn't want young LaPlante becoming anymore and any too soon the target of Conagher's ire than he needed to be. He would soon enough if he lasted that long. McGreevey, who'd mentored the boy personally for over year, knew he would last that long.

The young hand nodded but couldn't help hanging his shoulders as he fell back behind Nordic and McGreevey, Finn trotting along beside his partner. They booted their horses under the arch and down the pine- and fir-sheathed trail that dropped quickly, the broad valley of the Kawuneeche opening before them in the morning light, the cool blue, serpentine line of the Avalanche River, sheathed in willows and honeysuckle, curving through it.

"Ouch," Nordic said. "I know that hurt him. Been through it myself."

"Hell, we all have."

They rode to the bottom of the mountain and swung their own horses and the four they were trailing to the left. They jogged off down the west side of the valley to the north. Finn saw a rabbit, barked, and dashed into the woods along the river.

McGreevey chuckled at the dog.

To Nordic, he said, "I know you'd rather be alone, boss, but sometimes it ain't safe."

The river gurgled and chugged on their right, maybe twenty feet off the trail. Finn was scurrying around them, barking his frustration at his cunning pray.

The birds were singing again. Two elk with two younger ones, brown coats gleaming redly in the early light, were in the river, on the other side and downstream a hundred feet, drawing water.

"And, I might add," added the burly foreman, "I may not look like much, and I maybe can't make that shot your wife can with a .44, but I got a sniffer for dry-gulchers and can take one or two down, one and a half seconds apart, with my old New Haven Arms Company Henry repeater, from a hundred yards away. Can hit him so true they don't even have time for last rites!"

He chuckled and patted the worn walnut stock of the rifle jutting up from the scabbard strapped to the right side of his saddle.

"Besides," McGreevey added, "two Comanche Ranch

men can get in trouble in town a whole lot better'n just one!" He laughed.

"She told you about that, did she?"

"Your, um, *predilection*, as she called it, for *trouble*? Oh, yeah."

"That's why you're here," Nordic said, smiling and shaking his head. "To keep me out of Conagher's hoosegow."

"Oh, yeah." McGreevey laughed.

Nordic turned to him with a sincere look. "Zeb, I been huntin' with you. You made me look like a tinhorn up in those mountains. You have nothing to prove to me."

The foreman looked surprised beneath the brim of his weathered green hat. "Yeah?"

Nordic smiled. "Yeah."

As the morning light gradually intensified, he and McGreevey booted their mounts down the valley toward the Poudre River a few miles ahead.

Their pack horses followed with their grisly cargo.

———

N ordic and McGreevey had ridden three miles along the Avalanche when Nordic lifted his chin and sniffed the air like a dog.

He checked Apache down. His own chin lifted, sniffing, McGreevey turned his shaggy head toward the river on his right. Beyond the river lay several rises, the second higher than the first, the third one higher than the second.

All three ridges were a furry blue green with pine forest in the intensifying, high-country light. Dew shone like gold beads on the long, high grass rising along the river and the stream's tighter sheath of sage, willows, and honeysuckle giving off their pure, spring perfume that mixed with the verdant smell of the young aspen leaves. The perfume smells were tempered by the smell of a fire and roasting meat.

Charred beef.

Nordic and his foreman shared dubious glances.

Nordic jerked his head to indicate the far side of the river.

On this side of the river was Arapaho Mountain graze. On the other side of the river lay a long, broad stretch of open range. At least, officially it was open range…

Nordic and McGreevey swung down from their saddles and tied their packhorses to trees along the river. They remounted and crossed the river via a shallow ford they were both aware of. Finn splashed across the ford beside his master. They bounded up the bank on the river's opposite side and trotted their horses across a flat rising gently toward a forested mountain. They climbed a rise, trotted across another flat, then stopped their horses ten feet from the top of the next rise peppered with pines and Engelmann spruce.

Smoke rose from the other side of the rise. The smell of roasting beef was stronger now. The fire was close.

The men dismounted, dropped their reins, and ran crouching until they could edge cautious looks over the crest of the rise. Finn lay belly down beside Nordic, also edging a look over the ridge crest and into a narrow valley beyond, abutted on its far side by another forested mountain. The valley was bisected straight down its middle by a creek that, like the Avalanche River, eventually ended up in the Cache la Poudre another mile north.

Along the creek—Eagle Creek, Nordic believed it was called, him still being relatively new to these mountains and there being a stream of some kind in every canyon and swale—Indian women of various ages were washing clothes with a desultory, dreamy air, their long, black hair tumbling down their backs and glistening in the high-country sun.

Finn looked at his partner and gave a soft, inquiring moan.

Nordic petted the dog, calming him. All he needed was for Finn to charge down there, barking. Finn was as territorial as the old man was.

In that next valley, a good dozen or so adult women, children, and men of several different ages milled around four large tipis of bleached buffalo hides. The hides were almost garishly painted in designs of the sun, moon, stars, and, in one case, buffalo leaping over a cliff edge.

A large fire burned in the middle of the encampment, between the lodges and the stream, near which a separate fire burned and over which a large iron pot smoked and in which clothes boiled. A girl in twin braids and buck-skins was stirring the clothes with a long, oak paddle, occasionally shaking her damp hair back from her cheeks. One of the girls, maybe thirteen or fourteen, lolled naked and copper-skinned in the shallows near the laundry kettle, letting her black hair float in the water, resting back on her elbows.

Several covered wagons lay behind the fires and the tipis.

A couple of the men were chopping meat by the larger fire, on a large board resting over a pair of wooden, iron-banded water barrels. All were clad in a mishmash of buckskins and white men's clothes including old, threadbare suit jackets and wool or broad-cloth trousers. Some wore Stetsons. Some wore colorful bandannas on their heads. One man—tall and dark, with his long, grizzled, gray-black hair hanging loosely about his shoulders clad in an old, dark-blue army jacket, leaned back against a pole of the tipi behind him. He had his left foot propped back against the pole. A cigarette smoldered in his other hand. His mouth was moving, head slightly turned to the tipi's open front flaps, as though he were speaking to someone inside.

They all wore colors or designs or face paint or tattoos that marked them as Ute.

The Indian with his back to the lodge raised the quirley to his mouth, drew, and blew the smoke out toward the large fire before him and over which what appeared a yearling calf cooked on a spit with two iron, hide-wrapped handles, one off each end. Two boys in their teenage years sat on the ground near each handle, awaiting the order to turn the meat. An old man sat, clad in dark buckskins, legs crossed, ten feet back from the fire. He had long, blue-gray, flowing hair. His spindly frame was wrapped in at least two trade blankets.

He was smoking a pipe as he stared into the flames.

He was in his own world. Maybe only half conscious of the others around him.

At the same time, Nordic and McGreevey pulled their heads down behind the ridge crest and exchanged incredulous—no, flabbergasted—looks. McGreevey rubbed his eyes and shook his head.

He looked at Nordic. "Am I asleep an' dreamin'?"

"I was about to ask you the same thing."

"I feel like it's ten, fifteen years ago."

"What do you suppose they're doin' here?" Nordic

asked. "They can't be followin' the buffalo because there ain't no more buffalo to follow!"

"Should we ride down an' ask?"

Nordic thought about it and shook his head. "They might think we're threatening them. I don't want to do that. I didn't see any rifles. No pistols, for that matter. They're not on any war path." He glanced off, thought through his options, then returned his gaze to the Comanche Ranch foreman. "Those two braves who broke into our corral…"

"Likely from here."

"I saw several others their ages."

"The two you shot tried to shoot you first. Remember that."

Nordic nodded, then shook his head. "Never expected this many Indians. At least, it's not a war party."

"No, but maybe we ought to go back to headquarters, gather some more riders."

"No." Nordic shook his head resolutely. "We'll head to town like we planned, try to find someone who can identify those four dead men. Later, after I've pondered on this, I'll take those two dead braves to that encampment, have a little powwow with whoever the chief is. Tell 'em what happened."

"The old man is not gonna like this. Injuns back on the range again after all these years."

"That's open range, Zeb," Nordic said, pointedly. "You know that."

The foreman gave a gravelly chuckle. "Tell that to your father-in-law. Tell him about that beef on them Utes' spit down there, too!"

Finn whined, studying the two men curiously. But he

knew what they were talking about. Maybe not from their words but from their demeanors.

Nordic grabbed his hat, set it on his head, crabbed a little lower on the slope, then rose and walked back down through the forest. Finn ran ahead. McGreevey strode up beside Anders, both men taking long, pensive, slightly anxious strides.

The older foreman glanced at the taller man, the man from Dakota. He narrowed one eye with irony. "You missin' that line shack yet, Anders?"

Nordic stretched his lips back from his teeth, nudged his hat up from behind, and scratched the back of his head with his finger. "You know...?" He looked at the aging foreman whose thick mustache resembled some shaggy animal curled over his mouth. "I am."

CHAPTER SEVEN

Alex had gone into her and Nordic's bedroom to lie down for a bit.

She felt sluggish and, for some reason, world weary. At the same time, oddly, she felt discomfited. Unnerved. She'd gotten enough sleep the night before, before that telling silence. Maybe what she needed was to work a little harder around the house or the barn. Not like there wasn't enough to do on a working ranch but some days she had trouble picking out just one project.

The woman who came in to clean from time to time, the wife of a smaller rancher, didn't like it when Alex helped with the dusting or sweeping…and especially not the cooking! But Alex had a restless mind and the best way to put it to rest was to do manual labor. That usually put her mind to rest.

Often, she'd go out to the stable and organize and repair tack in the tack room though the hostlers made her feel like she was intruding. She knew she made them feel self-conscious, unable to fool around, to laugh and tell bawdy jokes as was their custom. She enjoyed cooking, though she knew she was no good at it and was secretly amused, not offended, at Nordic's and her father's reactions to her attempts at roasts and roasted chicken and stew. She had no finesse with spices—she either used too much or not enough. And she was forever overcooking roasts and chicken so they tasted like charred leather.

Her biscuits were so hard and tough they could be broken open only with a hammer.

Mostly, she left the cooking to Riley Otis, who doubled in that role when he wasn't needed on the range or working in the yard.

She'd just ruined a batch of oatmeal cookies. She chalked that up to her distraction at the current threat to the Comanche Ranch. There always seemed to be something reaching in, however subtly or unsubtly, to destroy. She remembered when the threat had belonged to the Ute warriors who'd resented having their ancestral home and hunting lands overrun by the whites who had also killed off their primary food source—the majestic buffalo.

The beaver once teeming in the streams had gone to the East Coast in the form of men's hats, foxes and wolves in the form of ladies' shawls.

She'd felt implicated, deeply implicated in the degradation of the West. She was white and belonged to a ranch family who'd taken over an Indian family's home to make it their own—their modern, "civilized" own— though Alex had known from a very young age she was only one of many thousands of despoilers.

She wore that guilt and self-consciousness to this day.

Still, her fear of the victimized Utes, driven to savage fury and blood-hungry attacks on the whites who were gradually—no, quickly—encroaching on their territories and ancient, rustic ways—was still keen in her heart. She had nightmares about the night raids and barn burnings and the massacres of surrounding ranch and farm families. Her father had had enough men back around the time Alex and her brothers were small to hold the "savages" off. But the smaller ranchers and farmers were scalped and killed, their women raped. Their ranches had sent pulsating glows high in the night skies as they'd burned.

Gradually, as the Utes had been forced from their land and onto government reservations in mostly arid lands, Alex's nightmares had started to abate. That was another source of her guilt but there was nothing quite so horrific as wondering if you were going to die that night only after being victimized in the worst ways known to humanity.

Oh, the Utes had gotten back at their usurpers. Make no mistake.

Alexandra didn't begrudge them. Well, she did, of course. You can't *not* begrudge someone wanting you dead. Not only dead but ravaged and butchered. At the same time, however, she'd understood their fury.

Those years back when she'd been very young had been terrifying times. Seeing those two young Indian men lying dead in the tall, blond grass and brush out by the ranch's original cabin had touched a raw nerve in her —one that hadn't been touched by anything except nightmares in a long time.

Where had they come from?

Where were the others?

There must be others. They'd tried to kill Nordic, pretty much baring their intentions.

A heavy thump and a man's loud groan rose from down the hall on Alex's left.

"Father!" she muttered and rose from the bed.

She hurried out the door and down the hall, her boots thudding. Even when she was indoors, she wore outdoor gear because it was the outdoors and her horses that always beckoned her. She tapped once on her father's door.

"Father?" she said, pressing her mouth up close to the panel.

"Oh, Lordy," came the old man's throaty, breathless voice. "Oh, Lordy...help me, will ya, girl?"

"Of course!"

Alex twisted the knob and stepped into her father's room.

She gasped when she found him lying on the floor in his longhandles and robe, half of a fat cigar smoldering on the floor near his outstretched right hand. A thick, leather-bound sketchbook and a chunk of charcoal lay on the floor near the book. The old man was breathing hard and groaning, his thick gray hair hanging in his face, partly concealing it.

"Father!"

Alex ran to the man, crouched down, and grabbed his arm.

He rolled onto his back, grimacing. "Ah, hell—you can't lift me. Get that big Norski galoot of a husband of yours!"

Alex grunted as, on her haunches, she tried to pull the gasping rancher to his feet. "My big galoot of a Norski husband is headed to town with those four men who bushwhacked him. He wants to get to the bottom of whose after him...or you. Or both."

She gently tugged on Deveraux's arm with her left hand, wrapped her right arm around his waist. Hoisting himself with one hand on the bed, he heaved up off his feet and Alex and he got him standing and leaning back against the bed, which he'd fallen from.

"Oh, hell! Oh, hell!" he groaned, waving his left hand to indicate the cigar on the floor.

"Oh, no, you don't!" Alex reached down, plucked the half-smoked stogie up off the floor, and promptly mashed it out in a carved driftwood ashtray on the table beside his bed. "I'm putting a stop to this. Why, your lungs are probably the size of raisins!"

"Harpy!"

Alex pushed her father back onto his butt on the edge of the bed. She nudged his left shoulder, got him somewhat turned, and then shoved him back on the bed until his head was against his pillow.

"What were you doing on the floor?" Alexandra asked her father.

Still trying to catch his breath, Garth Deveraux said, "I was tryin' to fetch the bottle." He glanced at the labeled bottle of Scotch standing with several other liquor bottles of various sizes and colors atop his walnut liquor cabinet, both small doors thrown open to reveal a plethora of other bottles of various sizes and colors.

He had a glass on the table to his right, beside a guttering lantern.

"Father, it's not yet noon!"

"I no longer recognize time. Fetch the bottle and my sketchbook and I'll increase your allowance by a dime a week."

Despite her anger and annoyance at the old man's self-destructive ways, she laughed. When she was little, he used to bribe her into doing things forbidden by her mother by offering to "increase her allowance by a dime a week."

He hadn't needed to do that.

He was a veritable god in his young daughter's eyes, as he still was, truth be known. Alexandra always followed his orders and suffered her mother's scolding for doing so. She knew, however, that her mother understood, for Louise Deveraux saw her husband the same way his daughter did.

As a god, of sorts. An angry, uncompromising god, but a god nonetheless…

"Unlike the hooch, the sketchbook I can do," Alex said, bending over to retrieve the leather-covered book of high-grade drawing paper from the floor. As she did, she glanced at where the book had fallen open—to two perfectly rendered small birds perched on a slender stump with a knot near the top poking up from the weed-spiked ground.

A slender little branch protruded from the knot, a shriveled leaf clinging to one end.

The birds had been rendered in the charcoal with loving precision, various shadings adding definition to the beak, eyes, to the feathers on the variegated wings, the bulging, downy breasts, and to the spidery feet, those of one bird—they were chipping sparrows—closed around a straw-thin branch protruding from the side of the stump. The feet of the other bird were set flat on the top of the stump, an inch above the slender branch.

Alex was dumbfounded at the delicacy and accuracy of the interpretation, and at the appreciation for the fragile little creatures portrayed.

"Did you draw this?"

"Give me that!"

"Wait."

Cradling the open book in her left arm, Alex riffled through the previous, coarse, ivory-colored pages with the thumb and index finger of her other hand. The book was half filled with similar natural images, including a perfectly executed moose standing in a river hemmed in with forest. The moose had its head up, and wet weeds drooped from its blunt snout to the water riffling around its hocks. The riffles on the moving water were also perfectly rendered.

Alex had no idea why, but a sudden spasm of emotion rippled through her. A sob broke between her lips. She placed a hand over her mouth, shocked at the poignance of what she was feeling...so out of the blue...and she clumsily gave her father his sketchbook back.

Deveraux frowned at her, his thick, wiry brows dropping down over his eyes. "Say, now," he said, understandably shocked by his daughter's inexplicable behavior. "Say now, it's all right." He placed his right hand on her left shoulder as she dropped onto the edge of the bed.

Shocked by her sudden onslaught of emotion, she clamped a hand down tightly across her mouth and was even more surprised when yet another sob burst from between her lips. Raw emotion continued to roll through her, making her shoulders quiver, until she buried her face in both hands, and cried.

"Say, now...Alex...honey...what's wrong? Was it... was it...?" Garth Deveraux glanced down at the thick, leather-bound book in his hands as though he wasn't sure what he'd found himself holding.

What had his dear daughter...his whang-tough, dear

daughter, as capable in the barn as she was in the kitchen —no, better suited to the barn than the kitchen!—had found so disturbing in his drawings?

Alex sniffed and shook her head as she started getting her emotions under control. "It's not that, Pa...Father... no, it's nothing there. They're all so lovely." She slid her glittery-eyed gaze to him, her own incredulity carving deep lines across her otherwise smooth forehead. "I had...no idea...what talent you so possess!" She shook her head, confounded. "Why didn't I see them? Did the boys see them? Did *mother* see them? Why, I get my own talent, for what it is, from *you*!"

He shook his head quickly. "No...no...of course not. Those are just...they're just little *pictures* I draw when I can't sleep or I'm ill...or like when that bronco you so loved tossed me into the corral...years ago...and I was in bed for two weeks." The rancher studied his daughter probingly. "What was it that...what was it that...?"

He didn't know how to finish.

Alex didn't know how to answer. She sobbed again. This time it was half sob, half self-deprecating laughter. "I don't know." She sniffed and shook her head slowly, staring across the room, as befuddled as her father was. "I've been doing that...lately. I'll be doing something around the house or in the stables or out riding the range...and...and suddenly I'll just break down in tears! I scared Riley and Fancy Dan half to death one day!"

Her stomach suddenly felt topsy-turvy.

Nausea built in her. *Oh, no... Not this, too...*

The nausea often came on the heels of the emotion.

Deveraux was rubbing his daughter's back with his big, right, open paw, sliding it up to gently massage the back of her neck. "What is it, Alex? What causes this?"

"I'm sorry, Father. I didn't mean to worry you. Oh, I know…I guess it's just that…Mother's dead, the boys are dead, so many of my pets are dead—Rufus, Clara, McGillicuddy." Tears washed over her eyes again as she slid her gaze back to her father, continuing with, "And you…don't take care of yourself…and…and you're going to be gone soon…" She looked at the large bedroom swirling around her, at the ceiling with its herringbone pattern and the heavy beams. "It's so big…and it's so empty, and it's under siege…*we're under siege, and…*"

Deveraux smiled. "It won't be empty for long."

She frowned. "What?"

The old man's smile grew broader, ever-so-slightly devious. "It won't be empty for long. In fact, I think you're gonna have your hands full before long."

She scowled. *"What?"*

"I ain't no sawbones or none o' that but I helped with enough mares an' heifers an' even sheep…for nigh on forty years…startin' way back to home…in the green pastures of my homeland…to know you got you a bun in the oven, my dear."

In his soft English accent, the "dear" came out as *"deahh."*

Deveraux's smile broadened beneath the large, sun-seasoned doorstop of his nose.

She knew right then and there that he was right.

Another wave of nausea rolled through her. She clamped her hand over her mouth once more, fighting it back. Her eyes were wide and round as silver dollars as she stared past the worn knees of her sun-faded denims and the scuffed, pointed toes of her riding boots at the floor.

She felt her father's smiling eyes on her, caressing her left cheek gently, softly, gazing lovingly at her profile. Another oddity for him. He'd never been the kind of father who'd gazed lovingly at his children. He'd never had the time. Besides, he'd been taught by his own father that gruff was the only way to be with your offspring. You couldn't coddle them. That would weaken them. In this tough world, your children had to be tougher.

He reserved his gentleness and cultivation for his birds, his rivers, his moose dining on the garden bottom of the Avalanche…

"What's the first one gonna be?" he asked her softly, continuing to gently massage the back of her neck, loosening the too-tight muscles and tendons. "Eh? What's the first one gonna be?"

She turned to him, shaping a devious smile of her own. "A *girl*!" she exclaimed. "A girl who wears little white dresses and ribbons in her hair and plays the piano all day when she's not reading. A bookish little girl whose favorite composer is Chopin!"

Deveraux grinned with one side of his mouth. He kept his eyes on his daughter. "Good," he said, eyes glittering once more. "We could do with a proper girl around here."

He chuckled.

Alex leaned down and kissed his cheek.

Straightening, suddenly her eyes bulged. The nausea was building to a crescendo. "Oh, *God!*"

She rose from the bed and went running across the room, out the door, down the hall, and into her and Nordic's own room just in time.

I'll be damned, she thought, fumbling the lid off the chamber pot.

I am. The lid clattered to the floor. *I'm...pregnant!*

At the same time, lightning bolts of terror crashed through her.

But he's not ready. It's too much too soon.

He'll run!

CHAPTER EIGHT

I t was a ninety-minute ride down out of the mountains to the town along the Cache la Poudre, Camp Collins, named after the army outpost, spread out along the river's eastern shore.

The post had been constructed in 1862 to protect settlers taking the Overland Trail across Colorado Territory to various points west, including Oregon and California. The long ride turned out to be mercifully uneventful save for the two men pausing to watch a fat grizzly male ford the Poudre and amble in its heavy-bottomed way up into the deep timber carpeting the ridge on the other side, pestered by a territorial pair of magpies it stopped every so often to swipe a huge, clawed paw at. It was well afternoon, shadows of cottonwoods, pines, and sandstone and wood frame business buildings growing long, when Nordic, Finn, the Comanche Ranch foreman, and the four dead men they were trailing rode into the dusty town that sat in the shadow of the Front Range of the northern Rockies.

Finn had leaped up onto Apache's back to ride into

the town behind Nordic, his memory having reminded him of the dangers of a busy town.

The large stone formation of Horsetooth Rock loomed in the west, the vertically split granite at its high crest looking nothing so much as the three giant horse teeth it had been named after. Sometimes Nordic rode into Camp Collins from that direction, straight west, but then you were traversing many intersecting canyons so deep and narrow that they were shaded nearly all day long, which made your return trip, unless you overnighted in town, challenging in the heavy mountain darkness.

Those canyons were also great places to get mistaken for a night-riding rustler and shot out of your saddle, never to be seen or heard from again. This was the outlaw West.

Any route traversing it was perilous, for owlhoots of every stripe haunted the trail for one reason or another. Some used the route along the Poudre to lose posses and bounty hunters up among the piney ridges tickling the underside of the vastly arching, cobalt sky. Others sat in wait for pilgrims they could accost for their riches, little as they would likely find, including guns, knives, tack, and stock. Comely females were ever the enticement for all matter of nefarious purpose including the money they would bring when sold to "lonely," stir-crazy mule skinners and rock breakers populating the mountains' numerous and usually smoky, muddy, wretched, and fetid mining camps.

Nordic and his foreman stopped at the jailhouse to speak with the county marshal, Frank Conagher, but neither the lawmen nor his two loutish deputies were there. Probably off on business or making the rounds around the town.

Nordic and McGreevey visited all four of the Camp Collins livery and feed barns, not finding a single proprietor, hostler, shoer, or farrier who recognized any of the four dead men or their horses. After they'd spent forty-five minutes traipsing around the busy mining and ranch supply town, leading the four horses, with Finn on their heels, not liking "town" one bit, the two Comanche Ranch men turned the four dead men over to the undertaker and split up.

McGreevey headed for a mercantile that doubled as a saloon.

He needed tobacco, busthead, and the lunch counter which was free with the purchase of a nickel beer. It was the best lunch counter between here and Laramie, laden as it was with pickled eggs, bean soup boiled with ham hocks, thick slices of ham, wheeled cheese, and sausage ground daily by a beefy German cook with a bib beard hanging to his belt buckle. The Kraut always smelled like a giant tube of bratwurst and had no better knowledge of English than Finn did. In fact, Finn was more fluent.

Anders headed for Lars Olson's Brewery & Saloon, now owned by his father-in-law—yes, he now, to his ever-renewing amazement, had a *father-in-law*—who had arranged for a friend of Nordic's, one of his few, to be employed as a serving girl.

Lars Olson had sold to Deveraux and semiretired but stayed on as the place's brewmaster, concocting his delectable ales—a swilling some—in a large shed out back.

Entering the place, Nordic almost ran into the girl, Sarah Nordstrom, he'd come here to see. Sarah was the daughter of immigrants from Anders's home territory of Dakota. Nordic held up quickly before he would have otherwise run over the slender blonde. She saw him at the same time and gasped, startled, then widened her eyes in surprise.

"Anders!" she exclaimed, color rising in her cheeks, her own blue, Nordic eyes flashing their delight in seeing him again. "What're you doing here?"

Finn knew the girl well. He'd followed Nordic into the saloon and was running around the girl—*woman*, rather, for she now had a one-year-old boy, Robert— yipping his own brand of greeting.

"Oh, Finn—you, too!" Sarah said, crouching slightly to stroke the happy dog's ears with her fingers. She held a large tray shoulder-high. Steam rose from the several platters it bore.

"Of course, Finn," Anders said. "You don't think he'd miss out on a trip to town, do you?" Nordic smiled at the young woman in her early twenties, glad to see her seeming happy now after having lost her parents and younger brother in the Never Summers, where'd they'd squatted on land which Anders's father-in-law—yes, *father-in-law*—had illegally claimed as his own.

Garth Deveraux hadn't carved out his vast holdings by being any less ruthless and venal than the rest of the larger ranchmen. Deveraux had not been responsible for Sarah's family's murders, however. Deveraux's foreman at the time, Wayne Bitterman, whom, Nordic had discovered, had been running his own rustling syndicate and was targeting his boss's own beef, had been responsible for that.

Nordic had killed Bitterman, whose dream it had been to marry Alex and take over the ranch, at the end of all that trouble. Finn had started the work of the man's killing, however. He'd attacked the man when Bitterman had been about to shoot Anders, causing Bitterman to blow his own toe off when the dog had fouled his aim.

The vile bottom-feeder's screams had been heard all across the Kawuneeche Valley that night when the sawbones from town had ridden out to the ranch to hack off the corrupt foreman's toe.

"A trip to town?" Sarah said, bending down to caress the dog with her loving gaze. Then she glanced skeptically at Nordic's canine pard. "Oh, really?"

Everyone who knew Finn knew the former stray had little use for towns. It was in a town in New Mexico where he'd been abused by stick-wielding urchins, including the red-headed son of the town's banker, where Nordic had adopted him, which had detonated a whole powder keg of trouble for the big man from Dakota.

Anders would do it all again, if he had to...

"I'll be right back!" Sarah said and hurried off with her tray.

She found Nordic and Finn a few minutes later. Nordic stood at the bar with a big mug of frothy beer before him. Finn sat at his feet, looking up expectantly for a bite of sausage or a cracker.

Anders loved beer. In fact, he often brewed it himself when he could find the ingredients—simply roasted barley malt, hops, and yeast—and had a good stretch of time on his hands. Early in the spring he'd planted a small, trellised garden of hops behind the Deveraux lodge, so later in the fall, after roundup, he could brew his own frothy, hoppy concoctions of Indian pale ale, which originated when the Brits were shipping beer to their troops in India. The hops—the more of it the better

—had been a necessary preservative for the ale's long treks across the stormy oceans.

Sarah set her tray down on the bar before her, caught the attention of the drink-slinging day manager, and jerked her head at Nordic, who gave the man a brief wave. The barman smiled at Sarah and nodded then continued to sling his drinks.

"Let's sit," Sarah said, nudging the big man with her elbow. "My feet feel twice their normal size!"

When they were seated at a round table near the bar, Nordic winced, shook his head, regarded the girl with concern, and said, "I'm sorry, Sarah. These serving jobs take a lot out of you. It was just the first thing I heard had come open, and..."

Sarah quickly placed her right hand on his large, brown left one flattened out on the table between them. "No, no, no," she said. "I wasn't complaining. I'm just glad to have a job...steady income for Bobby and me. Do you know this is the first job I ever had? Aside from milking and herding cows and tossing hay and straw, that is. And I didn't even get *paid*!"

She smiled warmly up at the big, red-blond-bearded Norski.

"Those jobs are no nap in the flower bed," he said as another serving girl brought Sarah a cup of coffee on a saucer and a bowl of water for Finn. Nordic, being the son-in-law of the saloon's owner, always found himself being doted on in town. That doting extended to anyone in his company, even his dog.

How strange.

He had almost always been treated like a big, temperamental, dangerous giant. Most folks had been a little afraid of him, and, because of his more than rustic, mostly homemade attire including skins and furs over the cooler months, repelled.

Now, he was the boss's kin.

How strange the twists and turns in a man's life...

Sarah and her little Bobby had lived for several months at the Deveraux lodge, after Nordic and Alexandra were married. The young woman didn't feel at home there, however. Nordic hadn't blamed her. No one, not even old Deveraux had not *not* wanted her to feel at home, but it was obvious that she and Bobby needed a place of their own.

Nordic knew the feeling. Of course, being surrounded by such luxury that belonged to him only by marriage, he often felt the same way. But he loved Alex with all his heart. He'd promised himself to her. He'd also promised the old man a family and to carry on the Deveraux tradition after Garth was six feet under.

Not that Anders didn't have his doubts about the life-changing decision he'd made, but he'd give it time. That's what he always came up with, when he felt the least at home and hungered for his old life on the range, falling asleep in the piney mountains to the serenading from surrounding ridges of coyotes and wolves...

Sarah and her colleague exchanged sisterly smiles and then the other one, an earthy brunette with a heart-shaped face, named Molly, who was from Nebraska, hurried off. It was afternoon, but there was still a good dozen or so customers sitting at the baize-covered tables and standing at the polished, brass-railed bar.

Sarah turned to Nordic with a warm smile and a vaguely puzzled frown. "What brings you to town?"

His hatred for towns preceded him. He rarely came but let his men haul supplies.

He shook his head and gave a grim, dismissive smile.

"Ah," she said, slowly spooning sugar into her coffee. "The usual."

"Yeah, unfortunately." Nordic sipped his beer and placed his right hand over her left one. "How are you doing, honey? How's our rough-an'-tumble little Bob?"

"Our rough-an'-tumble little Bob is as rough and tumble as ever. As he gets bigger, he gets rough."

"Well, he's a boy."

She dipped her dimpled chin and regarded the big man warmly. "He is at that. Getting to be more and more like his Uncle Anders."

Of course, Nordic was only an honorary member of Sarah and Robert's family, but he took the role very seriously just the same. He meant to look after them as if they were blood family. Such is the bond they'd grown between them when he'd taken her in when pregnant with the child, after her family of Dakota pilgrims, driven out of their homeland south of Bismarck by drought and large ranchers wanting more and more land for themselves.

Like so many homesteaders, they thought they'd find a better life farther west. The irony was, of course, that they might have legitimately filed their claim in a fertile valley in the Never Summers, but they'd filed it on land Garth Deveraux illegitimately claimed as his. Few if anyone had ever gone up against Deveraux and not paid the highest price for it. Lawmen both respected and feared him, so no Honyocker, as the rancher saw the Nordstroms and their motley ilk, stood a chance.

Nordic had found himself in a whipsaw between feeling the compassionate need to help Sarah and her baby while remaining loyal to the man who'd given him a job when jobs had been few and far between for a moody, reclusive wanderer like Anders Nordic. Back then, before he'd met the rancher's beguiling, beautiful daughter, Anders had found life livable only when he was living it on his own with his dog, as solitary and as at odds with life and with others as he was.

Deveraux had eventually seen his foreman's true, turncoat colors, a savage man working both sides against the middle—trying to make a stake for himself by robbing his employer blind under cover of darkness with others in his crooked syndicate, and then, keeping his ruse alive, by marrying the man's daughter.

Laughing all the way to the altar, as it were.

But then the aptly named Wayne Bitterman's luck had gone south when Finn had caused the man to blow his own toe off. Realizing his foreman's motives, Deveraux had backed Nordic and the young orphan mother and her newborn infant, whom Alexandra had delivered in Anders's humble line shack.

The rustling had been stopped, the instigators run to bloody ground.

Not that the rustlers would ever entirely be stopped.

Such men were attracted to the half-wild herds grazing the high, forested reaches as minks and ferrets were attracted to chicken coops.

"Why the sudden frown?" Sarah asked, shaping one of her own as she leaned toward the big Dakotan who had so improbably, given his rough countenance and customarily aloof ways, saved her and her child.

Suddenly self-conscious Anders shook his head quickly, trying to clear the barbed memories of that former war. Of all of them, for that matter. For when he'd come west to escape humanity, to live in the mountains with the pines, the elk, the coyotes, and the hawks and eagles, he'd ridden into one long war just as surely as had every man who'd donned either dark blue or dove gray during the War Between the States.

He was no longer surprised or disappointed by what his life had become.

Such was simply life, that was all.

But he'd met good folks along the way to where he was now, married to a woman he was deeply in love with, having formed an unlikely bond with her irascible father, and sitting here in a town he didn't like, because he didn't like any of them, but with a young lady he truly did and for whom he'd become her little boy's honorary uncle.

Imagine that life for him—the loner, Anders Nordic!

Sitting close beside him and reading his thoughts the dog had learned to do well, Finn mewled, barked over the water bowl, and thumped his tail, gazing up at his partner with the zest for life in his eyes.

The Dakotan smiled now, feeling his lips stretch inside his heavy, red-blond beard and lifting the high, flat plains of his cheeks beneath his eyes as blue as the mountain lakes high up near the craggy ridges late in the day and contrasted mystically by the threat of growing shadows. Shadows always grew, for sure. But only after the bright, lens-clear light that favored the Never Summers around Ander's ranch—yes, *his* ranch—up around his vast holdings surrounding Comanche Ranch.

Sarah gave him a warm, penetrating smile as she lifted her thumb and index finger out from beneath his hand and caressed his brown knuckles. "I know how you feel," she said.

Nordic raised his brows. "You do?"

Sarah nodded. "I know how it is...living up there. I appreciated the Deverauxs' hospitality, but I quickly learned how confining that way of life was. Despite their wealth, they're prisoners. I know you feel the same way, Anders. And I know how you feel about Robert an' me."

Her smiled broadened, her own blue Nordic eyes touched with the golden sparkle of—what?

Love.

"We'll be together and on our own soon," she said. "Out where we belong. Together."

CHAPTER NINE

Anders found himself staring at Sarah, tongue-tied.
She caressed his knuckles with her thumb and continued to gaze at him with that ethereal smile spreading her lips and glowing in her eyes.

Suddenly self-conscious, she quickly removed her hand from his and lowered it to her lap. She gave her head a dismissive shake. "I'm sorry." She glanced around the room. "I know we have to be careful. Rumors can get started by only two hands touching!"

She looked down at her hand and gave an ironic laugh.

His thoughts in a knot, Anders stared back at her, disbelief rising in him.

He'd given her the wrong idea.

Same old story between women and men. One ends up expecting more from the other than the other bargained for, and a sort of human discombobulation ensues.

He poked his hand through the big handle on the tall,

heavy mug, and took two big sips of his beer. He swallowed the thick, hoppy brew, getting some of it briefly stuck halfway down. He coughed into the end of his right fist. He slid his suddenly bewildered gaze, blond brows ridged over his eyes, to Sarah.

"Sarah, honey," he said, then silently scolded himself for calling her "honey." It had been words like that, so innocently voiced and meant only to assure her he felt affection and a brotherly closeness to her, an uncle-like bond with her baby boy, that must have given her the idea that they were more than what they were—*friends*.

This was due to his own inexperience with others, he realized now.

He hadn't realized before how careful a man had to be with his words. You couldn't just bandy them around like they were wooden nickels. You had to weigh each for the meaning they might convey.

She studied him, her gaze direct. Her lips quirked a smile. "That's why I left, you know."

"Why…?"

"To make it easier on you. I didn't want you to feel… I don't know…pulled in two directions. I knew you'd get out, as I had, in your own good time, having weighed your options." She jerked her chin to indicate the misty, dark-blue, lemon-green bulk of the Never Summers looming in the west, tipped with crags still showing the ermine of last winter's snow patches. "And, believe me," Sarah added, "that ranch…those people, God love them for taking us both in…is no option for you. Any more than it was for me and little Robert!"

Nordic didn't know what to say.

His mind was frozen.

Just as he opened his mouth to try and say something, the batwings clattered behind him and in the backbar mirror he saw two roughhewn men in equally roughhewn trail garb step into Olson's Saloon. They both wore long dusters well powdered by the trail, and pistols tied low on their thighs. Their eyes were dark and flat beneath the brims of their Stetsons. One wore a black hat and long, dark mustaches while the other one, taller, wore a high-crowned brown hat with a snakeskin band. He was clean-shaven save for sandy muttonchops running down both sides of his tanned, fair-skinned, angular face.

They both raked their flinty gazes across the big man from the Comanche Ranch then turned and strode slowly, with too much casualness, toward the bar on their right. As they walked, spurs chinking on the scarred, wooden floor, the shorter man in the black hat fiddled with his mustaches and said something too softly under his breath for Anders to hear.

That he hadn't wanted it heard, however, was obvious.

"I know them," Sarah said, placing a hand again on Nordic, this time on his forearm. "They're in here a lot."

He frowned at her. "They are?"

Sarah nodded quickly as she shuttled her gaze to the two newcomers just then bellying up to the bar, sliding the flaps of their dusters back behind the hoglegs holstered on their right thighs, rawhide thongs tied just above their knees.

"One of them asked me once...a few days ago... maybe last week...if I ever saw you in here."

Keeping his eyes on the backbar mirror, noting that the two newcomers were making an effort at not returning his stare, he said quietly, "Me, personally?"

"Yes."

"Hmm."

"They have a curious, seedy way about them, Anders. I mean, most men in here do, but…" She paused, lifted her cup to her lips with both hands, and sipped her coffee, which wasn't steaming anymore. "The one who asked me about you was drunk. Loose-tongued, watery-eyed. Otherwise, I don't think he woulda asked straight out like that."

"Which one asked?"

"The short man with the mustaches."

Again, Nordic sipped his beer, lowering his gaze to the table before him.

"What do you suppose they want?" Sarah asked, apprehension in her quiet voice.

Keeping his eyes on the table, Anders gave his head a single shake.

If Sarah hadn't been with him, he'd have gone up and asked the two newcomers flat out what they wanted. He'd have asked why the shorter man had asked about him. He couldn't do that now, however, because they'd know that Sarah had told him. He didn't want her getting messed up in trouble she had nothing to do with.

Nordic took another thoughtful sip of his beer and set the mug back down on the table. Men had asked around about him before. He'd shot plenty of rustlers in his time in the West and manning line shacks on his way here—in southern Dakota, Nebraska, and Kansas. Anywhere he could find a job that would hole him up in a remote line shack, far from other men.

Alone.

Just birdsong and the nightly yammering of coyotes. Warm and secure.

Relatives or friends of such men as he'd turned toe down for their crimes, had come for him. They'd asked around about him. That might be the case with these two. It might just be coincidental that four had ambushed him yesterday and these two had been asking around about him. The factions might be after him for entirely separate reasons.

Something told him they weren't.

They might be here for Deveraux, or they might be here for him.

Possibly, both.

Somehow, these two were related by mutual interests in the four men he and Alex had taken down on Comanche Ranch graze.

Just then, he glanced into the backbar mirror. The taller, sandy-haired man had been looking at him furtively, head turned to one side.

Now the man quickly dropped his gaze and turned absently around for his beer that had just been set down before him. His lips moved as he and the shorter man conversed, the short man taking quick, equally furtive glances at Nordic in the backbar mirror. He was the dumber of the two. He wasn't as cagey about glancing at Nordic in the backbar mirror.

That they were both interested in him, however, was obvious.

He needed to light a shuck. If these men wanted him dead and didn't care where they attempted the task, Sarah might get caught in the cross fire.

"I best pick up McGreevey an' hit the trail," he said to Sarah, tossing a nickel on the table then leaning over to peck the girl's left cheek.

It was their customary way of greeting and parting.

They were good friends. But what she'd told him earlier made him realize she thought they were more than that. But this was neither the time nor the place, in light of the newcomers who were taking a special interest in him, to get into a discussion about it.

Damn, life could get complicated.

Maybe he never should have left Deveraux's line shack...

"See you later, Sarah. Give little Robert a hug from his, uh...uncle." He tried to smile and make it appear genuine. He wasn't sure if he'd been successful.

Sarah touched his arm again and smiled up at him, a little color rising in her cheeks, a vague uncertainty in her eyes. "Goodbye, Anders." She patted Finn's head. The dog, who'd seen his partner sizing up the two suspicious-looking newcomers, turned his head to smile up at her, tongue drooping down over his lower jaw as he panted.

Too warm in here.

Too warm for Anders, now, too.

Sarah, he knew, had detected his sudden hesitancy, his confoundment that had come after what she'd told him. She'd been spilling her guts. It had to have taken a lot for her to do that. And all he could return it with was his inherent taciturnity.

Damn this life sometimes...

He smiled again, trying to make a better effort, saving the hard discussion for later. He pinched his hat brim, shouldered his rifle, crossed the saloon, and pushed out through the batwings.

He swung up onto Apache's back. Finn leaped up behind him. Nordic trotted the Appy along the main street to the east, returning the nods of passing men and some ladies who now knew him, of course, as Garth

Deveraux's very fortunate son-in-law. A lowly former line shack squatter now a man of wealth and power…not to mention husband of Deveraux's enchanting daughter.

Some guys…even big, standoffish former Norski farmers from Dakota…have all the luck.

When he came to a cross street a block east of Olson's Brewery & Saloon, he stopped for a lumber wagon turning in front of him and glanced quickly over his right shoulder. The two men who'd taken an interest in him were not giving up.

They stepped out through the batwings, mounted two horses at the hitchrack, and began riding slowly toward him—nonchalantly, of course. Ignoring the dust swirling around him kicked up by several large passing freight wagons, the tall man plucked a nickel-washed disk out of his vest pocket and opened the lid, feigning an interest in the time.

Doing so, he shot a quick glance at his quarry.

Halfway down the next block, Anders swung Apache over to the street's right side and stopped in front of the broad, deep loading dock fronting Emil Vossleman & Sons' Mercantile. McGreevey was having a beer at one of the three tables on the loading dock, with a stocky, bearded gent who could have passed for his brother but whom Nordic recognized as a driver for the Front Range Stage Line, making runs to remote mountain mining camps the narrow-gauge railroads hadn't reached yet.

From this vantage, the mountains appeared wonderfully remote, quiet, downright sublime. In fact, they were honeycombed with mines and miners and those who served them like game hunters, woodcutters, itinerant opera house actors and actresses, the Sons of Han with their opium pipes, cotton pants, gold-tasseled black silk hats, dreamy black eyes, and of course the obligatory *doves du pave*.

The thunderous, echoing detonations of dynamite in the mines carved into the stony ridges were so frequent they soon became as unnoticeable as a man's own heartbeat.

New towns sprang up seemingly every other day in some remote mountain canyon with a creek or stream running through in which gold panners stood in the knee-deep, bone-splintering cold mountain water, some of it still snowmelt and for which they would pay in the cost of the chilblains, bursitis, and arthritis in their later years which would come for so many of them all too soon.

McGreevey finished his beer, shook hands with the jehu, slung his saddlebags over his right shoulder, and walked over to the edge of the loading dock to stare down at Nordic.

The foreman smiled. In his deep, gravelly voice, he said, "I see you picked up a coupla shadows of your own."

Anders hadn't seen the experienced frontiersman glance up the street behind him, to the west where, out of the corner of his eye, he saw the two stalkers from Lars Olson's Brewery & Saloon now checking down their own mounts to seemingly admire the admittedly ornate and admirable front of the recently completed opera house constructed of large bricks of local sandstone and four turrets at each corner, like some ancient Spanish military outpost in the wilds of Old Mexico.

"You got a couple of your own?" Nordic said with a smile.

McGreevey smiled back. He jerked his chin to subtly indicate the mercantile's open door behind him. "They're in yonder discussin' the price of tea in China with old Vossleman." His smile broadened. "An' I ain't jokin'."

Again, Nordic smiled and swung down from Apache's back. "Gonna get some licorice for Alex. A few of them Cuban rockets for the old man."

He tossed his reins over the hitchrack and cast the foreman a conspiratorial wink.

McGreevey chuckled and leaned forward with his arms on the loading dock's rail.

Telling Finn to stay, Anders mounted the steps. Finn sat reluctantly on Apache's back but remained obediently with the Appy, who shook his head and switched his tail. The horse, like dog, was savvy. He knew when trouble was afoot. Finn kept his eyes on his human trail partner, knowing full well from experience that anytime the big, cantankerous man from Dakota entered any place in any town there was a good chance that violence would ensue and that they'd both be quickly on the run.

Worriedly, Finn shifted his weight and mewled softly at the mercantile's broad, open door, the thick shadows beyond which quickly consumed Anders.

With an apprehensive, darkly prescient cast to his dark-eyed gaze, Finn moaned and dropped belly down on Nordic's bedroll.

Apache glanced back at him and gave a foreboding whicker.

McGreevey looked at both the dog and the horse and frowned.

He jumped with a start when men shouted and a pistol roared.

Resounding through the mercantile's door were the thuds and chinks of bootheels and spurs on a wooden floor, the loud thumps of bodies tumbling off tables, the crash of breaking glass.

Sitting on Apache's back, Finn thumped his tail and gave a quiet, fateful howl.

Yep, the dog thought. *I knew it. I just knew it!*
You can't take him anywhere...

CHAPTER TEN

Nordic had taken three steps into the mercantile when he stopped suddenly.

Two men had been walking toward the door.

They stopped suddenly, now, as well.

One wore a sheepskin vest and black chaps, a pearl-gripped .45 positioned for the cross draw on his left hip. He was maybe six feet, lean and angular, dark-skinned. Maybe Mexican or Indian or both. He wore a high-crowned gray hat. The other man was the same height as the first, but he had a big gut and a fleshy, round, clean-shaven face save for the long, wispy mustaches that made him look like a catfish.

"Careful, Kairee," said the dark man, his voice low. "I hear he's fast."

"Catfish." Kairee smiled.

A second later, his right hand reached for the Schofield holstered low on his right thigh. He didn't have the revolver half out of its holster before Nordic's Russian roared. The other man scrunched up his eyes and shouted incoherently as he reached for his Colt. He got the fancy hogleg out of its holster but shot a hole in the floor just in front of his left, black boot an eyewink before Nordic blew a puckered, blue hole in his forehead, three inches above his left eye.

The man screamed and flew straight back onto a table at which two old former mule skinners with bib beards had been playing chess. They vacated their chairs quickly though haltingly on creaky knees, grabbing their beer mugs and shuffling back away from the table that broke in two as the dark man drove both halves to the floor with a *bang*!

The big German who ran the place, Emil Vossleman, had just been coming in from the kitchen with two big bowls of stew. He stopped suddenly and dropped them now as the explosions of Nordic's Russian continued to echo around the room, which had a counter with stools running along the room's left side. The bowls landed with a crash. Vossleman sandwiched his broad face in his large, paw-like hands and cursed loudly, following the curse with a diatribe which the man from Dakota did not understand, since he didn't have even a rudimentary knowledge of German.

The dark man was still twitching his feet and rattling his spurs on the wooden floor when Nordic, extending his Russian straight out from his right side, turned back to the door, where McGreevey was down on one knee extending his Colt .44 straight out from his right shoulder, popping off shots along the street to the left, where Nordic's own shadowers had been following him like shy dogs wanting treats.

A bullet cut through the air between Nordic and the Comanche foreman and plunked into the loading dock behind McGreevey, over his left shoulder. As it did, Zeb fired again, but this time his hammer dropped with a ping onto an empty chamber.

Finn stood barking loudly on Apache's back.

The horse whickered and sidestepped edgily.

Anders ran out and dropped to his own left knee beside the foreman around whose hatted, grizzled head his own powder smoke wafted as though from a quirley rolled with peppery Mexican tobacco. Nordic aimed the Russian westward, where people were shouting curses and clearing the street, horses at the hitchrails bucking, kicking, and pulling anxiously at their reins. Traffic came to a dead stop, clearing a fifty-yard stretch of the main drag fronting the mercantile.

Soon, the only man on that stretch of street lay belly down across a hitchrack before which a tethered palomino was pitching, clawing at the sky with its front hooves and whinnying shrilly, casting bright, fearful glances at the man slumping across the worn, splintery rail before it. Nordic glanced at McGreevey, who was shaking the spent rounds out of his six-shooter. They clattered onto the dock around him as he punched fresh cartridges from his shell belt through the Colt's loading gate.

"Where's the other one?" Anders asked.

McGreevey winced. Nordic saw the blood streak on the top of his left shoulder.

"He ran through that break on the other side of the harness shop. Last I seen of him."

"You're hit."

The foreman shook his head as he spun the Colt's cylinder. It made a shrill but solid winding sound. "Nothin' much." He heaved himself to his feet. Nordic could hear the older man's knees popping.

Anders straightened and, keeping his Smith & Wesson "Russian" aimed straight out from his right side, the hammer cocked, he moved slowly down the loading dock steps. Apache and Finn were both standing in the middle of the street about thirty yards west of the mercantile. Finn had likely fled the gunfire and Apache, pulling his loosely tied reins off the hitchrack, joined his companion. The horse and dog shuttled their wary gazes between Nordic and the dead man and at the mouth of the alley in which the second gunman had fled.

"Easy, fellas," Nordic said as he approached the pair.

Finn stood beside the horse. Apache had his head down and was switching his tail apprehensively. Neither the horse nor dog enjoyed a lead swap. Nordic didn't blame them. He didn't, either. He'd been through enough to have gotten used to them, but he never had.

Bad way to go.

He ran a reassuring hand along the Appy's long neck, moving slowly up close to the saddle. Keeping an eye on that alley mouth behind the dead man slumped forward over the hitchrack, he dropped the Russian into the holster thonged on his right thigh and shucked his Yellowboy repeater from the saddle sheath. He cocked it slowly, quietly, and McGreevey followed suit with his own long gun—a fine Henry, a few years old--make that ten or fifteen, its walnut stocks, front and rear, scarred from use from scuffling with rustlers, most likely—but a fine weapon, just the same.

Nordic crossed the side street between the mercantile and the harness shop, whose proprietor it appeared had doused any lamps within and drew the flour sack curtains across the window to either side of the front door.

When they were only a few feet from the harness

shop's front corner, McGreevey sniffed the wind like a dog. He drew his stretched and chapped lips inside his tangled beard and mustache. "He's still here," he said in a low growl that rumbled up from deep inside him. "He's close. I hit him."

Nordic looked at the older man, a curious frown stitching his brows.

The foreman nodded. "Pinked him on the side. Not bad but he's hurtin'." He glanced at the younger man. "Dangerous."

Anders nodded. "I'll take this side. You take the alley."

"I see blood yonder, near the shop's far corner. Sure enough, I pinked that polecat!"

McGreevey stepped onto the boardwalk fronting the harness shop. He winced at the groaning of the sun-bleached, splintering gray boards beneath his feet as he made his way slowly toward the alley mouth beyond where the dead man's spurred, brown boots hung down from the hitchrack, a foot and a half above the boardwalk.

Nordic approached the building's near front corner. A man's pale oval face appeared in the window as a large, bony hand inched the flour sack curtain aside. The man's eyes found Nordic and widened in surprise. The hand dropped, the face jerked away, and the curtain bounced back into place over the window.

Holding his Winchester straight up and down in front of his chest. Nordic moved down along the side of the small, mud-brick building toward the rear. At the rear corner, he stopped and inched a cautious glance around the corner and across the alley to the building's rear end.

A privy and a woodshed stood on the far side of the alley from the shop.

Against the shop's rear wall, split stovewood was stacked six feet high on both sides of the back door. The door was partly open, Nordic saw. A man lay in front of it, on his side, several chunks of split wood strewn on the ground around him. He had thick, curly hair and an untrimmed brown mustache. His brown eyes were open. Blood shone where his right temple had been smashed in likely by the chunk of bloody stovewood lying three feet from the dead man's head.

He wore a heavy, cracked leather apron from the pockets of which tools for repairing tack—snips, heavy sheers, and end-cutting pliers—protruded. A half-smoked cigarette smoldered on the ground near his right hand lying palm up beside him.

Nordic spied movement ahead of him, beyond the dead man. Nordic tightened his grip on the Yellowboy then loosened it as he saw McGreevey step out around the shop's opposite rear corner. The foreman was looking down at the dead man.

He and Nordic shared a dark glance then, both men hearing movement inside the building, moved toward the partly open door.

Nordic stepped over the dead man, paused, then jerked open the door.

"No—don't shoot me!" yelled the tall, bald man also wearing a leather apron standing a few feet inside the shop, a pencil wedged behind an ear, both hands raised palm out in supplication. He edged a terrified, squinty-eyed look around the hands shielding his face.

His eyes snapped wide as he flicked his gaze over

Nordic's right shoulder and the Yellowboy whose brass butt place he pressed hard against it.

Anders had just started to turn when the privy door thundered open and one of his original shadowers—the fair-skinned man with the sandy muttonchops burst out, tearing the door from its hinges. The door dropped in the brush. The man bulled forward, running at a crouch toward Nordic.

As he did, he fired each of the two, long-barreled pistols he extended straight out from his shoulders. One bullet caromed over Anders's left shoulder to evoke a yelp from the aproned man standing behind him. The fair-skinned man triggered his other gun at McGreevey, the bullet carving a ragged hole in the corner of the building flanking the foreman.

McGreevey and Nordic returned fire at the same time, each man blowing three rounds into their assailant from his right cheek to his left hip.

The man screamed. His step faltered. He triggered two more errant rounds as he struck the ground and rolled, piling up at Nordic's feet, the man's glassy eyes staring accusingly at biggest of the two men who'd killed him.

Nordic and his foreman looked around, tracking with their rifles, on the lookout for more would-be ambushers.

A few people poked their heads out the back doors of their shops then, seeing Nordic and the Comanche Ranch foreman extending their cocked, smoking hoglegs, drew their heads back into their stores and slammed their doors.

Running footsteps sounded up the alley behind McGreevey. More sounded behind Nordic, in the break between Vossleman's Mercantile and the harness shop that, with the only two men who had run the place dead, was for all intents and purposes defunct.

The town marshal, Glen Conagher—tall, lean, gray-headed and wearing his customary carefully trimmed gray mustache—stepped wide around the harness shop's rear corner flanking the foreman. He had his Colt out and cocked and slid it between Nordic and McGreevey. The lawman's thuggish deputies, one big-gutted and cow-eyed and whose nose Nordic had once knocked flat against his face, the other not as fat but just as cow-eyed —two former bank guards and ne'er-do-wells—about the only kind who'd work for Conagher.

Conagher was a former army man and scout who had helped run herds up from Texas. Not a bad man but the authority of the job, as it did so many otherwise semi-good men, had made him hard to get along with. So far after two years in this neck of northern Colorado, Nordic never had. Of course, that wasn't entirely Conagher's fault. Anders had a penchant for, when finding himself in town and unable to resist a beer or three or four, getting into fights. More than a few times, the big man from Dakota had rearranged the two deputies' faces and been taken down by the more furtive and subtle older lawman, Conagher, with a single rap of a pistol butt against the back of the big man's head.

More than once, both Nordic and Finn, like two peas in a pod, had woken up to find themselves both housed in the same cell in Conagher's jail.

"Figured it'd have to be him!" said the big-gutted, dark-haired deputy whose nose still had a ridge in it. He walked toward Nordic, aiming his double-barreled shotgun at him while thrusting his other open hand at

Anders. "Ain't seen him in a while," he added with a dry chuckle, shaking his head.

He stopped six feet in front of Nordic, gave a crooked smile, thrust his hand out close to the big Dakotan, and said, "Hand it over nice an' easy, Dakota."

Anders laughed. "Do you really think I'm going to give you my gun, you moron?"

The deputy flushed and hardened his jaws.

Anders said, "Haven't I broken your nose enough times?"

The other deputy chuckled at his partner's expense.

"And stomped the stuffin' out of both ends," Anders said to him.

That erased the smile on the slightly leaner of the two deputies' faces. He let the carbine in his hand sag groundward.

To McGreevey, Conagher said, "What happened here, Zeb? Figure I can get a straight answer from you."

The older Comanche Ranch rider glanced at the two dead, duster-clad men and said, "They was followin' us around like baby ducks." He glanced at the man lying dead a few feet beyond the rear, open door of the harness shop and then at his hired man who'd apparently come out merely to gather firewood so they could boil coffee, saw there was trouble afoot, and got laid out with a sharp-edged chunk of stovewood. "Woody and Shipman got caught in the cross fire, more or less."

Conagher shaped a sour expression, shook his head. "More or less." He looked at Nordic who had not lowered his rifle. Just because the law was here didn't mean trouble had left. "You're still attracting trouble the way a dead cow attracts flies," Conagher said.

Nordic shrugged. "Once it's in your blood."

To the lawman, McGreevey said, "We just turned in four dead men. They ambushed Anders...er, I mean *Nordic* on the trail near the Comanche headquarters yesterday. You might wanna take a look at 'em, Glen. Their faces might be on some of those wanted circulars hangin' in your office."

"Who are they?"

"We thought you might know," the foreman returned, impatiently.

Again, Conagher bunched his lips and shook his head. "You know, Zeb, more often than not the Comanche and that old man who owns it is a big ol' thorn in my side!"

"I'll tell him you said that," the foreman said with a slant-eyed grin. He jerked his chin toward Nordic. "I'll mention it to his son-in-law, too."

Finn barked.

The dog had come running just after the lawmen had arrived. Now, instinctively knowing who the bad men were, made water on the one lying six feet out from the privy.

The big-gutted deputy gave a repellent look and said to Anders, "Did you teach him that?"

"Finn's a self-taught man."

McGreevey chuckled.

Nordic said, "You know what I'm thinkin', Zeb?"

The foreman nodded as he set his Henry on his shoulder. "If there was four here today...just like yesterday... someone wants me out of his hair real bad."

"And they might be headed for the Comanche if they're not there already." To Conagher, Nordic said, "Hate to kill and run, but..."

Anders and McGreevey tramped quickly off through

the break between the harness shop and the mercantile, heading for their horses. Finn ran panting just off their heels. The old, tall, bony Vossleman, clad in a blood-stained apron, watched them from the loading dock rail and slowly shook his bib-bearded head in disgust.

"*Achter lever*," the big German said, and brushed a fist across his nose. He didn't appreciate his loading being turned into a battlefield.

"Anders!"

He glanced past Apache and the foreman's roan to see Sarah Nordstrom running at a slant toward him from the other side of the street, holding the hem of her conservatively cut print dress above her black ankle boots. Her blond hair and blue eyes flashed in the sunlight. Her eyes were cast with concern, downright trepidation.

"Anders! Oh, Anders!" she yelled in a pinched voice, half sobbing, as she approached the big Norski.

Oh, hell, Anders thought, reminded again of the hard conversation in his and the young mother's future.

A young lady he loved in a brotherly kind of way.

A young lady with a dead family, and whom he so desperately did not want to hurt further.

Sarah stopped before him and threw her arms around his waist and pressed her right cheek against his chest.

"Thank God you're all right!" she exclaimed. "When I heard the shooting, I just knew…"

"Yeah, it's a sure bet I'd be involved," he drolly quipped.

He turned his head to see Zeb McGreevey looking at him, one eye narrowed ironically.

The aging foreman was not too old to know the connection between Nordic and the girl he'd saved from

Garth Deveraux himself and the old man's former foreman. He gave an ironic smile, said tensely, "I'll get
started. You can catch up to me." He paused then added
dryly, "Unless you think you might need help…"

He winked.

Warm blood rose in Nordic's face.

McGreevey swung around and walked toward his
roan now standing with Apache at the hitchrack fronting
the mercantile, both horses' reins dangling. Traffic was
now resuming, albeit tentatively, on Horsetooth Avenue,
the town's main drag.

Finn ran in a circle around his trail pard and the
young woman he'd come to love, as well. As though
instinctively understanding the complication, he sat
several feet away from the pair, looked darkly off toward
the mountains rising in the west—where the complica-
tions had started—and gave a long, mournful wail.

CHAPTER ELEVEN

S arah looked at him and shook several locks of her windblown blonde hair out of her face. "There were more?" she asked. "I heard the shots, thought for sure I'd find you *dead*!"

She'd said this last with not so vague accusing, as though he himself were responsible for having gunmen on his trail. He understood she was just worried, however. Worry had a way of making you mad...especially when you were worried about someone you...

Well, someone you loved.

She couldn't love him, though. He hadn't realized that was happening. Or maybe he hadn't *wanted* to realize it. For God's sake, it looked like even McGreevey had realized it. If not him, who else...?

He let that thought go. He had enough to chew on. He had to settle Sarah down and get after the old foreman and get home. The headquarters might be in danger if the strategy of whoever had targeted old Deveraux and his ranch might be to get Nordic out the way first.

Deveraux had a good twenty men on his roll. The old

man's enemies would likely know the Comanche Ranch riders were gun-savvy men. A man like Deveraux, who had not only the ranch but many other business interests —so many that Nordic hadn't even started getting his mind wrapped around them all!—and with all those interests came enemies. Some, including other ranchers in the area and mine owners and railroad operators, to boot, Deveraux considered his *blood* enemies, the malice between them having festered so long it had become a part of each of them.

Like a slow-growing cancer.

Any cunning man targeting the ranch would have thoroughly investigated Deveraux's situation in the Never Summers and his business interests elsewhere. The aggressor would likely send plenty of men—seasoned killers, most likely, *professional regulators*—to move on the Comanche.

Nordic had to assume that such a man would know it would be no easy task. His strategy might be to take out Deveraux's notoriously gun-handy and wily new son-in-law first.

But how would the man…or men…known that yesterday Nordic and his gun-handy wife had won the day?

Unless he was close.

Very close, with spies around the Comanche Ranch reporting back to him…or them…every move made at the Comanche headquarters…

At least, Nordic had McGreevey to back him here.

Zeb might not look so formidable now, but Nordic had seen him in the mountains. Over the years, the tough old mossyhorn had acquired a reputation of his own as a man not to be messed with. An old frontiersman and

Indian fighter, one who'd led the immigrants from Council Bluffs across the Overland Trail all the way to California and Oregon. That took the prowess of a man to be reckoned with, a man who'd started acquiring his cool, calculating, and fearsome reputation even back then, twenty, thirty years ago…

When Nordic had first heard McGreevey had been hired to replace Bitterman and had seen him in the bunkhouse before he'd become foreman in the wake of Wayne Bitterman's deserved demise, the Dakotan had stood up and taken notice. Albeit as stove-up and worn down as McGreevey appeared—even a bit haggard, on the backside of fifty and losing ground fast—Nordic had known that, when shaking the man's hand and seeing the old luster remaining in his eyes, he'd been shaking the hand of a legend.

He needed to catch up with that man now.

McGreevey had backed Nordic's play. Now Nordic had to be there to back the foreman's play if he needed it.

"Well, you didn't find me dead," Anders told Sarah now and gave her a reassuring squeeze, despite the way she might take it. He had to go slow with her, break it to her slowly how things really were between them. First things first. Namely, McGreevey and the Comanche Ranch headquarters.

"Go on back to Olson's place. I have to get home. Somethin's happening." He gave the young woman an obligatory peck on the forehead then turned and grabbed Apache's reins. "Not sure what it is yet, but I have to get home. I'll be back soon!"

He pinched his hat brim to her, reined the Appy around, and gigged him into a hard run in the direction McGreevey had ridden, toward the Poudre Canyon that would carry them back up into the high-and-rocky where Comanche Mountain jutted, the Comanche Ranch headquarters spread out across it, like the jewel in the crown. He didn't look back, but his heart ached, knowing that he'd left the girl in the street, gazing after him, perplexed, hurt, maybe angry.

Finn barked as he ran to catch up with Nordic. The dog had likely said goodbye to the girl, whom he loved, then turned to catch up with his partner, the man he loved far and above any other, the man who returned that love and devotion in spades.

"Come on, Finn!" Nordic called automatically, because he knew the collie was expecting it.

It was nice in this new, more sociable life they were living, to expect things from others and get them.

He wished he could return the favor to Sarah.

This more sociable life had its bitter underside.

———

Sarah wasn't the only one watching Nordic and Finn heading out of town.

Marshal Glen Conagher was, as well.

He stood in the gap between the mercantile and the harness shop. The undertaker's wagon was approaching him, but he wasn't looking at the undertaker and the man's overall-clad helper driving the wagon.

Conagher stood leaning into his elbow resting against the side of the harness shop, staring toward where Nordic and his dog just now disappeared as they swung north along the Poudre.

Flanking him, the marshal's two deputies were staring that way, too.

The beefier of the two men, the one with the lumpy nose, turned his head toward Conagher and moved his mouth, saying something to him.

Conagher turned a fiery, gray-eyed glare at the man and, clenching his fists down against his sides, shouted. "Get back to work, damn you two worthless fools! Get back to work!"

They scuttled away like scolded dogs.

Conagher returned his hard-eyed gaze to Nordic's sifting dust.

———

Sarah had heard the man berating his deputies.

Now she turned in front of Olson's Brewery & Saloon's swing doors to regard the marshal staring after Nordic and Finn.

What a strange, angry...frustrated?...look he had on his face.

Conagher turned toward her.

His eyes met hers. She jerked a little with a fearful start and placed a hand to her breast.

Conagher looked away and abruptly turned and headed back in the direction of his jail office.

———

In her second-floor room in the sprawling lodge atop Comanche Ranch, in the heart of the ranch headquarters that her father and grandfather had both fought so hard for, Alex stopped brushing her hair.

Freshly bathed, her hair still damp and brushed back behind her shoulders, Alex lowered her hand holding the brush to the dressing table that had belonged to her mother. Alex had enjoyed watching her "make herself presentable" in her velveteen, scrolled cherry armchair seated before the German-built table and mirror. She'd loved brushing out Louise Deveraux's long, thick hair—chestnut-colored like Alex's own—and watch her apply oil to her eyelids and a subtle brush of peach rouge to her cheeks before a dinner party that would be attended by her husband's wealthy business partners and their wives. Louise Deveraux applied very strategic and conservative amounts of pale powder to her cheeks, tempering the rouge and adding depth to her eyes that were the clear hazel of the Avalanche River at sunset.

The lovely woman would add just a touch of darkening to her brows and a clear gloss from a delicate square jar that had accentuated the rosiness and richness of her lips. After those deft touches, she would then be ready for Alex to help her into a long, diaphanous, lime-green or soft cream gown that, in concert with her necklace and earrings and her rich, dark hair, would glint in the light cast by the great room's guttering lanterns, candles, and the flames dancing subtly in the hearth.

The servers would be fairly dancing around the room, with silver trays laden with small chunks of wild game to be nibbled with wild berry jam and Bavarian breads and crackers.

Times had changed at the Comanche Ranch.

Now Alex found herself staring in her mirror, worry, even fear stitching her brows.

She'd heard a strange sound followed by a soft thump from somewhere in the hall. She couldn't tell if the sound had come from up the hall or down. Or had it come from outside?

The wind's steady rush made it impossible to tell.

She shuddered with the feeling of a sudden, malign presence.

Alex's frown deepened, cutting lines across her ruddy tan forehead. Such color was unladylike. Most women of Alex's station didn't let the sun find them nor did they ride astride like a man. Alex had never fit in, nor had she tried to. Another odd, unidentifiable sound rose and, staring at her own troubled eyes in the mirror, she gently set the brush down on the table.

Had her father fallen out of bed again, chasing his heavy sketchbook?

Alex shook her head subtly. That wasn't it.

Keeping her ears pricked, listening, Alex rose from her chair, clad in only a sheer, pink nightgown that revealed everything she wanted it to reveal to her man. Which was everything. She was long, tall, and full-breasted, her hips nicely rounded. Her father often crudely quipped even around others that she was a Deveraux through and through, blooded for childbirth and gifted with the efficient energy needed for raising more Deveraux.

Alex's hands were fine and delicate but bearing the traces of the work she performed around the ranch, mostly to her father's disapproval. She roped, helped with the branding, and even helped rescue mired calves and their mothers, and she mended fence if a group of the men, separated out early in the morning for separate work details, needed an extra hand for tamping or lifting or pounding staples and nails.

Now, quickly, she lifted the gown above her head. Her damp hair rose with the garment then settled back down to her shoulders as the gown silently fluttered to the floor

Apprehension tickling her spine, Alex pulled on jeans and a shirt and grabbed her ivory-gripped .44 from her dresser. She opened the bedroom door and hurried down the hall toward the far end. She stopped at her father's door, turning her head to listen through the top panel, then squeezed the knob slowly, wincing, not wanting to wake him if he was asleep. On the other hand, she didn't want him to die on the floor alone.

The latching bolt clicked.

She slid the door open and stepped inside.

Her father lay on his back in his big bed, the sketch-book open on his chest. He snored softly, head turned toward Alex, lids fluttering as he dreamed. "Lou..." he muttered in his sleep, and gave a softy, incredulous cry. "Louise..."

Tears glazed Alex's eyes.

The old sot was dreaming about her mother.

She heard the vague sound again. She looked at the window. There were two panes that opened like French doors. One of the doors was partly open, the breeze making the gauzy curtain, glowing golden with late-morning sunshine, flutter out into the room from the sill.

Alex smiled. She knew what had made the thumping sound.

A fat, blue-eyed, mottled brown-and-white cat sat on the far side of the bed from Alex, near her father's ankles. The cat sat statue still. It blinked slowly at Alex, gave its head a slight tilt to one side, and gave a soft, plaintive meow.

Louis was a cat born and bred in one of the barns and had

been running around the headquarters for at least ten years. He pretty much kept to himself, Louis did, but he was known to climb the trellis outside Alex's father's and mother's room and somehow open the door and get inside. When Alex's mother had been alive, she and her father awakened some mornings to the fat tomcat curled in sleep between them.

When they stirred, he'd meow, leap to the sill, and disappear out the window, between the blowing curtains.

Louis stared at Alex now, and meowed.

Her father stirred slightly, sucking a ragged breath down his throat.

"Shh," Alex told the cat.

Odd that he'd come in this time of the day.

His eyes told her he'd been bothered by something.

Outside?

She walked on the balls of her feet around the bed to the cat, who did not skedaddle as he did around most people moving toward him. He'd always trusted Alex which whom he shared a certain bond. Alex wasn't sure what that bond was. When she was growing up, she'd see him maybe once or twice a week. He'd follow her into the woods, and they'd sit together by a creek. Usually, he sat beside her on a rock but occasionally he'd sit on her knee. Usually, he didn't like to be touched even by her but occasionally he'd let her pick him up, hold him against her chest, purring.

But only for brief times.

Then he'd go off and be his own man again.

He let her scoop him up off the bed now, however. Maybe he wanted a treat in the form of cool cream. Once or twice a month or so, he'd stop by for the cream. Almost always he'd enter the house by old Deveraux's window. That was a mystery to Alex. Her father was not a demonstrative man. Did he and Louis have a bond she didn't know about, one that either of them would want her to know…?

Like her father's sketchbook?

She smiled at the notion as she went out, her gun in her hand, Louis sitting on her shoulder, and quietly shut the door until the bolt clicked quietly.

Alex returned to her room and set Louis on her bed, where he watched her, sphinxlike, as she finished preparing herself for the day, which was already well on its way. Having been raised around men, her and her mother being the only women aside from a few female maids over the years, Alex never went downstairs without being fully dressed in her usual attire—blue denims, flannel shirt, suspenders, and boots. She knotted a bandanna round her neck and stepped into her hand-tooled riding boots as scuffed and brush-scarred as those of any of her husband's and father's cowboys.

"Here we go, Louis…thanks for your patience, *monsieur*."

The cat flicked its tail.

The cat following and purring again, Alex moved to the door, stepped into the hall, and stopped abruptly.

Again, she heard something.

A vague commotion muffled by distance.

Alex paused, listening.

Nothing more but the breeze and quietly creaking timbers.

"Come on, *monsieur*," she said as she descended the stairs.

Louis leaped down the steps beside her, anticipating those first few laps of that cream kept cool in a small cellar beneath a trapdoor in the kitchen and which Alex and a former maid, a bosomy Swedish lady who had helped Riley Otis with Alex's mother until Louise had passed. Halfway down the stairs, the cat stopped suddenly.

Alex turned to him, frowning. "What is it, Louis?"

The cat just stared into the light showing at the bottom of the stairs.

"Louis?" Alex said again. "What is it?"

The cat flicked his tail again, anxiously...angrily.

Alex drew a deep breath, pulled the .44 out from behind her belt, and extended it straight out from her right side. Slowly, she continued down the steps, saying in a voice she tried not to let tremble, "Hello?" She paused and walked down two more steps.

"Riley? Are you in here?"

Nothing.

"*Anyone* here?"

CHAPTER TWELVE

When Alex gained the bottom of the stairs, she stopped.

She stared straight down the foyer to the front door. A sashed window to each side showed nothing but noon sunlight and the dancing branches of pines and aspens. She strode ahead, looked into the parlor beyond which lay the great room where guests were entertained. *Had been* entertained, rather, when Alex's mother was still alive.

No sound. No movement.

She peered into the kitchen on her right.

Nothing there, either.

It occurred to her that in all the excitement earlier, she'd neglected to brew coffee and make breakfast for her and her father. He'd had a hard night, she knew. She'd heard him moving around in a restive sleep—grunting, groaning, yawning loudly as he tossed and turned.

She'd bring him something for lunch. She felt better. No more of the nausea she'd felt earlier.

She'd fix something if all was clear, that was. Something told her it wasn't, that something was wrong. The odd sounds. Maybe a man's surprised grunt followed by a dull thud?

Alex moved to the window left of the door.

She peered out onto the porch. There was no sign of the man who'd been assigned to stand watch there. No, there was a sign of him. Apprehensively, tightening her grip on the .44 in her right hand, she drew the door open with her left. Slowly, looking around carefully, not liking the trepidation that oozed like mud through her veins, she stepped out onto the porch and drew the door closed behind her.

She moved over to the object she'd seen through the window, crouched down and took the semi-wet, half-smoked quirley between her thumb and index finger. Still warm. A chair was parked against the lodge's front wall, to the left of the door. A Winchester carbine leaned against the wall beside the chair.

The rifle of the man who'd been posted as lookout here, to prevent anyone from getting inside.

Alex looked around, heart quickening.

A man's pain-pinched grunt rose behind her, somewhere off the end of the veranda. She glanced behind her. Nothing.

The grunt sounded again, the trill of a spur.

Alex's heartbeat increased, making her a little breathless. She rose quickly and, holding the .44 in her right hand, hurried down the porch steps, swung left, and walked down the side of the house, between where the pine-carpeted southern ridge swooped down into the yard, casting heavy shadows aromatic with pine and cedar tang.

After she'd walked slowly for fifteen feet, she stopped.

Denim-clad legs and spurred boots stretched out from between two thick evergreen shrubs Alex's mother had planted many years ago, after she and Alex's father had first been married. The man's booted feet moved, grinding the spurs into the ground.

Alex stood over him, stared down through the shrubs at him.

Case Sleighbaugh lay there. He was a quick, rangy man with a long elk-skin vest and knotted bandanna around his neck. His brown, sweat-damp hair was mussed and indented where his hat had been. His weathered Stetson lay to his right, turned onto its crown. The crown was caved in on one side—where a gun butt had been slammed down hard against it.

The realization of what had happened, that Case had been jumped, made Alex gasp. Her knees grew weak. She stared at Case's suntanned face carpeted in two-or-three-days of dark-brown beard stubble that contrasted the brick red of his sweat-glistening cheeks.

His brown eyes opened. They peered up at Alex, bright with misery.

He lifted his head a little, winced as pain racked him. He moved his lips, but it took a second or two for him to say, "Run!" He turned his head from side to side, wincing again. Then, a little louder, "I'm so sorry, Miss Alex. *Run!*"

Too late.

A shadow slid along the pine-needle-laden ground to her right.

She jerked with a start, began turning, caught a brief glimpse of the man behind her before a loud explosion rose from the porch, making Alex's ears clang and the ground leap beneath her feet. She'd just looked into the eyes of the tall, lean man standing behind her in a checked shirt and holding a gun by its barrel up near his right shoulder, ready to smash it down against Alex's head—before his own head shredded and blood flew.

The man blinked once before his head was torn off his shoulders and went bouncing and thumping around the scrubby ground to his left.

He dropped the pistol and staggered to his left. His arms flopped down against his sides. As his shoulders spurted blood where his head had been, he fell sideways onto his left shoulder and hip without breaking his fall.

Alex's ears kept ringing.

She clamped her hands over them and turned to her father, old Garth Deveraux himself, standing on the near end of the porch, aiming his trusty old Richard's gut-shredder straight out from his right shoulder.

Pale powder smoke curled from both barrels.

Alex released a deeply held breath as running foot-steps sounded from the direction of the bunkhouse and corrals.

"Oh...Father...!"

Alex stumbled backward, mind numb with shock.

Deveraux lowered the scattergun, scowled at his daughter with open reproof in those hard blue eyes, and shook his head slowly. "Let a man sneak up on you from behind like that?" Again, he shook his head. "Who *raised* you?"

———

A t the same time eight miles away, Finn ran around a curve in the mountain trail then up a low ridge fifty yards ahead of Nordic. The dog stopped at the top of the ridge and, tongue drooping over his lower jaw, gave a delighted bark, lifted his head, and howled.

Finn glanced back at his trail partner and wagged his tail.

Nordic knew what the dog was so excited about. It didn't take much more than seeing a friend he'd last seen less than an hour ago to put a spring in his step, a sparkle in his eye, and a big, friendly wag in his tail.

Dogs...

Nordic smiled. He wasn't much of a smiler, but nothing made him smile like a dog did.

"Get him, Finn," he said as he booted Apache on up the trail a few yards to the right of which the Cache la Poudre rushed through a thin screen of firs and aspens. "Get him an' give the devil the hindmost!"

He and Apache crested the rise, and there before him sat his middle-aged foreman on the ground beside his roan, leaning back against a pine bole. He had his legs stretched out before him, crossed at the ankles. He held a cigarette between the thumb in index finger of his right hand. He held a silver flask in his left hand, resting on his left thigh. His worn green Stetson was thumbed up on his forehead, revealing two large warts at the bottom edge of the pale strip of skin usually concealed from the sun.

Water dripped from the roan's snout. He'd just taken a drink from the river.

Panting, Finn ran up beside McGreevey, turned to face Nordic, sat down off the foreman's left hip, and curled his tail around behind him. He was glad they were together again. There was something about dogs and the idea of folks who liked other folks...and dogs...being together.

"Get that smile off your face," Nordic ordered.

McGreevey chuckled and shook his head. "What're you gonna do? Two women after you at once. I don't even have one!"

"Hell if I know." Nordic leaned out from his saddle fender to spit.

He scowled at his foreman who had also become his friend, the notion sort of sneaking up on him from behind. But there it was. He didn't know if it was supposed to work that way. He'd never been in such a position before. He was taking all this—being the head man behind his father-in-law of a large ranch—one day at a time. One hour at a time, truth be known. Just like he'd started out with Finn after he'd saved the dog from those abusive, little, male miscreants in New Mexico.

Though he saw the dog as much his own savior as he was the dog's.

McGreevey chuckled again. "Don't ask me. I always felt lucky just havin' one at a time. And, by God, that was enough!"

Finn barked, wagging his tail. He may not have known the gist of the joke, but he knew he was in on it just because he was in with these two men, both of whom, despite their outer gruffness, treated him like he was one of them. Finn hadn't known human kindness before the big man from Dakota had saved his hide in Chama.

Nordic looked at the flask resting on the man's thigh. "You know the rules. No drinkin' on the job."

The foreman raised the flask. "Oh, this? This ain't for me. This is for you. You're the one who needs it!"

He grinned as he offered the flask.

Nordic nudged Apache ahead, dismounted, slipped the Appy's cinch to let him blow freely and walk down to the water for a drink. Despite Nordic's impatience to get home, the mount needed a brief rest and water. Its rider accepted the flask from McGreevey.

He popped the top and took a long pull. He pulled the flask down, noted the soft, gentle burn inside him, filing some of the edges he'd felt on his ride out from town. Sarah Nordstrom's pretty face as she'd stared up at him curiously, incredulously, floated up behind his eyes again.

He raised the flask and took another pull, and the image slid away.

He sighed. "Does help," he admitted.

He thrust the flask at McGreevey. "Gentlemen don't drink alone."

McGreevey smiled again. "Was hopin' you'd see it that way." He took a pull, capped the flask, and shoved it down into a deep pocket of his buckskin, wool-lined vest. He studied Nordic ironically for a time, then said, "Don't fret. You got it way and above most men. Two beautiful women."

"I only need one."

"And you have one *helluva* spread here."

"And a lot of responsibility."

"Time slides up on a man."

"I know."

"You don't want to be alone. Like you, I've been alone. Thought it was the best for me, bein' the owly son of a bitch and all-around miscreant that I am." McGreevey gave his head a shake, his eyes darkly pensive. "Time slides up even faster when you're alone."

"I have Finn."

"You'll always have Finn. You'll always have her, too. If you play your cards right."

"Which is?"

"Gently, my friend." The wry smile widened on the old frontiersman's face. "Gently...with a close eye on your back trail!"

He tipped his head back and roared. He had a loud laugh, the foreman did, but the river nearly drowned it as it crashed between boulders, spraying white froth. The shade from the aromatic pines and the aspens felt fresh and cool.

"In other words," Nordic said, "I have to figure it out for myself."

"No guide has ever been written for what you have to deal with!"

Again, the aging foreman laughed.

Finn rose, turned to the man, and barked.

He was laughing along with the foreman, enjoying the camaraderie he felt here between two men and a dog even if one of those men felt he had the upper hand on the other one because he didn't have two women after him, a bunkhouse full of ranch hands, and a spread as big as some Eastern states or bigger.

McGreevey longed for something, Nordic knew. It was simple enough, he also knew. And he was old and wise enough to know what lay within his limits.

A good woman...and maybe a dog...to grow old with when he'd gotten too old to sit a half-wild horse and win the respect of a bunkhouse full of men, most of whom were half his age or younger.

You have my respect, you old scudder, Nordic said silently to the older man, staring back at him with his own thin, thoughtful smile half shaded by the broad brim of his cream sombrero. *You'll always have that.*

That was another thing he'd gained by coming here and taking over the Comanche Ranch for his wife's father. He had more than land and a big house and a bunkhouse full of men who respected him despite all his years riding alone—a loner from Dakota who usually only ever got noticed because of his size.

And because of the legend that had slowly grown around him and now preceded him wherever he went.

He had more than that.

He had a friend in Zeb McGreevey.

He hadn't known him long, but some friendships didn't take long to cultivate. He'd have McGreevey's friendship forever. A friendship like that didn't end when either of them died.

Anders turned to where Finn sat gazing at him. The dog was reading his mind. He was smiling his understanding with his eyes.

The dog knew as Anders knew that the friendship between them, man and dog, didn't end when either of them died, cither.

"Let's get back to the ranch," Nordic said, and tightened his saddle cinch. He looked over and above his saddle, gazing at the brassy sky above the arrow-shaped tops of the pines rising on the ridge to the southwest of the river. "Gotta…gotta bad feelin'…"

CHAPTER THIRTEEN

Thomas Ruddason, also known as Moon Runner, which was his original, Ute name, drew back on his rawhide reins braided with eagle feathers, stopping the sleek, black stallion he was forking. The markings on the stallion's neck, withers, and hindquarters marked it as the horse of a Ute warrior.

Ruddason was dressed in regular white-man's garb— denim shirt, brown leather vest, tight blue denims, and black boots. The main difference was that his clothes were in much better shape than that which most thirty-a-month-and-found white cowpunchers kept their own duds in. They were working garb, for sure, dusty and spotted with sweat stains here and there, but clean and crisp beneath the sweat and dust. Ruddason, could have passed for any on-Indian range rider in the Never Summers—aside from his distinctive Indian features and the tightly wrapped braids falling down his back, trimmed, as well, with eagle feathers.

His cream Stetson was banded in tooled brown leather—the fine tool work depicted charging buffaloes with their heads down, faces fierce, horns hooked. He and his companion were halfway up the two-track ranch trail from where the Avalanche River split the Kawuneeche Valley, one of the few places in the First Front of the Rocky Mountains—*Nuuchiu*—that had retained its Indian name. From here, Ruddason could see part of the eastern end of the Comanche Ranch headquarters—glimpses of outbuildings and corrals as well as a long, log bunkhouse with a shake roof and a large, stone chimney. He could also see through a screen of pines and aspens the ranch's grand sprawling lodge on a rise several hundred feet from the main yard with its centerpiece of a windmill and stone stock tank.

The windmill's metal blades turned lazily, winking gold in the afternoon sun. The Indian could hear the blades' faint squawking from here, nearly a hundred yards down the ridge from the yard.

He turned to Samantha Roman sitting her dapple gray mare to his right. The gray was fidgeting, lifting her head and chewing her bit. It whickered uneasily. Ruddason's own horse wasn't happy, either. It had its snout in the air, and big leathery nostrils contracted and expanded as it shifted, pricking its ears and switching its tail.

Samantha, a white woman in a cream blouse, gray riding skirt, and long, black riding boots glanced at Ruddason. A faint color besides her outdoor Utah tan rose in her cheeks. She wore a black box hat with a gauzy black veil and a white lace tail dropping down her long, slender back.

"Trouble here, Thomas."

"Yep."

Fifteen minutes earlier, on the southern breeze, they'd heard the unmistakable report of a large-gauge shotgun and the clamorous, frenetic yelling of many men. Now the headquarters was silent save for two dogs fighting over a branch in the yard near the windmill and stock trough.

In the aftermath of the shooting, the dogs gone back to their high jinks, which possibly meant the trouble expressed by the shotgun had passed and that Thomas and Samantha, the daughter of the Indian agent at the Uintah and Ouray Reservation in Utah, maybe hadn't just ridden into the middle of a shooting war.

Samantha scowled down at her dapple gray, who was tugging at the reins she held tightly in her black-gloved hands, and glanced at Thomas again.

"Maybe we should go back, come another day."

Ruddason shook his head. "My nephews are gone. Their trail led here." He glanced at her. "You stay here."

"Let an Indian man ride into a white ranch headquarters alone?" said the pretty brunette and booted her gray ahead along the trail beside her Indian lover. "I'm not that smart, I'm afraid."

Thomas and Samantha rode up into the yard and stopped when the two dogs dropped their stick and came running and barking, shaking their tails as well as raising their hackles. Both friendly and aggressive. They probably didn't like Indians any better than Indian dogs liked white people.

From the big, lodge atop the rise came the yell, "Company!"

A man on the lodge's broad front porch picked up a rifle and came down the steps. Several others followed, all of them spreading a good ten feet apart and canting their heads to get a look at the newcomers—a beautiful white woman and an Indian in white-man's garb and with long, thick, coal-black braids hanging down his back.

They looked at each other, confused by the nature of their visitors. Thomas started to smile at their consternation, trying desperately not to reach for the Sharps carbine angling up from the beaded scabbard strapped to his saddle's right side. An Indian around white men—especially white men who'd likely tangled with The People before—knew to keep his hands away from his weapons. So much as a twitch could get him blown out of his saddle.

If Thomas were dead, what would happen to Samantha?

He winced and shook his head, regretting one more time his having relented to her demand that she join him and his grandfather and many others in his extended family to travel overland by horse through the Rockies to the Never Summers, where Thomas's family was originally from.

Where most of them had died, in fact, in the sixties and seventies, when in the wake of the War Between the States the whites stormed westward to start new lives for themselves...

"Hold on! Hold on!" ordered a big, burly man—nearly wider than he was tall—stomping after the first men off the porch, most of whom, Thomas saw, were young enough to be the older man's grandsons. "Lemme get ahead o' this thing, gallblastit!"

He walked, stumbling on bandy legs, down the rise, throwing his arms out for balance. He was clad in a shapeless, dark felt hat and in a loose-fitting deerskin tunic on the chest of which an ancient hide tobacco sack bounced on the leather thong around his neck. He wore baggy denims and suspenders, an old revolver hanging low on his right thigh, which it slapped with every step he took.

With every step, which was too fast for him, he nearly fell.

He cursed under his breath.

By the time he'd made it to the windmill and the two dogs still barking and circling the newcomers, his leathery, round, mustached face was bathed in sweat. Breathing hard, he stopped and rested his hand on the grips of the old gun in its soft, leather holster. As the others, a good ten to fifteen men, mostly young, a few maybe in their late thirties, early forties, stopped to form a ragged semicircle behind him, this older man scrutinized the newcomers, appearing as though he couldn't believe his eyes.

"I understand your surprise," Thomas said. "We are accustomed to it."

The old man studied him and the pretty woman suspiciously, still breathing hard, sweat soaking his thick red mustache and beard.

"Odd pair, I know," Thomas said. "Don't worry—I'm not here to take any scalps. I'm looking for a couple of my nephews that left the encampment…against orders… late last night."

The thick-set, older man turned to the rail-thin younger man standing beside him, holding a Winchester down low across his thighs. He looked at the older man then returned his suddenly much darker gaze to Thomas.

Oh, no, an inner voice said to the Ute, who'd been raised as a warrior and still had the impulse, as much as he tried to suppress it, in his blood. *Don't let it come to this. Maykh.* He shook his head. *No.*

Keeping his gaze on the younger man, whose bleak eyes were riveted on Thomas, shifting quickly to the young lady on the fine gray beside him, the older one said, "They still out there, Sure Shot?"

The younger one scrunched up his eyes and gave an affirmative dip of his chin.

The older man cursed under his breath. To Thomas, he said, defensively, "They was tryin' to steal two horses out of our corral. Came at my boss the way the Sioux musta rode at Custer, slingin' lead." He paused, blinked once, dragged a sleeve of his buckskin tunic across one cheek, swabbing sweat. "They're dead."

"Where?" Thomas was not surprised. Heartbroken but not surprised.

The older man hesitated. He glanced at the younger, taller man then turned back to Thomas. "Want...I should have them brung to you?"

Thomas shook his head. "I want to see them."

The older man swallowed, glanced at the younger one to his left and then at the others, likely most of all the hands on the ranch out here by now—and sighed. "You men wait here," he said. To the younger one beside him, he said, "You try to backtrack the headless fella, Ryan. Where's Case?"

"Inside. Riley is doctorin' his head."

"The old man?"

"In his office with Miss Dev...er, I mean...with Mrs. Nordic."

The older man nodded. "Keep everybody here." To Ruddason, he said, "Follow me."

Thomas looked at Samantha. He looked at the Comanche Ranch men standing near the windmill, the dogs sitting nearby, tongues drooping, then turned back to the young woman. "Stay with me. Stay close."

She looked back at him, her brown eyes grave, and nodded.

The older man ambled across the yard and into the thick brush flanking the corrals, abandoned stock pens, woodsheds, an ancient chicken coop that had all but returned to the earth, and the bunkhouse. He walked maybe fifty yards before he stopped, his back to Thomas and Samantha riding beside him, and placed his fist on his hips.

He gave his head a single wag and turned to Thomas riding up beside him now.

His voice again pitched defensively, he said, "Like I said, they shot first. My boss had no choice."

"I don't doubt your story, mister," Thomas said, stepping down from the leather and dropping his braided reins.

Samantha dismounted, too, dropped her own reins, and followed Thomas over to where his nephew, son of his dead sister taken in childbirth, Rains Forever, lay in the bloody brush he had fallen into.

His young, brown, bare-legged body—his feet clad in badly worn white-man's boots with toes curled like those of moccasins—lay on his side, an anguished look on his pinched-up face. His chest and belly were covered in blood. His twin braids lay behind him in the bent brush.

Samantha gave a quiet intake of air, a strangled half sob, and snaked her left arm around her husband's waist. They stood together for a long time, staring down at the fifteen-year-old, whose father Thomas had had to kill when Six Clouds went after his wife, Thomas's sister, in a drunken rage with a bowie knife he'd bought for a horse from a white man.

Thomas sighed deeply then stooped, picked up the almost startlingly light body, and lay the young warrior over the backside of Thomas's horse, over his bedroll strapped behind the cantle.

Leading their horses, Thomas and Samantha followed the older man over to where the other young warrior, Still Nesting Eagle, lay much the same way—twisted and bloody, lips parted in agony even in death. As a toddler he'd been found swimming under a tree where two eagles were nesting, unbothered by the youngster's presence. Samantha sobbed quietly into her hands as Thomas lifted the boy in his arms and lay him like the other one, belly down across the rear of Samantha's gray, over her own bedroll which her deer hide rain slicker was wrapped tightly around.

"I can get you blankets to cover 'em with," said the older man, his defensiveness gone now, a gentle tone in his voice.

Thomas shook his head. "Won't be necessary."

He produced coiled rope from his saddlebags, cut it in two pieces, and used the two lengths to tie the dead braves' ankles to their wrists beneath the bellies of Thomas's and Samantha's mounts.

He swung up into his saddle. "Our encampment isn't far away." His expression hardened, his own brand of defensiveness entering his voice now. "We're on free range. I know it's still free. At least, your government owns it. That means it belongs to all—to even the Utes who were born and raised on it, who fought, died, and sustained themselves on it—for generations."

He shook his head and stared down at the older man.

"Mister, we won't be there long. And we are not looking for trouble. Please don't send anyone to harass my people…or there *will be* trouble."

He glanced at Samantha. She stared back at him, her brown eyes cast with apprehension now.

Thomas said, "If your boss would like to speak to me, he is welcome."

He reined his black around, trotted back through the brush where a much older man—even older than the one who had taken him and Samantha to the two dead young warriors—stood with the others. The older man, clad in a ratty robe over longhandles, held a double-barreled shotgun up high across his chest.

He stared at Thomas and Samantha without expression, with maybe a little shrewdness dancing at the corner of his old, slanted eyes.

Again, Thomas and Samantha shared a glance then put their horses down the ridge abutted on both sides by heavy pine and aspen forest, taking it relatively slow out of respect for the dead young warriors riding behind them.

It would be the young men's last rides on horses—in this world, anyway.

CHAPTER FOURTEEN

Nordic and Zeb McGreevey checked their horses down at the same time. They were halfway up the ridge to the Comanche Ranch headquarters. The men turned to each other, brows beetled over puzzled eyes, then returned their incredulous gazes to the two riders riding toward them, within sixty yards and closing slowly, holding their horses to walks.

Finn ran twenty yards ahead of Nordic, barking. Nordic called him back and, mewling his frustration, Finn returned and sat in the trail beside Apache's left front hoof. He yipped softly in frustration.

The riders each appeared to be carrying something on the backs of their horses, behind the two riders themselves...one of whom was a woman in a blouse, gray riding skirt, black boots, and with a box hat with a gauzy white stretch of fabric billowing out behind her as she rode. She was cameo-pin pretty with her heart-shaped face that had not a single wasted line, a proud nose, and straight, resolute mouth. She wore her blouse buttoned up to her neck, around the base of which, above her starched collar, she wore a single, black ribbon with a single, pearl stud.

She was as beautiful as a painting. Yet, not unlike Nordic's own wife, her deep tan overlaid against naturally smooth, alabaster skin, bespoke a curious young woman who did not confine herself to the indoors. No, she was often out with him, the regal, thirty-something Indian. Did she translate for him or was there something more there?

The question didn't linger long in the rancher's mind.

There was something more there.

"Now," McGreevey said, "who in the hell…?"

"Took the words right out of my talkin' box," Anders said, drawing Apache's reins up beneath his chin, stopping the mount.

They were an impressive-looking couple, he thought. He'd give them that.

The two visitors to the Comanche Ranch kept coming, faces stony. As they approached and then stopped their horses eight feet away from Anders and his foreman, it became increasingly apparent to Nordic that the man, who rode to the woman's left, Anders's own right, had at least some Indian blood.

Strike that.

With those high, flat cheekbones and inky black eyes sunk deep in finely chiseled sockets…those braids woven with feathers…the typically unreadable expression, he was pure blood if he was an ounce.

Both riders' eyes slid from Nordic to McGreevey then back again, and remained on the rancher, who held his reins taught against his chest. Apache was fidgety, smelling the death emanating off the two dead young braves riding belly down across the two newcomers' horses, behind the cantles of their saddles.

The Indian and the woman stared flatly at Nordic.

Neither said anything. They didn't have to. They knew what had happened. Old Deveraux or Alex or Fancy Dan, in charge when McGreevey was away, had told them. It was a solemn time for them. Nordic gave his chin a cordial, respectful dip, then turned Apache off the trail on his left. McGreevey followed suit, turning his own mount off the trail on his right.

The Indian and the woman, whose light-brown bangs slid across her forehead in the breeze, kept their mounts forward.

The man said over his shoulder as he passed, "Come. We'll talk. You know where we are."

"How do you know I know?"

"You know."

The man turned his head forward, and he and the woman continued down the ridge, the thick shadows of the midafternoon forest closing around them. Finn, mewling louder, instinctively wanting to give chase because he instinctively chased anything that moved— oh, what fun!—stared up at his trail boss, slitting his eyes. He wanted Anders to know he'd obeyed, but it hadn't been easy.

"Good boy."

Finn gave a proud snort, smiling.

At the bottom of the ridge, the Indian and the white woman swung to the left and headed north, toward where Nordic and McGreevey had come upon the Indian encampment.

The foreman turned to Anders. "Now, what do you think about *that*?"

Anders shook his head. "I haven't the foggiest idea."

"They look about as mismatched as you an' the missus."

"I know," Anders said. A smile tugged briefly at one side of his mouth, glinted in the outside of his right eye. "He's way purtier than she."

McGreevey gave a caustic snort.

They put their horses back onto the trail and continued to the top of the ridge. They rode through the headquarter's entrance portal with the large overhead crossbar and *COMANCHE RANCH* chiseled deeply into the age-silvered wood. The ranch's other two dogs came out, barking, but, as usual, Finn chased them off, with a nip to each one's butt, reminding both who was top dog in these parts.

Garth Deveraux stood in front of the stock tank at the base of the windmill. The shorter but far wider Fancy Dan stood beside him, staring darkly at Nordic and the Comanche Ranch foreman. Nordic reined up in front of both men and curveted Apache, who was still trying to rid his nose of the stench of death. Now, however, he was staring owlishly up toward the lodge over which lay the shade from the western pines as the sun angled toward the crags standing tall and touched with the salmon greens of the Rocky Mountain afternoon, and at the base of which sat the unseen, cool, dark waters of Lake Agnes.

Those remote, pristine waters beckoned to Nordic. Water always had called to him, especially after a long, hard day in the saddle, working cattle and shooting rustlers. Most of the shacks he'd lived in had been built near a water source—a lake or a creek. The Avalanche ran at the bottom of Comanche Ranch. Nordic always intended to swim in it, to clean off the trail dust and to regain his vigor, but he found that running the ranch and its vast acreage, nearly twenty hands including a blacksmith and wheelwright, a small bevy of stable boys mostly hired from surrounding farms, and thousands of cattle took every minute of every day, including many nights.

Deveraux held his trusty scattergun on his right shoulder. It didn't look like he'd gotten dressed for the day...again. If he was healing from his stroke, it was slowly. He didn't seem to be regaining his strength. That was probably due to his smoking and drinking and lounging around, feeling sorry for himself for having lost his wife, one of two grace notes in his life—his late wife and his precocious daughter—and for growing old.

"You saw our visitors," the old man croaked out, looking badly in need of a drink. He always looked drawn and pasty and desperate in the eyes when he needed a drink to quell the aching—both real and imagined—in his knees, his heart, and in his brain.

"Yep."

"Ever seen such a pair?"

Nordic glanced at McGreevey, who covered a chuckle by spatting chaw into the dust beneath his roan.

Deveraux said, "They're camped with others. *Injun* others, like him not her. Ride out tomorrow. Take Zeb and some others with you. I want 'em gone."

Nordic didn't say anything.

This was always the hardest part—dealing with old Deveraux who lived by the old ways, who regarded open range as his own. And who, out of long habit, used savage force, if necessary, to keep it his own.

Oh well, Anders thought. It wasn't him who caused the trouble. It was those two young braves likely trying to prove their manhood by sneaking in here this morning to steal a couple of Comanche Ranch horses. They'd shot at him, and he'd fired back.

End of story.

He'd let it go.

No, he wouldn't. He knew he wouldn't, because they wouldn't leave if he didn't take action.

Now he followed his father-in-law's gaze up to the sprawling lodge as two hands carted what was obviously a blanket-wrapped body down the hill toward the stables. Each carried an end on his shoulder. Some round object about the size of a man's head bulged out the blanket between the dead man's chest and his waist.

Both men grunted with the effort of hauling the load. Looks of disgust lined their faces.

As they passed, Apache and McGreevey's horse nickered edgily and shook their heads.

A good deal of blood from the bodies had soaked through the striped Indian blankets.

Nordic turned to his father-in-law quickly, the question in his scowl.

"A visitor. White man. Around noon. Knocked out Case an' would have knocked out Alex if—"

"Alex?!"

"She's all right! She's all right!"

Nordic neck-reined Apache hard left and booted him into a gallop up the hill through the pines. As he approached the house, Nordic heard the melodic strains of a piano.

Of Alexandra's piano in the parlor.

He leaped down from the horse and told the man standing there with a rifle to take his horse to the stable and see that the stable boys tended him well. The Appy would be needed the next morning. Anders wanted him rested. There was no other horse like Apache in the Deveraux remuda, despite how much the old rancher had paid for the stallions most of them had been sired with.

Nordic walked into the lodge's front door and right away heard a man say, "Ouch, you old scudder! You tryin' to heal me or kill me?"

He recognized the voice of the Canadian, Case Sleighbaugh, coming from the kitchen.

Nordic poked his head into the kitchen. Case sat in a chair at the table, his dented hat on the table to his left. The tall, Black man, Riley Otis, a liberal spatting of gray in his hair and beard, poked at the puncher's head with a damp cloth. A basin filled with bloody, pink water sat on the table nearby, steaming slightly.

"What happened?" Nordic asked.

Otis and Sleighbaugh turned to him.

Otis pulled a bloody cloth away from the Canadian's head and said, "I'm gonna shoot him if he don't hold still an' he don't stop his sissified caterwaulin'!"

Case said, "They jumped me, boss! Hornswoggled me good. I heard something out back, an'…ouch, Riley, you're kill me with all that pokin' an' proddin'!"

"Ah, hell," the Black man said, tossing the cloth in the basin. "He just needs a bullet!"

Nordic gave a frustrated chuff and left the room. He followed the soft, chiming of the piano through a lady's neat, red-carpeted tearoom with matching drapes over the windows and with its small table adorned with a silk cloth and silver tea server. Paintings in gilt frames on the walls hailed from another time and another place far beyond Nordic's understanding. Well educated and cultured, these Deveraux women. Imagine in such a savage place.

He walked past the marble bust of some man named Goethe...or however you said it...and through a pair of French doors, turning the brass handles slowly and swinging them partly open. Alex sat just beyond the doors, in the lodge's slightly more masculine parlor with wooden floors and game trophies adorning the walls, though there was more civilized trimming here, as well. Nice paintings of outdoor mountain scenes and horses and blooded bulls, two round wooden tables for late-night card games, cigars, and brandy snifters.

On the big liquor cabinet on the wall to Nordic's left, a decanter had been pulled out of alignment. Its stopper lay on the cabinet beside it.

Alex looked up from where she sat at the piano, a haunted look in her eyes. A cut-glass goblet lay atop the piano, near where she crouched over the keys, smiling dreamily—her eyes slightly glassy. Her hair had tumbled half out of its chignon and hung over her right shoulder.

"How was your trip to town?" she asked, sort of lolling her head and shoulders around with the music, above the keys she played beautifully, with nary an off note.

Anders sat on the bench beside his obviously distraught wife. "Later."

"Ah, sounds eventful."

"What happened here?"

Alex played for a few more seconds, smiling and closing her eyes. When she opened them again, she lifted her hands from the keys and looked at him with an odd, fractured smile. "Ever seen a man's head separated from his shoulders?"

Oh, hell.

He chewed off his right glove and set it awkwardly on the piano beside her glass. He placed his right hand atop hers.

"I have," Alex said, her dreamy, peculiar smile in place. "You'll see everything here, sooner or later!"

She leaned toward him and kissed his cheek.

CHAPTER FIFTEEN

"Oh lordy," Nordic said, his heart twisting for his young wife. He slid her tangled bun back behind her head and caressed her cheek with his thumb. He remembered the shotgun Deveraux had been wielding down in the yard, the dark but proud expression on his craggy, bearded face. "Your father."

"Someone call me?" a deep-throated voice broke in as the big old buff, Deveraux himself, pushed through the quarter-open French doors. "What can I do ya for? Oh, don't mind me. I was just needin' a little Who-Hit-John an' was too damn lazy to walk all the way back to my office!"

He lifted the decanter from the bureau, gave its open mouth a sniff, and smiled at his daughter, who held her own smile on her husband. Nordic removed his thumb from her cheek, his own cheeks warming with embarrassment though the old fella had caught them in plenty of embarrassing situations before. The lodge was large, but sometimes it wasn't large enough for the old bull buff, his lovely daughter, and big son-in-law.

Deveraux splashed brandy into a snifter and turned to Alex and Nordic still sitting on the piano bench.

"You all right?" Anders asked his wife, pitching his voice low, trying to pretend his intrusive father-in-law wasn't there.

Alex scowled. "Of course, I'm all right! Why shouldn't I be?" She rose and strode, smiling from ear to ear, to her father. She rose onto her toes and kissed the old man's cheek. "My father might be so old that when he enters a room the hills get up to offer him their chairs, but he's still got it, by God. If it hadn't been for him"— she turned to him and rubbed in the kiss she'd just given him—"I might be headed off to God knows where on some tough nut's hoss!"

She gave her father a genuinely appreciative, admiring smile then turned her glittering eyes to Nordic.

"Used both barrels," Deveraux said, a little incredulous. To Nordic, he said, "Don't worry—Alex was well out of the way, and I was close enough the shot went off tight enough."

"Tight enough?" Alex intoned, chuckling. "Why, they were so tight they tore the man's face off before ripping his head clear off his shoulders." She ridged her brows at Nordic. "You should've seen it. Bounced just like a ball!"

"I'm sorry, dear…that you had to see that," Deveraux said.

"I have to admit," Alex allowed, "that was a new one for me. I've seen men die in bad ways. Hanged, shot, burned, splattered beneath rockslides, worn like ornaments on the heads of bulls who gored them…trampled, beaten bloody, lightning-struck, rattlesnake bit…"

She planted her fist on her hip and turned to her husband, her warm gray eyes glittering with humor that,

Nordic knew, was all for her father. God, how she loved
that man. Wanted him to think she was as tough as any
boy he might have raised to manhood or had convinced
to stay on the ranch, to toil under his callused, ruling
thumb.

"Sure enough," she continued. "Papa hired a young
horsebreaker. A half-breed named Noah Three Crows.
Charming boy if a little sullen, but...helluva horsebreaker—eh, Pa?"

Deveraux shrugged, his pasty cheeks mottling red. He
wasn't sure he was being made fun of or fawned over.
Nordic wasn't sure himself. Maybe a little of both.

Maybe his wife, after seeing what she'd seen, had
gone a little off her nut.

The first time Nordic had witnessed such a grisly
scene he'd lost an entire day's worth of grub and had
been haunted by nightmares for years.

"Good horsebreaker," Alex said. "I was watching him
work the kinks out of a green yearling, leading him
around the corral, cooing to it, being ever so gentle, and
what does the horse do? Kicks out of a shoe that hadn't
been set right. The boy tripped over it. There was a
burlap sack of ropes nearby...only, one of the ropes was
a rattler that slithered out of it and bit Noah in the right
eye."

Alex drew a deep breath, shook her head. She
fumbled with the decanter, filled a snifter, set the
decanter down a little unsteadily, and brought it to her
husband. She narrowed one admonishing eye at him.
"Don't you worry about me. I was raised here...not
unlike where you were raised. Out there. Now, you take
that and join my father out on the verandah. You know he
dislikes drinking alone. As for me, I'd best go help Riley

with that sissified cowboy before he does more with his sewing needle than stitch that caterwauling Canadian's cut closed!"

She laughed.

She leaned down, kissed her husband, turned to her father, grinned, and strode out of the parlor, through the lady's tearoom, and into the kitchen, yelling, "Riley, let me finish this!"

Chuckling, Nordic strode with his father-in-law, who was chuckling, too, out of the parlor and through the lady's tearoom to the lodge's main hall.

In the kitchen, they could hear Case Sleighbaugh yelp and screech, "Easy, Miss Dev...I mean, Nordic. I always been especially sensitive to—*ohh, owww!*"

"Case, you've tangled with some of the nastiest rustlers this side of the Missouri River. I don't think a little needle and thread sewing you closed so you don't bleed out right here on the kitchen floor is gonna do you any more than they!"

Shaking his head and sipping his French brandy, Nordic followed his father-in-law out onto the veranda.

"That wife of yours," Deveraux said, easing his bulk into a wicker chair by a small, wooden table on which sat an ashtray carved by the old man himself from cedar, "has the bark on."

"She does." Nordic turned his back to the veranda's front rail, took another sip of his brandy, and said, "But that was for you."

"Oh, I know."

"Give us space."

The old man scowled, startled. "What?"

"Give us space. When you see us alone in conversation"—he pointed at the man with a finger of the hand holding his French brandy—"stay out of it. Hell, I don't care what you hear or see. She needs her own house, her own space."

Deveraux gazed back at him, slowly understanding. "Ah…I see. Orders, eh?"

"If this is *my* house where I'm going to raise *my* kids, them's my orders."

Deveraux stared at him coldly for another several seconds. Then he gave a crooked grin, sipped his brandy, and set the snifter on the table. "I understand," he said with an air of chastisement, turning his mouth corners down. "I'm sorry, Nordic. I, uh…I'm used to…"

"Riding roughshod over men."

Keeping his cowed gaze down, the old man nodded. "Yes."

"Four more in town," Nordic said, abruptly changing the subject.

The rancher raised his surprised, blue gaze at him. "What's that?"

"Four more. Zeb and I took 'em down. No one, including Glen Conagher, recognized 'em."

Deveraux fingered his bearded chin. "What the hell is—"

"Goin' on," Nordic finished for him. He strode forward, squatted at the old man's feet, holding his drink in one hand, patting Finn, who'd come over to sit beside him, with the other. "Eight men in two days," the man from Dakota prodded his father-in-law. "Come on. Think, Deveraux. Someone sent killers for you. They wanted me out of the way first, because I didn't recognize any of them. Now—"

"Now, look here!" Deveraux was suddenly furious, his eyes indignant. "You have as many enemies as I have.

And, seems to me, they were all after you! I don't care if you recognized any or not."

He let his voice trail off.

"But there was one. At least one, who tried to take Alex. If he'd wanted her dead she'd be"—his voice quavered as the thought was a punch to his solar plexus —"dead," he finished quietly, looking down at the veranda's worn floorboards.

Finn lifted his chin, turned his head toward the old man, and moaned.

Nostrils flaring slightly, eyes indignant, Deveraux said, "She's as much as yours as mine now. More so."

"They were here to take her from you. To hit you where you'd feel it most, or to hold her for some kind of ransom. They came after me—were *sent* after me—to get me out of the way." He glanced down toward where the men were milling around the bunkhouse, though several had been picketed in the woods around the lodge as well, some up high with a good pair of field glasses.

"If they've scouted the place, and they probably have —or whoever sent them has—they know she rides out by herself aplenty." Deveraux fingered his chin. "Why didn't they take her out there…on the range?"

Nordic shrugged. "They wanted to take her right out from under you. To burn you good." He shook his head. "No, it's you, all right. They were here for you. Whoever sent them, wants to get you good. Right where you live. They knew it would be easier if I was dead. No one can protect you like I can, since I live right here in your own house."

Anders looked around, scanning the yard and the bunkhouse, corrals, and other outbuildings. "This *place.*

They came *here*. Drew her outside, out of the lodge." He turned to his father-in-law. "Why?"

Deveraux just shook his head.

"What have you done?"

The old rancher looked at him quickly, frowning, flushing a little, vaguely sheepish.

"Who is it, man?" Nordic said, rising then leaning forward and placing his big hands on each arm of the rancher's chair, and squeezing, desperate to know who'd come for his wife.

Who'd come for *him*. But who they really wanted was Deveraux himself.

The old rancher looked up at Nordic apprehensively, taken aback by the fury, toughness, and determination in the man before him. Deveraux had wanted his former line rider here in the worst way, because he knew few could stand against him. It had been like that for Deveraux himself once. But now...beaten down by arthritis...confused and weakened by a stroke...he was a lone wolf whom the younger wolves were closing in on, to finish him.

To take everything he called his own.

His ranch. His men. His cattle. His land...

And his daughter.

He looked past Nordic at the high, spiky, dark peaks of the mountains to the west and behind which the sun was setting.

A sudden clarity washed into his eyes.

A dawning of sorts.

His spindly chest rose and fell heavily.

"Yes, who?" he rasped at Nordic. "Who?" He closed his own spidery hands down over those of his son-in-law and stared levelly into the younger man's eyes. "I know.

Deep down, I know." He glanced off again, brows hooding his eyes, deeply pensive.

Deeply troubled.

"I knew he'd come," he muttered.

"Who?" Nordic said, shaking the chair slightly, hardening his jaws.

Deveraux thought for a while longer. "I don't know." He touched his right index finger to his temple. "It's right here. It's in here. Buried deep. But it'll come." He nodded and looked at Nordic once more. "The name... it'll come."

Anders nodded despite his deep frustration.

He straightened and leaned back against the porch rail once more.

"We'll keep the men close to the house tomorrow."

Deveraux frowned. "What're you gonna do?"

"I think it's safe to assume that whoever's after you will take a break after what happened here today. He's lost nine men. Nine. He'll have to replace them. But in the meantime, he'll keep an eye on the place. I believe he's close. Whoever he is. Or, at least, he has a man close. Maybe in town. He'll give himself time to reassess. That's what I'd do. We'll keep the men close around the house. I don't want a fly getting into this house without someone seein' it. I'm gonna ride over to the Indian camp first thing, find out if there'll be any more trouble from that direction, and put a stop to it right then and there!"

"Hell!" Deveraux pounded the arm of his chair with the end of his age-gnarled fist in frustration. "Trouble from every direction!"

He didn't know the least of it, Nordic thought. He didn't know about Sarah...the young woman's intentions toward the rancher's son-in-law. It was a nagging thing Nordic couldn't get out of his head. It wasn't as fine a matter as the white attackers and the Indians, but, still, she would need to be dealt with sooner or later...

"You take McGreevey and some of the others with you tomorrow," Deveraux said.

Nordic shook his head. "I don't think the Indians mean trouble. Leastways, not the man riding with the white woman. I think he's the group's leader and somehow lost control of those two braves. He looked frustrated as did the woman. I'll ride down...just Alex an' me."

Deveraux arched his brows, incredulous. "You will not take my daughter into that bailiwick!"

"I want to go, Pa. If I can be of help, I want to do it."

Both men turned to see Alexandra standing with her back against the lodge's closed front doors. She had her arms crossed on her chest, one booted foot hooked over the other one, toe down. She'd returned her hair to its neat chignon but her bangs still slid across her forehead. She could have been the slightly older, raven-haired sister of the young woman who'd ridden into the headquarters the day before, sitting her saddle the regal poise in much the way Alexandra commanded her own, with the same casual deportment in her eyes.

Nordic would have bet silver cartwheels to mule fritters the woman with the Indian had been educated, as Alex had been, back East.

Alex slid her hard, determined gaze to Nordic. "Women can often talk reason when men can't."

Anders smiled.

"Them's Injuns, girl!" Deveraux intoned in exasperation. "What in the holy blazes...?" He shifted his wide, frustrated gaze between his daughter and son-in-law, lower jaw hanging. The old man was lost between worlds, unsure how to navigate either one. "An' whoever sent a man here yesterday, might send more!"

Nordic shook his head. "Not a chance. He knows we'll be ready for more. If he even *has* any more. Depending on how badly he wants to nettle you...or kill you...he'll wait till he thinks we've let our guards down."

"Well...what about them Injuns, fer cryin' in the Queen's ale!"

"They don't mean war." Nordic shook his head. "The Indian brought the woman here. A Ute warrior queen, she is not. She was here to keep everybody calm. To distract attention from possible shooting, for sure, but to keep everyone peaceful, too." He stared at his father-in-law with a knowing half smile. "She did that—didn't she?"

Deveraux looked away, an embarrassed flush rising in his cheeks. "Pshaww!" He rubbed the arms of his chair. "No, no...she weren't hard on the eyes, but..." He parried his son-in-law's level gaze with a hard, commanding one of his own. "If Alex is going, then I am going."

"No!" both Nordic and his wife said firmly at the same time.

Alex added, "Pa, you can't even get up and down these steps." She glanced at the porch steps. "How do you think you could get on a horse?"

Deveraux gave his own cunning half smile below heavily ridged brows. "With the help of my charming daughter and my son-in-law, who," he added, turning to Nordic and scrunching up his face into a swollen, red, sarcastic mask, "*adores me!*"

CHAPTER SIXTEEN

Senator James McClelland woke with a start.

He shot straight up in bed, breathing hard, sweat dribbling down his cheeks to dampen his thick, black, well-trimmed beard.

"Dear God," he yelled, blinking rapidly as he looked around the opulent bedroom in his hunting lodge at the foot of Long's Peak. He was not seeing this room with its log walls and heavy log beams, animal skins, game trophies including the massive head of an extraordinarily rare albino grizzly, adorning the walls. No, he saw the log and canvas hut with Indian trade blankets hanging from ropes breaking the single-room hovel into separate sleeping rooms for him, his older brother, and his father and mother. "Pa—fiirrrrrre!" he cried, hearing his own terrified words echo off the walls.

"Dear God is right," cried the woman beside him, sitting up as well and turning toward him, her long, golden-blonde hair flowing over her shoulders. "James," she said, voice trembling and placing a hand on the senator's shoulder, "not again!"

"Damn," McClelland said, still breathing heavily though the dream was dwindling and he could see the lodge's massive bedroom once more, for what it really was—his hunting lodge tucked deep in the fir and pine forests at the foot of Long's Peak, south of Estes Park, a ranching and mountaineering hub in the heart of the Never Summers.

He chuckled and rubbed his eyes with his thumb and forefinger. He threw the heavy covers back and dropped his feet to the floor. "When it comes, it really comes. When it goes away, it stays away for a long time. But when it comes…"

He fumbled open a bottle of Irish whiskey on his bedside table, splashed a goodly portion into a glass, and threw back half.

The young woman, Caryn Pritchard, granddaughter of Sir Frances Pritchard, industrialist and shipping magnate, sidled up to him, rested her head on his left shoulder, and rubbed his back. "Your heart's still beating awfully fast, James," she said in her faint Welsh accent. She'd been raised in Wales but educated in America. "Awful how it afflicts you so!"

McClelland was a big man of thirty-six, his handsome face seasoned by all the time he spent hunting in these mountains. He often led hunting parties comprised of his friends and associates from in and around the state capitol in Denver as well as Washington D.C. They'd go deep down into the Front Range's vast canyons and up high where the majestic and reclusive bighorn sheep lived, spending their lives negotiating narrow trails they cut themselves along the sides of sheer ridges. Such forays were as much drunken debauches as they were hunting excursions, and the senator lived for them just as his older brother had before Rob had been taken by a fever near his and his younger brother's mines which peppered the peaks above Leadville, farther south.

That's where and how they'd both started their fortunes, in the years after their family's ranch had been burned out by night riders sent by a man who'd deemed their property his own by way of water and mineral rights...

"So real," he said, shaking his head, gritting his teeth against the name festering like a cancer in his brain. "Just like it was occurring all over again." He turned to his lover, who'd been his paramour for seven months now— a long time for the married McClelland, who never stayed with one lover, usually the daughter or grand-daughter of a political collaborator or rival.

Procuring the lovely daughters or granddaughters of his friends and enemies was great fun for him. Especially landing those of his foes. That was every bit as rewarding as bringing down a house-sized, massively humpbacked grizzly from two hundred yards away with his big German Schuetzen hunting rifle with its double set triggers and its action heavily engraved with elaborate floral designs.

McClelland took another sip of the bourbon, which warmed him deep down in his belly though it took damn near a half a bottle of the stuff to file off the sharper edges of the recurring dream.

Nightmare, rather.

He rose and, holding his drink in one hand, pulled his heavy quilted elk robe off a wall spike beneath the ancient Hawken rifle mounted above the row of spikes— the Hawken had belonged to his mountain man grandfa-ther, who had first settled the stillborn ranch east of

Avalanche Peak in the Never Summers, overlooking the Cache la Poudre Canyon.

McClelland, six feet two and lithe, with long, sinewy muscles banding his back, chest, and belly—a horseman's body, his numerous lovers often told him—tied the robe around his waist with its belt of braided elk intestines and chucked aromatic, freshly split spruce onto the fireplace abutting the bedroom's north wall. He sank into a deep leather chair positioned sideways to the fire, giving him a partial view of the crackling fire and an entirety of the lovely young blonde adorning his bed.

She sat facing him, sitting up on her right hip, holding the covers modestly against her breasts. Her plump lips were rich red. Wasn't "bee-stung" the saying? Her eyes were as blue as the Welsh sky on a sunny spring morning. He liked how they flashed in the firelight, how the firelight danced shadows across her face that was far from cameo perfect. Her eyes, however blue and alluring, were not quite set in a straight line and her nose a little too wide. Her breasts were large and heavy, her rump a little broad, like the big cabooses on the village women who toiled in the Pritchard house, cooking and cleaning and hauling two wooden cream buckets at a time, of which McClelland doubted he could carry even one.

He'd seen these peasant women himself when he'd accompanied Caryn's grandfather, Frances, and her father, William, a couple times to the Pritchards' ancestral summer and hunting retreat, to shoot pheasants and red-legged partridge. That was where he'd met Caryn, whom he'd lured into his guest cottage by the second night he was there.

She was far from perfect in both appearance and in bed.

But he liked how she looked at him. He liked how she looked at him now, her eyes wide, deep, and cast with genuine concern.

None of the others had ever looked at him that way. None of them had ever made love to him the way Caryn did—clumsy and deferring but giving all, every inch of her heart and mind to him and, somehow, always fulfilling him.

Making him feel as though he'd really been made love to.

The others had wanted to entertain him, to fulfill him beyond what was naturally possible. They tried too hard. Their love had been manufactured. They'd made love like whores, as though their only intention had been to not get thrown out of his bed or shorted a nickel for his time. As for Caryn, her first word afterward was always, "Sorry," as she rolled away from him, giving him her back, raising the covers to her chin, and pouting.

He always slid up close beside her, the warmth of her body and large spirit rolling through him like the nearby Big Thompson River coursed between its banks as it made its way down out of the stormy mountains and onto the placid plains. That was what Caryn was to him. A placid river. He wished he could confess it to her sometime. How he felt. Such candidness was a foreign notion to him, however. He could no sooner express himself so openly as he could leap to the top of Long's in a single bound.

"Let's go home, Jimmy," she said now in her quiet, little girl's voice that she reserved for late at night, when she felt especially close to him...tenderly...devoted to him as she had no idea he was beginning to feel toward her and likely never would.

At least, not from his words which, unless drunk, he parceled out like pennies to children begging on Larimer Avenue in Denver.

"Let's go back to Denver," Caryn said, "I like you better in Denver. Out here, you have the nightmares!"

"I can't go home," McClelland said. "She's there."

"We can go to my flat." Caryn had her own suite of rented rooms in the tony Larimer Hotel.

"She ruins the whole town when she's there. Besides," McClelland added, throwing back the rest of his whiskey then studying the glass. "I have things to do here. Things I need to get done. Things I've waited a long, long time to do."

She'd noted the bitterness in his voice, he knew. She was smart, instinctive. More than the others. He could have had a conversation with someone about destroying the world and they wouldn't have reacted. Caryn blinked. Her expression was of deep apprehension.

"I don't like you here. I don't like how you *get* here. Your mood sours. You frighten me."

"I'm sorry," McClelland said with a sigh. He set his glass on a table, rose, and climbed onto the bed. He crawled to her, took her in his arms and kissed her forehead. "I'm sorry I do that to you. It's this thing I have to do. It will be over soon." He smiled and nudged her bottom lip with his thumb. "Maybe we'll move out here soon. Have a ranch of our own. Horses, cattle, chickens, goats—hell, anything you want!"

He knew how much she loved her family's animals on their estate in Wales. Over there, she laughed all the time. Here, she was too in touch with his moods. They affected her. They made her moody, too. That was how he knew she loved him. That notion rocked him back on his heels. But was it so bad?

Having a woman around who actually loved him?

Maybe in his case it was. In his heart, it wasn't. Still, he couldn't divorce his wife. A man in his position, state senator in charge of many committees not the least of which was overseeing the burgeoning railroads casting their tentacles across the West, could not invite such scandal. Besides, Heatherton wouldn't grant him a divorce, anyway. Nor would her family, her father being the lieutenant governor of Colorado.

If he were to try, her own family might ruin him, spread his scandalous misdeeds, of which there had been more than a few, to every ink-stained, hackneyed news-paperman in this country, Canada, and even Mexico!

"What will be over soon?" Caryn urged him, tugging on the sleeve of his robe. "What will be over, Jimmy? You are so lost in it all day. For a long time even before we came up here from Denver. You've been lost in it for sooo long! What is it?"

He stared at her, pensive.

He wanted to tell her. He'd never told another woman about his work. They wouldn't have wanted to know anyway. Least of all his wife. Hearing the first words of such nefarious deeds would have driven Heatherton to tears. She'd have gone to one of her wardrobes, yanked out a gown, held it up, and asked him what he thought.

Caryn deserved to know. She'd been by his side through the recent thick of it—through the planning of the trip out here, through the hiring and organizing of specialized men. He'd had to keep it all very secret. If even one hack from one of the scandal rags got wind of what the handsome senator whom many were calling the next governor—later, president?—had up his sleeve, he'd be finished.

But it was too late to turn back now.

He'd been planning every stage of this vengeance quest since he was twelve years old. Only Rob had known of his plans, because Rob had helped plan them, been a part of every aspect. Rob had taken that dark, forbidden knowledge to his grave.

Now James had no one left in his family.

All had been taken from him by one man.

He was the only one who knew of the plans he'd been concocting in his head since that fiery night thirty years ago, less than fifty miles from here, straight north as the crow flies, on the ridge above the drumming Poudre River.

"Jimmy…" Caryn said now, staring deeply into his eyes and frowning. It was almost as though she were reading his mind, and what she saw troubled her deeply. "Jimmy…please…let's go back…"

"Nonsense." He smiled, caressed her cheek with the backs of his fingers, and pecked her lips. "We were just starting to have fun!"

A sharp, warning whistle sounded outside the lodge.

McClelland's smiled faded. He lifted his head sharply, pricking his ears to listen.

Footsteps sounded in the hall outside his bedroom door. They grew louder.

Then stopped.

A light tap on the door followed by, "Riders, boss. Two of Conagher's men."

CHAPTER SEVENTEEN

M cClelland stared at the door, eyes wide, lips parted.

His heart fluttered.

"Just men?" he asked.

"Just men. Two."

McClelland cursed under his breath.

"What is it?" Caryn asked, her voice trembling. She rose in bed and turned to McClelland. "What is it, James? Who are they?"

"Stay here," he said, climbing off the bed and looking around for his slippers.

"Let me come!"

"No! No! No!" McClelland said under his breath, finding his slippers beside a large chest of drawers and slipping into them. "This is none of your affair."

"Just what kind of affair is it, James?" the girl wanted to know. "Are you in danger?"

McClelland's heart fluttered again. Anxiety rippled through him.

He looked at Caryn. She sat up, knees raised to her

chin, tenting the covers over them. Her eyes were wide, brimming with concern and fear.

What had he gotten himself into, he wondered.

A woman who cared.

The others—all of the previous others, too many to count!—wouldn't have given a damn about who was calling late at night. Or was it early in the morning?

"Dammit!" He hadn't realized he'd cursed aloud until he saw her beetle her brows severely. Injured. Her feelings hurt.

"Were you expecting a *woman*?" She stared at him, tears glistening in her eyes.

James moved back to the bed and sat on the edge of it. "I didn't mean to snap. It's just that I have certain things to do. Certain *private* things to do. You know that."

He placed two fingers under her chin, raised it slightly, and stared into her eyes. "I can't have you worrying about them!"

Nor pestering me about them! he silently added.

"James...dear sweet." Caryn wrapped her hand gently around his wrist. "I can tell you're upset. You haven't been yourself since we left De—"

"Enough!" Anger burst in him, cresting on a wave of frustration. He rose from the bed and glared down at her. "This is no business of yours. You have to stay out of it. Caryn, you must...or..."

"Or what?" she whispered.

McClelland glanced at the door. The man out there—Cleve Erskin, his lieutenant—was likely getting an earful. Oh well. Erskin could keep secrets. He'd been keeping McClelland's secrets for years now. He'd have to sit the man down in the near future and have a chat with him. Likely an unnecessary one, but one that must occur so McClelland didn't have to worry about what might slip out of the man's mouth when he was having drinks at the Jason Rand in Denver, where he and the other close associates—secretaries and valets and the like—of important men gathered for steaks and vodka.

McClelland stared into Caryn's eyes.

Again, his heart fluttered. He felt sick to his stomach, as though he'd chugged a bottle of sour milk.

Steeling himself, not wanting to say what he knew he had to say next, he said, "Or I'll have to send you back to Denver."

"But, James…"

McClelland raised a hand, stopping her. "That's enough. Go back to sleep. I'll be along soon. Now, Caryn—you mustn't concern yourself with my private affairs. No, you mustn't do so at all. I have secrets as do most men, especially those of my station in business and in government. We cannot take the time…we cannot be *distracted*…by the concerns of our…" Again, he glanced at the door. He finished, more quietly with, "Our intimates."

He thought she was going to cry.

Her eyes glittered. She turned her head a little to one side and stared at him with silent beseeching. For what? What did she want? He gave her everything. A new stole, a fur coat, shoes, boots, jewels…every week. He took her out to Denver's and the high country's finest restaurants…after his men had scouted ahead, of course, to make sure no spies or "journalists" were there.

He gave her the finest stallion that he himself had ever seen.

What more could she ask for?

The question lingered inside his head as he moved to the door, lowered the heavy brass handle, and opened it. The mustached Erskin with his dark eyes and pomaded hair stood there, his broad-brimmed black Stetson in his hands. He wore his big sheepskin coat against the high-country cold. He was no larger than McClelland—looked a bit of the dandy, even—but he'd been taught to fight in the Indian wars, and he was the senator's most prized bodyguard.

He wore two well-concealed pepperbox pistols that had destroyed the faces of several would-be attackers, usually sent by McClelland's political opponents or business rivals, in the senator's surreptitious past. The senator didn't care to reflect upon what the man had done to one man, twice Erskin's size and had easily doubled him in weight, with his obsidian-handled, razor-edged stiletto, one of a matched pair residing somewhere on the man's elegantly attired, compact person.

"Outside, Senator," the lieutenant said, holding out a large, hooded capote made from the hide of a bighorn ram and a pair of wool-lined, elk-skin mittens.

He helped McClelland into the coat and then they headed off down the burgundy-carpeted hall lit by two guttering, brass, wall-bracketed lamps.

What did she want? was the question that continued to echo around inside the senator's head, threatening to divert his attention from the important issues he had ahead of him, in the form of two men waiting outside.

"You, you fool," was the response.

He winced against it.

You.

———

McClelland followed Erskin to a landing on the second floor.

The bodyguard and secretary and lieutenant—whatever you wanted to call him—turned a shoulder to a stout door comprised of halved pine logs and winced a little as he pushed. He stepped out into the frosty mountain night choked in by a star-capped forest and darkness. It was still an hour away from dawn.

McClelland looked at the two heavily dressed men sitting two horses at the bottom of large, halved-log stairs. Their faces were concealed by the large brims of their dark hats. They each wore a heavy wool coat and thick leather gloves.

They did not have good news. McClelland saw it in their faces.

The girl wasn't with them.

Deveraux's girl.

The princess herself—Alexandra Deveraux, who was known to turn the head of every man who came within a hundred yards of her. She was as legendary as her father in her own, quiet, elegant, mesmeric way. It was said the mining magnate, James G. Fair, had once met her, her mother, and father in a tony hotel restaurant in Denver. He and Deveraux had once shared business ties.

One week after the meeting, a letter was hand delivered to the Comanche Ranch headquarters. The envelope bore the founder of the Comstock Lode's elegant letterhead into the fiber of which an ink ribbon had been hammered. In the letter itself, Fair had beseeched Deveraux for his daughter's hand in marriage, in exchange for a full quarter of the shares in one of his most lucrative railroad lines.

No one was privy to either the girl's or the rancher's response.

But there had been no marriage.

And she wasn't here, either.

He looked at Erskin.

The man looked back at him. His expression wasn't encouraging.

Neither were those of the two men staring up at him though he couldn't see their eyes.

Hunkering down inside his coat, McClelland moved down the steps, running his hand along the rail to his right. Erskin followed. When both were standing at the bottom of the steps, looking up at the two riders who had obviously ridden a long way quickly—steam from their horses' backs shrouded them and their riders.

"What happened?" the senator asked.

The man on the right shrugged. "It didn't happen. The Nordic's still kickin'…his wife's still at home." He paused and looked at the other man sitting his horse beside him. He turned back to the senator. "The old man blew Solaz's head off."

Solaz was an efficient killer who worked alone. He was well-known by railroad syndicates and ranchers and mine owners who often need special jobs done quietly.

Now, the man, it appeared, was headless.

McClelland stared up at Conagher's two men.

"How do you know?"

"The marshal sent another man to watch and report." The man on the senator's right shook his head. "He came gallopin' back to town like his horse had tin cans tied to his tail."

"It was the old man," the other man said.

McClelland scowled his surprise. "Deveraux?"

The other man nodded.

Unexpected even to himself, McClelland laughed. He clapped his hands, stumbled around, and laughed.

"My god…the old boy still has it."

"Apparently so."

McClelland sobered. He stared up at the two messengers from Camp Collins.

"That'll just make ruining him—burning everything he has…his men…his son-in-law…his lovely daughter… his beloved lodge…to the ground!"

The two messengers stared at him.

"Is Conagher still having the place watched?"

"Yep."

McClelland regarded the two men before him.

Like the others Conagher had hired, they were Southwestern gunmen who wouldn't be recognized this far north. They mostly worked in Texas and New Mexico.

But…were they any good?

Or, like the others who were no more, were they just cannon fodder?

"First thing in the morning, saddle fresh horses and ride back to town. Tell Conagher I'll be paying him a visit soon. Tell him we have to palaver," he added darkly.

The men glanced at each other, nodded, and rode away.

McClelland stared after them.

Conagher would answer for this. If the marshal thought he'd one day get anywhere near the territorial capitol in Denver, riding McClelland's coattails, he'd answer for this.

The senator looked at Erskin. His first lieutenant in his sundry, off-the-books affairs, stared back at him, expressionless.

Holding his coat closed at the neck against the mountain's night chill, McClelland started climbing the stairs to the lodge's second floor.

He did not see the forlorn face of Caryn Pritchard staring out at him from a window before she turned away and hurried back to their bedroom, shaking.

"Oh, Jimmy," she cried under her breath. "What have you done. What have you *done*?"

CHAPTER EIGHTEEN

"*Whoa!*" Sarah Nordstrom exclaimed as she walked out of the post office in Camp Collins and straight into a man who'd been walking by the place while looking down and rolling a quirley. Craning her neck to peer around the parcels stacked in her arms, Sarah had seen him too late.

The man and the one walking beside him had been laughing and talking and hadn't seen her.

Now, they did, however.

Her and her four boxes and paper-wrapped packages spilled atop the man she'd run into and onto the board-walk before him.

"Oh no!" Sarah exclaimed as she stooped to begin scooping up her freight from the boardwalk, before any of the passersby could step on them...or on her. It was eight o'clock—a busy time of the morning, people coming and going to and from the post office before starting work.

"I do declare, girl!" exclaimed the man she'd run

into, scowling down at her, holding his empty cigarette paper between the first two fingers of his right hand. His shirt was speckled with the tobacco he'd been trying to roll into a cigarette. "Can't you watch where you're goin'? You ruined my cigarette and injured my knee!"

Sarah didn't think she'd touched his knee.

He grinned at the other man, who grinned back at him, as the first man feigned a limp. "Oh lordy, it hurts! Someone fetch the sawbones...if he ain't already three sheets to the wind!"

He and the other man, roughly his size though a little taller, laughed.

Both were clad in the dusty trail garb of your average drifter or line rider. They were unkempt and reeked of whiskey. They'd likely been up all night playing poker and visiting the "hog pens," what the doves' cribs were so distastefully called.

Sarah had never lived in a town before, and she didn't like it one bit.

These two added to her dislike of it.

"I'm sorry! I'm sorry!" Sarah exclaimed, knowing the drover's knee didn't hurt. She hadn't touched his knee and none of the packages in her arms weighed over a few pounds—mainly the brewing supplies her boss, Lars Olson, had ordered from some brew supply store in Denver.

"Oh, it hurts!" The drover feigning injury turned to his partner and flexed his left knee tenderly. "I got me a game knee, Lem. You know that!"

"I know! I know!" Lem laughed beneath the brim of his weather- and smoke-stained Stetson. "She got you good—I seen it." He turned to a dapper gent in a business suit just then passing them on the boardwalk fronting the post office. "This little tart hurt my friend's knee!"

The dapper little man scowled at him and increased his pace, hurrying on past.

Sarah was holding three of the packages on her knee and was about to place the fourth one on top of the stack when the man she'd supposedly "injured" wrapped his rough hand around her left arm and jerked her too her feet so quickly that she lost all four packages once more!

She gasped.

The man, who had a narrow, dirty, bug-eyed face and long, straight, scraggly hair hanging down from his ragged green Stetson, drew her face up close to his and glared at her. "Didn't you hear what I said? You injured me!"

"I'm sorry," Sarah lied, terrified and anxious to get back to the saloon. "I'm very sorry. That was clumsy. But I need to get back to the saloon because Mr. Olson is about to brew another batch, an' he needs these—"

The ugly man's face brightened.

He was typical trail scum.

The kind too lowly to have enough ambition to rob stagecoaches. Farm supply wagons or aged prospectors, maybe, but mostly such men as this just drifted…into one small-town jail after another…

And now here one was, drunk all night, broke, badly hungover, and bored…

To his left, Lem laughed.

"Cole, she's the one who works for the Norwegian over to the brewery!"

"Sure, sure," Cole said, blowing his sour breath into Sarah's face. "I got it now. I see it, now…say, honey, you're right purty to look at!"

"Thank you," Sarah said tightly, trying to pull her arm out of Cole's iron grip. "I'll be runnin' along now…"

Cole drew her up close to him again. "I said you're purty," he said, glancing down at her chest well covered by her dark yellow day dress buttoned to her neck. "How come you dress so prim an' proper? Why don't you show some?"

Sarah gritted her teeth in anger and fairly spat into his face. "Because I don't work the line!"

"Hey!" came a girl's voice from behind Cole and the girlishly giggling Lem. "What's goin' on here?"

"It's all right, Lisle," Sarah said, seeing the pretty but street-tough doxie, Lisle, who also worked for Mr. Olson at his brewery and saloon. Only, Lisle worked the drinking hall and her upstairs crib and dressed far more skimpily, as she was now, clad in a corset and bustier but with a felt green stole around her shoulders.

She was the highest paid whore—there was another word Sarah winced every time she thought of it—in Mr. Olson's employ.

"I have it under control, Lisle," Sarah added, using her free hand to try to pry Cole's hand from around her left one. "Just a little misunderstanding is all." But she could hear the fear tremble in her voice. Anger bit at her, too. Rage. Cole was hurting her wrist. He had no call to treat her this way.

Lisle, her light-brown hair hanging loosely about her shoulders, blown back a little by the cool morning breeze, walked straight up to Cole and said crisply, "Cole Murkowski, you let her go right now."

Keeping a tight grip on Sarah's wrist, Cole turned to the tough doxie glaring up at him but with the usual calm in her eyes, as well. "Hey, Lem, look who's tellin' who what to do. A plain an' simple whore!"

He released Sarah's wrist and turned full around to stare directly at Lisle. He stepped up close to the doxie, leaned down and said with his nose two inches away from the girl's, "How 'bout we go out back"—he canted his head toward the rear alley running behind the buildings on his left—"an' you give me a free one. Maybe I'll buy ya a beer lat—"

He didn't get the "later" all the way out.

Lisle scrunched up her eyes and pursed her lips, pulled her right hand back, and slung it forward, smashing her open palm against Cole's right cheek. Cole turned his head to his left, glaring down at the doxie, stunned, a red welt already showing above his cheekbone.

Lem cackled. "Cole, she socked ya good! You gotta stay clear of the tough ones. They might be good in the ol' mattress sack, but..."

Sarah stood back, her packages scattered at her feet. She was trying to rub some feeling into her right hand but mostly she was trying to calm down. That hard slap Lisle laid on Cole had been no lighthearted slap of the slap 'n' tickle variety. No, that had come up from the doxie's heels.

Cole appeared to be still trying to wrap his mind around it, as well.

Sarah watched, breathless with dread, as Lisle walked straight up to Lem and grabbed him down low. She shoved her face with her chin jutting, wedgelike, up close to Lem's and said with a bowie-edged chill, "Wanna keep these, you cackling monkey?"

"Lisle!" Sarah cried. "Stop...don't!"

She was just making it worse. But that's how Lisle was sometimes. She prided herself on her toughness, of not taking anything from no man. At least, nothing she didn't want to take. Lisle may have worked the line, but she wasn't some hind-tit calf that anyone could abuse for the fun.

"Ohhh…ohhh…" Lem cried, his face swelling up and turning red. "P-Please, now, Miss Lis…"

He stopped when Cole, enraged, moved to the girl like a bull out of a chute. He picked up Lisle, who couldn't have weighed much over a hundred pounds, and raised her high in the air before slamming her straight down on the boardwalk.

Lisle landed with a screech, losing her stole.

She sat on her bent legs, head hanging, hair hanging straight down to hide her face. She grunted, groaned, then lifted her head and swept her long hair straight back with her arm. She drew the other one out in front of her.

Something shiny glinted in it.

The golden sun reflected off it so brightly that it momentarily blinded Sarah.

Lisle clicked back a barrel of the two-barreled little derringer. Sarah knew that some of the doxies at Mr. Olson's carried such "hideouts" in special pockets sewn into their dusters or dresses.

Lisle smiled wolfishly at Cole as she pushed up off the boardwalk.

He stared at her, his face crimson, jaws anvil-hard with rage.

Lem stood by, his face also red—with humiliation at having been assaulted so crudely, in the worst possible way, by a girl.

By a whore, no less!

He'd thought for sure, Sarah knew, that Lisle had been going to rip his manhood right off in front of half the town. Sarah had thought so herself.

Cole flared his nostrils, dipped his chin, and glared at the doxie from beneath his brows. "Don't never aim at gun at Cole Murkowski, whore." He took a step toward Lisle. "You understand me...*whore*?"

Lisle's smiled broadened. She slitted her eyes.

Oh, no, Sarah silently beseeched the doxie. *Oh, Lisle...please...do not...!*

"Understand this...scum!"

"Lisle!" Sarah screamed.

Her scream was accompanied by the sharp crack of the little pistol in the doxie's fist. The gun leaped in her hand. A blade of bright-orange flame stabbed from the over-and-under weapon's upper barrel.

Cole froze, lower jaw sagging.

Slowly, he dropped his chin to stare down at his belly from which dark-red blood oozed. His body tense, shoulders slumped, he sort of rocked back on his bootheels and cupped his hands over the wound.

"Holy!" exclaimed his friend Lem, staring in horror at his friend's belly. "Holy...*hob*!" He looked at Lisle. "You shot Cole!"

Sarah stared in mute shock at Cole. He dropped to his knees with a thud on the boardwalk, gray boards creaking against his weight. His face stretched into a horrible mask of raw agony, Cole crawled forward and swept his right arm out and to one side then brought it forward, swiping both of Lisle's feet out from under her.

She screamed and dropped to her backside, hair tumbling around her head, partly obscuring her face.

She dropped the derringer.

To Lem, Cole shouted, "Get her! Get that whore! I'm gonna gut her like a fish!"

Lem said, "Why waste time?" as he jerked his six-shooter up out of his holster, grinning devilishly down at Lisle, who stared back at the ugly man with a malign glare of her own.

"You better make that first shot a good one!" Lisle shrieked, all enraged bravado despite the horrific assault she'd absorbed.

"Oh, don't worry," Lem said, clicking his pistol's hammer back and aiming the barrel at the doxie's face. "I will!"

"No!"

Before she knew what she was doing, Sarah bolted forward, dropped to her knees ahead of Lem, and grabbed Lisle's gun. She rolled onto her right shoulder, raising the gun and, having learned how to shoot a derringer from Lisle herself, cocked the pistol, engaging the lower barrel. She aimed at Lem and squeezed her eyes closed.

Crack!

The gun bucked more than Sarah thought such a small pistol would.

Flames flashed.

A big man who'd just stepped between Sarah and Lem stumbled sideways with a pained grunt, his spurs chinking on the boardwalk, his shirt around his five-pointed deputy's star turning red. He was the larger of Marshal Conagher's two thuggish deputies. He winced, gritting his teeth and fell back into Lem, who dropped his own gun as he instinctively grabbed the big man. Lem stared in shock from the mortally wounded deputy to Sarah, who still held Lisle's smoking pistol in her hand.

"She shot Banner!" Lem cried. "She shot Luke Banner!"

Sarah had been in town long enough to know Banner was Conagher's nephew.

She stared in horror at the lumpy, thirty-something deputy she'd just shot, as the man dropped to the ground to lay on the boardwalk around Lem's ankles, his eyes blinking once then turning glassy before rolling back into his head. Her heart thudding against her ribs, Sarah dropped the gun from which pale smoke still curled.

She turned to Lisle staring at her, eyes and mouth wide.

The doxie glanced quickly along the street to the east.

She turned back to Sarah and her eyes opened wider.

Cole and the deputy lay dead.

Lem shifted his gaze from his partner—his *ex-partner*, rather—in shock, then he looked at Sarah and a fateful smile stretched on his lips.

"You're gonna hang, girl," he said in delight, shaking his head slowly. "Oh, you're gonna hang!"

Sarah had turned to see what Lisle was looking at.

It was the marshal, Conagher, and his other big, pot-bellied, bull-necked deputy striding this way, a block and a half away and walking fast.

Lisle kept her shocked gaze on her friend. "Sarah," she said, widening her eyes even farther. "Go! *Run!*"

Sarah hesitated, unable to move.

Her heart raced. Her mouth was dry.

"Run!" Lisle intoned. "Find a place to hide!"

Sarah said in a hushed, urgent whisper, "Take Robert to the Deveraux Ranch. Anders will know where to find me!"

With that, she ran to the nearest horse she saw, ripped

its reins from the hitchrack, fairly leaped aboard, tearing the skirt of her dress, and ground her heels into the gelding's flanks.

"You can run," Lem shouted behind her. "But you can't hide from Conagher! He *will* find you!"

CHAPTER NINETEEN

ancy Dan, who was anything *but* fancy, brought Deveraux's Overo stallion up to the main lodge. The young string bean, who pretty much did everything on the ranch and was trying his hardest to be an equal to the rest of the older men, Ryan LaPlante, led Nordic's Appaloosa and Alex's leggy sorrel mare, whom she'd named Catherine after a character in one of her favorite books.

Nordic believed the lady's last name in the book was Earnshaw. He wasn't sure why he remembered that. He didn't remember the title or much else about the book though he'd been interested when she'd told him about it. He'd always enjoyed hearing about what she read, though she read so much and told him so much, enjoying the retelling as much as the reading, it seemed, that he often got them confused.

If he remembered right, however, this one about this Earnshaw gal had the bark on. He didn't think most of the books Alex read had much of an edge to them, but this one sure did. A stormy romance, if you could even call it a romance. More like an obsession that sort of got the best of both main characters.

Nordic was out there on the steps first, watching Fancy Dan and young LaPlante stride down the hill through the trees, heading back to the bunkhouse. Secretly, young LaPlante still resented being relegated such menial tasks as leading horses, despite how fine the horses were. Didn't everyone know by now he'd one day be the Comanche's top hand?!

His skills were being wasted!

A half dozen men were posted on foot around the lodge. Six more were riding along the ridges surrounding the headquarters, on the scout for more interlopers though Nordic didn't think they'd see any.

Not soon, anyway.

Hopefully, never again.

If he knew how badly whoever had it out for the old man, he might be able to make a better guess.

He'd work on that later. He thought Deveraux knew. He had an inkling, anyway.

Something from deep in his past, maybe. Something he was ashamed about. That was why he couldn't bring himself to talk about it. Maybe he couldn't even bring himself to think about it.

Alex came out in a black leather jacket and black leather gloves against the morning chill. A stone mug of coffee steamed in her hands. She wore her hair down, spilling across her shoulders. As she moved to Nordic a stray breeze caught a curl of her hair and slid it across her cheek. She shook her head to toss it back and looked up at Nordic with an ethereal little half smile on her face, her eyes turned sideways and up, regarding him almost deviously.

"What's that about?" he asked her.

"What's that about?"

Alex shrugged a shoulder then looked out across the horses and the yard beyond, to where the western ridge rose, the pine forest clinging to its steep slope flashing lemon and gold as the sun's light, angling in from over the ridge to the east, intensified.

"What's what about?"

"You seem to be in a good mood for a young woman who…well…after what happened yesterday."

"You mean watching a man get separated from his head?" she said, wistfully. Then she stretched her lips back from her fine, white teeth and shook her head. "Yeah, that part I could have done without." She smiled up at Nordic, almost dreamily. "But I have my big Norski husband to protect me."

Finn gave a deep-throated moan where he sat at the top of the porch steps, beside Nordic, gazing up her a little indignantly.

"And his brave dog, of course!" Alex stooped down to kiss the collie on his long, black nose. "Who can forget Finn?" She straightened and favored her husband with another odd smile, as though she had a secret she was taking her time sharing. "But there's so much more than that. That will pass…as all the bad stuff passes. I've been a lucky girl. Someone's out to kill my husband and maybe my father, but I've been through enough in my relatively short life to know that, too, will pass."

She chuckled, sipped her coffee, swallowed, and turned her head forward again. "Then we wait for the next thing. It is an adventure, anyway—isn't it?"

Nordic smiled down at her. He'd be damned if her

mood wasn't buoying his own after having spent the night and morning thinking about the Indians.

"What?" he asked her. "Life?"

"Indeed," she said, rising onto her boot toes, and kissed his cheek. She pulled back and flicked his hat brim with her fingers. "Life."

One of the two double doors opened behind them, and Garth Deveraux strode out, saddlebags slung over one shoulder, his tightly rolled soogan clamped under that arm. In his right hand he held his Sharps .56. The rifle was the '74 model, which made it ten years old. He mostly used it for hunting these days, though a few rustlers and nesters had taken bullets from it, as well. He wore a heavy wool mackinaw and a blue wool scarf beneath his big, black, high-crowned Stetson.

He'd had Rosa sew flannel into the corduroy trousers he wore in the winter, and Nordic could tell from the thickness he was wearing a pair of those this morning, the cuffs stuffed down into his high-topped, black boots. From the top of the right one, a bone-handled bowie knife protruded and slapped that boot's mule ears as he came across the porch, somehow looking hale and hardy, which he rarely did these days.

The anticipation of an early ride, just like the old days, must have buoyed him much like Alex's unexpected cheerfulness had done for her husband.

"All right, all right," he grumbled as Alex pulled her lips away from her husband's cheek and turned to her father. "Enough o' that. Let's go see about some Injuns."

As he moved down the porch steps, favoring his right, arthritic knee a little, he added in a darkly wistful tone, "And that there is somethin' I never thought I'd hear myself say again. Injuns." He slung his bedroll over his Overo's hindquarters, behind the saddle, and strapped the sewn-together blankets into place. He shook his head. "Thought I had all o' them shot out of these mountains years ago!"

His English accent always grew pronounced when something had his blood up, as the idea of Indians moving into "his" territory had now.

Nordic and Alex had descended the steps and were sliding their long guns into the scabbards and checking their stirrups and saddle cinches.

"Pa." Alex glanced at her father as she stepped onto Catherine's back. "Be calm and cool, all right. We just want to see what they're doing here."

"What they're doing here on my land!" Deveraux said as he used the second step up from the bottom of the porch steps to mount his horse with a grunt. "Not to mention trying to steal my horses," he added, glaring at Nordic as if Nordic had been one who'd tried to steal his horses.

"Pa," Alex said in her impatient, plaintive tone, "nei-ther one of those braves—"

"Let it go," Nordic said, cutting her off.

He gave her a direct look that said, "Let's just wait and see what happens."

She got it, nodding.

They booted their horses on down the hill, following the cinder path through the trees at the edge of the main yards. Finn ran ahead, growling at and cowing the two ranch dogs who ran eagerly, barking and wagging their tails, out from the shade of the bunkhouse. The collie's aggression was short-lived. He got distracted by a barn cat and disappeared into the brush along the breaking corral.

Nordic rode with his wife and his father-in-law, wondering how in the hell he got himself into such a situation. Directly across the yard toward the bunkhouse, two hands sat on a bench oiling their rifles, their holstered six-guns and shell belt on the bench between them. As they passed one of the two stables, Zeb McGreevey came out from the shadows between the big double doors, leading his roan. His rifle angled up from his scabbard, and he wore his six-gun thonged low on his stout, right thigh.

Nordic reined up. "Not today, Zeb."

The thick-set, burly man stopped, hooked his bushy brows together above his scrub-bearded face. "Thought I'd tag along." He glanced at Deveraux, who stopped his own mount to his daughter's right. "You might need help."

The old rancher scowled. "With *what*? With *me*?"

The foreman shrugged his shoulders. "With anything. They are Injuns."

"You meant me, Zeb."

"Just don't want you to get your hands too full, boss."

"If they get too full, you'll hear the shootin'. Doesn't sound like that camp is too far away, this side of the ford. Keep a few men here with Rosa. Don't want that vermin...whoever he is," he added, casting his gaze around the surrounding ridges still striped with morning shadows and from which bird song lilted, "ridin' in an burnin' my house down."

"Who is it, Mr. Deveraux?" McGreevey asked him, his eyes grave.

Deveraux didn't answer for a few seconds. It was almost like there was a brief, unspoken communication between the two older men. Then Deveraux said, "We'll know soon enough." He brushed the cuff of his coat sleeve across his nose then nudged the Overo forward and under the crossbar of the entrance gate. Nordic looked at McGreevey. The foreman looked back at him, expressionless.

But there was something there. A thought, a dark idea was floating around behind the old foreman's poker face.

He was worried about something.

Now Nordic was once more, as well.

Alex looked at her husband. They, too, had a brief, silent conversation.

"What's going on, Nordic?" she seemed to say.

He silently said back, "I reckon we'll know soon enough."

He booted Apache ahead and they both rode under the crossbar and started down the ridge toward the blue Avalanche glinting freshly minted pennies beyond the pines and aspens in the valley below.

Deveraux led the way.

He was the boss here, just like the old days.

Finn trotted along behind him, between Nordic and the old rancher.

The old man rode straight-backed in the saddle, turning his head this way and that, keeping a special watch out. They weren't riding after just anyone. They were riding after Utes. That meant warriors to the old rancher. Nordic didn't blame him. He remembered those bloody years when the Indians were still trying to resist the white man's encroachment. And those two braves he'd shot were still fresh in his mind.

They'd not only rode out of that corral on stolen Comanche Ranch horses, they were out to kill *him*.

Why?

He thought he knew why. They'd likely heard his reputation for being tough. Deadly, even. They'd recognized him from descriptions they'd heard. They'd figured his infamous intransigence would lead to their killing if he caught them in the act, which he had. Also, they'd been out to prove their bravery against the formidable white man. Neither had probably fought white men before, though they'd likely come up against them in one way or another.

Both the whites and Indian harbored grave prejudices against the other and while open warfare was no longer as common as it once had been, it still happened. Further, the old hatreds still steamed and smoldered. The two dead braves had been raised with the stories of the white man's aggression. They'd probably had cousins and uncles, maybe even fathers and half-fathers killed when the wars still raged. Those histories hadn't had time to die.

Nordic had little doubt those braves had not only heard of his reputation but that of Garth Deveraux and the men the rancher employed, as well. That's what had compelled them to come hunting for trophies in the form of two of the formidable man's horses.

Nordic had to talk it out with the Indian who dressed like a white man.

There was a calmness about that man. Anders had seen the regret over what the braves had done in the man's eyes. He hadn't wanted that. He certainly didn't condone it. And he dreaded the possible consequences.

Then why were he and the others here?

Nordic's mind flashed on yesterday seeing the Utes gathered around the cook fires and hide lodges, some hastily erected with pine boughs he'd seen on the small tributary of the Avalanche. An Indian encampment, sure enough. One that did not look permanent, however. For that Nordic was grateful.

Still, why were they here even temporarily?

When they'd ridden a mile north of the ranch headquarters, Deveraux stopped his horse. He looked back at his son-in-law as Nordic and Alex halted their own horses, deferentially, off the rear hips of the old man's horse.

"Where?"

"Remember that ford another quarter mile north?"

"Yes."

"We cross there. The encampment is across a flat, on the bank of the tributary."

Deveraux turned his head forward and gazed into the trees lining the river on his right. "Deep Creek." He grinned and scratched his chin. "A Mex tried to put a road ranch up there once. To serve the woodcutters who used to cut wood along Avalanche Ridge, for the soldiers who had 'em an outpost at the base of the crags. They were watchin' the trail that cut over to the Western Slope and Utah. Utes used to gravel the migrants."

He flared his nostrils and scratched his chin again. "They was as bad as the Injuns."

"The Utes?" Alex asked.

Deveraux nodded. "If one of 'em was sick or they were out of supplies and couldn't afford any more, they'd just stop an' settle anywhere."

"Father, did you run them off?"

"A few times, yeah." Deveraux nodded as he gazed speculatively across the river, as though at one of those stranded prairie schooners where some migrants were trying to set up a camp—a canvas lodge and maybe a rope corral for their mules or oxen. He smiled as he gazed with self-satisfaction over his shoulder at his daughter. "My land...my rules. No nesters. Not Injun, not Meskin, not black, not yellow...not *white*!"

Alex glanced at Nordic. She pulled down her mouth corners and nodded.

She knew the rules.

She'd seen them enforced, too. And she didn't want to again.

As for Nordic, he ran nesters off because it had been his job, but he'd never shot or hanged any. That had gotten him crossways with his soon-to-be father-in-law last year, when Sarah and her parents had settled in a near canyon. They'd been on open range, but the only law out here were the ranchers, like Deveraux, who often claimed government graze as their own. Over the years, deputy U.S. marshals had wandered up from Denver or over from Salt Lake. When a few disappeared, however—one had been hanging from a tree and there hadn't been much left of him after the carrion-eating raptors, crows, ravens, and owls had had their fills—sighting of the federals had dwindled.

Now they were as scarce as buffalo.

A horse snorted off the trail to Nordic's left.

He jerked with a start but forced himself to make no sudden movement. Alex did, as well, as she turned her head quickly to stare at where the snort had come from, followed now by slow, soft thuds of approaching horses. Another whicker sounded from the thick forest on that side of the trail.

Deveraux heard it and reached for the Sharps angling up from the scabbard under his right leg.

"Easy," Nordic told him.

"No such thing as easy out here." The rancher rocked the breech-loading, falling-block's heavy hammer back and rested it across his knees. "Easy means dead." He cast an incriminating gaze over his right shoulder at his son-in-law. "You been out here long enough to know that, Dakota. Haven't you shot enough rustlers or broke enough heads in town lately…since you been married?"

The rancher smiled devilishly and turned his gaze back toward where they'd heard the approach of horses.

"Alex," he said, "untie this man long enough to get his grit back."

"Untie him?"

"Yeah…from your apron strings." Deveraux laughed.

He yelled into the forest from where the hoof thuds had dwindled to silence.

"Name yourselves!" the rancher shouted so loudly his horse gave a start. "Garth Deveraux here…with a cocked fifty-six!"

In the dense forest, a horse whinnied.

Oh, boy, Nordic thought with a sigh, keeping his right hand splayed across his thigh, resisting the instinctive urge to reach for his own fire stick. *Oh…boy…*

CHAPTER TWENTY

Alex didn't like her father's comment about the apron strings.

If there was one man in Colorado not tied to his wife's apron strings, that man was Anders Nordic, damn him.

She snickered.

Her father looked at her, one brow arched.

She smiled at him as she always had. Disarmingly. "Go to hell, you old reprobate."

She turned to stare into the shrubs and pines lining the trail's left side, the shrubs climbing twenty feet up the ridge, then only the pines climbing from there.

Finn gave a warning back from behind Anders's saddle.

"Take it easy, Deveraux," Nordic warned his father-in-law. "Whoever it is, they have us outnumbered." But he knew who it was, all right.

There was something about the slow, easy way the riders came that told him who they were…and who was leading them.

Then they emerged from the forest and rode out onto
the trail. They turned their spotted Indian ponies to face
Nordic's party, the handsome Indian in the white-man's
attire in the middle of the six-man pack, which consisted
mainly of full-blood Utes but a few half-breeds, as well.
They were all dressed in dusty Indian buckskins and
white man's trail garb. Most wore black or brown hats. A
young one—he couldn't have been over fifteen and baby-
faced but with cold, dark eyes—wore an ancient blue
cavalry kepi, a hawk feather poking up from the braided
guilt band around the crown. The brim had a nick in its
right side, likely from a Ute arrow or a Ute warrior's
Sharps or Springfield rifle.

Aside from the handsome leader and one other, who
had long, gray hair hanging down from a worn red
bandanna wrapped around his deeply lined, nut-brown
head, they were all under twenty.

Each Ute was holding a rifle, but they didn't seem
overly eager to use them. At least, not yet.

The handsome Indian stared at Nordic. Anders stared
back at him.

Alex glanced from her husband to the handsome Ute
and, wrinkling her nose in curiosity and impatience, said,
"We're sorry about your boys."

Deveraux gave a caustic laugh. "Like *hell!* They were
tryin' to steal our *horses!*"

"And they paid for their misdeeds," the lead Ute said.
"It will not happen again." He glanced at the men around
him. "They have been warned."

Deveraux said with such anger that it made Nordic's
belly clench. "Who the hell are you people, and what are
you doin' here? This is my land, Garth Deveraux's land,
and I do not allow nesting any more than I like rustlers."

The oldster turned his head to one side and narrowed one eye suspiciously. "You been long loopin' my beef?"

The others looked at the leader who sliced his hand out in front of him, palm down. "We took one beef when we first arrived here. We have one in our group, an old one, my father, who needed sustenance after the long journey here from where your government has house in Utah." He shook his head. "Not your land. Our land. We belong here."

"That's not going to work," Nordic said. "We have taken it now."

"We know it will not work. I am Moon Runner. My father is Red Bear. We brought him here…to his homeland…to die."

Nordic and Alex shared an arch-browed glance.

"I don't want him dyin' here. This is my land." The old white man thumbed himself in the chest. "It may have been your land once. But it is no longer. Now it is my land. You're trespassing."

Moon Runner looked back at him stubbornly. "I checked on the land office in Camp Collins. The land we have camped on is not yours. It belong to your government. That means we can camp there. My father can die there."

"Oh, you think so, do you, red man?" Deveraux said, putting even more steel in his voice. He fingered the rifle in his hands.

Finn looked from one faction to the other, trying to get the lay of the land, to understand the obviously dangerous situation.

The young braves stiffened and glanced at Moon Runner for orders.

Moon Runner raised a hand palm out and shook his

head. "We want no fight. We have the old among us. If we have to fight, we will," the Ute leader added proudly, "but we don't want to. We want to remain here in peace until my father passes."

Deveraux gave another caustic laugh. "You have a lot of gall, red man. Coming in here and telling me what you—"

"Hold on, Garth," Nordic said, one of the rare times he used his father-in-law's first name. "It can't hurt."

"They tried to steal our horses. They're rustling our beef…"

"Only one. My father needed sustenance. From now on we hunt game to sustain ourselves." Moon Runner paused then canted his head with his copper, severely chiseled face and dark-brown eyes to his right, indicating the Avalanche River beyond the trees lining the rolling, pine-peppered, sage-peppered graze—*Deveraux's* graze, to his old-world way of seeing it—beyond. "Come. You will be our guests. The women are grieving the deaths of their grandsons but they cook and wish to show you a good gesture for allowing us to once more occupy land that belonged to us for many, many years. For many more years than you are old, my friend. For more years than your father was old and his father before him."

"Well, it's my land now," Deveraux glowered back at him. "And we'll eat our own beef and game. That's our way. And you and your people are trespassing. You have to leave."

"We'd love to join you," Alex shot out of nowhere. "Your invitation is very gracious, Moon Runner!"

Moon Runner looked at the pretty, young woman. A faint smile showed on his mouth.

He reined his horse off the trail and into the brush and

trees along the river, his braves and the older man following him, the older man taking up the rear and turning his head to glance cautiously behind him at Nordic, Alex, and Deveraux.

Alex looked at her father who sat his horse, glaring at her, lips pursed, eyes dark.

Alex looked at her husband. He nodded then glanced at the rancher and booted the Appy toward the river. Alex rode up beside him. Finn held back, sitting, and called to the older, stubborn rancher with a single, beseeching bark.

"Think he'll come?" she asked Anders.

"Yeah, I do. Your pa is a curious fella, an' he's just mad enough to want to know what's happening over there at the Indian encampment."

Alex glanced behind them then said quietly, "Looks like you're right. But, boy, does he have a mad on!"

"Just hope he keeps that rifle down."

Finn ran just ahead of the old rancher as though leading the way, making sure that the older rancher came.

Nordic, Alex, and Finn followed the Indians over the ford in the river, the water lapping up around their horses' hocks. Occasionally, Finn held back and looked at Deveraux, who kept coming despite the glower on his red, age- and sun-seasoned cheeks. Finn looked happy that they were all three together though Nordic could sense the dog's apprehension. He'd probably seen Indians before, but Anders doubted they'd ever been this close to him.

They followed the Utes up the river's opposite bank and crossed two low, sparsely wooded hills. At the top of the second hill, they checked down their horses and sat to the left of Moon Runner and his braves. At the base of a higher ridge beyond them they saw the Ute encampment

—four or five buffalo hide lodges flanking two large cook fires on the other side of a tributary of the Avalanche.

Two of the women—there were four total, Nordic saw—all older with long, silver-streaked, dark-brown hair, were doing laundry in the river. They were crying bewitchingly, their bereavement startling in its stark expression. Two women cooking at the fires were also sobbing—a scratching, almost guttural screech. One had cut off her hair so that it hung only a few inches down from her scalp. Behind them, two little half-dressed girls sat on the ground and cried, pulling at the grass and sage before them.

One had painted her face probably in grief for a dead brother. Nordic was only distantly aware of the Ute people, but having grown up on the plains of Dakota, he knew that was one way the Sioux expressed bereavement.

To the right of the fires, on beds of pine boughs, the two braves were laid out naked, hair pulled back, their brown bodies glistening with fresh paint. The images would probably show them their way to the afterlife—a maps of sorts.

Finn looked up at Nordic and mewled uncertainly.

"It's all right, boy," Anders said.

Deveraux sat his horse to his right, on the other side of Alex. He sniffed the air. "I can smell beef," he grunted. "My beef!"

"Father…" Alex said out the side of her mouth, tensely.

To the rancher's right, Moon Runner sat his mustang staring down into the encampment. He turned to the braves lined out beside him, said something in their native tongue, and the braves booted their mounts on down the hill toward a rope corral in which a dozen mounts, some painted, stood grazing and eating feed from grain sacks drooping over the snouts.

Nordic turned to Moon Runner. "Sure this is gonna be all right?"

The Ute turned to him and nodded. He booted his own mount down the hill.

Nordic and Alex followed, Finn close beside his trail partner.

Deveraux rode sullenly to his daughter's right.

"Riding into an Injun encampment…into the encampment of Injun rustlers." He turned his angry gaze on his daughter. "Who rustled my beef…"

"Father, please cool off. This isn't twenty years ago. We have to get along with Moon Runner and his people if only because we're badly outgunned."

Nordic looked at her. She looked back at him with a nervous smile.

As they approached the Ute encampment, Anders felt that instinctive need to shuck his Winchester. It was a primal urge. The whites and Indians had been enemies for so long, both sides having killed the other viciously, as though they were still barbarians—barbarous, warring tribes.

Which they were, Nordic knew.

Not much had evolved in humans in millions of years. When encountering each other, they still felt compelled to kill each other. That wasn't true here, though. At least, not for Nordic. There were few wilder men on the planet, but he must have become a little more civilized since he'd met this beautiful, civilized, cultivated woman riding beside him.

Despite her warriorlike father.

He wanted to hear out Moon Runner, to meet his father who'd wanted to return to his ancestral homeland to die. Nordic had that urge himself. He'd left his home farm in Dakota because he'd felt the need to see the world and to experience adventure. But he had to admit if only to himself that he often felt homesick, that occasionally he longed to see his mother and father and his sister and brothers again. To see the grassland he'd been raised on, to watch the colorful Dakota sun rise and set beyond occasional trees and chalky bluffs silhouetted against it.

To fish for catfish and perch in Willow Creek that snaked across the part of the blond prairie sheathed in willows, box elders, and cottonwoods that his father and mother had staked a claim on.

To be planted near the old sod shanty and sod barn with its off-shooting stone corral, near the wheat, corn, and potato fields he'd been raised tending, the cows he'd been raised feeding and milking.

He hadn't been able to imagine longing for home when he'd left all that, near the little farming and river-boating hub of Fort Pierre. Now he felt it keenly but knew that when it was his time to return, he'd return. Maybe lying in the back of a wagon, chaperoned home by his own family—his wife, sons, and daughters, by his grandchildren and the family dog, as well.

He smiled at the notion.

It left his lips quickly, however, when he saw several of the young braves, finished corralling their horses, retrieving their rifles and turning to face him, Alex, and old Deveraux with hard, stony expressions on their dark-skinned, black-eyed faces. The women, only a few still sobbing, had turned to face the newcomers, as well.

One of these women picked up a rifle of her own.

She held it up high against her beaded buckskin dress over which she wore a frayed blue sweater.

Her dark eyes on the visitor, she called out angrily, gritting her teeth—the few she had left in her head—and wrinkled her nose as though against a foul odor.

She yelled in her native tongue—gutturally and angrily.

Finn ran ahead of Nordic, tail raised, and returned the Ute woman's angry tirade with one of his own.

She looked at the dog, spat to one side distastefully, raised her rifle, and cocked the Spencer's heavy hammer back.

Suddenly, Nordic, who'd checked down Apache, found his own rifle in his hands.

And he was racking a live round into the action…

"Nordic, no!" Alex cried.

CHAPTER TWENTY-ONE

Alex's cry brought Nordic back to his senses.

It was only then he realized what he'd just done so easily, so automatically that shucking the Winchester from its scabbard had been an unconscious act.

All the braves standing by the rope corral raised their own rifles to their shoulders and racked rounds into the actions. Two other old women also grabbed rifles and cocked them, aiming at the big, red-blond-bearded white man from their shoulders. The old woman who'd been going to shoot Finn had also now switched her target to Nordic.

Nordic saw movement in the doorway of the second lodge.

The white woman who'd been with the man known as Moon Runner stood in the doorway. She also held a rifle in her hands, aimed from beneath her right arm. Her eyes were flinty. Her man, Moon Runner, strode quickly toward Nordic gesturing angrily.

"Put it down! Put it down!" As he passed the old

woman who had aimed her own rifle at Finn, he said something in Ute, also gesturing angrily.

The old woman looked at him stonily over the rifle she had aimed at Nordic's canine trail pard.

She glared at Nordic and Alex, at old Deveraux, who said, "I hate to say it, son, but...you probably best leather that fire stick." He gave a dry chuckle. "Hard not to get killin' mad when your dog's threatened, isn't it?"

Finn stood facing the woman from six feet away from her, hackles and ears raised, tail up, growling.

"Now you know how I feel," the old rancher said out of the side of his mouth. "They only threatened your dog. They're threatening my *land*..."

Moon Runner looked at the rancher. "She will not shoot the dog. You have to understand—my people have different relationships with dogs than you do. At least, some of us, including Flying Hawk, does." He turned to the woman again and spoke commandingly in Ute.

She had her hard gaze on Nordic, said something in Ute, quietly but with loud menace. Nordic could read in her eyes what she'd said. "When he does."

Moon Runner turned back to Nordic. "Lower it now or there will be blood."

Nordic depressed the Winchester's hammer and slid the rifle back in its scabbard. "Come, Finn."

The dog looked at him over his shoulder, whined, then reluctantly came over and sat down beside Apache, who nosed the dog curiously, sniffing its defensive anger.

Anders held his hands palm out to Moon Runner. "Uh...sorry. Didn't even realize..."

"I know. That's how wars get started."

"He knows that, too," Alex said to the Indian leader.

She turned to Nordic and said with no little admonish-ment, "Don't you, my darling."

"I do," Nordic said to Moon Runner. "I do. I do." A hard expression returned to his eyes. "But understand this —my dog will not be harmed. I will shoot anybody who tries."

Moon Runner nodded and turned to the other rifle-wielding Indians around him. In Ute, slowly raising and lowering his right, open hand, he told them to lower their weapons and put them away. He said the words in English the first time, in Ute the next. Some of these younger men and girls probably had been taught English in so-called Indian Schools as their first language, learning Ute only after returning to their people.

The pretty white woman in the doorway, in a skirt, blouse, and high brown boots, lowered her rifle then, as well. She set it butt-down on the ground beside her and looked at Moon Runner. She said, "Thomas, bring them in."

Moon Runner, aka "Thomas," glanced at Nordic, Alex, and Deveraux, who chuckled dryly and said, "Thought I was the only contrary one here."

Nordic felt hasty but not ashamed. No man...or woman...messes with his dog. His and Finn's bond was a special one. They'd have fought to the death for each other.

When Alex was on the ground, she looked at Nordic and said, "Well, that was fun."

From the doorway, Thomas's woman called to Nordic with a welcoming smile, "Does your dog like bones?"

Nordic smiled back at her. "Mostly steak but in a pinch, he'll take a bone."

She looked at Finn and patted her thighs. She already

had a big leg bone—the bone of one of Deveraux's own beeves, no doubt—in her hand. Finn raced to her, tentatively slowing a few feet away.

"It's all right, Finn," said the man from Dakota.

Finn politely took the bone and scampered around behind the lodge to find some shade to dine in.

As one of the braves led theirs and Thomas's horses toward the rope corral, Nordic, Alexandra, and Deveraux followed Thomas to the lodge, where the woman awaited them. She held her hand out to Nordic.

"I am Samantha Roman, Thomas's wife." She turned to Alex and then Deveraux. Alex shook the woman's hand, smiling warmly, while Deveraux looked at her askance, skeptically.

A beautiful white woman married to an Indian?

Of course, the races had mixed for many years, but this pair confounded the old white rancher.

Miss Roman seemed to take a little devilish delight in his puzzlement. "We married in New York." She glanced at Alex and then Nordic and tossed her head back to indicate the lodge's dark interior behind her. "Come in, come in. We have stew and fry bread."

Nordic doffed his hat and stepped into the lodge behind his wife and father-in-law. He looked at the fire in the lodge's center over which a large pot hung from an iron tripod. The old Indian he'd seen when he'd first seen the encampment was there, sitting with his knees raised, a deerskin pulled across his shoulders. His silver-brown hair hung down his back. He stared at the newcomers blankly.

"Please sit," Samantha Roman said, holding a hand out to the hide pads situated in a ring around the fire.

Nordic, Alex, and old Deveraux sat, though the old

rancher had trouble getting down there. His old bones creaked and popped and he winced against the discomfort.

The old Indian looked at Deveraux then at the stewpot.

"One of your beeves," he said in broken English. He touched his chest with a gnarled brown fist and slightly bowed his head in thanks and appreciation. Then, keeping his eyes, which glistened slightly with emotion, on the old rancher, said, "You killed two of my grandsons."

Deveraux gave the old Indian an icy smile. "Yeah, well, old-timer, that's what happens when you sneak into my headquarters and try to steal my horses... They got off easy. I could have—"

Alex cleared her throat loudly, cutting off her father, abruptly.

He looked at her. "I said I'd do my part in keeping the peace. Didn't say I wouldn't speak my mind."

"That's why we're all here," said Samantha Roman as an Indian, maybe thirteen or fourteen, emerged from the deep, smoky shadows at the rear of the lodge, and, kneeling beside the old Indian, who was probably her grandfather, began using a wooden ladle to dipper up the succulent smelling stew into wooden bowls.

When she finished, Nordic, Alex, Deveraux, Samantha Roman, and Thomas sat around the fire, dipping up stew with round wooden spoons and small cakes of fluffy bread from a woven reed rack resting on a rock by the fire.

Thomas introduced his father, whose name in English was Red Bear. They ate in silence for fifteen minutes. Then Samantha rose, disappeared, and returned to the fire with a tray of tin cups that contained fresh water likely from the stream by the camp.

Samantha sat again and turned to her guests, tossing back her long hair. "As I said, I am Samantha Roman." She glanced at her Indian man. "Thomas Ruddason—his white name—is my husband. We've been married for two years."

Hesitating and frowning curiously, Alex said, "You met…in New York?"

Deveraux turned to Thomas who sat between him and Thomas's father, scowling. "Whoever heard of an Injun in New York?"

Thomas laughed. "Well, now you, Mr. Deveraux. I grew up in Boston."

"That's why you speak such perfect English," Alex said, nodding.

"When my family was killed not far from here, I was adopted by a minister and his wife. They took me to Denver, where I lived with them for eight years. I went to school there." He smiled and shook his head. "Boy, it wasn't easy, but I learned to get along. Doing so, I learned the white man's ways…and discovered literature. That love continued when my family and I moved to Boston, where my father taught in a seminary. The same seminary accepted me as a student. I continued to study the gospels, of course, but also European and American literature."

Samantha placed a hand on her husband's knee. "He translated Greek and Latin."

Thomas gave a shy smile.

"I taught at the seminary for a while, but I just wasn't comfortable in Boston. I never had been. I had many white friends, but there were too many people…their judgments." Thomas shook his head. "I'm glad I got the education I did but I moved back West when I turned twenty-six. I bought a small ranch in Utah, because I heard that was where my original family had been taken." He glanced at his grandfather. "My ranch was close to theirs, on the Uintah and Ouray Reservation."

"We ranched together," his grandfather said with a proud glance at his grandson. His smile broadened. "He was a good rancher. Better than the whites..." He gave Deveraux a sheepish smile. "And he was more civilized than the whites, too. Most of the white men were outlaws."

"Kinda whitewashing the barn—aren't you, Red Bear?"

"Pa." Alex found herself having to admonish her father once more.

Red Bear looked at his son, frowning. He hadn't understood the expression.

Thomas merely winced and shook his head.

Alex changed the subject, turning to Samantha. "How did you two meet?"

"I was a rancher's daughter," Samantha said, smiling knowingly at Alex, with whom she shared a similar upbringing. "Your father reminds me of mine."

"Pshaw!" Deveraux said. "Now you're just trying to flatter this old mossyhorn!" He looked at Thomas and said, feigning a puzzled scowl, "And I'll be hanged if it's not working!"

They all laughed. Even Red Bear.

Deveraux turned to Samantha again. "What did your...uh...your father think about that arrangement?"

"He disapproved. Especially when I went out to live with Thomas on the reservation."

"He fought the Injuns...er, uh...the Indians, did he? Back during the wars?"

"Oh, he still fights them," Thomas put in. "And they fight him. There is much unrest, but they are slowly learning to get along...to stop hating each other. Sam's father sells horses to my people and they sell horses and hay to him." He shrugged a shoulder. "For the most part, it works."

Red Bear dipped his chin to Alex and said through an ironic smile. "I never liked Richard Roman. And he never liked me. The only thing I like about him except he sired a daughter..." He glanced at Samantha and nodded. "A good one. She cooks menudo and tans hides almost as well as my first wife, who was many moons ago..."

"My mother," Thomas said softly, looking into his water cup.

"I teach on the reservation," Samantha said with a wry smile at Thomas. "I keep busy."

"She does it well," Thomas told Alex with a glance at Nordic. He wrapped his arm around his wife and pecked her cheek. "And my people love her."

Samantha shook her head. "They don't love me. But they do accept me, and I guess that's what matters most."

Nordic found Deveraux staring at her and nodding thoughtfully.

The old rancher caught Nordic looking at him and turned away, blushing.

After a long silence, Deveraux turned to Red Bear. "What makes you think you're gonna die, Red Bear?"

"I am old. And the doctors...tell me." The old Ute placed a hand on his belly, over the blanket. "I don't know what it's called, but...

He shrugged and glanced at his son.

"Cancer," Thomas said. "It has spread."

"Do not worry," Red Bear said to Deveraux. "It won't be long. When I am gone—in a week, maybe two—my son and the rest of my family, my sisters, grandsons, and nieces will put me in a hide scaffold high in a tree. It is my last wish to feed the birds here where I was raised." He shook his head. "I'll be gone by next spring. The winds will blow me away to *Sagmá-ci*."

"That is the next world," Thomas explained.

"Where I will sing with the birds I nourished on my journey from here," Red Bear said, pursing his lips and giving a fateful nod. "It is the way. It is right."

Deveraux looked into his cup again. It was his turn to purse his lips. He shrugged. "No hurry on that, uh, Red Bear."

Alex glanced at Nordic and smiled.

She placed her hand on her father's wrist and squeezed.

CHAPTER TWENTY-TWO

"Hey, that's my horse!" was the man's yell Sarah heard behind her as the last, straggling houses, cabins, and shanties of Camp Collins disappeared in the brush along the trail, falling away behind her.

Thank God she'd learned how to ride back home in Dakota or she wouldn't have a clue about what she was doing. She still didn't have much of one. She'd ridden her family's mules to a stream for water when they'd first homesteaded in the Never Summers, but she'd held them to walks. Now, as her appropriated horse—no, say it like it really is, *stolen* horse—galloped up the trail and into the first canyons of the mountains, all she could do was hold on.

She clung to the reins with one hand, to the horn with the other.

She'd been up and down the trail into the Never Summers on supply runs, so she knew the way. The horse must know where she was headed or knew where most people headed on this side of town—into the high reaches of the Never Summers—that he bypassed the side trail until the river came into view ahead.

Instead of taking the trail that would have taken her across the river and farther north, the horse took the slow bend in the trail and began the climb into the deeper mountains to the west. The Poudre River flowed cold and deep blue beyond the aspens and pines on her right. The river flowed through a deep canyon with a steep, gray, granite wall on the right, a hundred yards beyond the river. The canyon wall on Sarah's left rose less precipitously in places, more steeply in others. Between the trail and that left, southern ridge was blue-green forest and boulders as large as cabins.

Far behind Sarah, guns crackled.

They were coming.

Men from town were coming for her—likely, the marshal whose deputy she'd shot and several men he'd recruited to form his quick, makeshift posse. Likely the man she'd stolen the surefooted, fast-galloping buckskin from was part of that posse. Sarah knew the punishment for stock thievery in the West. She'd heard it over and over again on her family's journey out from Dakota, and she'd heard it many times since as her family had staked their claim and had begun to cut wood for their cabin.

They'd hang her.

The marshal would do nothing to stop them.

Sarah had shot his deputy, after all. Whether he believed it had been an accident, he'd want her to hang for that if not for stealing the horse.

Sarah shuddered.

My god—what had happened?

She'd only left Mr. Olson's Brewery & Saloon to fetch his brewing supplies from the post office. Then, out of the blue, she'd been accosted by two worthless men on the boardwalk. Lisle had come to her aid. Lisle had shot one of the men and Sarah had intended to shoot the other one to keep him from shooting Lisle.

Instead, she'd shot the marshal's deputy.

Oh, God! Oh, God! Oh, God!

Now she was a killer. The killer of a lawman.

If they didn't hang her for stealing the horse, they'd hang her for killing the deputy, for sure...

More guns cracked and barked behind her.

The reports were louder now.

They were getting closer.

She knew they were shooting just to frighten her silly, to make her stop the horse or fall off of it. Mostly, she knew, they were a pack. They were a pack of human wolves with the taste of blood on their tongues. They'd kill her once they caught up to her, but, being men, they'd have their own brand of fun with her.

Their own brand of torture.

She looked at the canyon wall on her left.

She had to get up there. She had to get off the main trail. They'd run her down in minutes if she and the buckskin stayed on it.

Somehow, she had to evade them. If she didn't, she would die. Robert would be orphaned.

She loved Robert so much! She couldn't leave him.

As the buckskin kept galloping up the trail, she could feel it tiring. The horse was slowing. Slowing gradually but slowing.

She glanced behind her. She couldn't see the human wolves behind her, but she could hear them. Their horses were tiring, as well, but they'd overtake her soon.

Think it through, Sarah told herself. You can do it. You can calm down and think it through.

You've been through so much before. The torturous trek out of the plains and into the mountains, attacked by bears, wolves, and human wolves as well. She and her father had fended them off. And they were attacked by Deveraux's men.

She was the last of her family. The rest were dead.

Don't tell me, she thought. She learned so little from all that…from fighting through…*that you haven't learned how to continue to evade death and worse.*

Hunkered low in the saddle, pressing her left cheek against the buckskin's sweat-lathered neck, she gazed down at the trail. It was rocky and gravelly and overlaid by several sets of horse tracks and the obscured furrows of wagon wheels.

Good.

They'd have trouble picking out her own tracks from those other tracks.

They'd figure she continued up along this main trail, which was the only one out here if she remembered right, though a few side trails angled off toward mining claims. They wouldn't figure she'd head for a mining trail. She wouldn't find salvation with lonely miners.

No, they'd figure she was heading for the valley that the Avalanche River ran through. They'd likely know that was country she was familiar with.

Good!

She saw some boulders lumping up along the Poudre, down a steep slope through pines and firs. The boulders obscured by heavy evergreen shrubs and the trees.

She straightened in the saddle and pulled back on the buckskin's reins.

She hipped around to peer behind her.

She could see the gang of riders, their heads bobbing back along a bend in the sloping trail and between the trees lining the trail's sides. Puffs of powder smoke rose in the air around them as they triggered their pistols wild, just trying to put the fear of God into her...which they'd done.

She reached down the horse's right side.

She had the rifle that had come with the horse.

Good.

When they'd been holed up at his line shack, Anders had taught her to shoot it. And, boy, she would if she had to!

She looked for a way down to those boulders and turned the horse off the trail's right side. She didn't think the riders had seen her yet. They'd have had a hard time picking her out of the rocks and trees around her. She gave the horse its head, picking its own way down the steep slope, jerking forward on its front feet, blowing, grunting, loosing rocks and gravel in his wake. He turned a hard right between two firs, then left, and finally they were nearly down to the river, holed up between the snag of three or four boulders, the trees along the ridge further shielding Sarah and the buckskin from the riders that would soon pass on the trail above.

At least, she hoped they'd ride on past.

She stepped out of the saddle, walked around to the horse's right side, and shucked the Winchester saddle carbine from its sheath.

She hoped they'd ride on past. But if they didn't, she'd come at a cost, by God!

She quickly tied the horse to a branch and sidled up to the backside of the boulders. She almost snickered despite her leaping heart and quivering knees. She hadn't realized a good part of the big, rough man who'd saved hers and Robert's hide up in the remote Never Summers had rubbed off on her. He was a stubborn, tough, defiant man. She'd learned from that, she suddenly realized, and she was damned glad she had.

Not one to curse, she cursed again, aloud this time.

"I'm damn glad I have!"

She jacked a round into the Winchester's action, hardening her jaws and gritting her teeth. She silently beseeched her dead mother for the "barn talk" as, pressing her back against the boulders, she half turned to gaze up through a notch at the top of one of the boulders. Through the notch she could see the trail at the top of the ridge.

The riders were approaching hard and fast, their shooting dwindling, however. Some must have stopped to reload. Others, the smarter ones, might have realized the foolishness of triggered lead with no target.

The drumming of the hooves grew louder.

Now Sarah could hear the squawk of tack and the jangle of bridle chains, the mutter of angry voices.

Then she saw the first riders move into view, jouncing with the sway of their horses. The one nearest Sarah was the town marshal, Glen Conagher, in his high-crowned black Stetson and neatly trimmed gray mustache. His severely chiseled features were set hard. On his far side rode the second, thuggish deputy—the blond one. The one she'd killed had brown hair.

The one she'd killed by *accident*, she reminded herself in a brief panic.

Oh my god—I am a killer, aren't I?

Everything had happened so fast, she hadn't had time to stop and consider the notion.

A killer.

If they caught her, she'd hang for sure. You couldn't get away with killing a lawman even by accident. Of course, she didn't know for sure about that, but something deep down told her that was true.

Her heart thudded as the riders passed, dust curling in their wake.

That much was good, anyway.

She pressed her back against the boulders once more.

She'd wait to make sure they were a good way ahead before she untied the buckskin and road back up the ridge. At the same time—her mind was a whirl of racing thoughts and emotions—she wondered what she'd do in the long run. She thought about Robert first and foremost, securing his safety.

And then she and he would have to go somewhere they couldn't be found. If they were ever found, Robert would be taken from Sarah, and she'd be hanged "by the neck until she was dead."

She'd heard those words spoken by the judge on the main street of her old town in Dakota, during the trials of particularly vile men. The words had repelled her, and she'd placed her hands over her ears to drive them out, but she'd heard them, all right.

And now they echoed like kettle-drum thunder inside her head.

When the drumming of the hooves had been silent for a minute, she waited another minute. The posse would soon know that Sarah was no longer ahead of them. They'd turn back. She needed to get back up the ridge, across the trail, and onto the forested, boulder-strewn ridge beyond.

Risky.

If she rode up there too soon, they might catch her if they were already on the way back. If she waited too long they might get back, see where she'd left the trail, and climb the side of the ridge for her.

"Here goes," she said, and slid the carbine back into the gelding's saddle boot.

She used a rock to help her climb into the saddle.

"Okay, boy," she said, hearing the nervous trill in her voice. "Let's go, okay. Let's go!"

At first, the horse seemed bewildered.

"Git up!"

The horse lowered his head and shook it.

"Oh, please, boy," Sarah urged. "We've come this far. We can't stop now!"

If she remained here, they'd find her for sure.

If she were alone, she would not care what happened to her. But she had to stay alive, and she had to stay free for Robert. He was everything to her.

Her and Anders.

Deep down, she knew he knew it, too.

Deep down, he felt the same way. He was just intrenched in the ranch and all his new obligations.

Finally, the horse moved forward. Again, he shook his head, confused, wary. Not at all sure about his new, female rider. Likely, the horse sensed her fear and desperation and was put off by it.

The buckskin retraced his route to the top of the ridge.

Once they were back on the trail, the horse stopped and shook his head again. Sarah knew the horse had probably easily anticipated his former rider's wishes, but he couldn't fathom Sarah, so he just stood there, waiting, wondering…

Sarah heaved a sigh of relief at having reached the trail.

She peered up trail in the direction the posse had come.

She neither saw anything nor heard anything. Just the sounds of the forest overlaid by the ceaseless rush of the river, and the pounding of the water over rocks. Birds pipped and flitted between trees, flashing golden in the sunshine. Pinecones dropped and landed with soft thuds.

The horse had turned down trail. It was wanting to go back to its town, likely back to its owner. Sarah reined it south, to the opposite side of the trail from the river and batted her heels against its flanks. Again, the horse shook its head. It didn't want to go that way.

"Oh, please, please, please," she urged the horse, lunging forward in the saddle and continuing to lightly though desperately touch her heels to the mount's flanks.

CHAPTER TWENTY-THREE

F inally, just when Sarah had resigned herself to the horse stranding her there, he gave a reluctant chuff. As though saying, "All right, but you're asking an awful lot, 'specially since we don't even know each other." It moved off the trail and began climbing.

It wove its way up through the trees, around outcroppings, and patches of slide-rock. She knew what the barren rock, its patched formed by former slides, was called because Anders had told her. Again, Sarah let the horse choose its own way, knowing it knew better than she, would sense the easiest way.

Occasionally, she glanced dreadfully down the slope behind and below her and was always relieved to see nothing, hear nothing. All was quiet. Just the forest sounds and the dwindling sound of the river far below her now.

The horse made its way up and across the slide of the slope, choosing the path of least resistance. Higher and higher they climbed until Sarah could start to see the open sky vaulting over the top of the ridge still a good hundred yards above her. Her heart beat eagerly, hope edging the terror away, at least slightly.

The horse was blowing hard again.

Sarah could feel its muscles contracting and expanding between her knees. Its lungs and heart were working hard. He needed a blow. After a certain amount of plow or hay work on their farm in Dakota, and on the long trail out here to Colorado, Pa had stopped his horses or mules every fifteen or twenty minutes to rest them and to give them water.

She pulled the horse up and around an escarpment shelving out from the slope and checked him down. She stepped onto the top of the dike padded thickly with long, red pine, fir needles, and branches.

Water.

She should have given the horse water before she'd left the river.

But then she saw the canteen hanging from a woven leather lanyard from its saddle. She picked it up, shook it. Water sloshed inside.

Again, her heart beating hopefully, she walked up in front of the horse who continued warily, its light-brown eyes cast with skepticism. He sniffed her neck, her ears, her hair until it tickled. She chuckled. He was just trying to get to know her. He was trying to understand what in the heck she was up to.

She uncorked the flask and dribbled water into her cupped hand and held that hand up to the horse's snout.

"Oh, you don't want to know what I'm up to," she told the mount, wagging her head. "Nope, that's not something you want to know." She leaned in close and spoke conspiratorially into the horse's left, twitching ear.

"Truth to tell, you've been *acquired* by a fallen woman. No run-of-the-mill fallen woman, either."

Pouring more water into her hand and giving the horse more—it eagerly drank from her cupped palm—she leaned back to peer around the scarp and into the forest below.

"No, this one not only works in a whorehouse... though I don't work the line, I hasten to add—but I shot man!" She whispered this last part into the horse's ear.

She gave a droll chuckle, unable to believe what she'd just said.

She'd *shot* a man.

She was wanted by the authorities.

On her way out West with her family, she'd seen wanted posters tacked to posts and on the outside walls of post offices and saloons. Hundreds of them. Maybe thousands. A few of the likenesses sketched on those circulars had been women. Cold-eyed women. With cunning looks in their cold eyes framed by usually long, straight hair.

Badger Lil had been one.

Eileen of Abilene had been another. Eileen had been wanted for shooting her husband while he'd sat in a privy in Abilene.

Sarah gave another caustic chuff and shook her head. She hadn't tried to remember those names. She just had. She hadn't even known she'd remembered them until now.

Fitting.

For she was one of them now.

Sarah the Deputy Killer.

WANTED DEAD OR ALIVE!

Would her eyes look the same as those other women's

eyes peering out from the yellowing paper of a wanted dodger?

She'd just given the horse one more handful of water when she heard something on the slope below.

A horse?

Then she heard a man's voice.

Then another's.

They'd caught up to her!

She peered up the slope rising steeply above her.

What to do?!

She stoppered the canteen, hung it from the saddle horn, then used the top of the dike to help her step into the saddle. She reined the horse around. Again, he was sluggish. He was probably smelling his rider down there and was tired of being manhandled by a girl!

But she managed to get him pointed in the right direction and booted him on up the slope behind her. She occasionally heard a man's voice and the chuff of a distant horse. A hoof clacked off a rock. She looked behind her and thought she spied movement through the branches but then the movement was gone.

They were following her trail, though.

The buckskin would have left a clear track in the soft forest dirt and pine needles.

The horse wove through the trees, rocks, evergreen shrubs, and boulders.

Sarah clung to the horn to keep from being thrown back over the horse's arched tail. Finally, they gained the crest of the ridge and stopped to get her bearings.

What bearings?

Around her was nothing but more brush, forest, rock, dikes, and ridges rising around her with high mountains looming cool and blue in the windy, sunny distance.

More voices behind her.

A man said, "...this way..."

"See a track?"

"Yep—she's climbin' up through here!"

Sarah shuddered.

She leaned forward to ease the horse's nerves, though she was really only trying to soothe her own. She was about to boot into fast motion but then stopped.

She heard the chink of a spur not far down the slope below her.

"Yep, she passed through here just a minute ago!" one man yelled to another.

"One comin'," said another.

The eager, excited voice was followed by the clomping of stumbling, running feet.

Sarah frowned and looked down the slope.

Were there only two down there? Had the group split up to track her?

That sounded about right.

Her heart beating so hard she thought it would explode from her chest, Sarah leaped out of the saddle and quickly led the horse to a pine twenty feet to the east. She tied the reins to a branch and slid the Winchester from its boot.

It felt as though she'd just grabbed a skillet out of a very hot fire.

It burned both her sweaty hands.

What was she doing? Yes, what in *hell* did she think she was doing?

What in bloody goddamned hell did this crazy Dakota farm girl think she was doing?

She'd killed a man and stolen a horse!

Was she going to kill yet another man?

"If I have to," Sarah said tightly to herself as she stopped at the lip of the ridge, just above where she and the horse had ridden up. "Bloody goddamn right!" She glanced up, sheepish. "Sorry, Mama. This is a special situation. I know you'd understand!"

She crouched behind a rock, rested the rifle over the top, and drew the hammer back until it stood cocked and ready to save her life.

To save the life of Robert's mom.

———

On the trail home after their visit to Thomas Ruddason's people, Alexandra Deveraux glanced at her father riding beside her, on her right side.

The old man stared straight ahead, expressionless. He appeared quietly pensive, one gloved hand holding the reins of his fine gelding, the other one closed light over the horn. Nordic rode ahead, and he'd seen the old man's inscrutable face, as well. He'd heard his silence.

"You all right, Pa?"

Deveraux took a couple seconds before turning his head to his daughter. He blinked. "Yes, yes—I'm fine." His mood seemed to lighten instantly. He even smiled, a rarity for him these days, having recently lost his wife and enduring a body that was failing him now in his later years. "In fact, I'm better than fine. That was nice, ridin' into that camp. Seein' those people. Talking with ol' Red Bear."

"Really?" Nordic asked.

"Yeah." Deveraux frowned suddenly. "I don't want 'em stayin' on, mind you. No, no—I won't tolerate that. But I can understand him wantin' to come home to die.

Funny…" He let his voice trail off as he looked up the steep, pine-carpeted ridge on his right. "When you live in a place for a long time…when you fight hard to acquire a place like I and my old man fought to acquire *our* place…once you have it you see it as only *your* home."

"How do you mean?" Alex asked him.

"I mean…you don't really think about the people seein' it as their home. I just saw it as a place that I conquered…that I made my own…for my own family. I never really looked at it through the eyes of, say, Red Bear." Deveraux shuttled his gaze to the Avalanche murmuring beyond the trees on his left. "I do now. I *can* now. God, how he must miss it."

"He sure enough does," Nordic said, swaying easily in his saddle.

For some reason, Finn had decided to jump up on Apache's back and ride with his master on the way home. The dog sat with a princely air on Nordic's blanket roll secured behind his saddle cantle, looking around, sniffing, on the scout, likely, for an afternoon snack in the form of a rabbit or a pocket gopher.

He hadn't entered Red Bear's lodge. Somehow, he'd sensed it had not been a place welcome to dogs, as some places weren't. He probably couldn't really understand that, as Nordic himself couldn't, for he didn't really see Finn as a dog but as his friend, on equal footing. But Finn knew when he was not welcome. He'd been waiting patiently, sitting with a princely air, as he was now, when Nordic, Alex, and old Deveraux ducked through the lodge's buffalo hide entrance flap.

"Yes, yes…I can understand that, now," Deveraux said, looking around at this pristine land around him as though with new eyes. Young eyes, like the eyes of Red

Bear when he'd been young. He turned his gaze to his daughter riding along on his left. "You know…I probably fought Red Bear many years back, when I was trying to carve out Comanche Ranch for my own….when I was older and I wanted to build a lodge of my own…for my own family."

"You might have, Pa."

Deveraux nodded. He glanced from Alex to Nordic and said, "You two take your time. I'm gonna ride ahead, check out an old fishin' hole Pa and I used to catch golden trout out of." He smiled, but there was a blush behind it, as well, embarrassed. "I haven't been out there for years."

"You do that," Alex said, giving her father a warm smile.

"I just will!"

The old man gigged his horse into a trot, and horse and rider were soon gone around a bend in the trail.

Nordic slowed Apache to a stop. Alex, who'd been riding behind him, rode up beside him now.

"Think he'll be all right?" he asked her, concern hopscotching his spine. "There're men after him, you know."

Behind him, Finn gave a soft whimper as he stared up the trail where the old man had gone.

Alex sat smiling as she stared in the same direction.

She nodded. "I think he will. I think that old mossy-horn can take care of himself." Her smile broadened as she turned to her husband. "Especially today."

Finn turned his head to her, listening intently, curious.

Nordic nodded but he was skeptical. He didn't like the old man riding off alone like that. There were very bad men after him. But this was an independent family he'd married into. As independent as he himself. Maybe even more so. He had to get used to it. To know when to let his guard down from time to time, to not worry about them.

To not worry about *her*. He had to know when to let her alone to be by herself.

"You know what else?" she asked.

"What?"

"I'm suddenly liking that old reprobate. I mean, I've always *loved* him, of course. He's my father. But…" She frowned, gazing ahead. "I like him today."

Nordic leaned out from his horse and kissed her on the lips.

She looked into his eyes. "What was that for?"

"I don't know." The big man shrugged. "You just seem extra special lately. There's a glow about you. Even after what happened earlier. There's something in your eyes."

"Nordic?"

He arched his brows, expectant.

"You think you're gonna hang around awhile?"

Again, he shrugged. "I reckon." He smiled, all irony gone from his eyes. "I kinda like it around here. Finn does, too."

Finn barked in the affirmative.

"Good. I needed to know for sure, Nordic."

"Why?"

She stared at him for a full fifteen seconds. "I'm pregnant."

For several seconds, he just stared at her. At first, he wasn't sure he'd heard her right. But, he had. Still it was hard to sink in. Her…his wife…pregnant?

He was…going to be a…*father*?

They'd been ordered to have kids, of course. But even before that, the minute he knew he was in love with her, he'd wanted them. He'd wanted them almost desperately. And he'd envisioned kids in their future, running about the house and yard. It had been such a foreign notion—as foreign as contemplating the moon and stars, which he would never understand.

But, now, here it was before him.

They were going to have kids. In fact, one of them... the first one...was growing inside her even now as he sat here in the saddle, lower jaw hanging, looking, he had no doubt, like a big, dump, deaf, mute idiot...

He couldn't find the words.

She just sat smiling at him. Her eyes flashed in the sunlight. Shade from the leaves on the trail's left side danced as gold as freshly minted pennies across her face.

Finally, she said, "Come on." She held his gaze as she reined her mare around him and started into the brush down the slope along the river. "I have a place I want to show you. A special place. Just for us."

She winked. That wink was like a hand reaching into his chest and twisting his heart one-quarter turn counter-clockwise.

The mare headed on down the slope through the trees, Alex leaning back in the saddle, holding her reins up high against her chest.

Behind Nordic, Finn moaned and thumped his trail.

"Coming?" Alex called behind her.

"Oh, yeah," he said finally, booting Apache down the slope. "I'm comin'!"

Finn barked.

CHAPTER TWENTY-FOUR

The man stepped out from around a large fir tree and stepped onto the top of the ridge. A .44-caliber bullet from the saddle-ring carbine Sarah aimed straight out from her right shoulder welcomed him.

He saw the rifle just as he lifted his chin, breathing hard from the steep climb. His eyes widened and he opened his mouth even wider to shout in protestation of his imminent demise, but he was dead before he could make a sound.

The man whom Sarah recognized as a bouncer from one of the saloons in town, threw his rifle away from him as the bullet punched through his chest and knocked him back down the ridge, into the trees and shrubs, out of sight.

To Sarah's right, the buckskin whinnied and pulled at his tied reins.

Flanking the dead man, another man yelled, "Stieg!" Running footsteps sounded as did the chinking of spurs. "Stieg, didja get her, you lucky devil!" The man laughed breathlessly as he ran and added, "You're buyin' the drinks tonight, ya lucky…"

He let his voice trail off when, apparently, he saw his friend Stieg lying unmoving on the side of the ridge. Sarah was already halfway to the horse and closing on the frightened beast fast. The horse whinnied again and stared in the direction of where she had shot Stieg. The horse pawed the ground with a front hoof.

Six feet from the horse, Sarah stopped and racked another round into the carbine's action. She dropped to a knee and raised the rifle to her shoulder. Her heart was racing so fast, and she was breathing so hard she felt as though she were trying to steady the rifle against her shoulder during an earthquake. The second man appeared —a short, stocky man in a bowler hat and suspenders. He held his own rifle straight out from his right shoulder, sliding it around, looking for a target.

When he saw her, he tensed. His eyes widened.

"Oh!" he said, glancing down the slope on his left. "She's here! She's he—"

Sarah's rifle punched back against her shoulder once more, knocking her sideways. She knew she'd missed her target but in the corner of her eye she saw the man, a faro dealer from the Black Cat Saloon, swing around and run for cover down the ridge. Sarah grabbed the buckskin's reins, led the horse closer to the tree, and used a knob of a branch poking out from the bole to help her step into the leather. Holding the rifle and the reins in both hands, she turned the horse around and booted him into the trees to the south.

The horse hadn't required much urging.

The two gunshots had been all the urging he'd required.

He ran hard, leaping deadfalls, wending his way through the forest.

Sarah could hear nothing behind her. The buckskin's galloping hooves and the horse's labored breathing were all she heard. The horse jerked her around so violently that, to keep from being thrown, she lunged forward, toward the saddle horn.

Doing so, she lost the rifle which clattered onto the ground and slid away behind her.

"Oh no!" she cried.

She turned forward.

Her eyes snapped wide in terror.

"Oh no!" she cried again.

She tried to wrap her right hand around the saddle horn but before she could, a low-hanging pine bough slid up before her in a blur of fast motion. She started to crouch, to get underneath it.

Too late.

The bough slammed into her chest just beneath her chin.

She screamed as she went flying over the horse's tail as though she were no more than a rag doll.

She hit the ground so hard on her belly she heard her breath punched out her lungs in a deep grunt and throaty exhalation.

Dust sifted around her.

Bells clanged in her head.

She lifted her chin from the pine needle-carpeted ground and peered ahead of her, back in the direction from which she'd come. She saw the buckskin running away from her, off to her left, reins bouncing along the ground behind him. The horse whinnied and buck kicked, tired of the whole ordeal.

He wasn't the only one, Sarah thought.

Her vision was blurry. She could make out the glitter of sunlight off pine boughs and aspen leaves, the soft ground rising away from her, back in the direction of the ridge.

A man's voice shouted, "There's Jake's hoss!"

Vaguely, she saw three men moving toward her, from up by the horse who had stopped about sixty yards away from her and curveted to face her.

The short, squat man in the bowler hat, who'd been the second one up the ridge after her, pointed at her and strode toward her, sort of crouching and aiming his rifle out from his right side. "There she is! Right there! Careful, she killed Stieg an' dang near blew my head off." He took several more steps in his bandy-legged fashion, the other two flanking him and moving in much the same way—very cautious and suspicious.

As though they were confronting a coiled diamondback though they should have seen she was no longer armed, flat on her belly on the ground, and badly soiled and disheveled.

Sarah grunted, groaned, and fought to get her senses back.

Fear overwhelmed her.

Her fear grew when the short, squat man in the lead said, "There's that immigrant little devil, part o' that nestin' family of squareheads from the plains. She came up here an' lived with old Deveraux and that big Dakotan who wriggled his way into the addled ol' jasper's family!"

"Married his daughter!" said one of the men behind him.

The other man gave a lewd squeal and made a goatish gesture.

The squat man stopped and aimed his rifle at Sarah, still struggling to gather her marbles.

"Let's give her a bullet," he said, raising his rifle and aiming down the barrel. "Why bother with her?" Then another idea came to him. "Less'n…"

One of the men behind him smiled deviously. "Uh-uh. *Uh-huhhh!*"

The squat man frowned suddenly. He lowered the rifle a little and turned his head to stare off behind Sarah and to her left. The others looked that way, as well. Sarah felt the drum of hooves in the ground beneath her before she saw a lean, tall man galloping toward her quickly. He crouched low in the saddle, his hat brim pasted against his long, angular face—a young face, Sarah thought, though her eyes were still blurry and her mind was still muddled from her unceremonious meeting with the ground.

"Who the hell…?" bellowed the squat man with the shaggy hair poking out around the brim of his bowler hat.

One of the men flanking him raised his arm to point and yell, "That's one o' them consarned Comanche Ranch men!"

Both him and the other men raised their rifles but not before the short, squat man snapped off a shot at the oncoming rider, who then snapped the butt of his own rifle against his shoulder. He held his reins in his teeth and triggered the Winchester in his hands. The crack of a shot sounded above the drumming of his horse's hooves.

The squat, bowler-hatted man yelped and stumbled backward, dropping his rifle as he crouched over his belly from which blood oozed, staining his striped shirt under his ancient brown, fringed, elk-hide vest. As he did, more hooves drummed, and more men yelled as a passel of more riders rode up from the ridge behind him. There were four more and—Sarah blinked her eyes to try to clear her vision that was still blurry at the edges—the man leading the small pack was the tall, gray-mustached marshal of Camp Collins, Glen Conagher, who reined his fine sorrel gelding back sharply as two bullets plumed the dirt and pine needles around his prancing horse's feet. Conagher crouched, wincing and scowling and raising one arm as though to shield his face from the unexpected onslaught.

The two who'd been with the short, squat man, who lay on the ground yelling and kicking wildly while trying to hold his guts in place, ran back toward the lip of the ridge where the four riders led by Conagher were just now dismounting in a hurry. They leaped from their saddles and dove for cover as the rifle behind Sarah barked three more times.

Then the rider was hovering over her on his black-and-white pinto pony, prancing beside Sarah with its head high, black mane buffeting and glinting in the late afternoon sunlight. A gloved hand thrust down toward Sarah and a young man's voice said, "Take my hand, Miss Sarah. Climb aboard. Them scalawags from town don't got the best plans for you, seems like!"

The gloved hand closed around Sarah's as she thrust it high. Then, suddenly, hearing her savior's grunt as he lifted her up off the ground and swung her onto the pinto's back behind him, she found herself seated on the man's blanket roll and saddlebag, her head still reeling.

Bullets sizzled through the air around her and her unexpected benefactor's head as he whipped the pinto around and sent the horse straight south through the pines and firs with, "Giddap, now, boy. If you ever needed to split the wind, now is it."

With a shrill, frightened but determined whinny the horse dug its rear hooves into the soft ground and, kicking two good-sized dirt clumps out behind it, cast itself forward into a hard gallop.

Sarah, still trying to get her bearings, felt herself thrown backward. To save herself from yet another unwelcome meeting with mother earth, she gave a desperate cry and threw herself forward to wrap her arms around the skinny, young man's waist, around his denim jacket, just above his dark-brown cartridge belt, and felt the pine-scented wind whip at her hair as they set off at a hard run across the gently downward sloping ground.

Bullets caromed threw the air around her.

Some cracked sharply into trees to either side of her, spraying bark in all directions. Others spanged off rocks while yet others thumped into the ground to either side of the pinto's scissoring hooves.

The crackle of gunfire and the heated shouting of her pursuers dwindled as the pinto widened the gap between her, the young man who'd saved her, and Glen Conagher's men who likely included his other deputy and the man who belonged to the buckskin.

They rode hard for what must have been a quarter mile.

Most of the shooting had dwindled to occasional staccato barks behind them, but the thumping of what sounded like at least two pursuing horses held steady. This seemed to frustrate the young horseman, who gave his head an angry shake and, chuffing with deep annoyance, drew sharply back on his rein, bringing his horse to a skidding halt.

"I'll be hanged! If I ever were to be hanged, these two'd do it!"

He curved the horse, jacked a fresh round into his rifle's action, and said, "Lower your head, Miss Sarah, and stick your fingers in your ears!"

Doing as she'd been told, Sarah turned to her right now to see the two riders galloping to within fifty yards behind then reining their own mounts to sliding, dusty halts, as well. The man on the left was Glen Conagher. The man on the right was his sole deputy now that Sarah had dispatched the other one.

The young rider canted his head, pressed his check up against the rifle's rear stock and said in a slight Southern accent, "I don't wanna have to kill you, Marshal—you bein' a marshal an' all. But I will." He slid the rifle slightly right, adding, "And I'll kill him, too. I don't see how Miss Sarah could have you and Lew Skully an' them other jaspers from town comin' for her that hard. No, sir, I don't! Now, you both turn them horses around and back the way you came, or they'll be goin' back with empty saddles!"

Conagher and the deputy both held their rifles on them. They were on unsettled perches, however, because their horses were prancing and sidestepping nervously. They held fire. The young rider before Sarah, whose own mount felt as calm as midnight after a storm, didn't even twitch a muscle.

Conagher lowered his own rifle slightly.

His gray-blue eyes blazed with fury and frustration below the crown of his black Stetson. He studied the rifle-wielding string bean before him, looked at Sarah, then turned to the deputy on his left, and yelled, "Pull back, Lew! Damnit, pull back!"

They reined their mounts around and as they booted them into dusty trots, Conagher looked behind him, jaws hard, and pulled his lips back from gritted teeth. "Go on. Git outta here." He swung his rifle out and back to point behind him at the quarry who'd frustrated him—no, humiliated him—so keenly. "But I'll know where to find you both!"

He turned forward in his saddle and he and his cowed deputy booted their horses into angry gallops back through the woods toward the ridge.

Still breathless, her heart still racing, Sarah looked at the young man sitting the pinto before her.

"Boy," she said, "you sure told him!"

He heaved a hard sigh and shook his head. "Boy, that sure was takin' the tiger by the tail!"

"Who are you?"

"Oh, uh…sorry," he said with an embarrassed chuckle, as though he'd thought it have only been proper if he'd introduced himself by now. He quickly chewed off his right glove and angled that hand back behind him. "Ryan LaPlante of the Deveraux Comanche Ranch at your service, Miss Sarah."

Sarah frowned. She didn't remember him, but she'd never gotten to know many of the hands at the ranch. She nodded dully. "Well, I thank you, Mr. LaPlante, but…"

"Oh, it's Sure Shot!"

"I thank you, uh, Sure Shot, but…you just saved the life of a cold-blooded killer and horse thief. I hate to say it"—she choked back a sob—"but the gallows might just be your reward!"

CHAPTER TWENTY-FIVE

A pache moved carefully down the slope.

The aspen leaves rattled around the horse, rider, and dog who sat behind Nordic, mewling softly and expectantly in his throat.

Near the bottom of the ridge, a path curved off to the right. It wound around the left side of an aspen whose roots were humping up out of the ground. It crossed the root then swung back right and descended gradually until Nordic found himself only a few feet from the river. Just beyond, upstream and around a slight bend, came the sounds of splashing and humming.

Apache followed the trail around the bend.

Nordic drew back on the reins, stopping the horse.

A hat lay in the brush to his right, crown side down.

Just beyond, clothes lay strewn in the brush on both sides of the trail—skirt, blouse, leather shirtwaist, ladies' undergarments including pantaloons, camisole, and then a pair of lacy pink pantalettes hung from the branch a what remained of an ancient, fallen tree.

Just beyond the pantalette guidon, a dark pool curved

in against the ridge, forming what appeared a deep, dark, backwater pool. A fallen spruce tree extended out from the bank on the pool's far side. It had been felled by lightning many years before—maybe twenty years or more. Its bark had been burned off. It's trunk and branches were charred black and riddled with the pock-marks of woodpeckers drilling for insects.

The big Dakotan's focus, however, was not on the pool or the tree.

No, his focus was on the lady in the pool, who leaned back against the half-submerged tree, her shoulders bare. He could see the pale shimmer of her thighs beneath the water as she treaded water slowly. She pulled her hair out of the bun behind her head and let it fall, rich and thick, down her shoulders and back. It floated on the gently churning, black water around her.

Her gray-eyed gaze held his.

"You're already a rotten leg," she said, and blinked once, slowly.

Nordic chuckled. He drew his right leg over his saddle horn and dropped straight, easily down to the ground. Finn remained seated behind the cantle, looking between Anders to Alex then back again, giving a steady, deep-throated, playful snarl. He lifted his fine snout and barked.

Nordic wasted little time in kicking his boots off, then his tunic, denims, longhandles, and wool socks. He enjoyed few things more than swimming, which he did regularly when he lived in the isolated shacks—alone until Finn came—all across the West, from the Bitter-roots in the north to the Sierra Blanca in the south, for more years than he cared to remember.

Behind him, he heard Finn leap down from Apache's

back with a grunt then thump off into the brush. The dog knew when three was a crowd. A rabbit would occupy him.

Nordic swam deep under the water nearly as cold as snowmelt even now in the mid-summer. He swam until he saw his wife's delectable body shimmering before him, long legs kicking slowly, her slender toes rising and falling as she moved. He moved to her, wrapped his arms around her legs, surfaced, and kissed her eyes.

She leaned her head back against the spruce trunk, eyes closed, groaning softly.

She opened her eyes, gave him that look he knew so well, and wasted no more time.

Though it took them a good, long time, as it always did.

Because even now, with trouble all around them, they were in no rush.

They had each other and a family on the way, and they had a long future ahead of them as long as they could keep it. They'd had to fight for it, but he knew what it was like to fight for his future...his life and, as pampered as she'd been living on one of the wealthiest spreads in the northern Rockies, she knew what fighting was like, too.

Sometimes, the more you had, the harder you had to fight.

They both rested back against the dead spruce, arms spread out along the tree above and behind them, holding them upright.

"How long," he asked, still trying to regain his senses after the bliss he'd enjoyed, his lady in his arms in what, he knew, had been a favorite swimming hole since she'd first learned how to swim.

It was where she and her brothers used to swim. He'd never been here before, but she'd told him about it. He'd wanted to see it, to swim in it, but he hadn't pushed. He'd wanted her to take her time in sharing it with him.

"I don't know. I haven't seen the doctor. Rosa thinks five and a half months."

"Here I thought you'd been having too much gravy on your potatoes."

She gave him a playful splash. "Happy?"

He nodded. "Yep."

She frowned. "You sure?"

"Nah, let's throw it back!"

She wrapped her long arms around his neck and gazed deeply into his eyes. "You're going to have a lot to throw back. I'm going to have many with you." She narrowed her eyes and pursed her lips with that Deveraux feistiness and determination. "I'm gonna fill up that whole lodge until the old bastard is finally satisfied. Oh, he'll only live to see one, if that…but I think he will, given who he is and who he sired"—she winked—"and he'll know about the rest. He and Mother both will up there, where they'll lie together in the little family cemetery overlooking the lodge, keeping an eye on things." She paused and her brows wrinkled a little, a slightly dark cast coming to them. "Where we'll lie someday, too…and our children after that…and theirs…"

He thumbed a tear from her cheek. "Don't get sad on me now. You know how it goes."

"I'm not sad." She smiled brightly, and he could tell it was real, not manufactured for him. "I'm happy. It's the way of all things…all life…and it will be ours, too." She looked around, tears of joy glittering like little gold beads in her eyes. "We'll be part of it all!"

He kissed her, then pulled his head back.

She studied him hard again, ground her fingertips into the back of his neck. "Nordic?"

"Yes."

"Let's find whoever's out to ruin him...*us*...our family...and kill the bastard hard."

"Okay."

"Let's do that together. Before we slap our firstborn to roaring life in his house."

"When do you want to get started?"

"Right now," she said, narrowing her eyes once more.

"Okay." He smiled and touched two fingers to his mouth. "Wait here."

She frowned and drew her head back a little. "What?"

"Shhh."

He turned, pulled his head under the water, swam across the pool, and climbed up onto the rocky, sage-peppered bank where their horses waited. He tramped barefoot, shaking the water out of his hair, over to Apache where the horse stood gazing skeptically into some shrubs on the river's far side.

Nordic shucked his Winchester, jacked a round into the action, turned, crouched, and emptied the Yellowboy —nine shots, one after another, the empty casings arcing and glinting in the sunlight as they sailed back over his right shoulder.

He lowered the smoking Winchester and turned to his wife staring at him in hang-jawed shock from the other side of the pool.

"There," he said with a resolute nod, staring toward the Avalanche's opposite side. "That's a start!"

He shoved the Yellowboy back down in its boot then gathered his clothes and dressed hastily. Alex swam from the pool's opposite side and, casting incredulous gazes at the thicket into which Nordic had emptied his Winchester, followed suit.

Neither said anything, and neither bothered to dry off first. They just pulled their clothes on over their wet skin. When Nordic had cinched his shell belt with matched, holstered Russians around his waist, they mounted up and swam their horses across the river. The Avalanche was neither deep nor as fast here as it was elsewhere.

They made the crossing in good time and a minute later they sat their horses looking down at the body lying belly down in the thicket.

Alex turned to her husband. "Who's that?"

Nordic was looking off, hipping around in his saddle to look behind them, at the forested ridge rising steeply a quarter mile away.

He turned to Alex. "I think I know, but I'll know for sure in a minute."

He dismounted, turned to his wife, extended his hand, and said, "Climb down."

She looked around, suddenly a little paranoid. "What? Why?"

Nordic shook his hand at her. "Just climb down."

When he had her on the ground, he turned to the river beyond the thicket in which the dead man lay. As he'd suspected, Finn swam across the river from the pool Nordic and Alex had swum in. He'd seen his trail pard pull his picket pin and didn't want to be far away from him. The dog was fighting against the current. The undercurrent was dragging him farther north than he wanted to be. Nordic walked downstream and when the dog was twenty feet from the bank, he waded in, grabbed the dog by the scruff of his neck, and pulled him ashore.

"You could've waited," he said to the dog with a sardonic chuckle.

The dog yipped and yammered, coyotelike, then spread his legs and gave a gigantic shake. He didn't make Nordic any wetter than he already was.

Looking around cautiously, warily, Anders walked back over to where Alex stood by the thicket. She gazed across the ridge behind her, knowing as much from what her husband hadn't said as by what he'd said that danger was afoot. Danger that took the living, breathing form as opposed to the dead or nearly dead form of the man lying belly down in the bushes, unmoving.

Alex glanced at Finn who was sniffing the dead man.

"He was just being loyal," she told Anders.

"He knows water better than that." Nordic stepped into the thicket and kicked the dead man onto his back, to lying beside his Sharps rifle in the brush. Two hazy blue eyes gazed up at him in terror from either side of the X that had been carved into the bridge of his nose, according to the story, late one night in the Sawatch Range in south-central Colorado.

The man's mouth moved as though he were trying to speak, but no words came out. Blood bibbed his chest and there were another couple of holes in his right thigh.

An eerie humming sounded.

Nordic's heart turned a somersault in his chest.

"Down!" he shouted and rammed his big body into his wife's, laying her out flat with a scream.

The heavy-caliber bullet chewed into a tree jutting from the middle of the thicket, just behind where Alex had been standing a half second before.

Finn barked as he stood facing the northern ridge, back legs spread, tail raised.

Nordic ground his knees into the turf on either side of the startled, addled Alex, leaped to his feet, ran to his horse, and shucked his Yellowboy once more.

"Damn!" he said, knowing the gun was empty.

He hadn't taken the time to reload after he'd killed the man with the grisly X carved into his nose.

"Alex, you stay down!" he shouted behind him. "Finn, stay with her!"

Finn barked and ran over to where Alex was sitting up, her wet hair streaked across her face, massaging her temples as she tried to regain her senses. Nordic ran forward and, thumbing fresh shells from his belt through the Winchester's loading gate, pressed his back against the broad bole of a pine. Reloading, he stretched his lips back from his teeth as he waited to hear that tooth-gnashing whistling sound a fifty-caliber round fired by a Sharps rifle made as it homed in on a person.

He racked a round into the action, thumbed one last round into the magazine, and, swiping his hat from his head with his arm, edged a look around the pine's right side. A man was moving on the ridge ahead of him. He'd fired the round that had almost struck Alex from a boulder thirty feet down the ridge from the top. He was climbing toward the ridge crest now, holding the Sharps "Big Fifty" in one hand, climbing with his face to the steep slope, legs spread, climbing with the inside edges of his feet.

Nordic snapped the Yellowboy to his shoulder and aimed.

His target just then crested the ridge, stood, glanced back over his shoulder at Nordic, then ran forward, out of sight.

Nordic loosened his trigger finger.

Cursing, he strode back to where Alex knelt beside the man Anders had shot from the other side of the river. Finn sat beside her, staring down at the dead man, showing his teeth.

As Nordic approached, he said, "Did he say anything?"

Alex nodded.

"McClelland," she said.

"Just that?" Nordic rested his rifle on his shoulder. "Just McClelland?"

"No."

Nordic frowned, waiting.

"He also, just before he died, mentioned Conagher."

CHAPTER TWENTY-SIX

"They can try to hang me!" exclaimed Ryan LaPlante. "But LaPlante don't hang so easy."

He grinned over his shoulder at Sarah sitting on the pinto behind him. "Besides, I got me the fastest hoss in the mountains. Now, don't go tellin' the boss I said so or he might hang me. Nothin' against his Apache, but Pegasus here could beat him at one full length in a quarter-mile run."

The young rider turned his horse around and put him south through the rolling forest which opened occasionally to reveal blue mountains humping all around.

"Pegasus?" Sarah said skeptically over the young man's shoulder, wide-eyed with surprise.

"Yeah, you know," Mr. LaPlante said. "The winged horse sired by Poseidon."

"Do you read Greek mythology?"

"I used to. Back in Oklahoma. We had us a real purty schoolteach—I mean, a real nice and very smart schoolteacher who read to us for twenty minutes each day before the bell rang to let us go." He shook his head slowly "Heck, I never wanted to."

"I bet you didn't…her bein' so *purty* an' all."

He chuckled. "That she was, that she was."

"Do you know where we're goin'?"

"Well, I figured I'd take you to the Comanche Ranch. Ain't that where you were headed?" Young LaPlante reined the pinto to a sudden halt and looked skeptically over his shoulder at the wayward young lady. "Say, what got you crossways with ol' Conagher, anyways? Not that it's a hard thing to do, but…he don't usually get his neck in a hump for purty girls."

"I shot his deputy."

"Say…*what*? You *what*?"

"I shot his deputy. The other one."

"Banner?"

"I don't know his name. But I shot him by mistake."

"Who was you tryin' to shoot?"

"Some ranny named Lem. He was about to shoot Miss Lisle. Ya see, they stopped me on the boardwalk outside the post office and…well…oh, never mind. I'm gonna hang, that's all. And my darling Robert will grow up without his mother!"

The sadness and terror of the whole evening in town washed over her again, on the heels of her desperate run from Conagher's men and then her tumble from the buckskin's back that sent all the marbles in her head to switching places. She didn't think they were still all in place. She couldn't think straight and, again, emotion was getting a grip on her.

"Say, say," Mr. LaPlante said, looking over his shoulder at her tenderly. "We'll get you to the Comanche

Ranch and the Nordic...the boss...I mean Mr. Nordic will know what to do."

Sarah sniffed and shook her head. "I can't go there. I'll only lead Conagher there. I'll bring trouble to the Comanche Ranch, an' I can't do that. Lisle's taking Robert there. No, I can't lead Conagher there. He'll go there, anyway, but if I was there, Anders would have to turn me over to them. He'd have no choice except to break the law."

Again, Sarah shook her head. "I won't do that to him. I won't put him in that position. He has enough on his hands...the trouble from town...the big ranch...his father-in-law...his woman...er, Miss Alexandra, I mean."

"Well, where would you like to go?"

"Do you know where his old line shack is? The one under Buffalo Mountain and just up the trail from the creek that shoots off the Avalanche?"

"Hell, I know...er, excuse my bunkhouse talk, Miss Sarah...heck, I know every nook an' cranny of this range. I been around it all many times, during roundups for spring branding and the fall gather and workin' the range, lookin' for herd-quitters an' lost calves. Yes, ma'am—I know where that shack is. Stayed there a time or two my ownself with the son of Harly Reed—you know the old Comanche Ranch rider who fell into that old, dry well pret' near twenty years ago now, drunk on the way home from town one night, an' the well turned out to be a—"

"Yes, yes—I heard the story," Sarah was quick to interrupt, not wanting to hear that old saw again. She doubted anyone in this stretch of the Never Summers hadn't heard the story of that cowhand who tumbled drunk late one night into a well that had become a rattlesnake den after the water had dried up.

There'd been so many snakes in that ancient cistern —someone had judged nigh on a thousand!—that the puncher's body couldn't be retrieved. Or what was left of it, that was. So they'd left it down there with those snakes, and now, as the story went, Harly Reed's ghost haunts that whole part of the—*oh, let it go for God's sake, Sarah*, she quickly castigated herself. There was enough to think about without bringing the dead cowhand's ghost story up that haunts the area of the well, an area that included the line shack she was heading for.

"My God," she groused, digging her fingertips deep into her temples. "Why do I let myself do that to myself?"

"Do what to yourself?"

"Let my mind wander so that I start thinkin' about more troubles than I already have before me!"

"Oh lordy—you're preachin' to the choir there, Miss Sarah!"

"So…you know where the line shack is?"

"Sure enough. We're headin' for it right now."

Sarah saw now that he'd swung the pinto slightly to the left, which was east, whereas the Comanche Ranch headquarters would be to the right.

"We'll join up with Harly Reed Creek—sorry, but that's what some o' the boys at the Comanch call it, jolly jokers—in about a mile or so. We'll follow that to the Harl—"

"Yes, I know—to the Harly Reed cabin." Sarah shook her head again. "Oh lordy, I never should've left Dakota…"

"What's that?"

"Never mind. How far away is the cabin?"

"Only about four miles, give or take." Mr. LaPlante

pointed to the southwest. "The Comanch headquarters is about six miles that way."

"I wonder if Conagher…"

"Knows about Harly Reed's cabin? I doubt it. Hardly anyone but a few of the hands from the ranch includin' Mr. McGreeley an' Fancy Dan and the boss himself an' old Mr. Deveraux, of course, know what it is."

"Good. That's why I want to go there. I need some time to get my senses back…to think through what to do. The main thing is to protect Robert."

"Miss Lisle is takin' him to the headquarters, you say?"

"If all goes well," Sarah said, a darkness entering her mood and into her voice, as well. "As long as she's not in any trouble in town over this. I don't know why she would be. If so, she'll find her way out of it. Some way she'll find a way to get Robert out of town and to the safety of the Deverauxs." She sighed, deeply frustrated. She'd been wanting to get Anders out of there and for him and her to get themselves and Robert out of here for good.

To carve out lives for themselves elsewhere.

Together.

But now because of that terrible trouble she'd run into in town, she was having her son be taken to that confining ranch, to those stiff, rich people who were nothing like them.

They were nothing like her and Robert and they were nothing like Anders, either, who'd somehow succumbed to them.

Well, Sarah knew how he'd succumbed.

Few men could not succumb to *her*…Miss Alexandra…

He was only a man, after all. Given time, though, Sarah was confident she could right his mind. Turn him to her and his adoptive son, Robert.

Only now, after all this...she had no idea what was going to become of any of them.

———

As Pegasus followed the creek around a bend in the blond grass and sage-carpeted bench country up on the east side of the valley that the Avalanche had cut —she'd learned while living at the Comanche Ranch headquarters that it was called the Kawuneeche Valley— Sarah felt mixed feelings.

She was glad she had a sanctuary to come to. She certainly saw the humble, low-slung cabin with slightly askew front stoop as a place of protection, ensconced as it was in her fond memories of her time here with the big man from Dakota, Anders Nordic himself and his loyal dog, Finn. But she did not like the reason she'd had to come here and now, in her addled, anxious state, she had no idea if the trouble was going to be resolved.

Unless she, Anders, Robert, and Finn pulled out of this country and traveled to where no one knew them.

She wondered if that was crazy thinking on her part.

Could she really build a life with the big Dakotan. Would he adopt Robert and become the father the boy needed so badly?

Would he just ride away from the Comanche Ranch and the glorious beauty he'd married...for her?

For Sarah Nordstrom, who didn't have a dime in her pocket. All she had was Robert, who, of course, was more than enough for her. But...

Had all she'd been through after leaving home made her, as her father used to call it, "a mite witchy?" Or soft in her thinker box…?

Back home, when women went mad they called it the "prairie sickness" or suffering from "*the wind*."

The wind alone had been known to drive many women…and more than a few men even…quite mad. The wind, the never ceasing wind.

For Sarah, since the day they'd left home and confronted one dangerous challenge after another, and then almost being raped in front of her family here where her family had tried to build their own ranch, had all these so-called "challenges" finally driven her mad?

Life in Camp Collins hadn't been easy, either.

She'd worked herself to exhaustion every day in Mr. Olson's Brewery & Saloon and then, when it came time to make her way back to the boardinghouse where the house's owner, Mrs. Ellingson, had taken care of Robert during the day, she'd been afraid of being accosted on the street and dragged into some alley leaving only God to know what happened to her.

Had it happened?

Had what she'd hoped and dreamed about—her, Robert, Anders…all be due to her own brand of "the wind?"

She didn't know.

For the moment all she wanted was to be inside the cabin where she'd known such safety, and imagine her handsome, rugged savior, Anders Nordic, cooking for her and Robert and bedding down on the braided rug on the floor…right by hers and Robert's side, with Finn curled in a tight ball by the door, on guard even at night.

"You wait here with Peg," said Sure Shot LaPlante as

he stopped by a lone, scraggly pine fifty yards out away from the shack. "I'll check it out."

He pulled Sarah down off the horse, dropped the reins, and cast Sarah a wink. "Peg'll stay right here with you. I train him well. That's what I do. I gentle and train wild hosses..." He reached out gently and slowly caressed the handsome horse's long, dusty neck. "A whole horde of screamin' Utes slingin' arrows an' lead wouldn't make him stray two feet from where I dropped his reins."

"Mr. LaPlante," Sarah said, looking along their back trail, "what if they follow us?"

"First off, it's Sure Shot," he said, keeping his voice low in case there was someone in the cabin. "Second, no one follows Sure Shot LaPlante." He thumbed himself in the chest with almost comical pride and shameless braggadocio. "I cover my trail. Did you see how I chose the hard ground and stuck to the creek?" He gave a cunning smile and shook his head. "They won't follow Mr. Sure Shot LaPlante. No, sir. None o' them are trackers. They're towners. And none o' 'em know where Deveraux's line shacks are. Big secret around here!"

He shucked his rifle from its sheath, gave it, too, a tender, almost loving caress with a gloved hand, then pinched his hat brim to Sarah. "Don't worry. I should be back in two jangles of a who...er, I mean..."

"Yes, I know the saying, Mr. LaPlan...er, I mean *Sure Shot*," Sarah said with a laugh despite her dour mood. "Two jangles of a whore's bell."

"Forgive this old sinner, please," he said with genuine humility and chagrin then swung around, hitched his baggy denims up on his lean hips, and strode off toward the shack.

Sarah laughed again, inwardly.

Old sinner, nonsense.

But if you are a sinner, Sure Shot LaPlante, she added, *you're a young one. And I'm not quite sure if you understand the predicament we are in.*

She glanced back in the direction from which they'd come.

Sure Shot's trail-covering skills notwithstanding, the young hand had humiliated Conagher and his surviving deputy. Conagher was not a man to take such an indignity lightly. Given time, he'd come…

She turned to gaze off longingly to the west, where the blue-green shrouded, volcano-shaped Comanche Ranch vaulted above two lesser peaks before it. She hoped that Lisle made it to the ranch safely with Robert soon.

She hoped that Anders would come for her soon.

Only he, the man from Dakota, could save her from this horror she'd found herself so deeply entrenched in.

CHAPTER TWENTY-SEVEN

Garth Deveraux reined in his Overo pinto.
He fittingly called the stallion Comanche, for he'd been born and bred on that very mountain. Deveraux had tried to gentle and train the horse himself ten years ago.

Even ten years ago the horse had been more than he could handle. That had been a tough year, realizing once and for all he couldn't do the things he'd taken for granted up to then.

He'd been a damn good horsebreaker and gentler in his day, when he'd had time. He hadn't been taught. He'd learned out of necessity. At first, he hadn't even realized what he'd been doing all those years in the corral.

He'd just been working with the wild horses he and his few men and father had brought in from the mountains' lower reaches and from the plains out east of Camp Collins and Laramie, to fill their remuda and to train and sell for extra money.

It had been a wonder to him how word of Deveraux's wild horses had spread—how well-trained yet feisty and purely game they were—so that eventually ranchers from Dakota, Kansas, and even Oklahoma and Texas had come to party with the rancher and to buy one or two or even, a few times, a half dozen to a dozen horses from him.

He could have made a living catching and selling horses, but that was a damn hard way to make a living. Men who broke horses didn't break them for long. No, eventually the horses broke them. They'd nearly broke Deveraux himself. His desire was to fill his ten-thousand-plus acres and the "free range" he'd always called his own, with the best beef in the West—longhorns and shorthorns bred with white-faced Herefords.

Deveraux had strayed a mile or two off the main trail. He was now well south of the headquarters and sat on a low knoll, staring off at a spring creek that ran down out of the mountains south of the headquarters to meet at a lovely, blue, flashing fork with the Avalanche whose own pure waters originated in the high mountains around Long's Peak, originally named after mountain man Louis Pierre Vasquez, who built a fort along the South Platte River, strategically placed between Fort Laramie and Bent's Fort, both of whom Deveraux had once herded his prized horses to.

"Back in the wild, old days," he said now, a fond smile shaping itself inside his scraggly, gray beard.

He stared down the knoll at a bend in the creek dropping down out of the mountains above and behind his right shoulder.

"Garth, come on—the water feels sooo good!" he heard his dear wife call, as she paddled around in the pool formed when a huge cottonwood had been uprooted by a rare mountain cyclone years before. He and his father had herded cattle to this crazy, up-and-down country, far from the trouble back home in Texas that had started when the carpetbaggers had moved in.

His dear Louise.

His wife.

She rode out here to swim alone and sometimes she managed to coax her wild husband down off his broncs and to join her to pick wild berries and roots including onions to add to her succulent stews and meat pies, the recipes of which had come with her family from Scotland. She made savory fruit pies with the berries, and they'd sip her wonderful wines on the porch of their small, humble cabin—long before they'd built the present, sprawling one—on crisp autumn nights with a fire burning, the cinnamon of falling aspen leaves perfuming the air.

Cooking and baking skills aside, whom did his dear Louise remind him of, he wondered with a wistful smile.

He gigged Comanche down the knoll and up and over the shoulder of the next ridge to the east. He used to hunt here with his boys. Deer had always been plentiful, for the creek ahead and on his right and the river behind him had made the Valley of the Kawuneeche as verdant as any in the Rockies. All game had always been plentiful here, especially after Deveraux had claimed this cut as his own and kept the nesters and farmers out.

He hated nesters enough to hang them. He, however, could abide a farmer as long as they cut hay for him.

Comanche lifted his fine head high, sniffed the warm breeze rich with the wine of pine and fir.

The horse stopped and whickered.

Deveraux reached forward to place his right hand on the stallion's neck. "What is…?"

He left the sentence hanging, for he smelled it, then, too—blood.

The blood of fresh game.

Not any game. An elk.

He lived and hunted in these mountains, shot any form of wild animal that could be eaten for so long that he could tell each one's own particular smell.

Elk, all right.

He gigged Comanche ahead, crossed a low ridge along the aproning slope of the mountain he was on, and drew back on the reins. Sure enough, a big bull elk hung from a tree up the slope about thirty feet to his left and a little ahead of him. The rack was enormous—big paddles that knew the wear and tear of several good ruts.

The big animal hung high. As it turned this way and that on two stout ropes, he saw that it had been dressed. The guts from its great cavity likely lay in a pile nearby —close but not too close. Not so close as to draw carrion eaters in too soon.

The big, dead carcass steamed in the cool, mountain, sunlit air. It had been hung there no more than an hour ago.

Deveraux's preternatural appreciation of the beauty of the great beast and the feast it would provide was tempered with the old, instinctual, well-practiced anger.

Who had shot this animal that, because it was on Comanche Ranch land, he deemed his own.

Voices rose ahead.

Men's voices pitched with anger and jeering.

Mocking laughter.

Deveraux looked over the brow of the hill ahead of him which humped up out of the slope, and to the south, his right.

Two big men dressed in hides and skins riding two beefy horses trotted around a finger of the creek. The man on the right was dragging a third man twenty feet behind him.

Deveraux couldn't see much of the dragged man. Mainly only the grass and sage he bent as he was pulled through it. A third horse followed cautiously a hundred feet behind the two men pulling the third man.

The third horse wore only a blanket for a saddle. Its halter reins were comprised of braided rawhide, painted blue and ochre in places.

The two big men stopped their horses abruptly.

One of the two big men's horses whinnied as the riders curveted them to look back at the third man. The third horse kept moving slowly forward. It lifted its head suddenly and returned the whinny. The two riders dismounted and walked back to where the dragged man lay now belly down in the sage, unmoving. Deveraux could see now from his vantage that the dragged man had brown skin and dark-brown hair. He appeared to wear a mishmash of clothing including animal skins.

The two big men laughed.

Then one of them—the larger of the two—reached under his thick elk-hide coat. A thick steel blade flashed in the sunlight so brightly that for a second or two it nearly blinded the rancher. Both men laughed as the one with the knife squatted beside the man on the ground.

He lifted the dragged man's head up out of the sage by his hair.

Deveraux had already unholstered his old cap-and-ball .36. He raised the old Civil War-model six-shooter high above his head and thundered off a shot. He cocked it and triggered one more.

That stopped both big men. They jerked their heads to him with starts. The one with the knife released his handful of dark-brown hair and, as the dragged man's head dropped into the sage once more, rose slowly to his feet.

Deveraux holstered the ancient popper, snapped the thong closed over the trigger, and clucked Comanche down the slope's steep shoulder. He rose easily, wincing only a little at the popping of the old, arthritic bones in his back. His blood was up. It coursed warmly through his spidery, old, half-clogged veins. His heart was beating smoothly. It wasn't chugging and missing beats like it usually did, and backing blood up into his ancient ticker.

It beat smoothly and resolutely, and his lungs worked without damn near choking him. They were suddenly the heart and lungs of a warrior.

As he bottomed out on the valley floor and heeled the stallion toward the two big men and their horses and the obvious Indian lying belly down in the sage between them, he cajoled himself with, "Now, watch yourself get shot out of the saddle, you cocky old bastard!"

A laugh bubbled up somewhere deep in his chest.

At least you can still laugh, you old scudder, he said to himself. *If you die, you'll die laughing and you've seen many who hadn't.*

Hadn't not died but hadn't died laughing.

As he drew within fifteen feet of the big men and their horses, who pranced around nervously, and Comanche blew and twitched his ears in disdain for them —the stallion hated all men and horses before giving them a chance—he saw a woman shimmer up out of the blond grass and sage behind them.

Behind the big men and the one who lay belly down on the ground.

Deveraux's gaze slid beyond the horses and the men. They widened.

His heart beat faster.

Incredulity and longing at the same time washed through him.

"Louise?" he heard himself say.

By God, it was her.

No, he was drunk.

Hell, he hadn't had a drink since breakfast!

Dressed in the old, cotton print skirt and wool work shirt she wore when she was cooking a big haunch or a pig outside and doing the laundry or pruning shrubs, she stood to face him, the skirt blowing around her long, slender legs, her long chestnut hair blowing in the wind.

A smile blossomed on her perfect face like a giant, spring rose, the first one of the season. She stretched her long straight arms out to both sides, drew her head back, and drew both hands to her lips, and held them there, her eyes burning through his with a passion he hadn't known since he'd shoveled dirt on her coffin.

She flung her hands and arms away as she threw him a big, loving, everlasting kiss.

The kind of kiss from the kind of love that wouldn't die until long after the sun had burned out and was floating around the heavens like one vast black ball of papery ash.

Then she shimmered away as suddenly as she'd appeared.

"Lou...Louise?" he muttered. "Don't...don't...go..."

The laughter of the men before him broke the spell.

He turned to them.

Louise was gone. Only they were here. They and the Indian and the horses, the Indian's horses looking skeptically on from a hundred feet down creek.

He felt as though he'd taken a brief trip to heaven only to return to a ruined world.

One of the beefy men turned to the other. "Why...we got us one lost, addlepated old fool..."

"You think so?" Deveraux glowered at him. He reached down to flick the keeper thong from over the hammer of his ancient horse pistol. "You want me to drill you one through your muckin' head to show you who's the addled one?"

CHAPTER TWENTY-EIGHT

D everaux was still flushed from his daydream.

He blinked to clear the image of his beloved, deceased wife from his vision, because he knew she wasn't really there.

Was he, like the beefiest of these two beefy hardtails before him had said, just an addled old fool.

He looked down at the old cap-and-ball he had aimed at the two men in hide coats and buckskin pants. They both wore pistols and knives—one had an ivory handled bowie jutting up from the top of his right, high-topped moccasin. Both wore their pistols in wide shell belts over their coats.

They were no men to mess with.

Bounty hunters, most likely.

Still, Deveraux saw that the revolver in his hand was steady. His heart was steady, as well.

"You're on my land," he said now, the old steel in his voice that might be a tad on the raspy side but he still had the old, stubborn steel, by God. "Shootin' game on my land."

"What game?" said the man on Deveraux's left, the smaller of the pair of obvious hard cases though he was small by no regular standards.

"The one up the slope. The elk."

The beefiest of the two shook his head. "We didn't shoot no elk. We was lookin' for Injuns. Peskey said his men saw Injuns on the range, and he brought us in to clean 'em out!" He glanced at the man struggling on the ground behind him. The Indian, one likely from Thomas Ruddason and Red Bear's bunch, lifted his head and arms trying to free himself from the rope binding his wrists which was tied around the beefiest man's saddle horn.

"Norman Peskey sent you, eh?" Deveraux said. He didn't have much truck for any of his neighbors, Peskey most of all. He and Norman Peskey had gotten into an all-out fistfight in the Bullhorn Saloon in Camp Collins about five years ago. Their men had had to separate them before they'd have killed each other.

Two bulls just didn't belong in the same corral. The Never Summers were the same corral.

"He promised a five-hundred-dollar bounty for every scalp we bring him," said the less beefy of the two.

Deveraux raised his pistol and narrowed a steely eye as he aimed down the barrel at the man who'd just spoke. "You tell Norman that Garth Deveraux said to go to hell. Now get off my land."

Both men studied him, cunning in their eyes.

They looked him up and down. The dull light shimmering in their eyes and the sets of their mouths inside their tangled beards—still owning the remnants of a recent lunch—was as though they'd encountered some living relic from the past.

Deveraux didn't get to town much anymore.

He'd become somewhat of a recluse. He'd been hearing rumors that he was dead for years, the rumors diminishing when he showed himself on the range now and then. But he rarely went out. He preferred his memories of the wild old times when there were far fewer people in this range he saw as his own—yeah, the whole damn range because he was here first! Such reflections were fueled by his Scotch and his fine French brandy he had sent by the case from Denver.

"Garth Deveraux, eh?" said the beefier man.

"Hell," said the one with a sneer making his mouth crooked, "I thought you was dead."

"Looks dead—don't he, Igor?"

"Sure does, Whiskey."

Deveraux smiled. "Igor Kaminski and Alvin 'Whiskey' Green. I hazed you two off my land ten, twelve years ago."

Both men set their jaws and glowered at him.

"These whole damn mountains ain't yours, Deveraux," groused Igor Kaminski, the bigger of the two tough nuts, his stringy, red-blond hair that hung down from his shapeless leather hat slithered across his face and mouth.

"They are"—Deveraux hardened his own jaws with tauter threat—"and I want you out of 'em. Get the hell out." He rose in his saddle with a sudden burst of fury he knew all too well—that old Deveraux fury that could blow a man out of his saddle with a drop of the hat. "Now!" He shouted so loud his old voice couldn't handle it. It came out as a strangled wail.

Tears of emotion shimmered in his hard, gray eyes.

Tears of emotion and frustration that he couldn't make himself clear anymore.

He glanced down at the pistol in his hand.

The gun was still steady, though, by God…

The two hard cases stared at him. They looked at the gun in his hand and then into his eyes.

"What about him?" asked Whiskey Green, hooking a thumb over his shoulder.

"Leave him."

"He's an Injun!" protested Kaminski.

"Leave him."

"Where's your men?" asked Green, canting his head to look behind Deveraux. "Didn't think you went anywhere without a half dozen men."

"I don't need 'em," the rancher growled. "Now, turn around and get the hell off my land before it's only your horses doin' the leavin'."

They both looked down at the pistol he was, by God, holding steady in his right, gloved fist. They could see in his eyes he meant business. He'd empty their saddles if they pushed him. They might not have thought, a few minutes ago, the old buffalo still had it in him, but they saw now he did…by God.

Still, it would be hard to ride away from one so old and obviously stove-up.

Could they live with themselves?

If not, though, they might not live at all.

"Shit," Whiskey cussed, glancing once more at Deveraux's old cap-and-ball.

Both men mounted their horses.

Whiskey Green released the rope from his horn, let it drop to the ground, and reined his dun away. "Let's go, Igor. Let him solve his Injun problem himself! Hell, let 'em all move back into the country!"

Kaminski cursed, spat to one side, and reined his own horse away.

They rode past the Indian, Green kneeling out to spit on him, then booted their mounts into lopes, following the curve of the bending creek to the south.

Mad as old wet hens. Being cowed by an ancient old relic of the frontier past armed with a pistol nearly as old as he was.

With a grunt mostly out of fierceness now rather than weariness, Deveraux stepped down from the saddle. He didn't leap down as he would have ten, fifteen years ago after winning such a standoff against men half his age—just stepping down without help was enough. He walked over to where the young Indian glared up at him, still straining against the rope binding his wrists together.

"Who're you?" he demanded.

"The old renegade who just saved your life." Deveraux squatted as best he could, trying to make the effort not show on his face. "Around here, when a man's life is saved…or even just his topknot though they likely would've cut your throat, too—he says thank you."

The Indian studied him through deep, dark eyes. With his chiseled, red-brown features and short hair, a thick lock of it hanging down over his sweating, dusty forehead peppered with weed seeds and bits of sage, he looked vaguely familiar. Deveraux pulled his own bowie knife out of the sheath hanging off the left side of his cartridge belt. He held the blade over the ropes, between the wounded man's wrists, and stared into the Indian's defiant eyes.

He waited.

The Indian stared back at him.

Finally, he sighed and looked down and said half-heartedly, "Thank you."

"What's your name?" the rancher asked as he sawed through the thick ropes with his knife.

He spewed something in Indian, again defiantly, his eyes boring into Deveraux's.

"Now in English," the rancher ordered, casting the cut ropes away.

"They shorten it to Wild Runner."

"Your brother's Moon Runner."

The boy looked at him uncertainly. "Yes." He lifted his proud chin. "He is older...but I am wilder," he added with a grin.

Rubbing his wrists, he tapped his thumbs against his chest.

"How old are you?"

"Sixteen."

Deveraux said, "Get up. Can you, wild man?"

"Wild Runner." He stood fleetly, proudly.

He wore buckskin breeches and a beaded buckskin tunic, fringe sloping down from the shoulders, over a collarless duck shirt. Indentations in his hair marked where a hat had been. It was gone. They were durable clothes, not too beaten up except at the knees and elbows. One of his boots—a white man's stockman boot was half off. Wild Runner stooped to pull it on as though embarrassed by his dishevelment.

His chin and nose were badly scraped and burned, his lips cracked and oozing blood. The nubs of his sharply hewn cheeks were scraped and bruised, as well. He moved a little uncertainly, sort of trying to maintain his balance.

"You from Ruddason's camp?"

"Moon Runner's and his white woman's, yes."

"Why aren't you there?"

"I heard there might be whites coming."

"And you don't like whites."

The kid wrinkled his nose. "Why should I? They keep me...or try to keep me...on the reservation. My brother says this is my home!" He stomped one moccasin-clad foot.

The boy's features were nearly identical to his older brother, though the kid had a few years before he grew into his. By that time, he'd be one, strapping buck, one to ride the river a few times with.

Deveraux glanced up the slope over his left shoulder. "You shot that buck on my land."

Wild Runner gave a bold curl of his upper lip. "This isn't your land. No man can own the land. Not even a white man. Besides, I shot him." Again, he thumped himself in the chest, jutting his proud, bloody chin forward. "He is mine!"

"Your brother has more up here than you do." Deveraux tapped his hatted head. "He knows how to try to get along."

"That's because he is white." Wild Runner scowled at him. "They lured him away—that preacher and his wife. They made him white. I stayed behind. I am Indian!"

"You want a job?"

Wild Runner looked as though he'd just been slapped in the face. He stared at Deveraux as though he'd been asked a trick question.

"I got me a feelin' you're good on that horse." He looked at the brown-and-white pinto who'd moved up close and stood, head hanging, regarding his master and the old white man uncertainly. "Would you work for a white man?"

Again, Wild Runner just stared at him.

"Twenty a month and found until you prove what you're worth." Deveraux shrugged. "You'll be home, anyway. Away from the res…"

"I don't muck out stalls for no white man."

"You will the first month. The second month you'll work with our blacksmith. If you haven't ravaged any women in town or got drunk and tore up a saloon, you'll get regular wages. You'll ride the range tending my herds"—he glanced at the obviously loyal pinto—"on that horse. You'll have a string of 'em…for when he gets tired of your sharp tongue."

Again, Deveraux looked at the horse.

Then he smiled.

He rose, ignoring the popping in his knees, and grabbed his reins. He grabbed the horn, jumped once, trying for the stirrup, and missed. He cussed, chewed his lip, and tried again. His face swelled until he thought it would explode.

Damned embarrassing, getting old. Especially in front of a damn rock-worshipping renegade.

He reined Comanche around. "Fetch your game and follow me."

Deveraux rode up to the knoll he'd descended an hour ago. He was not surprised to see his daughter, son-in-law, and Thomas Ruddason sitting their horses atop the knoll, incredulous looks on their faces.

They'd tracked him here. Ruddason had tracked his brother here.

Nordic's lips curved a whimsical smile. Alex stared at her father, hang-jawed. She'd wanted to ride down and save the old fool from himself. Nordic had kept her from doing so.

The old rancher wasn't done.

He just had to prove it to himself.

"About him," Ruddason said, gazing at where his younger brother was riding the pinto up the slope toward where the elk hung from the tree. "I am sorry I slipped away…"

"Because he could." Deveraux stopped beside Moon Runner. "No offense to your ma, but that's a son of a bitch, that one!"

Ruddason stared at the old rancher in surprise. Then, shaping a slow smile, he nodded.

"I gave him a job. I'll likely be sending him home to you, but I'll give him a year an' see if he's man enough." Deveraux rammed his heels into Comanche's flanks. "Hy-yahh, Comanch. Time for a whiskey or two!"

He loped off along the creek toward the Avalanche.

Alex turned to Thomas Ruddason. "That all right with you?"

Moon Runner turned to her. Again, he smiled. "I saw how your father turned the horns in on those two hard cases. I reckon it has to be!"

He and Nordic chuckled.

Wild Runner reined his horse around and put it into a northward gallop toward his people's encampment.

CHAPTER TWENTY-NINE

That night over a supper of elk roast marinated and basted in chokecherry wine and cooked wild carrots, potatoes, and wild onions, Alex turned to her father sitting at his place at the end of the dining room table, and said, "You might have let him eat with us on his first night at the ranch."

Deveraux was cutting into a thickly cut slice of elk meat swimming in its own dark broth on his plate. He brushed his fingers on the napkin hanging down from his shirt collar and poked the meat chunk, nicely charred on the outside, into his mouth.

Chewing, he said, "He's a savage. He'll feel more at home with savages!"

That tickled the old devil's funny bone. He swallowed the meat, slapped his thigh, and had a hardy, wheezing laugh.

Nordic looked at Alex sitting beside him.

Riley Otis, who'd cooked the supper just as he did most nights when outdoor work wasn't more pressing, sat at the opposite end of the table from the rancher. He looked up from where he was smearing his own chunk of meat into the dark gravy poured over his mashed potatoes. "Oh, Mistuh boss," the Black man said, furling his black brows and slowly shaking his head as he chewed, "that ain't no way to talk. He's a human being first, an Indian second."

"Yeah?" Deveraux said. "We'll see about that."

"Pa," Alex also admonished her father. "Riley's right. That's no way to talk about the young man you just recruited."

Nordic bathed his own meat in potatoes and gravy. "I think it's a good thing you did, Deveraux. He looked happy to be here. I don't doubt he hates that reservation he's been forced to grow up on."

"He is. He loves the idea of workin' on a ranch. Believe me, he knows the Comanche Ranch's reputation." The old man chuckled proudly and shook his head. "He's smart. He's cunning." As he worked on his plate, he turned to his daughter. "He knows where he is. He realized the opportunities here."

"He looked scared," Alex countered, sipping her coffee.

"He's not scared." Deveraux laughed.

"He might be," Nordic agreed with his wife. "But he'll grow out of it. He'll make his way in the bunkhouse."

"I turned him over to McGreevey and Fancy Dan. They won't coddle him, but they'll make sure the others get along with him. They're good mentors, them two. He'll get along just fine."

Alex sighed and dug into another meat chunk. "I suppose you're gonna start him out mucking stalls and forking hay."

"Right along with the other stableboys," Deveraux said, chewing again. He pointed his fork at his daughter. "Ain't that the way you started out there? An hour in the stables and barn for an hour ridin'."

She looked at her husband in disgust beneath her brows.

Nordic smiled. It was a tough world, the world of a ranch. Everybody starts at the bottom as he had himself back on his family's farm. When you had milk cows, you pretty much fed, watered, and swamped stalls and barn alleys all day long. They had a small herd of beef cattle that had needed tending, too. He made a mental note to go out and check on the kid before bedtime, make sure he wasn't getting into any fights. Make sure he wasn't being harassed, which he'd already warned the men about as he knew Zeb and Fancy Dan had, as well.

"Don't worry—I was strategic in my decision," Deveraux said, pouring himself another glass of Riley Otis's delightful chokecherry wine which made the elk haunch, cooked with the wine, as well, almost tingle on the tongue.

"Strategic, eh?" Riley said, skeptically. He rose with his empty plate and picked up Alex's plate, as well. "How so, boss man? How was you strategic?"

He glanced at Alex. They shared an ironic smile and the cook carried their plates and empty coffee cups to the dry sink in the kitchen across the hall from the large, well-outfitted dining room with its long, oak table that could seat twenty in a pinch, and once, a few years ago, had. Especially on holidays or when her father's business associates and wives or local ranchers—those he didn't hate, that was—were invited for germans, as parties were called up here in the western mountains.

Now Deveraux aimed his fork at Riley and then at his son-in-law and added with brows raised in self-satisfaction at his shrewdness. "With him here...Running Moon's brother...we won't have trouble with any more of those feisty savages back at his people's encampments." With false sheepishness, he glanced at his daughter and said, "Uh...I mean...feisty Injuns..."

He glanced at Nordic and smirked.

Anders shook his head at him.

But it was hard, indeed, to get a zebra to change its stripes.

He'd learned that from other oldsters he'd known. Hell, he knew how hard it was for he himself to change his attitudes. He wouldn't pretend he didn't harbor, deep inside, albeit reluctantly, many of the rancher's own prejudices.

Alex glanced at her husband. "What're we gonna do with him?"

"Ah, hell," Deveraux said, dropping his fork and knife on his empty plate and tossing his napkin onto it, as well. "I'll be dead soon...layin' out on that manure pile you warned me about, sweet daughter of mi—"

The rancher stopped when one of the pickets yelled from the yard below the lodge and over which the mountain dusk was closing quickly.

"Riders! Two!"

The call was followed by the crying of a small child.

Nordic looked at his wife, scowling. "What in holy blazes...?"

Alex slid her chair back and rose from it, turning toward the door.

As Riley removed Nordic's plate, silverware, and

coffee cup from the table, Anders rose and followed his wife out of the dining room and into the foyer.

Deveraux looked at Riley who was scowling his own befuddlement as he continued clearing the table.

"A child?" the rancher said. "Who's bringin' a child to the Comanche Ranch this time o' the night?"

Riley paused, listening to the child's cries. Swinging around and heading for the kitchen with another load of dishes, he said, "By Jim, I believe I recognize that caterwaul!"

Nordic grabbed his hat off a gold wall spike and followed Alex out onto the porch. So did Finn, who'd been lying on the rug in front of the door but was now on his feet, mewling and wagging his tail at the delighted prospect of visitors.

The sun was down behind the high crags jutting in the west but enough green light remained that he could see two riders approaching the house as they rode up the hill from the ranch yard. Not two riders. Three. The young woman riding a blue roan to the left of where Thomas Ruddason rode his stallion along beside her was holding a small child in her arms. Not a baby but a toddler. The young woman looked worn out, and Nordic didn't blame her. The child was too big to be carried by such a small woman.

Finn ran around both horses, barking, but fell silent when Nordic told him to. He kept his eyes on the visitors, though, just in case his help should be needed.

Nordic recognized the child in the girl's arms, and his heart quickened in dread—if little Bobby was here, where was Sarah? Alex must have recognized the child, too. She hurried down the porch steps and stopped just as the roan halted before her. She reached up and accepted the bawling child from the young woman's arms. She was obviously exhausted. Her hair was a tumbleweed around her head and her face showing through the mussed locks was drawn, her eyes weary. Clad in men's trail clothes including boots and an overlarge denim jacket, she slumped in the saddle.

She looked almost ready to pass out.

Alex stepped back with the child in her arms, bouncing him gently, soothingly. "There, there, Bobby. It's all right. You're all right. You're at the Comanche Ranch. Remember me—she drew the child close and cooed in his ear--your Aunt Alexandra?"

Riley Otis had walked up beside Nordic. Now the big man came halfway down the steps, reaching out to Alexandra.

"Here, here—hand that chil' over. I'll take him inside, get him warm, and get this chil' something to eat! There, there, boy," he said, the blanket-wrapped boy in his arms and, rocking him gently, took him back up the steps, across the porch, and into the lodge. His crying still issued from inside, muffled by the oak front doors.

"I'll go help with Bobby," Alex said, and followed the Black man into the lodge.

"I found her off the trail, riding cross-country. Heard the child's cries from the camp," Ruddason told Nordic. "She said someone might be following her and she needed to get the boy to the Comanche Ranch." He looked at the young woman whose name, Nordic knew from his frequenting Larson Olson's Brewery & Saloon, was Lisle. "She's exhausted," Moon Runner added. "And frightened."

"What happened?" Nordic asked, reaching up to pull the young woman down from the saddled livery horse.

She pulled away from him, shook her head. "No...I have to get back to town. Mr. Olson'll fire me. Sarah's at the line shack. Go to her!"

"You're not going anywhere," Nordic said. "You'll never make it back to town."

He reached up and pulled the girl down from her saddle, hefted her in his arms, against his chest, and turned to the house, vaguely wondering why in blazes Sarah would go back to the line shack.

"No!" Lisle cried, trying to push away from him.

"No, no, no," Nordic said, climbing the steps. "My wife's right. You'll never make it. You stay here tonight. We'll get some brandy and food in you." As he moved up to the door, Riley pushed one of them open, stepping out to hold it. As Nordic passed through it, he said, "What happened to Sarah? Where is she?"

After all that Sarah had been through, he was expecting to hear she was dead.

He was relieved when Lisle, obviously reading his mind, her arms around his neck, clinging to him now instead of fighting—realized now just how whipped she really was—"She's not dead. But Conagher is after her. She shot his deputy, Banner. It was a mistake. She meant to shoot the man who was about to shoot *me*." She turned to glare into Anders's eyes. She hardened her jaws and gritted her teeth. "That son of a bitch! Banner was nothing special but it's Clem Dawson who should be dead on that boardwalk in front of the post office!"

Nordic swung through the French doors leading to the ladies' tearoom, then into the parlor beyond. His father-in-law had been waiting at the door, befuddlement on his craggy features. Deveraux followed him while Riley had gone off to tend to the child whom Nordic could hear crying on the lodge's second story. He had probably taken him into a bedroom. He'd give him food and water and probably some milk.

Poor Bobby was most certainly every bit as tired as his savior was. Probably more so. That was a long, hard ride for a toddler. He was likely badly disoriented and terrified to be without his ma.

"What happened?" Deveraux asked as Nordic sat Lisle down on a divan in the parlor.

He turned to the old man. "Fetch her some water."

Deveraux looked astonished. He'd probably never been told to do anything. Hell, everything had always been done for him! Aside from hanging rustlers, that was. No, that was a job he didn't mind doing himself.

Not one bit.

"Wh-What?" he said, looking at his son-in-law as though Nordic had spoken in a foreign tongue.

Annoyed and impatient, deeply worried about both Robert and Sarah, Nordic glanced at him. "Fetch her some water from the kitchen!"

Deveraux threw up his hand, turned, and strode, deeply indignant, through the ladies' tearoom to the kitchen, muttering angrily.

Nordic went to the liquor cabinet and held out a goblet of brandy to Lisle. "Here. Take a swallow. A small one."

She looked as though she could barely keep her head up. But she lifted her hands and took the brandy in both.

"Obliged," she said.

She sipped the liquor, swallowed, and shook her head. "Whew. What a ride! Poor Bobby!"

Tears glinted in her eyes, reflecting the light of two

hanging lamps and the fire that had been laid in the hearth.

Deveraux brought a half a glass of water.

Lisle was tough. Nordic had seen her bean a man over the head with a length of split stovewood. He'd been getting too fresh with her at Olson's place. As he lay on the floor, shaking, losing consciousness fast, she'd blown a wisp of hair from her lips and said, "Next time, act like a gentleman."

But having the both famous and infamous, feared and respected old rancher bring her a glass of water, shocked her. She was slow to take it, so Nordic grabbed it out of Deveraux's hand and gave it to her. She looked up at the old rancher, hesitant, reticent. "Thank you, Mr. Deveraux."

"You're welcome, girl."

Deveraux looked at Nordic, wonderingly.

Nordic said, "I'll talk to her."

Deveraux turned his mouth corners down in chagrin. The young wolf was usurping the older one. He'd known it would come to this. The way of the world and the reason the big Dakotan was here.

"I'll be in my study," Deveraux said, ambling off to his carved horse-head chair and a goodly portion of Scotch.

Nordic turned to Lisle. She took another sip of the brandy and told him everything that had happened in town, right up to Sarah's stealing the horse and heading for the line shack and Lisle slipping away in the crowd, returning to her room, dressing quickly, renting the horse with what little savings she had, and retrieving little Robert from the boardinghouse that he and his mother roomed in.

She'd told the old lady who ran the place that Sarah wanted Robert and Lisle to join her for a late breakfast. She didn't think Mrs. Ellingson, the lady who ran the place, had believed the story, for she scowled skeptically as Lisle had hurried off with a blanket-wrapped, gooing-and-gawing toddler in her arms, and headed for the mountains on her rented horse. She'd ridden mostly cross-country in case, after the dust in the wake of the deputy's demise had settled, someone thought to look for her and possibly follow her.

She'd been raised in the Never Summers by a family who'd cut hay for the mountain ranchers. She knew them well, and she knew every route in and out of them well, too.

She'd been intercepted by a concerned Ruddason, who'd heard the child's cries from his camp, only a few miles north of the ranch.

"Sarah went to the line shack, you say?" Nordic asked her, thoughtfully rubbing his jaw.

"Yes," Lisle said, worry flashing sharply in her otherwise tired, dull eyes.

"She'll never make it," Anders said, still rubbing his jaw nervously, half to himself. "She might think she knows these mountains, but she doesn't."

"Anders." Alex had just entered the room and looked down at him, shuttling her wondering gaze between him and Lisle and back again. She shook her head. "What... what?"

"How's Robert?"

"He had some water and fell asleep. I think he'll be all right. I'll stay up with him. Both I and Riley will."

"Good." Anders rose and took his wife's hands in his own. "I'm going to the line shack."

"Now? Why?"

He glanced at the doxie. "Lisle, you tell her." To Alex, he said, "I hope to be back by morning but...I don't know."

He released her hands and strode quickly from the room. Finn followed him closely, panting with excitement.

"Anders!" Alex called to him.

But then he and the dog were gone.

CHAPTER THIRTY

"Riders!" came the shout from another picket hidden in the shadows somewhere in the main yard.

Nordic had just stepped onto the porch, Finn beside him.

Thomas Ruddason had left. He must have taken Lisle's horse with him or, more likely, taken it down to the stables to the stableboys who would tend it until Nordic could get the horse back to town. He didn't want Lisle riding alone when she went back. She was in danger. Conagher would not take lightly the killing of his deputy, Banner, who was also Conagher's sister's son.

A no-good nephew, but a nephew—blood—just the same.

Anders stopped and turned to look down the hill toward the bunkhouse. As he did, a half dozen horsemen rode under the headquarters' entrance arch and entered the yard. Two men rode ahead of four others. They were all shadows in the darkness relieved only by a remaining faint glow in the sky and by the lit windows of the bunkhouse. But Nordic knew one of the two lead riders, sitting tall and lean in his saddle beside the slouching one, was Glen Conagher. Stray light winked off something shiny on the man's chest as well as off the chest of the man riding next to him as they both turned from the west and rode up the southern hill toward the lodge.

Skully was the deputy's name. Lew Skully. A few years ago, he'd ridden right here at the Comanche Ranch for Deveraux, who fired him and, according to the old man, who'd chuckled during his telling, had given him a good kick in the behind as the useless fool had tramped sullenly off to the corral for his horse.

Now Conagher and the deputy drew their horses up to the bottom of the porch steps. Finn walked up to the top of the steps and barked.

"Finn."

The dog looked over his shoulder at Anders and cried, chagrined.

The marshal held a rifle barrel up from his right thigh. Nordic could feel the fire of rage radiating off the man, a former outlaw himself after several years in the army fighting the Sioux in Dakota.

Nordic stared down at Conagher. The marshal looked over and behind Nordic as one of the lodge's front doors opened and Alex stepped onto the porch, old Deveraux following her, his double-barrel barn blaster in one hand, a short glass of Scotch in the other hand. The glass was short, but the Scotch was not. Alex had her .44 wedged behind her wide, brown leather belt.

Neither Nordic nor Conagher said anything as Alex stepped up to Nordic's right and Deveraux stopped to his left, raising his shotgun up high, the rear stock snugged against the crook of his right arm. Nordic, his wife, and father-in-law stared down at the six horseback riders, the deputy fidgeting a little, nervously, in his saddle. The horses were nervous, too. The riders had to keep tight grips on their reins. The mounts could sense the dislike in the air.

Finn could, too. He growled very softly, almost inaudibly, deep in his chest.

Most folks saw Camp Collins as Deveraux's town, since the old man had an interest in so many businesses and in the mines around it. Conagher didn't like that. To his way of looking at it, the town was his. The county, on the other hand…

Conagher spoke first, not beating around the bush. "Is she here?"

"No. Lisle from Olson's place is here. She brought Sarah's baby."

Nordic threw it all right out to Conagher. The marshal knew that none of them were to be messed with. Nordic saw that knowledge in the man's hard eyes.

"And Sarah…the one who shot my deputy?"

"Go home, Conagher."

Both Deveraux and the old man's daughter looked at Nordic quickly. The old man smiled.

Conagher bunched his thin lips and flared his nostrils. "She—"

"Shot your fat, worthless nephew by mistake. She wouldn't have had to shoot anyone if you'd been doing your job, you worthless pile of horse dung."

Finn stretched his lips back from his teeth and growled at Conagher.

Conagher switched his hard glare from Nordic to Finn. "That dog still needs a bullet, I see."

"You better hope nothin' happens to this dog," Nordic

warned the lawman. "Anything happens to him…even an infect gopher bite…I'm gonna ride to town and shoot you dead."

The men around Conagher shifted nervously in their saddles.

The marshal's deputy looked at his boss. An angry flush darkened his face touched by the lighted lodge windows behind Nordic.

"You push it," Conagher said. "Just like that old man has." He shook his head. "Don't push it too hard."

"Or what? You'll send more worthless riders after me?" Nordic gave a hard-jawed smile.

Now it was Conagher's turn to shift a little, nervously, in his saddle.

The five men around him looked at him.

"You workin' for McClelland now?"

Conagher glared at him, chin down, his chest rising and falling heavily behind his green plaid mackinaw coat. Nordic thought he could almost hear the man's heart beating.

Deveraux had turned in shock to his son-in-law. "McClelland?" Deveraux said.

No one said anything.

Least of all Conagher. The marshal looked as though he'd had his tongue in a knot by those treacherous Sioux squaws up in Dakota.

The silence stretched.

Nordic could hear the boots of the five men who included McGreevey and Fancy Dan, spread out across the trail down from the lodge to the yard. Zeb and Dan were muttering out the sides of their mouths to each other, likely having a hard time wrapping their minds around what they'd just heard about Conagher and McClelland.

"I don't know what you're talkin' about," Conagher broke the silence. "You don't, either."

"You still havin' my place watched?" Deveraux asked. The cunning, old mossyhorn had glued the pieces together in his still-sharp mind. He knew more than what Nordic and Alex knew.

Nordic wanted to know what that missing piece was.

Why did Senator McClelland try to kidnap Alex?

Why did he want Deveraux dead?

Where was he? Was he pulling Conagher's strings from Denver?

Nordic glanced at Finn standing stiffly, tail up, hackles raised, glaring at Conagher.

"Stay, Finn."

He moved down into the yard and over to the marshal. "If I shot you right now, put a bullet right here" —he reached up and pressed his right index finger on the lawman's badge—"I bet I'd put an end to it, wouldn't I?"

Staring down at him, Conagher clenched his jaws so tight, their hinges dimpled.

Deveraux laughed and said, "Only one way to find out, son. Only one way! Hah!"

Alex gave him a scolding look and his laughter and the delighted smile on his face died quickly.

"At least, it would give the senator something to think about, wouldn't it? Until I hunted him down and shot him, too." Anders shoved his thumbs down behind his cartridge belt. "Tell him that. Tell him Anders Nordic is comin' for him. Tell him I know he wants to kill me, kill him...and her...and I'm gonna kill him for it!"

He stepped back and drew his cross-draw Russian.

He aimed it up at Conagher and cocked it. "Now, get out of here before I decide to test my theory!"

Jaws so hard they appeared about to break, eyes so wide they looked as though they'd pop out of the man's long, angular face, Conagher leaned toward Nordic. He opened his mouth to speak but before he could get a word out, Nordic slid his Smith & Wesson slightly to the right.

It barked, stabbing smoke and flames.

Conagher jerked his head up and clapped a hand to his ear. He pulled the hand down and saw blood glistening on his glove. It also glistened where Nordic's round had torn a .44-sized notch out of the man's ear.

The deputy jerked his right hand down to his right side.

"Uh-uh."

This from the old man who'd raised his double-barrel twelve-gauge one-handed and thumbed one of the rabbit ear triggers back.

Alex had already pulled her own gun. She aimed it straight out from her right shoulder at the lump deputy, whose face grew pale in the lamplight from the windows, and he carefully removed his hand from his holstered six-shooter.

Nordic slid his gun back toward Conagher, who flared a nostril, neck-reined his horse around, rammed his spurs into the mount's flanks, and galloped down the hill toward the main yard. McGreevey and Fancy Dan each stepped to one side, making way for the deeply grieved lawman, whose riders turned their own mounts and followed him down the hill, through the trees, into the yard and then out under the entrance portal and off down the ridge in the darkness toward the Avalanche.

Finn stared after him and barked. He looked at

Nordic, who smiled and said, "I know—I should've given you a go at 'em."

The dog sat and mewled in frustration.

Nordic looked at Alex.

"Wait till morning," she said, shoving her pistol back down in her pants. "They might see you, follow you to Sarah."

"They won't follow me. Not in the darkness. Besides, Sarah is the least of his worries now." He shook his head. "Conagher's gonna go back to town and throw whiskey on his wounds, try to figure out what to tell McClelland."

He looked at Deveraux.

His face a mask of deep-lined, shadowy consternation, Deveraux lowered his eyes and moved his lips, mouthing the name with a dark frown, "McClelland..."

Alex looked at him.

Nordic moved up the steps, kissed her cheek, then strode off down the hill toward the men still gathered there with their rifles.

Finn barked and ran along behind him.

———

When Alex had put Lisle to bed and checked on Robert, who seemed to be sleeping peacefully and whom Riley Otis had assured her he would check on throughout the night, she walked to the rear of the lodge and into her father's office.

Deveraux was standing at the study's French doors, the drapes pulled back to show the black night beyond shrouding the forested ridge climbing steeply to the south. Lamplight reflected off the glass but Alex could

see a few stars kindling beyond the arrow-shaped silhou-
ettes of the spruces and firs at the ridge crest.

The old rancher held a stogie in one hand, a glass of
Scotch in his other hand.

As Alex removed the stopper on the glass decanter
and grabbed a glass off a pyramid, he turned his head to
one side. He drew on the stogie and let the air out in a
thick wreathe before him.

Alex slumped into a deep, leather chair near the
hearth and sipped the Scotch.

She watched her father stand there at the doors, head
turned to his left, smoke billowing above and around him
in the study's deep shadow beyond the light of two lit
lamps—one on his desk, one hanging from the ceiling
over the low, cherry coffee table before Alex and on
which, leaning forward, she set her glass.

She leaned back in her chair and crossed her legs.

"Who's McClelland?"

Deveraux quirked his mouth inside his mustache at
the name.

He took another sip of his Scotch and puffed the
stogie once more. Smoke ambled toward the near side of
the room, under the bleak stares of a dozen game trophies
and wood and glass cabinets displaying antique books
and weaponry and armor including a Viking helmet he
had discovered as a young man on his family's estate in
Staffordshire.

He eased himself creakily into the chair across the
table from Alex, grunting, and leaned back in the chair.
His face was swollen and red. His cold gray eyes shimmered with angst. His breathing was labored. All this had
started at the name "McClelland."

Sunk back in his chair, stogie smoldered in the hand

of the arm he rested on the chair's right arm, his glass in the other hand, his red plaid robe tied over his still-lean waist, he just stared at Alex.

"Why does he want you dead?" Alex said. *Like so many others* she did not say aloud.

He drew a deep breath.

"He's from…or was from…a family of nesters." He canted his head to indicate north. "Just over the ridge."

"Avalanche Ridge?"

"Yes."

"You ran them out?"

"Burned them out." Deveraux's lips quirked and his cheeks twitched as though with a pain spasm. "Burned them out…"

Absently, he brushed cigar ash from the chair arm, staring at it with a befuddled look. In the firelight, his deeply wrinkled forehead resembled worn, red leather, the lines dark with shadows.

"Why?"

"They were nesters?"

"Had they staked a claim."

Deveraux shrugged.

"Did you kill his family."

"They died in the fire. His parents, a sister, I think…"

"You don't know?" Her voice was sharp with derision.

Even hatred. Yes, there was a large part of her that hated a large part of her father. She tried to hold it at bay as best she could, but it came out at times like these.

His arrogance. His old, blooded…*cold-blooded*… English entitlement.

"I know that James and his brother survived it. I told them that night that if they stayed, I'd hang them."

Deveraux sipped his Scotch and forced himself to meet the cold, hard gaze of his daughter directly. "It got out of hand," he said, his voice a little shaky. "I and the fellas had been drinking."

"You and the fellas had been drinking and got all heated up…no fault of yours…and decided to go night riding. And a family got burned out. Murdered."

"I didn't mean for it to go that far, surely."

"You mean you don't know?"

The old man shook his head. "I don't know." He met her gaze again with a wavering, weak one of his own. "It was crazy in those days, Alex. You've no idea what it took to hold this place I've now turned over to you and Dakota. It didn't come cheap either in money nor lies. Many dead Indians as well as whites. They were all closing in…threatening me…my family…my *land*!"

"How did James go from being burned out by you to a territorial senator who, I've heard, seems the likeliest candidate for the governor's job?"

Deveraux puffed his stogie, staring at the table, deeply pensive.

"I don't know. He and his brother prospected together…got lucky…invested their money in mines. Their fortunes exploded. And then his brother died somehow—I don't remember—and James, who had one hell of a will on him, I'll give him that, invested in more and more. Here in Colorado…Wyoming…and back East…"

Again, thoughtfully, staring down at the table as though at the devil laughing at him there, he puffed the cigar.

"And now he's a senator."

Deveraux chuckled dryly.

"And he wants you dead."

The old rancher arched a brow. "Oh, yes, of course he does." He smiled at her, irony in his large, sad eyes. "Wouldn't you?"

"And he'll kill every man who stands between him and his goal."

"Including the Nordic, yes."

Alex frowned, puzzled. "And me?"

"He wanted you to hurt me. He probably intended to take you over to that big hunting lodge he built…"

"By Estes Park. Many bigwigs go there…dine… drink…hunt." Deveraux took another sip of his Scotch and smiled. "They all come with expensive women."

"Women not their wives, I take it?"

"Oh, of course not!" He gave a brief, raking laugh.

Alex shuddered at the thought of the rich, powerful man's intentions for her. She leaned forward, plucked her glass off the table, and took a deep sip.

"So, now," she said, crossing her legs again, and resting her arms on the chair arms, "we have to kill him, don't we? A territorial senator with his hat set for the governor's office."

"Look around, Alex." He raised his hands from the chair and looked around as though at all of his holdings, all of his investments…his cattle…mines…railroads… his sprawling land. "Is it worth it?"

Alex finished her drink. She heard little Robert stirring upstairs and Riley Otis cooing to the boy, probably rocking him gently. The ceiling creaking above Deveraux's study.

She set her glass back down on the table, rose, and strode to the door. Fire burned in her veins, in her heart. It burned all around her. She couldn't escape it. She was trapped here, in the secure luxury that was all she'd ever known.

At the door, she stopped and looked back at the man she suddenly hated more than any other man she'd ever encountered, including a few in the East when she'd been going to school, who'd wanted to acquire her...to add her to their holdings...

Deveraux held his rheumy, grave, inquiring eyes on her.

"Is it worth it?" he repeated.

Did she want to live elsewhere...to make her own way far from the Comanche Ranch and all its freedoms and trappings?

"No, it's not," she decided.

Did she want to raise children here...possibly, more like *him*?

"But what choice do we have?"

Deveraux smiled wolfishly, devilishly satisfied... amused...by himself. By the dilemma his life had passed on to his daughter.

"And so it continues," he said.

Alex walked away.

CHAPTER THIRTY-ONE

Nordic followed a series of cattle and ancient Indian trails east of the Comanche Ranch headquarters.

They would be a bewildering maze of interconnecting trails to anyone but Nordic, who'd taken this concealed route to the old line shack he'd lived in until a year ago many times. Alex knew it because he'd shone her. Deveraux had no doubt found it long ago, when his father had built the line shack itself, well concealed by the steep, forested ridge jutting behind it and a low saddle in front of it.

He didn't think any of his current riders knew about it.

Sarah had been here, and she'd apparently headed for it to escape but...Anders shook his head in dread now as he put Apache up one of the last rises...there was no way she could find it from town. He'd told her, in case she and her baby had needed to escape to the shack when he was away, but there was no way she'd remember. In her desperation, she'd probably thought—

"Boss?"

The voice came out of nowhere just as a dark shadow had slid out from the shadow of a stout spruce. A tall, man-shaped shadow with a hat. A rifle glistened in the starlight, held in the man's hand crossways in front of his chest.

Taken aback by the shadow and the voice—the voice of a young man—Apache gave a sharp whicker. He pitched suddenly. So suddenly that the buck took Nordic as off guard as the voice and the shadow had.

The horse reared, clawing at the stars with his front hooves, and gave a shrill whinny.

The sudden move ripped the horse's reins out of Nordic's gloved hands. He lunged for the horn, but the horse's pitch had tossed him too far back in the saddle to reach it, and then he was flying almost ass over teakettle over the Appaloosa's left hip. The dark ground peppered with sage and pine needles also glinting in the starlight came up around him fast.

"*Gushh-aw-wahhhh!*" came his breath as it was punched out of his lungs by the ground that assaulted him mercilessly about the back of his head and shoulders.

The horse dropped back down on his front hooves, whickered again, ran a ways up the trail, and stopped.

Familiar yipping sounded amid the loudening running of padded feet and then Finn was at Nordic's side, yipping and moaning and licking his trail partner's left cheek.

The big Dakotan sat up, feeling as though he'd been beaten senseless by a big man—a professional, barefisted fighter he'd once fought for drinking money in Paddy O'Neil's Saloon in Ogallala, Nebraska. The big bruiser, bald as an egg, had struck so fast despite his size that his fists had been a blur.

He'd been the only man to ever beat Nordic in a fair fight, and Anders had thought he'd put that humiliation behind him. And he had. Until now.

"Oh, jeepers! Oh, jeepers!" Anders heard above Finn's mewls and barks as the dog continued to lick his lips and cheeks. The thumps of more running feet. The shadow that had landed Nordic so unceremoniously here grew before him in the darkness.

The young string bean and horsebreaker, Ryan "Sure Shot" LaPlante, knelt beside him, resting his rifle across his knees. His face was a long oval beneath his broad hat brim.

"I'm so sorry, boss. I'm so sorry. I was just tryin' to be quietlike. I didn...I didn't realize it was you until..." He groaned in defeat and released Nordic's left arm which he'd been tugging on, trying to help his boss to his feet. "Oh lordy! You're way too big. I can't...I can't help you up, I'm afraid."

"That's okay," Nordic said. "I ain't ready to make the climb just yet. Gotta find my brains. You see 'em layin' anywhere around here?"

"Huh?"

"My brains. They're scrambled!"

"Oh! Ah, jeez...I'm so sorry. I thought you mighta been Conagher or one of his...one of his posse riders. Wanted to be careful."

"Yeah, well, you were, you were. Easy, Finn." Nordic shoved the dog away from him. "Leave a little o' the beard on my face, will you? It comes in handy in the winter, don't ya know?"

The dog yipped and sat before him, canting his head from left to right and back again, softly thumping his tail.

Apache came over—one slow clomp after another—and extended his neck to touch his leathery snout to Nordic's jaw, sniffing.

"I'm still alive." He pushed the horse's head away. "No thanks to you. I thought I trained you better'n that!"

The horse stomped, blew, and hung his head low as though in chagrin.

He switched his tail and stomped again.

"Here," Nordic said, extending an arm to the kid who rose to a crouch before him. "Let's try it again."

The kid placed both his hands under Nordic's right arm. He dug his bootheels into the ground. Nordic did the same, and both heaving up from their feet, managed to get Anders standing. Planting his fists on his hips and bending back at the waist, trying to figure out what kind of damage he incurred, he looked at Sure Shot, frowning curiously.

"What're you doin' out here?"

"Mr. McGreevey told me to ride out and check that old Basque sheepherder's place, see if it was bein' occupied. On the way back to the headquarters I ran into Miss Sarah." He paused and looked pointedly at his boss. "Did her son make it to the Comanch?"

Anders nodded. "Sound asleep when I left. Lisle's there, too. Sarah's here?" He glanced toward the cabin. "With you? Have you seen Sarah? Miss Nordstrom?"

The young man nodded. "In yonder. Sound asleep. I been out here, keepin' watch for Conagher."

"Conagher won't be comin'. He and his posse are on their way to town with their tails between their legs."

"No, kiddin'?"

"Would I kid you?"

"I coulda shot him right out of his saddle. He must be hoppin' mad at both of us, then."

"Reckon so." Nordic turned to the cabin. He could smell pine smoke issuing from the chimney, see the gauzy rise of the gray smoke against the night-dark, star-bright sky. Turning to LaPlante, he said, "How is she?"

"Dead-dog tired! I gave her some jerky and coffee and she was so sleepy she pret' near passed out before I could catch her and lay her on the cot."

"All right, she's sleeping. Good."

"Conagher told you what happened, I suppose?"

"He told me." Nordic was slipping Apache's saddle cinch, Finn sitting nearby, looking around at the old, familiar haunt where he'd caught a good many jackrabbits and gophers. He'd catch mice and flip them in the air, playing with them like a cat.

When the rancher had his gear on the ground, he looked around.

He watched and listened. Only the usual night sounds. If a man were about, the animals would have told him by now. And his finely honed instincts would be warning him. He turned to the east, saw a faint lightening between the high, black ridges and a fading of the stars between them.

"Be dawn in ninety minutes or so. You take the chair on the porch. Try to get a little sleep."

That appeared to be just fine to young LaPlante. He was young and fit and as game for anything as he always was, but he needed sleep, too, and his body was telling just that. He set his rifle on his shoulder, pulled the front of his hat brim down, and strode off toward the small, low, shake-shingled cabin with its small front stoop. An ancient, hide-bottom chair sat to the left of the door, near the pot Nordic had always kept on the porch for Finn's water.

Nordic stretched his neck, winced at the ache in his right hip and shoulder, both of which had struck the ground first. He needed rest as much as LaPlante did. It had been a long day. He couldn't help but smile.

By God, on this day he'd been told by his lovely bride he was going to be a father.

He needed to catch a few weeks, but with the news in his mind, his brain would never give him release.

He turned to look at the creek running along the base of the low, hogback ridge he was on. It glistened like a snakeskin in the starlight, dimpling with the current and the breeze. It made a gurgling as it parted for the rocks and slid around and around the ancient, sun-bleached trees and large branches that had long ago fallen into it.

On the far side of the stream, ahead a hundred feet down the slope stood a large cottonwood, fluttering its dark leaves in the darkness, making little whispering sounds. There was a nice hole in the creek beneath that tree.

The soothing coolness of the water beckoned Nordic.

He'd swam once today. But he'd always counted it a special day when he had the time to swim twice.

Besides, that chill water fed by deep springs south of here and around the high slopes of Long's Peak would sooth his aching joints and his aging body, in general.

He walked down the slope leisurely, the smile in place on his mouth.

His horse and his dog followed dutifully, wondering what this strange, big man they'd found themselves sharing life with was up to now.

He stopped at the edge of the screen, across from the deep hole that cut into the opposite bank beneath the cottonwood. He swiped his hat off his head, kicked out of his boots, and unbuttoned his shirt.

Aging body.

Yeah, it was aging on him as it did every man.

He'd started being aware of it roughly seven, eight years ago.

Now he had given his wife child. That made him even more aware of it. He had to keep healthy. According to old Deveraux, one would be just the start. That old coot—*how in the hell had he got himself targeted yet again?*—wanted a whole passel of them. He'd know, too, if he had them or not.

He claimed he'd know from clear up the hillock where his dear wife and youngest boy had been planted and where Nordic often caught him, wandering up to the top and looking down at the two low mounts, hands in his pockets, toeing rocks…

The smile faded from the younger rancher's face.

That would be him someday, wandering up there to visit whom he'd lost.

He hoped he never lost anyone but he was old enough to know better. He'd already lost so many back in Dakota that when he finally did go back for a visit, he'd be visiting mostly graves.

He shook his head and squeezed his eyes closed. He'd be damned if he wasn't fogging up.

For cryin' in the lutefisk, you simple bastard, you got it good now.

Think about that.

Think about that beautiful woman you just made love

to. The young goddess who is right now at this very moment growing your first child in her womb…

He shucked out of his balbriggans, looked at the dog standing on the bank to his left, and then at Apache standing to his right, looking at him with their typical skepticism…dubiousness. If they lived to be a hundred, they'd never understand humans. As hard to fathom as the rocks, the clouds, the trees in the sky…the sky.

"Be right back," Nordic said. "Keep an eye out. If I get my hide perforated while I'm in there, I'm holding you both responsible!"

Apache shook his head and switched his tail, then gave a whicker.

Finn was up to the challenge. He looked at the big Dakotan and gave a single, resolute bark.

Nordic dove in and swam, every nerve in his body screaming out in protest of the cold, cold night water.

He came up blowing water, dove again, swam back and forth across the twenty-by-twenty-foot pool, and dove deep. He pushed off the sandy bottom with his fingers, swam upward until his head broke through the skin of the pool, blowing water. He kicked and paddled into the gap between two stout roots of the old cottonwood. Angling down the side of the bank and into the pool, they were like a mother's arms opening for a beloved child.

He rested back against the bank, raised arms resting on the roots to either side of him. Apache and Finn stood watching him expectantly. Finally, Finn gave a groan and sat down.

Nordic stared past the hogback hill to the east.

The cabin sat slumped—a vague, boxlike shadow in the darkness.

He could smell the woodsmoke of the fire that he hoped had Sarah sleeping peacefully.

Sarah...

Again, he frowned.

The talk they had to have was not going to be easy.

Apache turned to look behind him, over his right shoulder.

Finn leaped to his feet, turned full around, and barked just once.

"Shh!"

The voice came from the near side of the knoll down which a shadow limned slightly by the vaguely growing light moved down the hill toward the creek.

"Shh!" came the young woman's voice again and she ran a little awkwardly down the hill in a tight dress, a coat dropping to down below her knees. The old deerskin Nordic had left here, hanging on a hook by the door. Finn ran to her, she stooped to pet him, laughed, and ran to the edge of the creek.

She looked up and down the stream, looking for him.

"Anders?" she called.

Oh, no. Oh, no.

Nordic pressed his back up tighter against the bank, hoping she wouldn't see him.

"Anders?" she called again.

Finn turned to him.

Don't bark, dammit! Don't bark!

Finn barked.

CHAPTER THIRTY-TWO

Sarah followed Finn's gaze to Nordic.

Oh, hell.

"Here," he said, feeling foolish and a little tired of living with the trappings of a so-called civilized life. He used to walk out here with no one around to see him but Finn and his horse. "Just takin' a swim. I'll be out in a minute."

She turned to him quickly and slapped her hands to her mouth. "You *did* come!"

"Of course, I came. Now, turn around. I'm gonna climb out."

He could see her smile in the thinly fading darkness. "What if I don't?"

"Sarah."

"Oh, all right!"

Nordic swam across the creek and when the water grew shallow, he looked at her watching him.

"Sarah."

"Oh, all right!"

She turned around.

Nordic climbed out of the creek and with Finn running around him and Apache idly cropping grass, he dressed wet as he had earlier. It was a tad cool, this early in the morning, the dawn not yet here, but it would keep him invigorated.

"All right," he said, setting his sombrero on his head and stepping into his boots.

Sarah ran to him, wrapped her arms around him, and looked up at him beseechingly. "Bobby's all right?"

"Bein' spoiled right now by my wife and Riley Otis."

"Oh, thank you! Thank you, Anders. I knew we could depend on you"—she smiled up at him lovingly, her eyes flashing like the creek in the starlight—"to take care of us."

She pressed her cheek against his chest and tightened her hold around his waist.

Anders looked down at her. "Sarah?"

She looked up at him, still smiling.

"Let's sit down here, honey. We have to have a talk."

"Yes," she said, sitting down and drawing her knees up beneath the torn skirt of her dress. "I think we should."

He sat beside her and also raised his knees.

She turned to him and placed a hand on his shoulder. "Anders, I want you to know I know why you married Alexandra. She's a wonderful lady! She and her father offer a wonderful home. An incredible ranch!" Her eyes grew very serious. "But I also know you don't belong there."

"I do."

She frowned, looked at him as though she must have misunderstood. "What?"

"I belong there, Sarah."

She removed her hand from her shoulder, placed it atop her knee, and stared down at it. He placed his hand on hers, atop her knee.

"I love Alex, Sarah. I know that's hard for you to hear, but I'll be staying on at the Comanche Ranch."

At least, he thought he would. Sarah was right. It was a lot to take on. Such a heavy load he'd have never considered before he'd met Alex. But he had met her. And he'd fallen in love with her.

Finn, sensing the gravity of the situation, whined softly as he sat behind them, tail curled around him.

Staring down at his hand resting atop hers, Sarah said, "Anders...I thought...I thought..." She looked up at him suddenly, her eyes soft with emotion. "I thought you loved me."

"I do love you."

Her eyes widened hopefully, and she opened her lips to start to speak but he cut her off with, "But not in the way that you think. I love you like a sister. A much younger sister. I love Bobby as though he were one of my own. But we can't be together, Sarah. We can't be a family. I'm sorry that I led you to believe we could." He shook his head and inwardly winced as he said, "But we can't."

She stared deeply into his eyes and the dejection in her gaze broke his heart.

Softly, very quietly, she said, "You don't belong there, Anders. You're no more at home there than I was."

"I am." He wasn't yet certain that was true. He'd likely know soon enough, once this McClelland and Conagher conflict had been resolved. After he learned what he'd have to do to resolve it. After learning what might be coming next out of his father-in-law's murky past.

But whatever happened, he would be with Alex.

Not only did he love her, she was carrying his child.

Their child...

"I received a letter from one of my aunts in Dakota," Sarah said, looking up at him longingly, sadly, but still determined that they not only belonged together but would eventually be together. "She said there was a farm for sale near them. I thought we...you, me, Bobby..."

Nordic squeezed her hand beneath his. "No."

Her eyes shown with the start of tears. "Anders..."

"I know you're lost. Your family's gone. And you're lonely. Very lonely. I know how that feels firsthand. I didn't have to endure it the way you have...at your young age..."

"I'm not so young," she said, her voice tightening.

"You are. And you have a baby. A little boy. He needs a father, and you need a family. But Sarah." Squeezing her hand beneath his even more tightly, he shook his head. "That isn't me."

She looked down at his hand and sniffed.

"I love you, Sarah," he said. "I'm gonna look after you the whole rest of your life. You an' Bobby...just like he was my own. You'll always have that—me...and Alex if you like. I'm gonna find you your own place...in town because, though it doesn't seem like it now, you'll be safer there."

She shook her head. Tears rolled down her pale cheeks below her dark, stricken eyes. "Conagher... he'll..."

"He'll do nothing to you. I told him if he came near you or Bobby, I'd kill him." Nordic's eyes bore into her with a dead certainty that rose up from his very soul. "He knows I will. I'm probably gonna have to kill him, anyway. Leastways, you don't have to worry about him. Now, I want you and Bobby to stay with me and Alex and her father at the Comanche Ranch until I can find you a good home. A safe one."

She sobbed into the back of her wrist, sniffed, and looked up at him again.

"You'd do that for me?"

"I would give my life for you and that little hellion-to-be, Bobby."

She sobbed and laughed at the same time. She wrapped her arms around his neck. Her tear-wet cheek pressed against his. He felt her body tremble as she sobbed. "Thank you."

"Pshaw." Nordic gave her a loving squeeze and kissed her cheek. "Thank me after you've spent another month around that old devil father-in-law of mine!"

They both laughed.

———

Early the next morning, Nordic sat in the wicker chair on the porch of the Comanche Ranch's main lodge, a mug of stout, smoking coffee in his hand, his sombrero hooked over his knee.

Finn sat to his left, taking in the morning along with his trail partner. His snout slightly lifted, black nose working as he sniffed the slight, chill breeze tanged with the winey scents of the high forest and the piñon smoke issuing from the kitchen fires and from the chimney rising from the old man's office. Still wearing his snug night sock, Deveraux was resting back in his chair, sipping his coffee laced with Scotch, his thick, callused fingers, twisted from arthritis, danced gracefully across the pages of his heavy, leather sketchbook. It bore his monogram on the cover—a gift from his late wife, dearly missed by the old man and his daughter.

Nordic had never met the woman, but her presence filled the house as, he knew, so would Deveraux's in a year or two, after his passing. He'd join Louise and his youngest boy, killed by a horse. The oldest boy?

No one, including Alex, talked about him.

Nordic had heard via whisperings in the bunkhouse late one night, when he'd been playing stud poker with the men, that he'd gone outlaw a long time ago.

Anders's Winchester Yellowboy repeater leaned against the chair on his right, loaded and ready for travel.

For the time being, however, he wanted to just sit here and bask in the first gold rays of the sun rising behind the Nokhu Crags to the northwest of the head-quarters—great bastions of solid granite that were the crown jewel of Poudre Canyon, up high near Larimer Pass. Lake Agnes lay cool and blue at the formation's bottom, its usually still skin kissed gently from below by rainbow trout. Forested ridges, all the colors of a painter's palette in the fall, sloped up like an apron in all directions around it, toward the solid rock of the Crags whose highest reaches were lost in clouds on rainy and snowy days.

Here at the headquarters the mornings were sublime.

From the bunkhouse beyond the trees halfway down the slope to the main, working yard, he could hear the men milling in and around the bunkhouse. Conversations and laughter, occasionally a bawdy voice peeled followed by the scuffling sounds of rough man's play or the beratement of the cook for stealing biscuits.

The stableboys were out forking hay over the corral fences for the horses.

The blacksmith had his doors thrown open and was building a hot coal fire in his bellows. Nordic could hear the man talking to himself, grunting, and cursing as he moved barrels and implements around in preparing to ring the wheels of the wood dray parked before the open doors with iron rims.

A cat hunted along the base of one of the open doors, hunkered low, tail stiff, the tip occasionally twitching.

The two ranch dogs barked as they chased rabbits or wild turkeys in the tall brush behind the bunkhouse. Finn had no use for either. He knew his station was far and above theirs, though the hands kept them both better than well fed. They were constantly fighting over the bones of a recently butchered elk or deer.

From behind the stout doors behind him came the soft, delicate notes of Alex's piano, which she liked to play, meditatively, with her first cup of coffee.

Nordic yawned, stretched his legs out, crossed them at the ankles, and sipped his own steaming mud.

His mouth quirked a satisfied smile inside his thick, red-blond beard.

He couldn't live in a better place.

Still, a war was coming. As sure as he was sitting here. Soon.

As if to validate the thought, the clomps of hooves rose from the direction of the yard.

He turned to see two horsebackers leading the saddled Apache up the slope through the trees.

Zeb McGreevey and Ryan "Sure Shot" LaPlante reined up at the base of the porch steps.

Apache stopped and whickered.

Finn gave an eager moan. Something was about to happen...finally. He looked up at Nordic and wagged his tail.

"The kid again?" Nordic said, scowling at young LaPlante.

The kid flushed.

Nordic frowned. "Look, Sure Shot, I appreciate what you did for Sarah, but, when you drew that bead on Conagher, he drew one on you. I don't wanna have to haul you back here belly down across your horse."

"He's got one on you, too, sir," Sure Shot retorted defiantly.

"I'm used to it."

Zeb said, "Don't be so hard on him, boss."

"He's twenty-two. I want him to see twenty-three."

McGreevey smiled like the cat that ate the canary and looked sideways at Sure Shot. "He's our secret weapon. An' not just for his shootin' skills, neither...though they don't hurt."

Nordic's frown grew more severe.

"I know where McClelland's hunting lodge is," said young LaPlante, proudly.

"Not many folks know about it," McGreevey said. "The senator's the secretive sort. He's made enemies sort of like..." He let his sentence trail off as he glanced at the lodge door out which, coincidentally, came the gray-bearded old man of the Comanche Ranch, followed by his daughter in jeans, boots, and with her shirttails hanging out, suspenders down.

They were flanked by Sarah in a house robe and holding little Bobby in her arms.

"Sorta like me," Deveraux said, looking at McGreevey then sliding his hard gaze at his son-in-law. "I make no bones about it. Doubt the senator does, too. I have to kill him before he kills me. Or worse..." He glanced at his daughter standing to his right, beside Sarah and Bobby rolling a finger in his mother's hair.

He looked at the Comanche's youngest hand, "If the shaver here knows where his hunting lodge is, take him, for heaven's sake. Every man who signs on here knows each day might be his last. I tell 'em that right up, so there won't be no—"

"No misunderstanding," the young drover said with a smile. To Nordic, he said, "Yep, he told me that first off. I know what it's like. I been here long enough. I know it ain't no piece of cake, holdin' the wolves at bay."

"Especially when you've teased them," Alex said to her father out the side of her mouth.

He wrinkled his nose and grunted.

"Sure Shot sure held Conagher at bay," Sarah chimed in, smiling proudly at the young man. "If not for him, God knows where I'd be."

"I know where you'd be," said Deveraux with a dark scowl.

Sarah glanced at him and grimaced.

"Pa," Alex admonished him.

"All right, all right," Nordic said. "You can't fight the Sisters of Christian Charity." He looked at young LaPlante. "You could just draw us a map and stay here and continue gentlin' that blue roan you're so fond of."

"Wouldn't be near as much fun as ridin' with you,

boss," Sure Shot said through the excited smile on his lips, glancing at Sarah, who smiled back at him.

"You be careful, young man," she admonished him.

McGreevey looked offended. "What about me?"

"You, too, Zeb," Alex said.

She cut her worried gaze to her husband. "You're taking a big chance, not riding with more men backing you."

"More men, more chances of bein' seen." Nordic glanced at Sarah. "You all right?"

A hell of a thing she'd endured in a short time.

But she nodded.

"She's fine," said Deveraux. "Don't worry—I started her off with some o' the Scottish grain in her coffee."

Sarah grimaced and shook her head distastefully.

"Pa," Alex admonished again, but her eyes were on her husband, telling him to be careful without saying so aloud and risk embarrassing him.

Nordic pinched his hat brim to her. "Be seein' ya."

"You'd better."

She lifted her coffee to her lips and gazed at him through the rising steam.

CHAPTER THIRTY-THREE

"Men in the rocks up yonder," Sure Shot said the next day, midmorning.

He reined up a fine leggy sorrel, a bronc he'd caught, gentled, and trained himself in front of where Nordic sat Apache. "Not sure how many, but at least five," the young man added. "They're guarding the entrance to the canyon the senator's lodge sits in."

Nordic stared beyond the kid, at the rolling, forested slopes beyond him and into which he'd disappeared over an hour ago. They sent Sure Shot to reconnoiter the canyon entrance because he was a sure shot for good reason. He had good eyes, to boot.

"I think there's five," the kid added, leaning forward in his saddle, both gloved hands on the horn. "I just ain't sure. Mighta been one holed up in the rocks beneath another one. I couldn't get that close or they woulda seen me, though I was on foot. Left Number Two here in a little side canyon."

"Five, then," McGreevey muttered, crossing his own gloved thumbs over his own saddle horn.

"I said I think there's five," Sure Shot told him, desperately not wanting to be held to a guess.

"All right, all right," Nordic said. "Maybe five."

McGreevey chuckled.

"Just don't wanna be wrong and get either of you two old me…er, I man, fellas shot out'n your saddles." Sure Shot flushed the colors of a Colorado sunset.

"Me," Zeb said, grieved, "I ain't old! Hell, you might be able to shoot the gonads off a flyin' pheasant at two hundred yards, but I could pull you off'n that saddle and kick the stuffin' outta both ends…boy!"

Nordic chuckled.

Sure Shot flushed a deeper red and looked down, a little crushed.

"Easy, Zeb," Nordic said. "That was the first time I been called old…leastways, to my face"—he cast the kid a phony glare—"but I reckon I'd best start gettin' used to it."

"Ah, hell," said Sure Shot.

"How far ahead until we should leave our horses?" Nordic asked the kid.

"At the bottom of the next ridge." He cast a quick look at McGreevey. "Then we climb. I know a way to skirt the men in the rocks, but like I said," he added with another dangerous glance at the fifty-plus foreman, "It involves climbin'."

"I can climb!" said the Comanche Ranch foreman, aggrieved again.

"Ah, hell!"

"Let's go," Nordic said and booted Apache ahead.

They were on a steep shoulder of a forested mountain. They rode across the shoulder and through dense forest, ducking under low pine boughs and aspen limbs, letting the well-seasoned, mountain horses pick their own way around fallen trees and rocky debris including a couple of dangerous-looking talus slides.

The pure air, lens clear, was crisp. The men's and the horses' breath frosted the air before them. It frosted the air around Finn, too, who was currently investigating a long dead, fallen pine that had been hollowed out rot and likely served as a home to raccoons. Finn moaned and wagged his tail as he tried to push deeper into the hollow.

As they rode down from the crest of the next ridge, Nordic turned to Zeb riding beside him. "Five men," he said, keeping his voice down so Sure Shot, riding about fifteen feet behind them, wouldn't hear. "He must be expecting trouble or just paranoid. Either way, I don't like it."

"For us or him?" Zeb said, jerking his head to indicate the kid.

"Him."

"I can hear you," Sure Shot said behind them.

McGreevey looked back at the kid, grinned, and touched two fingers to his hat brim.

Nordic gave a wry snort.

Finn ran ahead of them, climbed a rock, and when Apache and Nordic rode even with him, he leaped onto Apache's back, behind the rancher's saddle.

The dog could run up one ridge and down another and, even in this high, thin air, hardly ever stopped to blow, but they'd been traveling through this rugged country where there were few trails other than those leading to widely spread-out ranches or mining camps, and Finn thought it was time for a breather. Also he'd caught and eaten at least one rabbit. He wore the dark-red blood bib proudly on his scruff.

At the bottom of the ridge, Sure Shot trotted Number Two up beside Nordic and McGreeley. "I'll lead the way now, if you two don't mind. I know where we can get up that ridge behind plenty of cover, so those five...at least five...won't see us or wind us."

"Be my gues..."

Before Nordic could finish his response, the kid reined his bronc to the right and put him into a jog.

Anders glanced at McGreevey. "I think he's set his hat for your job, Zeb."

"Hell, he can have it," the foreman quipped. "Especially if that old bull buff father-in-law of yours has any powerful men after him."

Nordic smiled and nodded.

They followed Sure Shot around a bend in the narrow, forested canyon which was threaded by a spring-fed creek running along the ridge on their right. Once around the bend, Sure Shot stopped his sorrel and glanced at the two older men riding up behind him.

"Best dismount here. The lodge is about a quarter mile straight on, at the mouth of this canyon and at the base of that big rock yonder."

Sure Shot jerked his chin up to indicate a bastion of solid gray stone that glowed nearly white in the high-altitude, late-morning sun. From here it looked the prow of an enormous ship, one built of solid rock. Over the blocky crest of it, two bald eagles soared in lazy circles, their white heads glowing even more brightly against the massively arching cobalt sky.

The men dismounted.

Sure Shot led his horse ahead, turned to look into a gap in the ridge on his left, then turned and beckoned to the men.

Ten minutes later, they'd tied their mounts, slipped their saddle cinches and, each holding his rifle, started to climb the ridge along a slanting deer and elk trail. Finn followed close on Nordic's heels, not running off to chase rabbits or deer. He sensed they were on a mission of some seriousness and wanted to stay close to his trail partner.

It was a tough climb. The slope was steep enough that they'd have to push off their knees. At one point, Sure Shot paused, grimaced, flexed his right leg, and said, "Kinda hard on the knees."

"Pshaw," Zeb funned him. "I don't feel a thing."

He smiled at Nordic walking ahead of him, behind Sure Shot, who knew this area better even than McGreevey, who'd at one time prospected in the general area before building a small ranch of his own and which he'd lost to a wildfire.

Sure Shot looked at Nordic, smiled, and continued walking.

When they gained the crest of the ridge, all breathing hard and sweating—though McGreevey no more dramatically than his younger trail mates—they stopped in a niche of rocks from around which a couple of wind-gnarled pines rose. Sure Shot scouted ahead a few feet, peeking around a large rock, then moved back to Nordic, Finn, and McGreevey.

Sure Shot lifted his neckerchief to quickly swab the sweat from his forehead and said, keeping his voice very low, "We'll cross the top of this ridge. It's only ten, fifteen feet or so. But it's sorta exposed. If there's more men up here than the ones I saw, they might see us. Looks to me it drops after fifteen feet and we'll head straight west then. The senator's lodge won't be far. He might have posted more men close around it, if'n he's…"

"If he's thinkin' we might be bringin' his war to him," Nordic acknowledged with a nod.

"Yep."

"Maybe your wife was right," McGreevey said to the rancher.

"Oh, she's always right," Anders said. "But if we'd brought more men, we might have been found by now, and there's no way we could get more men up close to that lodge. Or…" He removed his hat and, holding it, swabbed his forehead with the sleeve of his elk-skin jacket. "Get inside that lodge, which is my plan."

"Kill him in there?"

"Yep."

The foreman gave him a skeptical look. Sure Shot did, too.

"My father-in-law might have started the war when he did the unthinkable, burnin' a whole family off a homestead they'd registered all proper an' legal. But that man has tried to kill me and kidnap my wife. He'll burn my ranch…the ranch I aim to raise my family on…to ruin and kill one old man who's on death's doorstep already."

Nordic spat to one side and looked back at McGreevey. "I don't blame him for the frontier justice he's waited all these years to bring. But he's brought it to me now…to my family…and two can play that game."

"Yep." Zeb nodded, drawing his mouth corners down. "I don't like it, but I know you're right."

"I don't like it, either. But there you have it."

Finn sat at his feet, looking up at him, sensing the dismay in his partner's heart.

Not too long ago, it had been so much easier. When it had just been them.

Man and dog.

Now, it was far more complicated and, like McGreevey had said before, cloaked in gest, how many more men like the senator, wronged savagely by Deveraux, would come calling and threaten Nordic's family?

This is what he got, he thought.

For dancing with the devil.

He looked at Sure Shot and nodded.

Then he looked at the dog looking expectantly up at him, from his feet. "Quiet, Finn. You know how it goes."

He could tell by the dog's eyes, he understood.

He nodded at Sure Shot, who peeked around the rock on his left, then told the two men behind him it was all clear with his eyes, then ran, crouching, holding his rifle low in his gloved, right hand, across the crest of the rocky ridge and into the pines and firs that peppered the downslope on the crest's far side.

Sure Shot swung right and they moved along the side of the ridge, wending their way around rocks and trees, heading west. This was easier, flatter going, and they made good time.

They'd walked nearly a half hour, the sun hammering down at them, dust rising around their boots, when Nordic heard the metallic scrape that could only be a rifle's cocking mechanism. The sound made his spine tingle between his shoulder blades as he waited for the shot...

He stopped and looked behind him.

Zeb, ten feet behind Nordic, had stopped, too, and was looking behind at a man standing on their back trail, holding a Spencer repeater against his shoulder, his mustached upper lip stretching back to shape a cunning smile.

"Anders Nordic," he said, narrowing an eye as he aimed down the barrel, "the senator done put a bounty on your head"—his eyes flicked slightly as he looked at the Comanche Ranch foreman and then at Sure Shot—"and every last man on Deveraux's roll." His smile broadened. "And I just got me three."

Nordic's blood turned to ice.

He stared at the rifleman over McGreevey's right shoulder.

His brows knotted and his lower jaw started to slacken when in a blur of fast motion something sprang out from between two boulders on the rifleman's left side. The man screamed, face crumpling in shock and dread as Finn, whom Nordic had thought was still at his feet, closed both his toothy jaws into the man's left forearm.

Finn growled and snarled. While hanging from the stunned man's arm, he shook his head, laying the man's forearm open to the bone.

The man cursed and flung the dog away.

Finn flew back against the side of one of the boulders he sprung from.

"Vermin cur!" the man bellowed as he drew a Remington from his holster.

He didn't get the gun cocked before McGreevey, standing in front of Nordic now as both men faced down their back trail, snapped his hand up beside his right ear. A knife blade glinted as it flew end over end in the air between him and the rifleman who jerked sideways, dropping his gun with a clattering thud on the rocks and gravel. He clutched the right side of his neck with that hand.

Blood oozed thickly up from beneath the hand that reached for the staghorn handle of the blade embedded hilt-deep in his neck.

He staggered sideways, boots grinding gravel.

Finn rose from the base of the boulder he'd slammed into, shook, and leaped onto the rifleman's chest, driving him to the ground on his back.

Nordic and Sure Shot, who'd come up to stand beside him, both gaped at the dead man with the dog on his chest, growling deeply, hackles raised.

McGreevey smiled in delight over his shoulder at Nordic and Sure Shot, chuckled, then walked up to where Finn stood on the man's chest, teeth bared, growling down at the man who raised his hands to the dog's sides. His intention was to try to throw Finn off him again but his feeble attempt, as his life pumped out of him with the blood spurting from around the razor-edged blade of the Arkansas toothpick, looked more as though he were merely petting the dog lovingly.

Nordic and Sure Shot walked up to McGreevey.

All three stared down at him.

Finn still on his back, he stared up at them.

The light was leaving the man's eyes fast.

He looked at the dog who wanted to rip his teeth into his neck but under the circumstances of the man's imminent demise didn't see the point.

The man's lips moved. "Good...doggy..." he said thinly, deeply dazed and at his last. "Good...doggy...."

CHAPTER THIRTY-FOUR

Standing on the dead man's chest, Finn looked up at Nordic.

The big Dakotan shook his head. "I reckon your work is done here, boy."

Finn yipped and stepped down off the chest of the dead man whose pale blue eyes, half rolled back in their sockets, stared at the sky.

Nordic looked at McGreevey. "Zeb, where in hell did you…"

Chuckling, McGreevey placed his left foot on the dead man's chest, wrapped his right hand around the blade embedded in the man's neck, and pulled it out with a grunt. He turned to Nordic and Sure Shot and smiled, eyes glittering. He held up the knife, blood dripping down its razor-edged blade.

"You're lookin' at the first-place winner of the ninth annual knife-throwin' championship at the Tumblin' K." He winked. "Back in the day."

He cleaned the blood-coated toothpick's blade off on the dead man's elk-hide jacket.

He hadn't finished the job before a bullet spanged off the boulder to his right.

It was followed by the crash of the rifle that had fired it.

Finn leaped and snapped at the air then lay belly down and stared up over the top of the boulder before him and into a nest of rocks that towered above it.

Zeb and Sure Shot had both hit the ground and lay belly down, whipping anxious looks at Nordic, who stood crouching, resting his Yellowboy on his knee.

"Did you see where it came from?" the foreman wheezed out.

"No, but Finn did! Stay, boy!"

Nordic ran through a gap between two more boulders on his left and found himself in a narrow corridor between both rocks. When he came to the end of it, he poked his head out from behind the rock on his left, staring up at the nest of rocks forming a pillar of sorts of rock and tufts of tangled scrub brush growing out of cracks. A hatted head slid out away from one of the rocks about halfway up the pillar.

A rifle barrel glinted in the sunlight.

Nordic jerked his head back into the gap between the boulders.

As he did, he felt the warm curl of air in front of his forehead.

The bullet barked shrilly against the boulder on his right, spraying rock dust. The rifle's whipcrack followed.

Nordic leaped out of the gap and ran a winding course through rocks and scrub. He angled around a towering spruce and leaped onto one of the rocks that littered the side of the pillar of rocks, and began climbing, breathing hard, scissoring his legs and arms, holding the Winchester out to his right for balance. He hopscotched the rocks and leaped gnarled cedars and pines growing up between them. Seeing movement roughly fifty feet ahead of him in a niche in the rocks comprising the pillar, he dove over a flat-topped rock to his right.

A bullet screeched then tore into the rock he'd just leaped from, the screech of the ricochet making his eardrums ring.

He rolled to his right and came up on his belly, raised the Winchester, cocked it, and fired three quick rounds into the niche in which he'd spied movement and a rifle barrel. The Yellowboy bucked and roared, the ejected casings flying over his right shoulder and into the rocks and brush behind him.

A man grunted.

A man fell out of the niche, his rifle flying out of his right hand.

Down he came, as though floating, the flaps of his duster winging out to each side and behind him.

He struck on the gravelly slope, lost his hat, and rolled wildly down the steep incline, arms and legs flying, until he came to rest five feet in front of Nordic, who glanced at the man only long enough to see his blinking eyes and open mouth, blood trickling from a corner of it. Anders pushed to his feet, ran halfway up the slope, and dropped to a knee as another bullet screeched toward him and slammed into the slope a few feet behind him.

Another bullet spanged off a rock.

The barks of both rifles, one after another, echoed wildly off the near formations and higher ridges.

Nordic continued running up the slope.

He stopped, raised the Yellowboy, and fired.

Jacking another round into the chamber, he ran again, breathing hard, his legs aching, calf muscle grinding.

He raised the Winchester, fired again, and on the heels of the thundering report, he heard a man scream and say through a groan, "Oh...son of a...son of a bitch...killed me!"

A thud.

The man rolled down the steep incline toward Nordic who leaped the body, which continued to roll down beyond him before thumping up against a rock. There was a final gasp of death.

Anders jacked another round into the Winchester's action and, holding the rifle straight out from his right shoulder, continued climbing the rise. At the top, he stopped and peered into the circular, turretlike cleft in the rocks. A man in a long, black coat and black Stetson wearing small, steel-framed spectacles stood with his back against the stone wall behind him. He had his right hand clamped to his throat. Blood oozed out from between his fingers.

A Sharps rifle lay on the ground at his feet.

He had his head thrown back and was grunting and wheezing.

He lowered his chin. His spectacles glinted in the sunshine angling into the turret from behind Anders.

Nordic recognized him.

Charlie Kitchen. Regulator from Denver. He once shot a rancher while the man was sitting down at his dining room table, having supper with his family.

"Can't..." said the gunman. "Can't...believe...I'm gonna...die like...this..."

"Better than you deserve."

The gunman stared at Nordic. He opened his mouth to speak but before he could say anything, Nordic finished him with a round through his forehead.

Nordic counted in his mind.

One...two...

This was the third man of the five Sure Shot had reported in these rocks guarding the mouth of the canyon in which the senator's hunting lodge sat.

A shadow slid up across the rocks and gravel to Nordic's left.

The shadow of a man in profile.

Something slid forward of the shadow.

A gun.

Nordic glanced over his shoulder to see a man standing behind him, grinning. The long-barreled, silver-chased Remington in his black-gloved fist clicked as the man thumbed back the hammer. The maw yawned wide, cold, and black. It was pointed at the back of Anders's head.

He heard that ominous whistling again.

The man behind him must have, too.

He'd just started to lose his smile, staring incredulously into the rancher's eyes, when a fist-sized chunk of bone, blood, and brains exploded out of the right side of his head. His head jerked to that side. His right arm jerked, and the man's Remington barked, the slug blowing up sand and gravel to Nordic's left. He flew sideways and rolled, his hat bouncing along the ground beside him.

As he did, Nordic spied more movement ahead and above.

He looked up. His heart lurched into his throat when

he saw a man standing atop a boulder a hundred feet from him, aiming a rifle at him.

I might've avoided the last one, Nordic thought, knowing the man on the boulder had him dead to rights.

Two quick rifle blasts sounded to Nordic's hard left.

The man atop the boulder triggered his rifle, smoke and flames lapping from the barrel. The bullet barked off the face of the turret behind Anders just before the man opened his hands and the rifle dropped out of them. It dropped straight down to land with a clattering thud on the ground at the base of the boulder.

The rifleman stumbled backward, eyes widening beneath the broad brim of his cream Stetson. Holding his belly already glinting red with fresh blood, he stumbled forward and dropped headfirst over the side of the boulder. He turned a somersault in midair. He, too, lost his hat and it followed him down. Two or three seconds after the man himself had landed on his back, the hat dropped very lightly on his belly, crown up.

All laid out like a dead man in a coffin...

Nordic recognized him, too. Sanders or some such. Another gunman from Denver.

Anders fingered his chin in thought.

The Senator sure did cotton to gunmen from Denver. He'd probably hired them all before at one time or another.

Finn came running from where he'd been sitting at McGreevey's feet, a hundred feet and up a gravelly grade from Anders. The foreman slowly lowered his smoking Spencer and turned to Nordic, grinning inside his tangled beard. He jerked his chin up to indicate something or someone behind Nordic now as Anders had turned toward the foreman.

"He maybe the *surest shot* around here, but this old man ain't so bad his ownself!"

Nordic turned to where Sure Shot knelt at the turret's far end, leaning forward on his Winchester. He smiled in triumph.

"That should be all of 'em," the kid said, lifting his chin to cast his gaze beyond Nordic and McGreevey. "*If* there was only five. Now, I ain't sure, so..."

Nordic turned to Zeb. The foreman was smiling at where Finn was just then making water on the dead man lying spread-eagle at the base of the boulder. "That dog sure don't got much respect for the dead," he said, and chuckled.

"I don't either. Not when..."

He let his voice trail off. He frowned, befuddled, as he stared at Sure Shot.

Or at where Sure Shot *had been.*

Nordic had turned to the kid, too. Only, the kid wasn't where he'd been only a minute ago. His rifle, however, lay on the ground where he'd been kneeling. An ominous sight—the rifle lying there all alone.

Anders glanced warily over his shoulder at Zeb.

He racked a cartridge into the Yellowboy's action. He'd taken two steps down the gravelly grade fronting the turretlike formation where the three men had fired at him when Sure Shot reappeared. Only this time he wasn't alone.

A tall, straight-backed man with a high-crowned black Stetson and a carefully trimmed, gray mustache mantling his thin upper lip, was holding him taut from behind, his left arm around the kid's lean waist, his right, black-gloved hand holding a long-barreled, silver-chased Colt taut to the kid's right temple.

Nordic's guts churned.

His voice pinched with anxiety and no doubt the pain of having that gun barrel pressed against his head, Sure Shot said, "Yep, there was another one, all right."

As if voicing his own incredulity, Zeb said atop the grade behind Nordic, "Well...I'll be jiggered. *Conagher*!"

CHAPTER THIRTY-FIVE

"Throw 'em down," ordered the Camp Collins marshal, hardening his jaws, narrowing his narrow devil's eyes inside their deep sockets, and ramming the barrel of his Colt even harder against Sure Shot's head.

The kid winced and stretched his lips back from his teeth. He was back on his heels, his spurs grinding into the sand and gravel.

His long, clean, boyish face tense and pale with fear.

He knew that Conagher would just as well shoot him as look at him after how he'd turned the man with his rifle a few days ago, when Sure Shot had come upon the man and a posse from town trying to run down Miss Sarah. He expected to have a bullet drilled through his head. The reason it hadn't already happened was because the corrupt lawman needed him.

"I said throw 'em down!" the lawman bellowed, pushing the kid forward a little just from the momentum of his own desperation.

Yeah, he was desperate, all right.

All the other men the senator had sent out here to protect his hunting lodge were dead.

Now, it was only Conagher.

Where was the senator, Sure Shot vaguely wondered beneath the cold fear sweeping through him in heart-pounding waves.

Nordic stared hard at the lawman, his rifle still raised in his hands.

His hands were sweating inside his gloves.

He'd do it, he thought, staring into the killer's slate-gray eyes. Yeah, they were killer's eyes. He'd known it before. He'd always know Conagher wasn't a straight lawman and that he was probably working with some of the rustling syndicates in the area who were trying to rustle Deveraux's cattle clean off his range. No doubt the senator had been doing that, too.

Nordic glanced at Sure Shot.

His heart ached for the kid. He couldn't see him killed.

He could not.

Anger and frustration were a poisonous froth inside him. He could feel it oozing out of his pores with his sweat.

He squeezed the rifle in his hands as he stared hard into the rogue lawman's eyes.

"What's he payin' you, Conagher. Cattle? Maybe *my* cattle. *Deveraux* cattle?"

"Don't be so high-an'-mighty, Dakota. You're a common cow nurse." Conagher glanced up at the kid before him. Sure Shot was a couple of inches taller than him. "You got lucky. Now, you're ridin' high an' smug…drinkin' Deveraux's liquor an' smokin' his fancy cigars!"

His gray eyes flashed contempt. He stretched his lips back from his small, square teeth.

His words bit Nordic deep. He hadn't said anything he hadn't said to himself.

Still, it was hard to hear from others. He knew it wasn't only Conagher thinking it. Others thought it and said it among themselves.

"Throw 'em down," Conagher said, more quietly, tightly, ominously. "First the long guns then the pistol rigs."

"No!" Sure Shot yelled in a half-strangled voice. "Don't you dare, boss. He'll kill me, anyway. I don't hurt his pride. I scared him. Had him dead to rights and was about to kill him when he was after Miss Sarah!"

"Shut up, you little dung beetle!" Conagher railed, bunching his lips with fury.

Nordic didn't know where it came from, but the kid still had enough pluck in him—now, when he could die with just a twitch of the lawman's trigger finger—to laugh goadingly and to roll his eye up at the man behind him.

"He plumb turned green when he saw my rifle sights lined up on him!"

Again, the kid laughed.

Nordic said, "Sure Shot, shut up!"

He looked back at McGreevey who had a terrified look on his face.

Nordic bent his knees and set his rifle on the ground beside him. He nodded for Zeb to do likewise. The foreman did.

Finn sat halfway up the grade between Nordic and McGreevey. He was showing his teeth and growling steadily at the man threatening Sure Shot.

Sure Shot shook his head and shuttled his fear-bright, defiant gaze between Nordic and the foreman. "Don't," he pleaded. "Don't. Kill him! He'll kill me, anyway!"

"Shut your mouth, kid!"

Sure Shot laughed mockingly again. "I made him look like a damn fool. It's probably all around town!"

"I said shut up!" His face red with rage, Conagher pulled the kid a foot to his left and slammed the barrel of his Colt against Sure Shot's right temple.

The kid grunted and leaned sideways, the lawman holding him up by his shirt.

Finn barked angrily and went running past Nordic, hackles raised, making a beeline for the lawman.

"Finn, no!" Nordic shouted.

Conagher aimed the Colt straight out from his right shoulder, drawing a bead on the dog who was within ten feet of him and closing fast.

"*No!*" Sure Shot bellowed.

The kid closed his hand around the gun and drove it down.

It barked, blowing a fist-sized chunk of sand and gravel out of the ground.

Sure Shot wrestled the pistol out of the lawman's hand and threw himself hard left.

As he did, Finn took a running leap and dug his teeth into Conagher's throat.

"Nooo!" the lawman cried. "Get him…get him… *off me!*"

Conagher flew back and struck the ground hard, Finn on top of him, chewing and tearing, snarling like a wildcat.

Sure Shot sat half up, leaning back on one hand, the lawman's pistol in his other hand, staring wide-eyed at where Finn was making fast work of the lawman, who lay writhing and kicking under the dog's brutal assault.

"Finn!" Nordic said, moving forward. "That's enough, boy."

Finn stopped, stepped down off the man, walked six feet away, and sat down, licking the blood from his chops.

"Good work, boy," Nordic said. "Good work, boy."

"Good work?" Conagher screeched, sitting up and cupping both hands to his bloody throat. "He almost killed me!"

"You're already dead."

"Wha—you…" The lawman shook his head, gritting his teeth, frightened eyes on the rifle growing larger and darker as the man wielding came toward him. "You… can't…I'm…"

"You got in with the wrong crowd, Conagher."

"I, uh…I uh…"

"What'd he promise you?"

Conagher stared at him, keeping his hands clutched to his bloody throat. He suddenly had a long-faced look of dejection, hopelessness. The game was over. His part in it, anyway.

"The lieutenant governorship." He flushed with embarrassment. Suddenly, it seemed, he saw himself for what he was. And he didn't like it a bit.

His eyes were on the ground.

"I can do him one better than that."

"Boss," McGreevey said, stopping near where Sure Shot sat on the ground, the dog right beside him now, too. The foreman looked incredulous. He glowered at Conagher. "If you want, I can finish the son of a—"

"I can let you live," Nordic said, keeping his icy gaze

on the lawman. "But then you're mine. No one else's. You're mine." He thumped himself in the chest with his finger. "You belong to the Comanche Ranch."

Finn barked and snarled.

The dog didn't like the idea any better than the foreman did. Nor than Sure Shot did, judging by the disbelieving look in the kid's eyes.

"It's either that," Nordic said, shoving his rifle down close to the lawman's forehead, "or I can finish it right here. Believe me, I'm never gonna hear the end of it from my father-in-law if I don't."

Conagher drew a deep breath and let it out slow. "Yeah." He nodded. "All right."

"You belong to me."

Again, Conagher nodded.

"Say it."

Conagher drew another deep breath. "I belong to you. To the Comanche Ranch."

"To Garth Deveraux."

"To Garth Deveraux," the lawman spat out like an unwieldy prune pit.

"Was it worth it."

Conagher shook his head. "I been a lawman a long time. Denver looked good."

"Was it worth it?"

Again, the lawman shook his head.

Nordic canted his head in the direction of the lodge. "Where is he?"

"He's there. Has a girl with him."

"He alone?"

Conagher shook his head. "His lieutenant's there. Erskin."

"They inside or out?"

"When I left, they were inside."

Nordic set the Yellowboy on his right shoulder, his right hand around its neck. He glanced at McGreevey. "Zeb, you stay here. See if you can get that bleeding stopped."

He glanced at the lawman.

It didn't look like Finn had torn his throat all the way out.

Zeb looked at the man distastefully and wrinkled his nose.

Sure Shot looked up at his boss, eyes wide.

"You're comin' with me," Nordic said, adding with a wry smile, "Sure Shot."

The kid smiled, gained his feet, picked up his hat, picked up his rifle, dusted it off, and set it on his head.

"You stay, Finn."

The dog barked once, defiantly, ears pricked as far as he could prick them.

Then, seeing the commanding look in his master's eyes, the dog dropped belly down, crossed his paws, and stared at Anders, pouting the way a shepherd dog can pout when he's told he's no longer part of the work.

Too dangerous.

Nordic chuckled and walked away, Sure Shot hurrying to keep up with the big man from Dakota.

———

Nordic squatted in a cleft near the long, stone escarpment he and Sure Shot had followed for a couple of hundred yards since leaving McGreevey and Conagher.

The lodge lay below the scarp, in a large clearing in the pines.

The main trail to the big cabin—three stories high and with balconies running all the way around all three floors—lay to Nordic's left another hundred yards away. McClelland's men and Conagher had been watching the entrance to the canyon where the trail cut down the middle.

The lodge sat on a forested mountain, and the sun shone crisply down from a cobalt sky. Stables, barns, and corrals lay to the west, or the rear, of the impressive lodge. A gravel drive formed a horseshoe shape at the front. Anders imagined all the snazzy rigs and fine, blooded horses that had ridden up that drive to the big, green, halved-log front doors outfitted with large, glistening brass handles in the shapes of snarling grizzlies standing on their back legs, ready to pounce on their prey.

Two large, carved wooden bears, the same green as the doors, stood to each side of the main entrance, greeting the senator's moneyed guests thrillingly. Smaller bears had been carved into the logs beneath the house's four eaves, recessed beneath the roof's broad overhang. Green shutters were closed over all the windows and French doors except over the windows on the narrow balcony of the lodge's third story, which formed a widow's walk of sorts at the very top of the massive, barracklike structure.

Nordic appraised the two windows he could see from this vantage, the one at the front of the third floor and the one at the near side, which was the north side of the lodge.

Both windows were open, yellow curtains fluttering to each side.

He'd just slid his gaze to the window at the front of the third floor when Sure Shot whispered urgently, "Boss, down!"

Nordic glimpsed a flash of sunlight on a rifle barrel jutting from the third floor's north window. He pulled his head down into the gravel-floored niche in the escarpment he and the kid were kneeling in. A bullet smashed into the stone wall of the niche behind Nordic and Sure Shot with a hammering wail like the crack of near lightning.

The deep-throated report followed a half second later, echoing like thunder on the heels of the lightning.

"Damn!" Sure Shot said, then, being a good boy, hastily added, "Pardon me, boss, I meant dang!"

"I'll be a son of a *bitch*!" Nordic said when he saw the fist-sized crater the bullet had punched in the rock behind him. "That's a thirty-two forty with a hell of a lot of firepower behind it!"

"A Schuetzen," the kid said.

"A *what*?"

"Big fuckin' gun!"

Nordic chuckled and lifted his head to peer at the lodge again.

The rifle appeared once more, poking out the window at the front of the third story.

"Down!"

He and the kid had no sooner dropped the crowns of their skulls below the rock wall before them that another bullet came whistling eerily in, like a midnight demon with a grudge to settle.

The bullet hammered the stone wall before them followed by the thundering report.

Rage burning in him—yeah, the man was seeking revenge for an injustice, but Nordic was going to kill him, just the same. The man had sent men for his wife who was carrying Nordic's child. He rose and triggered three quick rounds at the window from which the crazy son of a buck had just fired his sporting rifle. All three bullets caromed through the window although the senator himself had pulled his head down.

And then Sure Shot went to work with his own Winchester at the north window, which he must have seen the senator switch to. Nordic thought he heard a startled grunt on the heels of Sure Shot's last shot.

Grazed the man.

The kid pulled down his head and smoking rifle.

"Think I might have pinked him!" he said.

"Well, you're Sure Shot." The rancher placed a hand on the game kid's shoulder. "Can you keep him distracted while I try to work my way over there?"

Sure Shot pumped a fresh round into his Winchester's action and said, "Watch me!"

Another bullet came winging in, slamming into the rock wall before Sure Shot.

The kid rose, pressed the rifle's butt against his shoulder, aimed quickly but carefully, and fired.

CHAPTER THIRTY-SIX

N ordic scrambled through a gap in the niche's rear wall.

As the senator and the kid exchanged rounds, Nordic walked fifty yards back east then followed a crack in the side of the formation, a flue of sorts twisting around protruding rock and stunted cedars, to the ground. He moved north, wending his way through thick forest another fifty yards before swinging west, heading toward the north edge of the cabin.

There was a stable and another corral there, a couple of large, high-paneled drays on skis which were likely used for winter woodcutting.

He jogged through the thick pine forest.

He came to the clearing in which sat the corral connected to a large, log, tin-roofed stable on the other side of it.

The blasts of the Schuetzen continued, punctuated by the flatter, distance-tempered reports of Sure Shot's Winchester.

Nordic stopped at the edge of the forest and looked around, surveying the house and the area around it, looking for signs of the senator's lieutenant, Erskin.

Spying no movement, he moved toward the lodge slowly, keeping the forest close on his left, holding his cocked Yellowboy straight up and down before him. He scanned the outbuildings and other corrals on his right. If Erskin was out here, he was keeping out of sight.

Nordic moved toward a door on this side of the lodge, atop high, broad steps that rose to the veranda on the lodge's first floor. The trees pulled back behind him on his left, open ground stretching to his right and behind him. Slowly, he moved up the steps. He crossed the porch to the door, tried the large, brass latch, this one, too, in the shape of a snarling grizzly.

Locked, of course.

Holding the Winchester straight up and down against his chest, Nordic stepped quickly across a large window to the left of the door. As he did, there was a glassy *ping!* followed by the blast of a rifle inside the lodge. The bullet sent several glass shards spraying from the window onto the porch floor.

Nordic hardened his jaws, swung the Yellowboy to his right, and rammed the barrel through the window and fired four times quickly, triggering and cocking, triggering and cocking. He thought he heard a grunt from inside. More distantly, a girl screamed.

Before the echo of his last shot had died, Nordic threw himself headfirst through the window. He flew over a table on which cooking utensils were arranged and landed on a hard wooden floor in a rain of shattered glass that poked into the heels of his hands and elbows through the buckskin of his tunic. His hat tumbled to the floor.

Immediately, he lifted his head and was up, scrambling forward across what he saw was a large kitchen with a range and cupboards. He dropped behind a long, wide food preparation table. Jacking another round into the Winchester's action, he looked around and brushed broken glass off his clothes.

The Schuetzen's reports thundered around the house, but the kid's Winchester had fallen silent.

He could hear a man's enraged, distant shout.

It was coming from the third floor.

The senator.

Had he lost his target?

The hunting rifle had fallen silent. Eerily so.

Had one of those bullets powered by a heavy load of black powder taken out Sure Shot?

The idea stabbed Anders like a rusty knife. Before he'd gotten himself entangled in the Comanche Ranch, he hadn't known such worry for anyone except his dog. Now he had a whole bunkhouse full of men. He had a wife…a child and likely many more on the way…

The man shouted again, then fell silent. Nordic could hear creaks in the ceiling of someone moving around up there.

He turned to a large pine swing door ahead of him and on his left, right of one of the kitchen's two large, black ranges.

A wet sink and a pump sat to the left of it, under shelves neatly arranged with foodstuffs.

Nordic had heard something beyond that door.

He heard it again, the faint creak of a floorboard.

Anders raised the Yellowboy and pressed his cheek to the neck curving up toward the cocked trigger. He aimed down the barrel, drawing a bead on the small, square window in the door's upper half.

The door blasted open with such force it slammed against the sink, pump, and cabinets with a resounding *crash*! A tall, dark figure came storming through the open door, a muscular man impeccably dressed wearing a neat mustache, goatee, and side whiskers.

He wailed like a demon as he ran toward Anders, firing the two gold-plated, Civil War-model Confederate LeMat pistols in his hands, the bullets caroming around Nordic and chewing into the table before him. Nordic shifted the Yellowboy slightly and emptied it into the chest of the impeccably dressed and barbered gent who continued running and shooting until both pistols clicked empty. He shot past Nordic and by the force of his momentum went hurling headfirst through the window whose glass the Dakotan had broken out when he'd gained entrance.

Outside, a dog barked.

In a black, white, and fawn-colored blur, eyes wide, Finn leaped from the veranda through the broken window, landed on the kitchen floor with a grunt, and ran up to Nordic, panting and wagging his tail.

Anders placed two fingers to his lips.

The dog sat down beside him and pinned his ears back, groaning his excitement at being with his partner again, and shifted his weight from one foot to the other.

"Dammit, boy, you were supposed to…"

He let his voice trail off when the kid appeared in the window, looking in, holding his Winchester. His eyes met Nordic's and then he stepped through the window and came over and dropped a knee beside the rancher and Finn. He pointed at the ceiling.

"I hit him. If he ain't down, he's close." Sure Shot paused. "The girl's with him."

"I heard her." Nordic set his rifle on the floor, unsnapped the keeper thong from over the hammer of his left-side Russian, and pulled the gun from the leather. "Stay here," he told Sure Shot and then looked down at Finn and said, "You, too."

Finn gave a little, disgruntled yip and slid his front feet forward as he dropped to his belly.

Nordic rose, crossed the kitchen avoiding the blood the senator's lieutenant had left on the floor, and made his way slowly through the swing door and into a large dining room outfitted with a stout, walnut table that could seat the entire territorial senate for a New Year's Eve gathering. Nordic moved around the table and left the room by a door in the opposite wall, then passed through several more, large, cavelike rooms until he reached a broad staircase rising from the stone-floored foyer fronting the stout entrance doors.

He climbed the stairs to the second story, turned and continued climbing to the third-floor landing.

He stood in the landing's shadows. Varnished rails surrounded him beyond and below to the second and first floors.

Nordic extended the Russian up at an angle.

Light shone above, coming from the open windows on the third floor.

A figure staggered into Anders's field of vision.

The senator, silhouetted against the light behind him.

He wore a suit and a red bow tie. A tall, handsome man with rings on his fingers.

And a bullet in his neck.

Blood glinted as it oozed out from beneath the hand McClelland cupped over it.

He had a long-barreled, ivory-gripped Bisley in his right hand which he held low along his right leg. He leaned against the wall, drew a ragged breath, and glared down at Nordic.

"He killed my family," he said, voice taut with pain. "Burned us out."

"My wife didn't." Nordic paused. "I'm sorry for what he did. And I don't blame you for comin' after him. But I blame you for comin' after my wife. For comin' after me."

Nordic started climbing the stairs, slowly.

"Had to...had to...get you out of the way!"

Nordic stopped five steps down from McClelland. "You didn't."

He aimed the Russian at the man's head slick with sweat. "Time to end this," he said. "I got work to—"

A gun popped behind McClelland.

The man's eyes snapped wide. He lowered the hand that had been cupping his neck. Blood oozed from the ragged hole. McClelland stumbled forward, onto the steps. He turned his head to see behind him. "You..." he whispered. "You..."

He turned forward and Nordic stepped aside as the man fell forward and rolled violently down the steps all the way to the bottom where Sure Shot and the dog stood, staring at the dead man at their feet and then up at Nordic.

He turned to see the blonde young woman clad in a red robe and rabbit fur slippers standing ten feet away, near a massive desk cluttered with books.

She lowered the smoking derringer and stared wide-eyed at where the senator had been standing.

Nordic frowned at her in disbelief. She was young, maybe not yet twenty. Almost pretty.

She slid her own shocked gaze to Anders and tears glittered in them.

"I had to kill him." She sobbed. Tears streaked her cheeks. She looked down at her slippered feet. "I had to kill him." She looked up at Anders, her blue eyes deeply grieved. "I loved him." She placed the hand holding the derringer over her heart. "I had to be the one!"

She lowered her head again, closed her eyes, and bawled.

She wavered on her feet, trembling. She dropped the derringer.

Nordic holstered his pistol and hurried up to catch her in his arms just before she fell. He carried her to a long, leather sofa over the back of which a lion skin was draped. He laid her down, knelt beside her, and took her hand in his.

He heard creaks and ticking sounds on the stairs.

He turned to see Sure Shot and Finn gain the top of the stairs and stand there, staring.

The girl opened her eyes and looked at Nordic. She sobbed once more, her chest heaving behind the velvet robe, and said, "What…what…was it…*about*…?"

Nordic looked out the window to his right abutted on each side by oil paintings—one of a mountain lion about to spring on its prey, the other of a bucking, black bronc with fire in its eyes. The kind of fire McClelland had been harboring since he was just a kid, too young to have gone through what he had.

His family murdered. His home burned.

What have I gotten myself into? Anders thought. *How many more of the old bastard's enemies will I have to confront?*

He turned back to the girl staring up at him searchingly.

"The past," he said. "It was about the past. Like everything else."

A LOOK AT:
LOU PROPHET: THE COMPLETE WESTERN SERIES, VOLUME ONE

THIS PROPHET IS RIDING TO HELL AND BACK.

Lou Prophet's life as a bounty hunter has taught him one rule—
you don't stop riding till the job is finished. Repeatedly caught
in bloody crossfires, Prophet is determined to show outlaws that
justice doesn't always wear a badge.

Join along as this bounty hunter searches for a gorgeous
showgirl, chases down a brutal gang, protects his partner at all
costs, escorts a Russian noblewoman on an Arizona trail, and
captures stage-robbers.

Lou Prophet: The Complete Series, Volume 1 embraces the
relentless pursuit of justice and proves that—in the unforgiving
Wild West—true heroes are forged in the fires of perseverance.
This collection includes The Devil and Lou Prophet, Riding
with the Devil's Mistress, The Devil Gets His Due, Staring
Down the Devil, and The Devil's Lair.

AVAILABLE NOW

ABOUT THE AUTHOR

Peter Brandvold grew up in the great state of North Dakota in the 1960's and '70s, when television Westerns were as popular as shows about hoarders and shark tanks are now, and Western paperbacks were as popular as *Game of Thrones*.

Brandvold watched every Western series on television at the time. He grew up riding horses and herding cows on the farms of his grandfather and many friends who owned livestock.

Brandvold's imagination has always lived and will always live in the West. He is the author of over one hundred lightning-fast action Westerns under his own name and his pen name, Frank Leslie.